NEAR DARK

NEAR DARK

A THRILLER

Brad Thor

EMILY BESTLER BOOKS

—

ATRIA

New York   London   Toronto   Sydney   New Delhi

EMILY
BESTLER
BOOKS

ATRIA

An Imprint of Simon & Schuster, Inc.
1230 Avenue of the Americas
New York, NY 10020

This Emily Bestler Books/Atria Paperback Canadian export edition July 2020

EMILY BESTLER BOOKS / ATRIA PAPERBACK
and colophon are trademarks of Simon & Schuster, Inc.

For information about special discounts for bulk purchases, please contact Simon & Schuster Special Sales at 1-866-506-1949 or business@simonandschuster.com.

The Simon & Schuster Speakers Bureau can bring authors to your live event. For more information, or to book an event, contact the Simon & Schuster Speakers Bureau at 1-866-248-3049 or visit our website at www.simonspeakers.com.

Manufactured in the United States of America

1 3 5 7 9 10 8 6 4 2

Library of Congress Cataloging-in-Publication Data

ISBN 978-1-9821-5280-2
ISBN 978-1-9821-0408-5 (ebook)

To all those we lost.
And to all those who bravely served so that the rest might live.

"He whom love touches not walks in darkness."

—Plato

PROLOGUE

A cold rain slicked the poorly paved streets. Aging Russian hydrofoils banged against rotting piers. Crumbling French architecture struggled with leaks. Life in Vietnam's third largest city was miserable. Inclement weather only made it worse. Andre Weber couldn't wait to leave.

Looking at his host, he commented, "Counting machines are quicker."

Lieu Van Trang smiled. "But they are far less attractive."

Weber shook his head. Trang was known for his eccentricities. A coterie of young women, stripped naked so they couldn't steal while tallying his money, was completely on brand. It was also a total waste of time.

Electronic currency counters could have done the job six times faster and would have eliminated any human error. They also didn't steal. But Trang liked to play games. He liked to fuck with people's heads. He knew his visitors wouldn't be able to take their eyes off the girls.

As far as Weber was concerned, it was unprofessional. They were here to conduct business. There was a shit ton of money on the table and that's where his team's focus needed to be. The girls were distracting. Even he was having a hard time not looking at them. And if it was difficult for him, it had to have been almost impossible for his men.

This was not how he liked to do things. Weber preferred encrypted communications and washing money through shell corporations or cryptocurrencies. Trang, on the other hand, was old-school. So old-school, in fact, that he refused to conduct any business electronically. Everything was in cash and everything was face-to-face.

The two couldn't have been further apart in their approach. Even in their appearances they were strikingly different. Weber, the Westerner, was tall and fit. With his short hair and his expensive, tailored suit, he looked like a young banker or a hedge fund manager. Trang, thirty years his senior, was impossibly thin with long gray hair, a wispy beard, and translucent, vellumlike skin that revealed a network of blue veins.

The only thing they shared in common was a lust for money and a talent for taking care of problems. While Weber didn't want to be here, he had been paid a huge sum of money, a sum equal to what Trang's girls were currently counting out, for this assignment.

When all was said and done, it would be the highest-value contract killing ever to hit the market. It had already been deposited in a secret account and would be payable on confirmation of the subject's demise.

But like Weber, Trang was just a middleman—a headhunter, skilled in identifying the right professionals for the right jobs. His fee, payable up front, was a fraction of what the successful assassin would receive. It was quite fair as he was taking only a fraction of the risk.

Anyone whose murder commanded that sort of a price had to be very dangerous and *very* hard to kill. Trang would have to take extra steps to make sure none of this blew back on him.

Once the girls had finished counting the money and had confirmed the total, he dismissed them. Every set of male eyes, including Trang's, watched them as they filed out of the room. Several of Weber's men shifted uncomfortably as they adjusted erections.

"One thousand dollars each," said Trang, enjoying the men's pain. "Best money you will ever spend. I will even throw in rooms for free."

The man had just collected a ten-million-dollar fee, yet he wasn't above pimping out his girls for a little bit more. He also wasn't shy about his pricing. *One thousand dollars?* No matter how good they were, Weber doubted they were worth a thousand dollars—not even for all of them at the same time. Trang was as shameless and as sleazy as they came.

It was time to wrap things up. Weber didn't want to stay a minute longer than he had to. Removing the folder, he handed it over.

Slowly, Trang leafed through it, employing the freakishly long nail of his right index finger to turn the pages.

When he was done, he closed the dossier and asked, "So what can you tell me about the client?"

"Only that it's someone you don't want to fuck with."

"Apparently *somebody* fucked with whoever it is or you wouldn't be here opening this kind of a contract. What transgression, what sin, could be so egregious that it would call for a one-hundred-million-dollar bounty on a man's head?"

Weber had his suspicions, but as his employment had been shrouded in secrecy and also handled by a cutout, he couldn't say for sure. Not that he would have, even if he had known. He prided himself on discretion. It was a necessary part of his business and absolutely critical in his line of work. The kind of clientele who hired men like him didn't appreciate loose talk. It was the surest way to a very similar sort of contract.

Weber changed the subject. "How long?" he asked.

The Vietnamese man arched one of his narrow eyebrows. "To complete the contract? That's like asking how long is a piece of string. Every professional is different. Each has a different way of going about their craft."

"The client wants it done quickly."

"I have a list of certain professionals in mind. I guarantee you that any one of them will be eager for the job. With a fee like this, whoever I task won't drag their feet."

"Task all of them," said Weber.

"Excuse me?"

"You heard me. Task them all. Whoever gets to him first, and kills him, wins. That's what the client wants."

Trang smiled again. "He really did fuck with the wrong people, didn't he?"

Weber nodded and, standing up from the table, prepared to leave.

"Is there anything else you can tell me?" asked Trang. "Anything that's not in the file?"

"Only one thing," Weber replied, as a torrent of rain slammed against the windows. "Don't underestimate Scot Harvath. If you do, it'll be the last mistake you ever make."

CHAPTER 1

L ooking back on it, Scot Harvath probably shouldn't have punched the guy. Flipped him on his ass? *Sure*. Put his wrist into a painful, yet harmless joint lock? *Even better*. But uppercut the guy so hard that he knocked him out cold? *Not one of his better decisions*.

And therein lay the problem. Lately, Harvath seemed to be out of the good-decision-making business altogether.

Forget for the moment that the other guy had it coming. A wealthy Wall Street type, he appeared to take great pleasure in verbally abusing his female companion. The more the man had to drink, the worse it got. It was uncomfortable for everyone sitting nearby. What it *wasn't*, though, was any of Harvath's business.

People got into relationships for all sorts of reasons. If she was willing to sit there and get berated by some jackass, that was her problem.

At least it had been until she took off her shawl. The moment she did, everything changed.

On such a warm evening, in the resort's open-air lounge, it had seemed odd to be wearing a wrap. Then Harvath noticed her bruises. She had tried to conceal them, but to his discerning eye they were unmistakable, running up and down both arms. Apparently, Wall Street could get rough with more than just his words.

In Harvath's book—hell, in any decent human being's book—men who beat women were scum. Did this guy need to be taught a lesson? *Absolutely*. Did Harvath need to be the one doing the teaching? *That was de-*

batable. Karma would catch up with the guy eventually. It was one of those things from which you could run, but never hide.

Nevertheless, Harvath felt for the woman. Maybe it was all the cocktails he had consumed that were talking. Maybe it was the amount of personal trauma he had unsuccessfully been trying to escape. Either way, the emotional and physical pain radiating from her was undeniable.

And so, when Wall Street next popped off, Harvath didn't even think. He just reacted. Standing up, he walked over to their table. Her problem had just become *his* problem.

"That's enough," he said.

"Come again?" the man replied, an angry look on his face as he rose to confront Harvath.

"You heard me. Leave the lady alone."

"Mind your own business," Wall Street snapped, giving him a shove.

That was when Harvath laid him out.

It was a dramatic escalation of the situation and drew a collective gasp from the other guests. The punch could have killed him. Or, he could have hit his head on one of the tables as he fell. A million and one things could have gone wrong. Thankfully, nothing did.

And while Harvath could have made the legal case that Wall Street had made contact first, it hadn't come to that. He wasn't interested in involving police or pressing charges. That didn't mean, though, that it was over.

The staff at Little Palm Island Resort liked Harvath. He was a repeat customer known for his easy smile and engaging sense of humor. But on this visit, something was off. Something had happened to him; something unsettling.

He was withdrawn and quiet. A dark cloud hovered over him wherever he went. He rose early to work out, but other than that spent the rest of his time drinking, heavily.

Had the resort been empty, the management might have been able to ignore his self-destructive behavior. It wasn't empty, though. It was at full occupancy and none of the upscale clientele wanted to spend their luxury vacation watching a man drink himself to death in the bar.

Harvath didn't care. He knew his alcohol consumption was dangerous, but after everything he had been through, all he wanted was to be released—released from the guilt, the shame, and the pain of what had happened.

The real problem was that there wasn't enough booze in the world to wash away what had happened. His wife, Lara, was dead. His mentor, Reed Carlton—a man who had become like a second father to him—was dead. And one of his dearest colleagues, Lydia Ryan—who had stepped up to helm his organization when he wouldn't, was dead. All of them had been killed in an effort to get to him and he hadn't been able to do a single thing to stop the carnage.

With all of his training, with all of his counterterrorism and espionage experience, he should have been able to protect them. At the very least, he should have seen the attack coming. But he hadn't.

Helpless to save them, he had been forced to watch as they were murdered. Horrific didn't even begin to describe it. The physical torture he was subjected to afterward paled in comparison.

Dragged by a foreign intelligence service back to their country for interrogation and execution, he had managed—through sheer force of will—to pull himself together long enough to orchestrate his own escape. Then, on behalf of Lara, Reed, and Lydia he had carried out his own bloody revenge.

It turned out to be a devastatingly empty accomplishment. He felt no better at the end than he had at the beginning. It gave him no pleasure; no satisfaction. In fact, it had only hollowed him out further—eating away at him like an acid—dimming the already sputtering flame of humanity that remained.

Losing the people closest to him—simply because he had been doing his job—was the absolute worst-case scenario someone in his line of work could ever expect to face. It was worse than torture or even death—fates he would have gladly suffered if it meant that Lara, Reed, and Lydia could have all gone on living.

Instead, he was the one expected to go on living. He would have to "soldier on," carrying the pain of their murders as well as the guilt of knowing that the deaths were his fault.

• • •

And so, once he had completed his revenge, he had traveled to Little Palm Island—a place where he had found solace in the past. This time, though, rejuvenation lay beyond his grasp. He was simply too broken; too far gone.

The only comfort he could find was when he'd had so much to drink that he was simply too numb to feel anything. He would get to that point and keep going until he blacked out. Then he would get up and do it all over again.

If not for his long runs in the sand and punishing swims in the ocean, he would have begun drinking at sunrise. As it was, he was still hitting the bottle well before noon. For someone with such a distinguished career; someone who had given so much in the service of others, it was no way to live.

But Harvath didn't care about living. Not really. Not anymore. While his heart continued to pump alcohol-laden blood throughout his body, his ability to feel anything, for anyone, much less himself, was gone. He had given up.

As such, he wasn't surprised to learn that he had eventually come to the point where he had worn out his welcome at Little Palm Island.

Considering his sizable bar tab, the manager had made him a deal. In exchange for cutting short his stay and departing immediately, a portion of his bill would be comped. Harvath agreed to cut his losses and move on.

Packing his things, he rode the polished motor launch back to Little Torch Key, revived his abandoned rental car, and drove until he came to the end of the road in Key West.

There, in a less touristy part of town known as Bahama Village, he took the first room he found and paid for two weeks, up front, in cash.

The carpet looked to be at least twenty years old—the paint even older. The whole place smelled like mold covered up with Febreze. He was a world away from the high-thread-count sheets and hibiscus-scented air of Little Palm Island. Like Icarus and his melted wings, the once "golden boy" of the U.S. Intelligence Community had come crashing down to earth. Cracking a window, he opened his suitcase.

Having served as an elite U.S. Navy SEAL, it had been drilled into him to properly maintain and stow his gear. After hanging several items in the closet and placing the rest into a battered chest of drawers, he carried the wrinkled Ziploc bag he was using as a shaving kit into the bathroom.

There, he lined the contents on the shelf above the sink and stared at himself in the mirror. He looked terrible.

Though his five-foot-ten-inch body was still muscular, he had lost weight. His sandy-brown hair might have been sun-bleached and his skin tanned a deep brown, but the cheeks of his handsome face were sunken and his once sharp, glacierlike blue eyes were tired and bloodshot.

If any of his friends could see him, his transformation would have been shocking. Decay was a powerful force. Once set in motion, it went quickly to work.

Returning to the bedroom, he walked back over to the suitcase. There was only one item remaining—a photograph in a silver frame. It was his favorite picture of Lara. She stood in a sundress, her long dark hair falling across her shoulders, with a glass of white wine on his dock overlooking the Potomac River in Virginia.

Lara's parents were Brazilian and she had grown up speaking both English and Portuguese. After her first husband had drowned, she said she had been plagued by a feeling known as *saudade*.

When he asked her to translate it, she had said there wasn't really an equivalent. In essence, it was a longing for someone or something you know you will never experience again. She had been terrified that Harvath, the first man she had loved since her husband's death, was going to cause her to relive those feelings.

As a police officer, she had understood that the majority of people were sheep—gentle creatures largely incapable of protecting themselves. To defend them from the wolves of the world, they needed sheepdogs. As a homicide detective, she further understood that sheepdogs would never be enough. The world also needed wolf hunters—brave souls willing to go into the darkness to take down the wolves before they could attack. That's what Harvath was—a wolf hunter. And that's what had scared her.

While he claimed to want a family more than anything else, he continued grabbing the most dangerous assignments that came his way. He would leave at a moment's notice—sometimes for days, weeks, or even months at a time.

He was working for a private intelligence agency named after his mentor: The Carlton Group. It had been tasked with providing the CIA room to breathe as it rebuilt itself into a leaner, better-focused, and more efficient organization along the lines of its predecessor—the OSS.

To many D.C. insiders, it felt counterintuitive to approach America's modern, rapidly evolving threats by looking to the past. But to those spearheading the renovation, they knew that's where the answers lay. The Agency was dying—choking on its own bureaucracy. Like a hot air balloon falling out of the sky, the only way to fix it was to toss anything and everything that was unnecessary overboard.

By stripping it down to its bare essentials, they could focus not only on what needed to be done, but also the best ways to do it. For far too long, brave men and women at the CIA had been prevented from doing their jobs by risk-averse middle managers more concerned with their next promotion than with conducting the nation's most dangerous business.

But, like any large, government entity gorging itself on ever-increasing budgets and layers upon layers of self-inflicted rules, regulations, and red tape, many things at the CIA weren't going to be easy to change. They were going to take a lot of work, a lot of patience, and a lot of time— during which the threats to America were only going to grow deadlier. Enter The Carlton Group.

As the man who had come up with the idea and had created the CIA's Counterterrorism Center, Reed Carlton had seen the writing on the wall long before most. When he finally tired of no one on the seventh floor listening to him about what was coming, he left and started his own endeavor. He staffed it with highly accomplished, former intelligence and Special Operations personnel. Carlton had a scary eye for talent. And, as with everything else in his career, he had been way ahead of the curve.

During the Agency's struggle to remake itself, some of its riskiest, most sensitive work was quietly contracted out to The Carlton Group. Just as they were picking up speed and more jobs were being funneled their way, they received dreadful news. Reed Carlton—the heart, soul, and brains of the entire organization—had been diagnosed with Alzheimer's.

Once he had gotten over the initial shock, he had only one request—that Scot Harvath, his handpicked successor, the man he had poured all of his wisdom, experience, and know-how into, give up field operations and take over the running of the business.

In a move that stunned everyone, Harvath had said no. It didn't matter how much Carlton threatened or cajoled his protégé, the answer remained the same. At least it had been until the Old Man, as he was known by those closest to him, had brought Lara into it.

He knew how much Harvath cared for her and her four-year-old son, Marco. He knew it was only a matter of time before they settled down and became a family. He also knew that no matter how often Harvath said that was what he really wanted most in life, it wasn't true. Not completely.

Harvath had an addiction. He was addicted to the lifestyle—the constant scrapes with death and the heroinlike highs that came from the massive adrenaline dumps they provided. And like any drug addiction, it needed to be constantly fed and continually took more than the last time to reach the same high. It also had the same outcome waiting for him at the end. Sooner or later, it would take his life.

Harvath was no ordinary junkie, though. He was highly intelligent, which meant he was exceedingly good at coming up with justifications for not getting out. *No one was as experienced, nor as skilled as he was. No one had the human networks he had. No one was as good at developing assets. No one was willing to take the risks that he did. No one could adapt as quickly on the ground.* And on and on.

It was all true, but it didn't mean that others couldn't be groomed to do the same—and that was precisely what the Old Man had wanted him to do. Harvath had stayed in the game far longer than was safe. He put way too much at risk each time he went into the field. In a word, it was *selfish*. The fact that he depended on a cocktail of performance-enhancing drugs just to remain at peak performance should have been a bright neon sign blasting the message that his days were numbered.

The Old Man's admonishment to think of Lara and Marco had pissed Harvath off. It was emotional blackmail and a professional low blow. It angered him most, though, because he knew Carlton was correct. He needed to make a tough decision. But like any junkie, he would first try to negotiate his way out of it.

Despite what the Old Man thought, Harvath honestly believed that he had several more years left of kicking in doors and shooting bad guys in the head. The sports medicine group he had found that rehabbed top professional athletes and Tier One operators had been a godsend. If not for them, he might have been reluctantly inclined to agree with Carlton that it was time to move from playing to scouting and coaching.

The docs and exercise physiologists he worked with, though, had upped his game to levels he hadn't even thought possible. Through their program, he was stronger, faster, and had better reaction time than he'd had in his thirties. The advances they had developed were incredible. So, with all due respect to his mentor, he had proposed a compromise.

Instead of abandoning operations altogether, he had spent half his time in the field and half his time at The Carlton Group incubating new talent.

This was not the outcome the Old Man had been gunning for. He needed somebody steering the ship on a full-time basis. He also knew Harvath—maybe better than anyone else. He knew that if he gave him an ultimatum, Harvath would jump ship and freelance for whoever would pay his quote—and with his skillset, there were plenty of opportunities. He might have been able to get him blacklisted at the CIA, but the Brits or the Israelis would have scooped him up in a heartbeat.

Whether Harvath would have agreed to work for a foreign service was an unknown. In the end, like a son, the Old Man wanted to keep him close. He wanted to know that the ops that Harvath undertook were as well planned and professional as possible. If he kept him in-house, he could guarantee that they would be—something he couldn't say if he let him put himself on the open market.

This left Carlton with the problem of who would actually run the organization. After discussions with the President and the Director of the

CIA, he was given permission to approach the Agency's Deputy Director, Lydia Ryan. She had been an exceptional intelligence officer and understood the game from top to bottom. Lydia was an excellent hire.

The Old Man, despite having Alzheimer's, was a walking history of the espionage business. He knew where all the top secret "bodies" were buried. Lydia and Harvath had taken turns sitting with him, recording every piece of valuable information he had stored in his brain before it all slipped away.

When his capacities began to fail and he started revealing some of his sensitive exploits to his housekeeper and friends who would call up or drop by to check on him, Harvath decided it was time to silo him.

Carlton's fondest memories had been of spending summers at his grandparents' cottage on Lake Winnipesaukee in New Hampshire. It was off-season and easy for Harvath to find an available home for rent. As the oldest memories were usually the last to disappear, he thought it would be a comfortable and familiar place for Carlton.

With the President's approval, a team of Navy corpsmen—all with top secret clearance—was detailed to the Old Man. On rotating shifts, there was always one in the house. Harvath flew up to see him as often as possible.

He had just returned from a particularly harrowing assignment overseas, during which he had made up his mind about what he wanted. While he couldn't promise that he would retire from fieldwork anytime soon, he knew that he loved Lara and her son and would for the rest of his life.

Following a romantic meal, he had walked her down to the dock and had proposed. She had lovingly and excitedly accepted.

Knowing that the Old Man was slipping away, Harvath had asked her to elope with him. He wanted to get married at the cottage, quietly, by his bedside. Ryan would be their witness.

Lara knew how much Reed Carlton meant to her fiancé. She had come to love him like a father as well. Including such a special man in such a special moment was the right thing to do. And so, she had agreed.

To keep it under wraps—until they could do a big church wedding with Lara's family, his mom, and all their friends present—they hired a local judge to conduct the ceremony in private.

Everything had been perfect. The Old Man had even been more engaged and energetic than they had seen him in long time.

Harvath couldn't have asked for anything more. The walks around the lake with Lara, the laughter, the lovemaking; those couple of days—from the secret wedding until the attack—had been the happiest he had ever known. Then it had all come crashing down.

After the murders, the torture, his escape, and fighting his way across a frozen foreign landscape to freedom, much of who he had been was stripped away.

Since the funerals, his colleagues had backed off, showing their respect by giving him space and letting him grieve.

Nevertheless, he couldn't shake the feeling that someone had been keeping tabs on him. He figured it had to have been somebody from the office. They were more than just coworkers, they were family. And spies, after all, never stop spying—especially on each other.

They all knew where he had been staying. In fact, a colleague had done him a favor by shipping a suitcase full of his clothes down to Little Palm Island in advance of his arrival.

But now that he had decamped for Key West, he'd be harder to find. Harder, but not impossible.

He still had his phone, which never left the room and which he only turned on to scroll through photos, old texts, and voice messages from Lara. Lest anyone catch him while the phone was on, he had it set to "Do Not Disturb," disabling the chime and sending any new calls straight to voicemail.

Once his unpacking was complete, he had spent the next several days making the rounds of local watering holes until he finally settled on one. Not that his standards were particularly high. They weren't. All that mattered was that the air-conditioning was cold, the bar quiet, and the clientele a particular class: hard-core, professional drinkers who just wanted to be left alone.

The place he ultimately selected was a quintessential dive bar. Dimly lit, with blacked-out windows, its air was redolent of urinal cakes, spilled beer, and wasted lives.

Nobody paid him any attention. In fact, no one had given him so much as a second look. It was the perfect hole in the wall to continue his slow-motion suicide.

And though he could have continued to drink top-shelf as he had at Little Palm Island, he instead went for the worst stuff they had. He wanted it to burn all the way down. He wanted to torture himself. Glancing around, it was pretty obvious that he hadn't cornered the market in self-loathing.

Imagining the backstories of the people he was drinking "with" didn't take too much creativity. All of them had been drawn to the southernmost point in the U.S. by something. There were probably more than a few failed marriages, failed businesses, and outstanding warrants in the room. Anything was possible. They didn't call Key West a "sunny place for shady people" for nothing.

The bartender was an attractive woman in her forties. Twenty, even ten years ago, the top bars on the island would have been cutting each other's throats to hire her. She was not only sexy, but she was also adept at slinging drinks. More importantly, she knew when, and when not, to make conversation.

When it came to Harvath, she could tell that he was not looking to talk. He was polite, and tipped well, but he kept to himself.

He came in every day with a newspaper he barely read, sat in the same scarred booth where he ordered the same drink over and over, as he stared toward the front door. It was as if he was waiting for someone. But whoever that someone was, they never came.

She felt sorry for him. He was handsome, close to her age, and a man who obviously needed to be put back together. She had always been drawn to guys who were screwed up. "Broken Bird Syndrome" a friend had once called it.

He wasn't like the other customers. He seemed like a "somebody." Somebody, who at one point in his life, had prospects; potential. She had a lot of questions. *Where had he come from? What was he doing here? How long was he going to stay?* Most of all, she wondered what he was like in bed.

When it came to her advances, though, the man was immune. Whoever had wounded him had done a bang-up job.

Still, she liked having him around. There was something comforting about his presence. The strong, silent type—he struck her as a guy who could handle himself.

Maybe he was an ex-cop, or possibly ex-military. It didn't matter. All she knew was that having him in the bar made her feel safe.

Not that a lot of bad things went down in Key West. But, like every other resort town fueled by alcohol and an "anything goes" attitude, sometimes things got out of control.

It was at that moment that the door opened. And as it did, no one inside had any idea how out of control things were about to get.

CHAPTER 2

Harvath was a detail person and had developed a good feel for the bar's rhythm as well as for its customer base. So, when the front door opened and two out-of-place men walked in, his Spidey sense immediately began tingling.

The two gorillas looked like a pair of bikers who had picked up the wrong bags at the airport. They wore stiff, new boots without a scuff on them. Their shirts were also new; the sun-blocking, SPF kind that sport fishermen wore and which could be found all over the island.

Despite the heat outside, they had their sleeves rolled down to their wrists and buttoned tight—as if they were trying to hide something. *Probably tattoos*, he thought.

Neither wore any jewelry, but as they passed his booth, he noticed they each had pierced ears. And from the white stripes on one of the men's fingers, Harvath could tell that he spent a lot of time outside and normally wore several thick rings.

Beneath the other man's shirt, he caught a flash of silver chain attached to a wallet. Somewhere, better hidden, they were each probably carrying a knife, and maybe even a firearm.

It wasn't that he begrudged anyone their right to self-defense. He had spent a career carrying and using weapons. But these weren't your garden-variety Florida rednecks down in Key West for a good time. The bearing of these men suggested something different—something dangerous.

Yet unless they were dumb enough to walk over and put a gun in his face, he didn't care who they were or why they were here. In street parlance, he was all out of fucks to give.

That voice in the back of his head, though, kept asking questions. *Why had the men removed their jewelry? Why were they keeping their arms covered? Why the new boots? What the hell were they up to?*

Trying to ignore his gut, he took another sip of cheap bourbon, opened the newspaper, and attempted to mind his own business.

His instincts, though, weren't done raising the alarm.

Throughout the animal kingdom, when Alphas crossed paths, there was always eye contact. Both of these guys were definitely Alphas and both had observed him, but neither had made eye contact. The omission was like a white-hot, phosphorous flare sailing across the animal portion of his brain.

They hadn't made eye contact because they knew that doing so would trigger a response. It was the only possible explanation.

He had always been adept at reading people. It was like a sixth sense. The worse someone's intent, the better he was at picking up on it. He could sum up a situation and get off the "X," as it was known in his line of work, faster than just about anyone else.

Whatever the men were planning, it wasn't good. He could feel it in every fiber of his being.

Seating themselves at the bar, the men each ordered a shot and a beer. Tossing back their whiskeys, they then clinked mugs, knocked back the beers, and ordered another round.

It didn't take long for them to get loud. And as they did, they began to grate on Harvath's nerves.

All he wanted was to drink in peace, but they were making it difficult. For some reason, when their second round arrived, they decided to start giving the bartender a hard time. He couldn't believe this was happening all over again.

Adjusting his position in the booth, Harvath angled himself so he could keep a better eye on the situation.

As she set the drinks down, they tried to touch her. One of the men even attempted to push money into her jeans. From the other side of the bar, she swatted the guy's hand away and gave him a warning.

Harvath wondered why the hell she didn't just throw them out. This wasn't a strip club. But it also—he reminded himself—wasn't his bar and, therefore, wasn't his problem. At least it wasn't his problem until he got to the end of his drink and needed a refill.

Holding up his empty glass, he signaled that he was ready for another. To her credit, she noticed.

Grabbing the bottle of bourbon, she stepped out from behind the bar. But despite giving the two problem customers a wide berth, she couldn't avoid a clash.

As she walked by, one of them leapt up, grabbed her around the waist and pulled her to him.

He had his thick arm around her so tightly that even if she had wanted to smash the bottle against his head, she wouldn't have been able to.

"Get the fuck off of me," she ordered, but it only seemed to delight the man and encourage him further. Burying his bearded face against her, he kissed her neck as his buddy howled his approval.

Harvath watched, still hesitant to get involved. But just like at Little Palm Island, he knew he was going to have to. It was the way he was wired. He couldn't let crap like that go.

Taking the section of newspaper he was reading, he set it on the table, rolled his empty rocks glass in it, twisted the ends together, and took it in his fist. These guys had obviously come looking for trouble. Now, they had found it.

He slipped from his booth, a bit unsteady from all the alcohol he had consumed, but not so bad—he hoped—as to put him at a disadvantage.

Holding his makeshift weapon behind him, he headed toward the bar. He doubted either of these two were going to listen to reason and he had no intention of fighting fair. He was inebriated, it was two against one, and both men were much larger than he was. The element of surprise needed to be heavily in his favor if he hoped to come out on the winning end of this one.

It took about a microsecond to realize that any chance he'd had of surprising them was lost. They both not only saw him approaching, but also figured out he was holding something behind his back.

"Hold up, motherfucker," the buddy said. "What do you think you're doing? And what's that you're hiding?"

As was his fashion, Harvath ignored questions he had no intention of answering. You didn't answer questions when you were taking charge of a situation, you gave orders. "Let go of her," he demanded.

The man holding the bartender sneered at him. "Fuck you," he replied. "Mind your own fucking business."

Harvath nodded at the bottle she was holding and said, "That *is* my business."

The men looked at each other for a moment, almost unsure of how to respond, and then burst into laughter. He wasn't trying to save the bartender, he was trying to rescue the booze.

"Sit your ass down," the buddy ordered. "And whatever you've got behind your back, this is the last time I'm going to tell you to drop it."

"Let her go," Harvath repeated. "Then we can all get back to drinking and nobody gets hurt."

"You mean *you* don't get hurt."

Harvath smiled. "It's up to you. Let her go, I'll get my drink, and like I said, nobody'll get hurt."

"And if we don't? What are you going to do about it? There's two of us, dumbass."

"I see that," said Harvath. "Listen, why don't—"

"Why don't we what?" the man interrupted. "Let you buy us a drink? Is that what you were going to say, pussy?"

The rage that Harvath had been harboring; the rage that he had been trying to cap, with glass after glass of bourbon, began to bubble up again and was about to boil over.

If he was honest with himself, he had been spoiling for a real, knock-down, drag-out fight since Little Palm Island. He wanted to vent all of his anger in one great purge and it looked like he was about to get his chance.

Smiling, he replied, "I wouldn't piss on you losers if you were on fire, so there's no way I'm going to offer to buy you drinks. I will, though, offer for us to take this outside. Let her go and we'll see if two against one makes a difference. Or not."

With that, Harvath set the glass he had wrapped in newspaper on the bar and smiled at the men.

They looked at him and smiled back. The larger man took one more sip of his beer as the other let go of the bartender.

Stepping a safe distance away, she announced, "I'm calling the cops."

"Better call an ambulance first," the buddy said as he gestured toward the door.

"Good idea," Harvath agreed, as he headed toward the exit. "In fact, call two."

CHAPTER 3

Harvath knew better than to fight inside the bar. There were too many things that could go wrong. There were also too many witnesses—any number of whom could have whipped out a phone, filmed what was taking place, and posted it to the internet, or worse—shared it with the police, who would share it with a jury. No matter how justified Harvath might have been, his fighting style was brutal. For average people unaccustomed to violence, it was difficult to watch and would win him little, if any, sympathy in a courtroom. It wouldn't matter who had started the fight, all a transfixed jury would be focused on was how he had ended it. Taking it outside was the smart move.

Outside there weren't any cameras. Outside he could do whatever he wanted. Outside he could let his rage off its chain.

Whoever these assholes were, he was going to make them pay for everything bad that had happened to him.

It didn't matter that they had nothing to do with any of it. They were begging for an ass-kicking and ass-kickings happened to be one of his specialties. Suggesting the bartender call for two ambulances wasn't hyperbole, it was a courtesy. He was going to beat the shit out of both of them. The sooner they got this over with, the better.

The night was thick with humidity as they squared up behind the building. Harvath did a quick scan for any cameras he may have missed, as well as for any stray items that might get picked up and used as weapons. *Nothing*. It was time to get to work.

Already taunting him with a string of insults, the smaller of the two men had made a critical error. Puffing out his chest, he had also foolishly raised his chin. Harvath stepped right in and delivered a devastating throat punch.

The man's hands reflexively flew to his neck as he stumbled backward, struggling to breathe.

Harvath spun to face the guy's partner, but didn't move fast enough. The larger man had already shifted to the left and landed a massive punch to the side of his head that caused him to see stars. He felt his knees buckle as he fell to the ground.

It was a stupid mistake. Harvath should have seen it coming, but his rage and his ego had gotten the better of him. He had been overconfident and now he was in trouble. *Big* trouble.

In a street fight the ground was the deadliest place to be. His opponent, well aware that he had the upper hand, took full advantage; kicking him over and over as hard as he could.

Within the first couple of kicks, the smaller man—having recovered his ability to breathe—reappeared and put the boot to him as well. It would only be a matter of time before one of them began kicking him in the head. Once that happened, the fight would be over. Harvath had to do something. *Fast*.

He rolled onto his side, and as he did the two men increased the intensity of the kicking.

Rocking onto his elbow as he absorbed the blows, he used his hand to brace himself and began to push up and off the ground. As soon as he had his legs beneath him, all he needed was enough space to get back onto his feet.

As his attackers moved in a circle around him, Harvath spun as well. Using his free arm to parry the punches and kicks, he searched for an opening. When it presented itself, he exploded into a standing position, hammering the larger man in the groin on the way up.

The move took both assailants by surprise. Harvath was back in the fight and showed no mercy. Slipping away from a poorly aimed punch by the smaller man, Scot pounded him with a vicious jab-cross-hook combination.

There was the crack of cartilage and a spray of blood as he broke the man's nose with the first punch and sent him, unconscious, to the ground with the hook.

Careful not to make the mistake he had made previously, he kept both of his hands up to protect his head. He was already moving as the bigger man closed the distance and slammed him with a series of heavy punches. No matter what he did to stay outside his reach, his opponent still found a way to land his blows.

The man was an exceptional fighter and Harvath was forced to keep his hands up to protect his face and head. As he did, he left his body exposed and took a wave of painful strikes in many of the same areas he had already been kicked. When the man landed two solid kidney punches, Harvath was sure he'd be pissing blood for a week.

This fight had been much harder than he had anticipated. He needed to bring an end to it.

As his opponent stepped forward to deliver another series of punches, Harvath unleashed a blistering side kick, destroying the man's left knee. From there, he moved in and lit the guy up.

It was a flurry of knees, fists, and elbows. Every single blow found its target. As each strike landed, Harvath's rage erupted out of him like an uncapped oil well.

The assault came so fast and from so many different directions that the larger man couldn't even defend himself. When he put up his hands and arms to protect his head, Harvath attacked his body. When he tried to protect his body, Harvath went after his head and face.

All the while, the man kept his remaining good knee protected, knowing that if Harvath connected with it, that would be the end of the fight.

Sensing what the man was doing, Harvath feigned dropping his guard.

It presented such a perfect target, that even in his bloody, battered state, the man couldn't resist taking one powerful, final swing in the hope of knocking Harvath out. It was the last mistake he made.

No sooner had he stepped into his punch, than Harvath pivoted off the line of attack and took out his opponent's right knee with another side kick.

As the giant fell, Harvath met his face halfway down with an enormous uppercut, snapping the attacker's head straight back, knocking him unconscious. The fight was over.

Or so Harvath had thought.

One of the number-one rules in a street brawl was to always watch for other assailants. Just because you couldn't see them, didn't mean they weren't out there—friends of the combatants, eagerly waiting to jump in, or even sadistic onlookers hoping to land a cheap shot when your guard was down.

Usually, Harvath had good situational awareness. He knew to look for these kinds of things. This time, though, he had failed to.

Maybe it was the bourbon. Maybe it was the sweat stinging his eyes. Maybe he had simply lost a step.

Whatever it was, when a figure stepped out of the shadows and pointed a suppressed pistol at him, he knew he was going to die.

CHAPTER 4

Harvath had no idea who had come to kill him. He had made so many enemies over his career that it could have been anyone, or any organization, or just a random asshole.

He had cheated death so often, though, that it was hard to believe it had finally caught up with him. He only hoped that it would be quick. And, that if there was a heaven on the other side, that Lara would be waiting for him there. Straightening up, he turned to fully face his killer.

The man holding the weapon stood about five-foot-ten, so they were essentially eye-to-eye. He was slim but fit, with brown hair, brown eyes, and pale skin. His features were nondescript and of indeterminate origin. In a word, he was utterly forgettable—a quintessential "gray man" if Harvath had ever seen one.

He radiated an icy calm. His breathing was steady and his weapon didn't tremble. Clearly, he was a professional and had done this kind of work before.

There was nothing in his eyes, nothing in his face that signaled a motivation—no rage, no vengeance, no passion. He didn't look like someone Harvath had directly wronged. No, this was a *transaction*—cold, detached, and impersonal.

While Harvath wanted to know who had sent the man and why, he refrained from asking. He wasn't going to give the killer, or more importantly his employer, the satisfaction.

Besides, there was no need to drag the whole thing out. If this was how his life was going to end, he planned to exhibit some modicum of stoicism. Might as well just do it and get it over with.

Stopping just at the edge of the shadows, the killer maintained his distance, bolstering Harvath's assessment that he was a professional. He didn't need to come any nearer. He had watched Harvath fight and would know that getting too close could end badly. Better to stay where he was, take the shot, and disappear back into the darkness before anyone knew what had happened.

What's more, if he was a pro, he would have done his homework. He would have known Harvath was too smart and too well trained to have risked sneaking up on him.

Sending two knuckle-draggers to lure him outside was smart. They'd probably been paid to beat him within an inch of his life and take off before the cops got there. What the hooligans wouldn't have known, was that once they had fled, the hitter's plan was to materialize and finish the job. Smarter still, the cops wouldn't have been looking for a lone, mysterious gunman. Based on the accounts of everyone in the bar, the knuckle-draggers would have been the prime suspects. The hitter would have walked away clean. Harvath had completely thrown a wrench in that plan.

No doubt, the two bruisers were expendable. Whether they regained consciousness and escaped before the police arrived was their problem. The killer had only one priority at this moment—taking out his target.

In the distance, the klaxons of emergency vehicles could already be heard. The assassin was running out of time. It was now or never.

As if reading his mind, the man took a deep breath, looked down the slide of his pistol, and adjusted his sight picture.

Harvath wasn't afraid to die. He didn't look away or close his eyes. In fact, he kept them locked right on his killer.

The assassin began to apply pressure to the trigger and Harvath knew the moment had arrived. He braced for the worst. And then it came.

There was a muffled pop followed by silence. That was it. He felt no pain. In fact, he was still very much alive.

How was that possible? Had the assassin missed? Had his weapon malfunctioned? A fraction of a second later, Harvath had his answer.

Blood began to trickle from a hole in the would-be killer's forehead.

And as he collapsed to the ground, Harvath realized the man had been shot by someone else. *But by whom?*

Suddenly, four men carrying suppressed weapons appeared out of nowhere. Their faces were obscured by balaclavas and night vision goggles. *What the hell was going on?*

"Time to go," one of them ordered. Harvath instantly recognized the voice.

Before he could reply, two of the men had grabbed him under the arms and were steering him toward a narrow gangway.

Glancing over his shoulder, he caught a glimpse of the other men swiftly unfurling a body bag and placing the dead man inside.

When they emerged from the gangway, a dark panel van was idling at the curb. As they approached it, the door slid open and he climbed in. The two men with him stood guard outside. It smelled like disinfectant.

Seconds later, the other men arrived with the body bag. Once the corpse was loaded, everyone piled in, and the van took off. As it did, the occupants began removing their night vision goggles and balaclavas. One by one, the faces of his teammates were revealed.

The first one belonged to the man whose voice he had recognized— Mike Haney. With his square jaw and close-cropped hair, the six-foot-tall Force Recon Marine looked like he had stepped out of a recruiting ad.

"What the hell just happened?" Harvath asked.

"We saved your life," Haney replied. "*Again.*"

The man was right of course. If it hadn't been for them, Harvath wouldn't have made it back to the United States from his last mission alive. *But what were they doing here?*

Tyler Staelin, the team's de facto medic, removed a penlight from his medical kit, clicked it on, and asked Harvath to follow it with his eyes. Once the five-foot-ten former Delta Force operative was satisfied with his colleague's neurological function, he began running through a checklist of questions to assess other possible injuries.

Harvath replied to about three of them before growing frustrated. "I'm fine," he said. "Answer my question."

Staelin cracked a pair of cold packs and handed them to him. "Place these wherever you need them."

Harvath slid them under his shirt and, with great discomfort, held them against his rib cage. "What the hell's going on?" he repeated. "What are you doing here?"

Their silence was unsettling. Gallows humor came with the territory and ran deep with this crew. Normally, he couldn't get them to shut up. The fact that nobody was answering could only mean one thing. They had bad news.

It was Chase Palmer, the team's other ex–Delta Force operative, who finally spoke up. In addition to looking like a younger version of Harvath, he had also been personally recruited by the Old Man. "We got a tip from the Norwegian Intelligence Service," he stated.

Harvath's frustration was growing. "What kind of tip?"

"Carl Pedersen was murdered."

CHAPTER 5

It was like being hit by a truck. Carl Pedersen was not only Harvath's best intelligence contact in Scandinavia, but he had also been a friend. The Old Man had introduced them and, despite their age difference, they had become close. Pedersen's loss was devastating, especially on the heels of losing his wife and two dear friends.

"When did it happen?"

"Four days ago," Chase replied. "Maybe more. His body wasn't discovered until today. A neighbor found him. At his country house."

"How was he killed?"

"From what the Norwegians say, it wasn't pretty. He had been tied up and tortured. Then he was shot, once, in the chest. The round went straight through his heart."

Not one prone to showing his cards—particularly his emotional ones—Harvath blanched. That was a shitty way to go, especially for someone like Pedersen.

He had been a good man. Old-school. Willing to bend and even break a few rules here and there if it meant saving lives. He had been a spy's spy. There weren't a lot like him at the Norwegian Intelligence Service. Sharing a border with Russia—and all the malign activity therein—Norway had been lucky to have him. He wouldn't be easy to replace.

It sounded like a professional job. What didn't make sense, though, was why the Norwegians had notified them. "What prompted the call?" he asked. "Why reach out to us?"

Reluctant to let the other shoe drop, Chase didn't respond. He knew what a blow it was going to be.

Piloting the van toward Naval Air Station Key West, Sloane Ashby was the team's lone female operative and also another one of its youngest. Ex-Army, she had been recruited by the Old Man as well. She was not only attractive, but she could also be quite funny. Now, though, wasn't a time for jokes. It was time to tear the Band-Aid off and give it to Harvath straight.

"The working theory at NIS is that Pedersen was tortured in order to get access to his phone and laptop."

Harvath caught her eyes in the rearview mirror. "Why? What for?"

"According to their computer forensics people, the killer was building a dossier."

"On what?"

"Not on *what*. On *who*."

As a pair of police cars went racing past them, it all came crashing down on him. "Me?"

Haney put his hand on his friend's shoulder. "That's why the Norwegians reached out. They wanted to warn you. The killer accessed Pedersen's phone, his laptop, and the secure NIS database. Every recent search appears to be related to you."

Harvath didn't want to believe what he was hearing. *Not because of him. Not another murder.*

It was like having the truck that had just hit you, back up, and do it all over again. He needed another drink—a big one. Probably more than one.

Turning his gaze to the body bag, he managed, "So that's the guy."

"We think so, but there's not much to go on. The killer didn't leave any evidence at the scene in Norway."

It had to be him, Harvath thought. He didn't believe in coincidences.

"How did you know he was going to be here, tonight, on Key West?"

"We didn't," said Haney.

"Then how did you find me?"

"When you didn't pick up your phone, we were worried it might already be too late."

"I've had it turned off. It's in a drawer back in—"

"Back in your room," Haney said, interrupting him. "Yeah, we know. We found it. That's the first place we hit when we got here."

Harvath knew that the phone didn't need to be turned on for it to be tracked.

"In order to get word to you," Haney continued, "we asked Key West PD to go by and do a wellness check. They did, but your room was empty. Eventually, they tracked down the property manager, who said he'd seen you earlier and everything appeared fine. The cops left a note in your room, as well as with the property manager to call Uncle Paul."

Call Uncle Paul was a distress code. Had Harvath received that message, he would have known that he was in danger and should make contact as quickly as possible.

"How did you figure out to come by the bar?" he asked. "I've never brought my phone there and I always pay cash."

Haney withdrew the receipt upon which the bartender had written her name and cell number and handed it to Harvath. "Her phone wasn't turned on either."

"Probably because she was tending bar," said Harvath.

"We didn't know what to think. Because it was off, we couldn't call, but we could track it. Once we got a lock, we headed straight over."

Harvath had thought about throwing the woman's number away, but in the end had hung on to it. He wasn't planning on sleeping with her. At least he hadn't thought he was. But in all of his despair and loneliness, there was part of him that craved the touch of another human being.

That phone number had saved his life. And even though The Carlton Group had its own private jet, they must have moved heaven and earth to get to him as fast as they had. A few seconds later and he would have been dead. At the very least, he owed his teammates a thank-you.

"Thank you," he said.

"You're welcome," Haney replied. "No more funerals."

Harvath nodded. It was a noble ambition, but he didn't know how realistic it was. Death was an occupational hazard in their line of work. It came with the territory.

The goal, of course, was to make sure the bad guys were the ones doing the dying. But, as evidenced by Lara, the Old Man, Lydia, and now Carl Pedersen, that wasn't always possible.

Gesturing toward the body bag again, Harvath stated, "This has got to be the same guy. There must be something that ties him to Carl."

Haney agreed. "This is priority one for the Norwegians. Who knows what evidence they've developed since we last heard from them. We'll take prints, a retinal scan, and photos for facial recognition on the flight home."

Home. The term didn't resonate with him the way it once had. Home used to be a place he longed to return to after dangerous assignments abroad. It was what he had been building with Lara and Marco—a life, a family—something worth living for and coming back to. Now, he had nothing.

As he teetered on the edge of an all-consuming darkness that threatened to swallow him whole, he needed to face his demons—in his time, in his own way. If he survived, great. If not, then so be it. It wasn't time for his self-imposed exile to end.

"Drop me off at the next corner," he ordered.

Sloane caught his eyes in the rearview mirror and then flicked her gaze to Haney.

"Scot," said Haney. "It's not safe for you to stay here."

"I don't plan on staying. But I'm a big boy and can handle myself. Maybe I'll follow in Hemingway's footsteps. Head down to Cuba. Do some fishing." *And a hell of a lot more drinking.*

"That'd be a bad idea," Staelin interjected.

"Why's that?"

"Besides Cuba being a communist dictatorship and you being one of the most anticommunist people I've ever known?"

"Yeah, besides that."

Staelin glanced at Haney as if seeking permission to answer the question. But before he could, Chase jumped back in. "There may be more than one assassin out there looking for you."

Harvath turned to him. "What are you talking about?"

"We have a piece of information that the Norwegians don't."

CHAPTER 6

Sølvi Kolstad was tall, very good-looking, and had made a lot of bad choices. She was lucky to have been allowed back.

Standing up, she stretched her long legs. It felt good to get the blood flowing. She was exhausted and her mind worked better with movement.

Outside, beyond the thick forest of pine and the clear, cold lake, she could feel the thrum of the city. It was always worse late at night. The pull of the different neighborhoods. Places like Grünerløkka, where she used to go for MDMA, or Brugata for cocaine, as well as Hausmanns gate for heroin, and Grønland for meth.

She could feel them all calling out to her as sure as she could feel her lungs inflating as she breathed, and the beating of her heart in her chest. It was a struggle. Day by day. Hour by hour.

The treatment counselors had told her that if she didn't give in—if she remained strong—that over time the powerful longing would fade. Fade, but never completely disappear.

The closest thing she had found to the euphoria of illicit drugs was intense, lung-searing, muscle-burning exercise. The flood of endorphins released into her system transported her, albeit all too temporarily, to another plane of existence. The only thing better was a mind-blowing orgasm. But for those, she needed a partner—and ever since her divorce, which had sent her spiraling, she couldn't be bothered to put in the effort.

Intimacy wasn't very high on her checklist anymore. Walking over to the window, she studied her reflection in the glass.

When her blond hair was pulled up in a high ponytail you could see the beginning of a tattoo. It was a line from Sartre in delicate, thin blue script that ran from the base of her neck down to the midpoint of her spine. *Il est impossible d'apprécier la lumière sans connaître les ténèbres. It is impossible to appreciate the light without knowing the darkness.*

Above her right hip was a scar from a bullet that had gone straight through. A couple of millimeters lower and it would have shattered her hip, sabotaging the mission she had been on at the time. While she had bled profusely, she had managed to accomplish her assignment. The scar in front and in back were reminders—both of the dangers she faced in her job and that she should never take anything for granted.

Her striking appearance was rounded out by large blue eyes, full lips, and impossibly high cheekbones. For all of the damage she had done to herself, she hadn't lost her looks. In fact, some were saying that she looked better now than before her leave of absence from NIS.

It was amazing, she supposed, what being high as fuck and losing your appetite could do for your appearance. There was only one obvious place the drugs had taken their toll—her teeth. Carl Pedersen, though, had fixed them. Or more appropriately, he had paid to get them fixed. A private dentist in Bergen—someplace far away from anyone she may have known or bumped into from Oslo. That was also where he had gotten her into a private drug treatment program. Quite simply, he had rescued her.

When everyone else had given up on her, when she was at her absolute lowest, rock-bottom moment, and most needed saving, that's when he had appeared.

Gathering her up, he had taken her away to some safe house—halfway between Oslo and Bergen—a place she doubted even the NIS knew about.

It was a gorgeous ski lodge in the town of Geilo and obviously belonged to someone with a lot of money. Who, though, he never said.

That was just like him. Carl Pedersen knew people everywhere. Not just in Norway, but around the world. He was either the best friend or the worst enemy a person could ever have. She couldn't believe he was gone.

The pain caused by his death felt like someone had shoved a glowing fireplace poker through her chest. He had not only saved her, but he had also helped her sober up and had gotten her reinstated. If not for him, she didn't know where she'd be right now.

Scratch that. She knew where she'd be—if she would have still been alive—and it wouldn't have been pretty. She owed him everything, including her life. He had been her second chance.

And unlike other men she had known, he had never asked for or had expected anything in return—only that she do her absolute best. That was why he had brought her into NIS in the first place. He had seen the potential in her. And she had delivered on that potential. Big-time.

Sølvi worked harder than anyone at NIS. She understood the threats Norway was facing. The *real* threats.

While governments and their pet political initiatives came and went, she saw the bigger picture. Because Norway was so wealthy, it could afford to be both high-minded and kind. Those were noble attributes, but only if the nation was prepared to be narrow-minded and tough when it had to be.

For instance, calling out China for their human rights violations and awarding the Nobel Prize to a dissident critical of Beijing was all well and good, as long as you were ready to punch back twice as hard once Chinese hacking of Norwegian banks, businesses, hospitals, and critical infrastructure went into overdrive.

That was one of the most important things Carl Pedersen had taught her. As the Soviet Union had begun to dissolve, Norwegian politicians had cheered. While it was indeed worth cheering, Pedersen urged the powers-that-be in Oslo to consider what was coming next.

Stripped of its global superpower status, Russia was going to become even more dangerous. Its belligerence would increase and Norway, as a member of NATO, and as an immediate neighbor, would be a target.

Everything Pedersen had predicted had come true. Cross-border incursions, increased espionage, political and cultural influence operations, interference with Norwegian military exercises, indiscriminate and non-

attributable sabotage operations—all of it. His warning had been chill-
ingly prophetic.

But, where Norway hadn't taken Pedersen as seriously as it probably
should have, Sølvi had. Having grown up in a military family, she had long
been exposed to dinner table conversations about Norway not taking its
freedom for granted. As a young girl, talk about Norwegians remaining
"ever vigilant" was all around her. Nevertheless, the moment the chance
to spread her wings and leave Norway had arrived, she had taken it.

What started as a semester abroad in Paris, led to a summer job as an
au pair, which led to being scouted by the owner of a modeling agency
who lived in the building. She didn't go back to school, or to Norway, for
the next two years.

The money had been fantastic. The travel and the places she saw were
even better. But it was during this time that her penchant for choosing
bad men and making other, even worse decisions began to show itself.

At first, the attention was intoxicating. Handsome photographers, ad
execs, and fellow models. She got invited to the hottest clubs and was introduced to even more men, as well as even more opportunities to get
herself into trouble. Her mistake of choice—cocaine.

All of the models were doing it. It gave you lots of energy, helped you
stay super thin, and was always available. She was having too much fun to
notice how tightly the addiction was taking hold.

In the end, her father had flown to Paris and rescued her. Bringing her
home, he had gotten her cleaned up and had given her an ultimatum—go
back to school or join the military.

School had seemed like the easiest choice, but she chose the military
instead. No one could believe it. *Sølvi the fashion model in the Norwegian
Army?* It had shocked everyone—especially the friends who had jokingly
egged her on in that direction.

She had felt guilty about how she had let her family down and, most
importantly, her father. She had been embarrassed that he had to come
and bring her back home. He had been disappointed in her. She had
seen it every time he had looked at her. The shame had been impossible
to bear. She wanted him to be proud of her. She still did. The military

would make him proud. It would also provide her a means to be proud of herself.

In all honesty, it had been one of the best things to ever happen to her. She had needed the military's structure and its discipline. Had she returned to university in Oslo, she was convinced that she would have only been dragged back into the suffocating world of drugs.

Instead, she had gone through basic training and then set her sights on a new unit she had heard the army was toying with codenamed *Tundra*. It was rumored to be an all-female Special Forces pilot program. Very little was known about it and because it was so highly classified, very little was being said.

She had applied and had been rejected three times. Each time they had given her a different excuse. *Too tall. Too skinny. Too weak*.

While there was nothing she could do about her height, she could improve her body and overall physical fitness, which was exactly what she did.

She lengthened her runs, added in sprints and cross-training, began lifting heavier weights, and completely changed her diet.

When she applied a fourth time and they tried to reject her, she was pissed. And she gave it to the panel with both barrels—telling them to start thinking up new excuses now because she was going to apply again and again. She wasn't a quitter. It was precisely what they wanted to hear. She was given a slot to try out for what would be known as Jeger Troop— the Norwegian word for huntress.

The ten-month program was grueling, but she relished it. The more they threw at her, the better she did. No matter how hard they tried to break her, they couldn't.

From the eighty-eight female soldiers initially invited, only twenty were able to complete the training, and from there just thirteen went on to form the first unit.

Sølvi was proud of herself. And just as important, so was her father. She had been made for Jeger Troop. Or so it had seemed.

Despite being deployed multiple times, she had never fired her weapon. None of their operations had gone kinetic. It seemed that Jeger

Troop spent the majority of its time either conducting surveillance or interacting with Muslim women in Afghanistan—hoping to develop actionable intelligence.

Shit assignments came with the territory—even for Special Operations forces. Sølvi, though, had been led to believe that they'd be undertaking the kinds of missions similar to the male commandos'. The fact that Jeger had been regulated to "safer," second-tier operations didn't sit well with her. That wasn't what she had signed up for. And so, she had started looking around for other opportunities.

It didn't take long for her to come to Carl Pedersen's attention. The moment he met her he knew she'd be perfect for NIS. There was something about her—a street smarts, a savvy that couldn't be taught. She was intelligent and quick-witted; perfect for the espionage business. She was also a very striking woman, which would discount her as a threat. Lots of men were going to drop their guard the moment they saw her. In Pedersen's opinion, she was being wasted in the military.

Nevertheless, poaching her from Jeger was going to ruffle a lot of feathers. They had spent a boatload of time and money training her. It took some serious string-pulling to get her transferred, but string-pulling was something Pedersen was quite skilled at.

She was an exceptional student. Privately, he liked to joke that she had the "Three Bs." Beauty, brains, and huge brass balls.

From the moment she had shown up at NIS, she had been eager to prove herself. She was a risk-taker, but not a foolish risk-taker. Pedersen was confident that as long as he could help her channel her passion, she'd be one of the best intelligence operatives Norway had ever seen—maybe even better than him. And, he had been right.

No matter what kinds of assignments he sent her on—no matter how complicated, or how dangerous—she always found a way to succeed. Yes, she got knocked on her ass. She also got battered, bloodied, and bruised. On a handful of occasions, she had even come close to losing her life. But that was what the job required and she had thrown herself into it with everything she had until a devastating, personal loss had sent her tumbling back into the realm of drugs.

Of the many mistakes she had made while living abroad, the biggest involved a night of heavy partying where she ended up in a rough part of Milan with a horrible man who had slipped something into her drink. By the time she realized what was going on, it was too late. Though she tried to push him off of her, she was unable.

Although that night would fade into the background of her life, it would never disappear—not completely. Years later, it would come roaring back.

Happy and challenged with her job at NIS, there was only one area where she felt unfulfilled, empty. Most men, if not intimidated by her looks, were intimidated by the demands of her career—of which she could discuss very little.

That had all changed, though, when friends had introduced her to Gunnar, a good-looking Norwegian tech exec. Everything about him had been perfect, especially how she had felt when they were together. He had laughed at her jokes, had never been jealous or insecure about her frequent trips abroad, and had always complimented her. They had made a remarkable couple and it had only made sense that they would get married. Both of them had been certain that they were ready.

They'd had a beautiful ceremony at Oslo Cathedral, followed by an extravagant reception on the roof of the Norwegian National Opera and Ballet, and then had honeymooned in Portugal.

After a year, Gunnar had begun talking about having children. Sølvi had known that it would impact her career. But he had wanted children more than anything and she had wanted to make him happy. So, she had given in.

But no matter how hard they tried, she couldn't get pregnant. Eventually, they had gone to see a specialist.

The news hadn't been good. Because of a prior medical procedure, Sølvi was incapable of conceiving. They had both been devastated, but for Gunnar, it had been the absolute end of the world.

Things had only gotten worse when, in a moment of candor after a bottle of wine, Sølvi had confided in him about the night she was raped and confessed to the abortion she had sought once she had learned she was pregnant. The operation had brought about a terrible infection, which, only now, did she realize had rendered her infertile.

But instead of being her rock, instead of being the best friend she thought she would always have to lean on, Gunnar had left her.

She had come home from work and he was gone—along with the dog they had bought together. A week later, he served her with divorce papers. Her spiral back into drugs didn't take long from there.

When Carl Pedersen found her, pulled her out, and forced her to get clean, she made herself two promises. One, she would never, ever touch drugs again. And two, she would never, ever fall in love again.

Turning away from the window, she began to pace, her thoughts returning to Pedersen's murder. There were many avenues of investigation she could take. While there had been no physical evidence discovered at Pedersen's home, that didn't mean they wouldn't turn up something, eventually.

The problem was that the first forty-eight hours after a murder was the most crucial for finding clues and tracking down the killer. After that, the odds turned against investigators—dramatically so. People's recollections of what they saw or heard began to fade. Physical evidence started to degrade. Short of a confession or DNA showing up in a database, the crime wasn't very likely to be solved.

Because Pedersen's corpse had been in the house for days before being discovered, the killer already had a significant head start. Worse than that, the killer appeared to be a professional, someone who had targeted Pedersen because of his position as an intelligence officer. Whoever the assassin was, he probably wasn't the type to offer up a confession or to allow his DNA to be uncovered.

With Kripos—Norway's National Criminal Investigation Service— leading the murder investigation, there were plenty of experienced hands ready to run down even the smallest of leads. That left Sølvi and NIS the freedom to get creative.

She already had their best teams combing CCTV footage from bus stations, railway stations, border crossings, and ports of entry. Anyone suspicious was run through facial recognition and compared against their databases, as well as all Interpol red notices from the last decade.

The killer hadn't always been a pro. At some point, somewhere, he must have made a mistake. As far as she was concerned, no stone was too small to overturn. She was going to find that mistake.

But to find it, she was going to have to come at the case from a much different, much more personal angle.

Walking over to her desk, she glanced at the enormous etching hung on the wall behind it. It depicted Huginn and Muninn—*thought* and *mind*—the two mythological ravens said to bring the Norse god Odin his information.

She sat down, logged onto her computer, and thought for a moment. Then, she tapped out an email. Reading it back, she shook her head, deleted it, and tried again.

Ten minutes and three drafts later, she finally had something that struck the right tone.

It was a big ask—on a lot of levels. It was also embarrassing. She had to do it, though. Carl Pedersen would have done it for her.

Looking at the time, she debated whether she should head home or just crash on the couch in her office. It was late and she was wrung out—both emotionally and physically. The pull from Oslo's seedier neighborhoods as she drove back to her apartment would be strong. Probably too strong to resist. She convinced herself it would be better to stay.

In the morning, she'd go for a run around the lake and then shower in the NIS locker room. There was a spare change of clothes in her office closet. By all appearances, she looked like a hard worker—and she was. Get far enough under the surface, though, and you saw that working—sometimes even spending nights at the office—was how she walled off her demons.

But there was no reason for anyone to suspect what she was wrestling with. Carl Pedersen had seen to that. He kept her drug use secret and had made sure that when she returned to work that she aced her physical and no residual traces of illicit substances were detected in her system.

That was the kind of friend he was. He had not only helped her weather her own particular storm, but he had lashed himself and his career to her. Sink or swim, they were in it together. He believed in her that much.

Ever the espionage chieftain, he had prepared a cover story for her. As far as anyone at NIS was concerned, her leave of absence had been due to the dissolution of her marriage. Dropping hints in the right hotbeds of office gossip, many coworkers suspected that she had gone through a period of depression. It explained everything without rendering her disqualified for her position. Human beings were logical creatures. Give them a simple, plausible explanation for an issue and, absent any contradictory evidence, they'd accept it.

And despite her fear, everything had worked out—just as Pedersen had said it would. There was only one wild card: the person who had suspected her drug use and had reported it to Pedersen.

They hadn't spoken. They hadn't even seen each other since she had returned to NIS. But that was the person she needed a favor from now. It was why she had agonized over the wording of her email. She was only going to get one shot, if at all.

The CIA's Oslo station chief was as buttoned-up and professional as they came. There'd be a lot of questions. There'd also be some painful recriminations. They had been friends. Good friends. But a lot of murky, not-so-nice water had flowed under the bridge since.

Making up her couch, she turned out the lights and lay down. She tried not to think of Pedersen, but as soon as she closed her eyes, her mind was filled with him. The thin gray mustache, the chain-smoking, the turtlenecks and perfectly creased trousers. She remembered his smile, and his warmth, and his patience.

At the corners of her eyes, she could feel tears beginning to come. She fought them back. *Not now*, she commanded herself. Giving into grief only created a dangerous on-ramp. It was what had propelled her into the world of drugs when Gunnar had left her. She couldn't risk that again. She needed to sleep. She needed to be sharp for tomorrow. Because it was going to be ugly.

Whether the CIA liked it or not, they *were* going to give Scot Harvath to her.

CHAPTER 7

The Carlton Group's G650ER touched down and taxied to a revetment area on the far side of the airfield. There, a Black Hawk helicopter—rotors hot—sat waiting to take the private jet's passengers on the next leg of their journey.

Testifying to how fast the team had moved to get down to Key West, the aircraft hadn't been catered. The only food in the galley were shelf-stable items like granola bars, bags of chips, and beef jerky. That didn't matter to Harvath. He hadn't been interested in eating. Only drinking.

There was plenty of bottled water and energy drinks in the fridge. The bar area, though, had looked like a grocery store an hour before a hurricane was scheduled to hit. Every shelf was bare, all the booze having been consumed on the flight home from their last assignment. "Work hard. Celebrate harder," was one of the group's many maxims. Harvath, therefore, prided himself on always having a Plan B.

Tucked away in the crew closet was the plane's "bribe box," a locked, hard-sided Pelican case that contained luxury items the team might need overseas in order to secure cooperation from foreign customs, passport control, military, or police officials. Inside were envelopes of cash, sleeves of gold coins, cartons of cigarettes, boxes of high-end cigars, and bottles of exceptional booze.

Opening it up, he had withdrawn a bottle of Jack Daniel's Sinatra Select Tennessee Whiskey, discarded the gift box, and headed back to his seat, pausing only long enough at the bar to grab a glass, a few cubes of ice, and a bottle of water. His plan was to continue keeping reality at bay for as long as possible. After all, he hadn't asked to be scooped up and he'd be damned if he was going to stop drinking. They could force a rescue on him. They couldn't force sobriety.

Positioning himself in the very back of the plane, he made it clear he wasn't interested in interacting with anyone. He simply wanted to be by himself. There'd be plenty of time for talking once they got to wherever it was they were going.

If they had been headed to The Carlton Group, they would have landed at Dulles International. If the White House, Harvath's house, or some other D.C.-area location had been their final destination, the closest airport would have been Reagan. You chose Andrews Air Force Base for secrecy or security. Considering that they were carrying a dead body, he supposed both probably applied.

He had no idea how they were going to move the body bag, out in the open, and honestly, he didn't care. This was not his op and, therefore, not his problem.

Stopping by the bar on his way off the plane, he dumped his drink into a plastic roadie cup and followed the team down the air stairs. Sloane, who had always had a soft spot for Harvath, walked with him toward the helo.

When she had been brought on board, the Old Man had made it clear to Harvath that he didn't want him dating her. It hadn't been necessary. She was good-looking, *yes*, but he was a good twenty years older. That wasn't his thing.

Not that the bedroom concerned him. It was finding common interests outside of it that would have been the problem.

Some men might have been able to make it work, but he wasn't one of them. The age gap was just too wide.

It was all for the best anyway. She was a hell of an operator and he had nothing but respect for her. What's more, he understood her.

To a certain degree, she was the female version of him—especially in the "using humor to diffuse dark situations" department.

She was complicated and had a chip on her shoulder. He'd been the same way—young and in a hurry. Confident, yet with something to prove.

He trusted Sloane, as he did all his teammates, with his life. But his trust went even further than that. He also trusted her with the keys to his house.

When he had disappeared overseas to avenge the deaths of Lara, Lydia, and the Old Man, she was the one who had buttoned up his place, pulled together a suitcase of clothes, and had it waiting for him down at Little Palm Island by the time he arrived back stateside. She had also included the framed photo of Lara that sat next to his bed. She was a good person and knew him so well.

Hooking her arm through his, she walked with him to the Black Hawk, held his cup as he climbed aboard, and then handed it up to him.

"You're not coming with?" he shouted, as she smiled from the tarmac.

Nodding toward the jet she replied, "I'll catch up. Got a little dead-weight to take care of first."

He understood. This was her operation and that made the dead body *her* problem.

Placing his drink between his legs, he strapped in and put on a headset as one of the crew members slid the door shut. The craft then began to vibrate as the pilot applied power to the twin GE turboshaft engines. Seconds later, they were airborne. There was no feeling in the world like it.

No matter how many times Harvath had experienced it, and he had experienced it a lot, lifting off in a helicopter was always an incredible sensation.

The Black Hawk banked northwest toward the Anacostia River. Soon, he could make out the lights of Nationals Park. Off in the distance, on their left, was the Tidal Basin and the Thomas Jefferson Memorial.

As they flew over the National Mall, depending on which window he peered through, he could see the Washington Monument and the Lincoln Memorial beyond, as well as the Capitol on the other side of the helo.

D.C. was beautiful at night, particularly from the air. He had no idea where they were going.

After passing the White House, they continued northwest, flying over the Adams Morgan neighborhood and then the towns of Chevy Chase and Bethesda. Rockville and Gaithersburg slipped beneath the dark belly of the Black Hawk next.

Once they passed Frederick, Maryland, he had a pretty good idea of where they were headed. Years ago, as a Secret Service agent attached to the Presidential Protective Detail, he had made this trip many times. He knew the terrain below them like he knew the scars on his kitchen table. If the helicopter went down right now, he could lead everyone to safety, as well as to a handful of supply caches and covert redoubts.

Closing his eyes, he took a sip of his drink and listened to the chatter over his headset. It was all so familiar—the radio communications, the pounding of the rotor blades as they sliced through the pine-scented air, the bounce of the airframe as it was buffeted by updrafts from the mountainous forest several hundred feet beneath them.

Maybe it was the alcohol, or maybe it was the nostalgia, but he couldn't help but be taken by what a gorgeous night it was to be in the air. He was sorry they weren't flying with the doors open.

When the pilot gave the two-minute warning, he opened his eyes and looked at his watch. Twenty-eight minutes since they had passed the White House. Just as he remembered.

After checking his seatbelt restraints, he peered out the window and drained what was left in his cup. They were about to land on hallowed ground. It would have been disrespectful to hop out of the helo with a drink in his hand.

When the big bird came in, it came in hard and fast. It quickly flared and then touched down on the concrete helicopter landing zone. The rotor wash blew dust and small clumps of dirt in all directions.

Harvath glanced at his watch again. From the White House to Camp David, it had taken exactly thirty minutes. When everything had been absolutely turned upside down in his world, it was nice to return to something from his past that was still the same.

Sliding open the heavy door on the right side, one of the crew members hopped out and made sure all the passengers kept their heads low as they headed toward a line of waiting golf carts.

Piloting them was a team of young Marines. Harvath headed toward the nearest one.

The name on the driver's perfectly pressed uniform was Garcia. He introduced himself to the Lance Corporal and she checked her list of berthing assignments.

Known officially as Naval Support Facility Thurmont, the two-hundred-acre Camp David retreat was established in 1942 under the FDR administration. Prior to the outbreak of World War II, the President's favorite retreat had been the presidential yacht, the USS *Potomac*, also known as the "Floating White House." But concerns over attacks, be they by air or by German U-boats, made it necessary to locate a safer getaway for the President.

The National Park Service had been charged with finding the right location. In addition to being extremely private, it also had to be at a high-enough elevation to remain cool in summer, so as not to exacerbate FDR's asthma and allergies.

Despite the two-and-a-half-hour drive from the White House, Roosevelt had fallen in love with the site, calling it his "Shangri-La." The name stuck—at least until Dwight Eisenhower was elected President. He found the name a little too fancy and changed it to "David" after his father and grandson. It had been known as Camp David ever since.

Scattered amongst the twenty-plus rough-hewn oak cabins painted moss green were a massive aircraft hangar, indoor and outdoor swimming pools, a three-tee, one-hole golf course, tennis and basketball courts, a horseshoe pit, an archery range, a field house, a bowling alley, a movie theater, a bar and grill, a gift shop, a fitness center, a chapel, a fire department, a health clinic, a shooting range, a mess hall, and an underground bomb shelter, as well as barracks and support structures for the sailors, Marines, and other military personnel who staffed and secured the facility.

"You're going to be in Hawthorn, sir."

Harvath knew it well. Considering that his previous visits to Camp David had been as a Secret Service agent guarding the President and as such had required him to sleep in the barracks, it was an honor to return as a guest and be staying in one of the cabins. Hawthorn in particular.

Hawthorn was next to Holly, the cabin where Winston Churchill had stayed in 1943. He had been the first foreign dignitary to visit Camp David, then Shangri-La. Legend had it that he and FDR had planned the D-Day invasion right on the Holly cabin's porch.

Harvath was fascinated with Camp David's history. Arguably, one of the most famous things to have happened there were the Camp David Accords—brokered by President Jimmy Carter and the heads of Israel and Egypt. But there were so many other, lesser known stories that he found intriguing—particularly from the days of the Soviet Union.

When Nikita Khrushchev visited in 1959, he shared President Eisenhower's cabin with him. It turned out that, like Eisenhower, he was a big fan of American Westerns. The pair got better acquainted over movies such as *High Noon*, *Gunfight at the O.K. Corral*, and *The Big Country*.

In 1973, President Nixon presented Leonid Brezhnev with a dark blue Lincoln Continental—donated by the Ford Motor Company. The Soviet leader was so excited, he had Nixon hop in, and they sped off—without their protective details.

Barreling down one of the perimeter roads at over fifty miles an hour, Nixon tried to warn his guest of a dangerous curve up ahead. Brezhnev either didn't hear him or didn't understand. He kept accelerating. Only as they entered the curve did he realize his mistake. Slamming on the brakes, he managed to steer through it, but just barely. Once safely out of the turn, Nixon paid him a wry compliment on his "excellent" driving skills.

Camp David was also the secure location Vice President Cheney was evacuated to on 9/11. Three days later, President Bush arrived with several cabinet members, advisers, and generals. The mood, as one would imagine, was said to have been quite dark. The next night, before dinner in the Laurel cabin, Attorney General John Ashcroft joined National Security Advisor Condoleezza Rice at the piano where they sang hymns.

Despite that mournful period, the camp's overall history was quite positive and uplifting. It was the one place the President and other influential world leaders could truly relax—even if just a little—and deal with the weighty issues of the day.

One of Harvath's favorite quotes about the retreat came from a book about President Ronald Reagan, who, after having left office, said, "The days I liked best were those Fridays when I could break away a little early, three or three thirty, and take off for Camp David." Those were some of Harvath's favorite days at the White House as well.

As they drove from the helipad, they passed the Aspen cabin, which was reserved for the President and his family. None of the lights were on. This didn't come as a surprise to Harvath. Not only because of the late hour, but also because there'd been no sign of the President's Marine One helicopter, as well as all the other security measures that got put in place when the President was on the property.

Harvath didn't know who he was there to see. He also didn't know what piece of intelligence The Carlton Group had that the Norwegians didn't. According to his teammates, they didn't either. All they had been willing to say was that this was for his safety, and everything would be explained once they got to their destination.

Pulling up to the Hawthorn cabin, Lance Corporal Garcia put the golf cart in Park and said, "Here we are, sir. Would you like me to walk you inside and demonstrate how everything works?"

"No, thank you. I'll be fine," he answered.

"There's a phone on the nightstand, along with a list of extensions, if you should need anything. Stewards are available twenty-four/seven."

"Roger that."

"Have a good stay."

"Thank you," Harvath replied as he stepped out of the golf cart and walked up to the cabin door.

He thought about asking if the Shangri-La Bar in the Hickory Lodge could still be accessed, after hours, via a bad window in the back, but that had been a Secret Service "secret." They were the ones who, long ago, had rigged the window in the first place. He wasn't sure the Marines had been read in on the caper. Better to keep it to himself.

Stepping inside Hawthorn, the first thing he noticed was the smell. *Oranges*. Back when he had been working the President's detail, all the cabins had smelled like soap. Irish Spring to be exact. This was definitely an improvement.

The furnishings, though, were still the same—simple and understated. The bed had crisp linens. There were bottles of water. The bathroom, though dated, sparkled. It wasn't the Ritz. Not by a long shot. Harvath didn't care.

Inside the slim wardrobe, an array of clothes had been left for him. Someone had obviously been alerted that he would be arriving without luggage.

What they hadn't been alerted to was that in addition to needing something to wear, he would also be needing something to drink.

Just because he hadn't wanted to step off the Black Hawk with a roadie in his hand, didn't mean that now that he was in his cabin he didn't want to recommence his pain management routine.

Walking over to the telephone, he was about to ring for a steward, when there was a knock at his door.

The stewards at Camp David were good at anticipating guests' desires, but he doubted they were *that* good.

Crossing to the door, he opened it. There, standing between two enormous dogs, was the person he had been brought to see.

CHAPTER 8

The dogs whined, eager to get at Harvath. Their owner, though, was having none of it. He issued a quick, one-word command and the incredible animals fell silent.

Standing less than three feet tall, the little man—who suffered from primordial dwarfism—didn't even come up to the shoulders of his two, massive Caucasian Ovcharkas. The physical juxtaposition was impressive. Even more impressive was the intelligence, discipline, and fealty shown by the creatures.

"I thought you might want a nightcap," said the little man. "Along with some answers."

"I could use both," Harvath replied.

Nicholas smiled and, with another quick, one-word command, released the dogs from discipline and allowed them to rush Harvath.

Throughout global intelligence circles, the little man was known as the "Troll." To his friends, he was known simply as Nicholas.

He had once been one of the world's leading purveyors of black-market intelligence. He had also once been Harvath's nemesis. Time and circumstance had a way of changing things, as well as people.

It was an odd, crooked path—filled with treachery, deceit, retribution, and penance—that led to where they were now. They had gone from being directly opposed to each other; combatants to comrades in arms. As their mutual respect and appreciation had grown, they had formed an unbreakable bond. They had become like brothers. Family.

After greeting Argos and Draco, and doling out plenty of head patting and behind-the-ears scratching, Harvath let Nicholas know he was ready for that drink.

Their party decamped for the cabin next door where Nicholas and his dogs had been installed.

Per their training, Argos and Draco stayed close to their master as they traversed the short distance through the trees. The little man had made powerful enemies over his career. The fact that he had joined The Carlton Group and had changed many of his ways made no difference to them. There were certain grudges, certain wrongs that could never be forgiven. Lives had been destroyed by the information he had trafficked in. The dogs were in place to protect him should anyone show up on his doorstep looking to settle an old score. As Harvath was currently being hunted down himself, he completely understood.

They made small talk as they walked—Harvath dreading the inevitable question he knew was coming. *How are you doing?*

It was why Key West—and Little Palm Island until he had been kicked off—had been good. No one knew him. No one asked him difficult, painful questions. In a way, it had felt as if he had outrun his old life. Then, just like that, it had caught up to him again. And now here he was.

Nicholas, who had been born in Soviet Georgia, abandoned by his parents, and raised in a brothel, was no stranger to pain either. He had no desire to inflict any, unnecessarily, on Harvath.

The Carlton Group had become the little man's home. The losses of Reed Carlton and Lydia Ryan had been devastating for him too. He had also cared very deeply for Lara and his heart broke for his friend at losing his new wife. With that said, they had a serious problem to deal with— and Harvath needed to face it head-on.

Entering the Holly cabin, Nicholas led his friend out onto the screened-in porch. There, he had an ice bucket, bottles of water, a bottle of Blanton's Gold bourbon, and a box of Cohiba cigars.

"You got the best berth at Camp David," Harvath remarked as they sat down.

"I wanted Aspen," Nicholas joked, "but President Porter said no."

A brief smiled flashed across Harvath's face. He wouldn't have put it past Nicholas to have asked for the President's personal cabin. He was a man of incredibly fine taste and boundless appetites—particularly when it came to food, wine, and, until recently, extremely expensive women. He had been tamed—or so it had appeared—and Harvath felt terrible for not having asked about his girlfriend, Nina.

They had been on again, off again so many times, it was hard to know what the exact status of their relationship was. Before everything had gone upside down at The Carlton Group, Lydia had told Harvath that, in her opinion, the volatility in the relationship was what drew Nicholas and Nina so passionately to each other.

"How's Nina?" Harvath asked.

Nicholas paused for a moment before responding, searching for the right words. Finally, he replied, "She's good."

There was something about the little man's expression, something that caught Harvath's attention. "Just *good*?"

"We don't know yet."

"What does that mean?"

Nicholas picked up the box of Cohibas and offered him one. "It looks like I'm going to be a father."

Harvath was dumbstruck and, for a moment, didn't know how to respond. All Harvath had ever wanted was a family of his own. He had almost, finally, had one with Lara and her son, but it had been snatched from him.

Now, here was Nicholas, on the verge of being given that priceless gift, yet the downbeat tone with which he delivered the news suggested he was anything but happy.

"What's wrong with you?" asked Harvath. "That's wonderful news. You make it sound like you've just been diagnosed with a terminal illness."

"What's wrong with *me*? All you have to do is look," he said, waving his hand over his body, emphasizing how small he was. "What if the baby is born like this?"

"What if it isn't?"

"What if it *is*?"

Harvath understood his friend's concern, but the chances that Nicholas and Nina's baby would also suffer from primordial dwarfism were so small they were almost nonexistent. The condition required a mutant gene from *both* parents and therefore was incredibly rare.

"Everything is going to be okay," said Harvath as he chose a cigar. "When is she due?"

"In seven months. Give or take."

"Your baby is going to be beautiful. Trust me. You're going to be a great father."

Nicholas began laughing so hard, he nearly dropped the box. "From Marquis de Sade to Mother Goose. Sounds like a seamless transition."

Again, Harvath smiled. He had missed him. "I didn't say it would be easy. I said you'd be great at it. And you will be. Congratulations."

"Thank you for the vote of confidence," he replied. Selecting a cigar for himself, he then placed the box on the small table between them and offered Harvath the cutter.

"You first," his friend said.

After Nicholas had snipped his cigar, he tossed the cutter over to Harvath followed by the lighter.

The tips of their cigars glowed a bright orange as the men puffed away in the semidarkness of the porch and blew heavy clouds of smoke into the air.

Nodding toward the bourbon, the bottled water, and the ice, Nicholas intimated that it was time for Harvath to pour.

Once the drinks were made, they quietly clinked glasses and then settled back in their chairs. There was no toast. Neither wanted to break the silence that had settled over them. For the moment, they enjoyed not saying anything at all.

It could last only so long. Finally, it was Harvath who spoke. "Okay, what the hell is going on?"

CHAPTER 9

With the Old Man dead, Lydia Ryan dead, and Harvath not interested, the management of The Carlton Group had fallen upon Nicholas. Right after the murders, when Harvath had gone missing, he had proven himself more than worthy of the challenge. He had worked tirelessly to get him back. This new threat they were facing, though, frightened him even more—and he didn't scare easily.

Exhaling a cloud of smoke, he asked, "Where do you want me to start?"

"Who was the assassin in Key West?"

"We don't know, yet."

"Is it the same person who killed Carl Pedersen?"

"We don't know that either."

"Chase said there may be more than one assassin. He also said we have intel the Norwegians don't."

Nicholas set his cigar in the ashtray and looked at his friend. "It's only RUMINT. Nothing confirmed."

Harvath was familiar with the term. RUMINT stood for Rumor Intelligence. He waited for Nicholas to fill him in, and when he didn't, he cocked an eyebrow as if to say, *spill it*.

"Allegedly, someone, or some organization, took out a one-hundred-million-dollar contract on a single individual. At this point, it's just whispers. Barely audible chatter on the Dark Web and in other re-

mote places. We didn't share it with the Norwegians because in our opinion it was too vague."

"And you think the subject of this contract is me?" asked Harvath.

Nicholas nodded. "That's my concern. That's why we brought you
here."

"But why not one of our safe houses? Or one of the Agency's?"

"Do you want the tactical or the practical answer first?"

"Tactical," Harvath replied.

"One hundred million dollars can buy even the worst kind of person
a lot of friends. It's such a huge bounty, we didn't know whom we could
trust."

"Even within our organization?"

"Somehow, an assassin picked up your trail and tracked you to Key
West. Only a handful of us knew you were in Florida."

"I had my cell phone. Used my credit cards now and then. I wasn't exactly trying to disappear."

"Nope," said Nicholas. "But if there really is this kind of a contract
out on you, we have to assume it's only being shopped to the best."

"More than one assassin, though? That's not normally how this is
done."

"That's part of the RUMINT as well. Supposedly, the contract was
put out to a pool. Whoever closes it out first, gets the bounty. That's why
we came so hard and fast to get you."

"So, out of an abundance of caution, you said no to our portfolio of
safe houses, no to the CIA's, but yes to Camp David?"

"That's the practical side of this. I wanted one location with no additional movements. None of the 'different bed every night' scenarios like
some sort of Mexican drug lord or Middle Eastern dictator. Place you and
encase you. That's the plan.

"What's more, I didn't want to be cooped up in some house, especially
not with the dogs. Here, we've got two hundred of the most secure acres
in the world. A squirrel can't even get within one hundred feet of the perimeter without the Marines knowing about it."

"Aren't you afraid of one of *them* being bought off?"

"A, no, and B, by whom? No one knows we're here except for McGee, who made the request, and President Porter, who gave his approval. I guarantee you, neither of them is going to be bought off."

Nicholas was right about that. Bob McGee was the Director of the CIA and Lydia Ryan's boss before she had moved over to The Carlton Group. Harvath trusted McGee. He also knew that the Marines who served at Camp David were not only exemplary, but also rigorously vetted.

"Plus," Nicholas continued, "only if we were camped out at the NSA or the Situation Room back at the White House, could we access faster and more secure networks. This is the perfect bolt-hole."

Harvath agreed. It made sense on several levels. Nodding, he steered the conversation back to his earlier questioning. "Let's say the contract does exist and I'm the target. Who's behind it? Who have I pissed off badly enough to put up one hundred million dollars to take me out?"

"Even at their most flush, bin Laden and al Qaeda wouldn't have been able to come up with one hundred million, much less give it away. ISIS, though, is a different story."

"How so?"

"They're the Goldman Sachs of the terrorism world. They may have lost the land that made up their caliphate, but they didn't lose their bank accounts. According to an Iraqi Intelligence report, they still have access to over two and a half billion dollars. *And*, they hate your guts."

Harvath began to make a mental list. "Okay, they're contestant number one. Keep going. Who else?"

"As far as terrorism organizations?" Nicholas asked. "Ones that have those kinds of funds and enough reason to want to spend that kind of money on you? That's all I've got at the moment."

"How about non-terrorism-related organizations?"

"There are various crime organizations around the world that could launch a hundred-million-dollar contract. But to be honest, I can't think of one you've pissed off badly enough to warrant it."

"So what does that leave us with?"

"You've dispatched some exceedingly wealthy bad actors. These people left behind enormous sums of money. If their heirs were smart, they'd be out living it up, but sometimes heirs aren't smart, they're vengeful."

Harvath swirled the ice in his glass and said, "You could probably track that money, though, correct?"

"I've already started looking into it."

"Good."

"Which brings us to state actors," said Nicholas. "And there's one country in particular that jumps right to the top of my list."

Harvath took a long pull off his Cohiba and then slowly blew the smoke into the air. "Russia," he stated.

The little man nodded. "They hate you even more than the jihadists."

"The feeling is mutual. Believe me."

"It doesn't make sense, though."

"Why not?" asked Harvath. "I killed the Russian president's son."

"And he was a sociopathic monster. He deserved it—as did the rest of them. But you had been absolutely clear what would happen to President Peshkov if he sent anyone after you. You even put it in writing to him."

"We're still watching all of his money, aren't we?"

"Day and night, but that's the thing. *None* of it has moved. Not a ruble, a dollar, a euro, a rand—none of it."

"Could he have a hundred million we don't know about?" Harvath asked.

"Is it possible? Sure. Anything's possible. He's been stealing from his country for decades. But is it *likely*? With how hard we've worked to uncover every single one of his assets? I just don't know."

"What about a cutout? Somebody close to him. An associate of some sort."

Nicholas thought about it. "Someone willing to put up one hundred million dollars of their own money?"

"It would definitely get his attention. Who knows what kind of favor that would curry?"

"In Russia, doing the president that kind of a service could buy almost anything—a ministry position, mining rights, who knows?"

"This sure feels like the Russians to me," said Harvath, refilling his glass. "Carl Pedersen helped me to not only halt their Baltic plot, but also to snatch their chief of covert operations for Eastern Europe."

Nicholas nodded. "Two for one. They got whatever intel they needed to track you down, *and* they killed Pedersen."

Harvath felt the pain over his losing friend stab at his heart once more. He took a long sip of bourbon before responding. "Why put out a contract then? Why not just assign it to Russian Intelligence—GRU or FSB—and let them handle it?"

Nicholas shrugged and picked his cigar back up. It had gone out and he needed to relight it. "If," he said as he activated the lighter, "Peshkov really didn't want this to look like it came from him, he'd have to carry the charade all the way through—a cutout for the money and a cutout for the killing."

It was a good point. "Okay, let's say that's what happened. How did the Russians know Carl and I were connected, much less that he helped me with everything?"

"Simple. He messed up."

Harvath shook his head. "No way. Not him."

Turning his attention away from his Cohiba, Nicholas looked at his friend. "Everybody makes mistakes. I've made mine. The Old Man made his. And you've definitely made more than your share."

"I'm not saying he was incapable of making mistakes. I'm just saying I never saw it. I never heard about any, either. The Old Man said Carl was one of the best he'd ever seen. The Norwegians are neighbors with the Russians. They can't afford mistakes. Not even small ones."

"Okay. For the sake of argument, let's say Carl Pedersen was perfect. He never made a mistake. What does that leave you with?"

Harvath swirled the ice in his glass again as he reflected. "Someone else made the mistake. Someone close to him."

The little man nodded and went back to puffing on his cigar. "If that thread exists, then you need to find it so we can pull on it. *Hard.*"

Even in its alcohol-soaked state, Harvath's brain began running through the possibilities, ruling in and out a myriad of different scenarios.

What quickly became clear was that as with any complicated equation, if you were missing data, it made it nearly impossible to solve the problem. Harvath knew Carl Pedersen, but he had no clue who Pedersen trusted and may have talked to. They had kept their relationship tightly compartmentalized—for the safety of them both.

With the dogs sleeping nearby, the porch fell quiet again. Harvath and Nicholas, captive to their own thoughts, smoked their cigars and sipped their drinks in silence.

After a few minutes had passed, Nicholas said, "There's something else I need to tell you."

"What is it?" Harvath asked, staring off into the darkness.

"When the murders happened and you disappeared, Bob McGee brought me a copy of the documents the Old Man had drawn up. They laid out how he wanted the company run after he was gone. It turns out that I was his third choice. And like a good prodigal son, I stepped up. I felt it was my duty, especially after everything that had happened."

"And?"

"And now I'm stepping down."

Harvath, somewhat shocked, turned to face him. "You're what?"

"I have zero qualifications to run this organization; or *any* organization, to be honest. I appreciate the faith he showed in me, but this isn't my métier. Where I excel is behind a keyboard, in the ether, moving highly sensitive pieces on a digital chessboard. That's why you brought me in to begin with. You gave me a chance to be part of something bigger than just myself. And I'll always be grateful."

"So, you're quitting?"

Nicholas shook his head. "You guys are my family. I'm not going anywhere except back to the job I was brought on board to do. I can't track money, listen to the whispers of the Dark Web, and run down leads while I'm dealing with payroll questions, quarterly projections, and sales targets."

Harvath waved his hand like he was brushing off a mosquito. "That's not what you're supposed to be focused on. That's why we have a CEO and a CFO—to deal with all the C-Suite issues. You're supposed be the heart and the brains of the outfit. That's why the Old Man selected you."

"That's why the Old Man selected *you*," Nicholas reminded his friend. "I'm not a leader. You *are*. I stepped up when there was a void, but

I never intended for this to be permanent. Now that Nina and I have a baby coming, my capacity for added responsibility is going to diminish pretty quickly."

This was the last thing Harvath needed. He had been done caring—about everything. He didn't want to be responsible for Reed Carlton's legacy, much less the direction of his namesake company.

It made him feel guilty. Not enough to jump in, grasp the mantle of leadership, and save all of it, but guilty nonetheless.

"If you step down, who's going to take over?" he asked.

"Well," Nicholas replied, "per the Old Man, the company can be put up for sale and the new owner can decide. Or, you and I can agree to bring somebody else in to do the job."

"Right now? In the middle of everything that has happened? In the middle of everything that *is* happening?"

"I would argue we need somebody now, more than ever."

Harvath had always carried a certain burden of guilt for not agreeing to replace the Old Man. But he had made it very clear that he wasn't ready to leave the field. Now, with Nicholas saying he wanted to step down, he felt even worse.

"Where in the world are we going to find somebody? It's not like we can just post this kind of a job on the internet."

"I've already got somebody in mind, but let's discuss this in the morning. You look exhausted."

"I am."

"Can you do seven a.m.? The Hickory Lodge?"

"I'll be there," Harvath replied, grinding his cigar into the ashtray and standing up.

Nicholas gestured toward the bottle. "It's yours. If you want it."

"No thanks," he said as he left for his cabin. "I'm done."

CHAPTER 10

Not wanting to miss breakfast, Harvath had set the alarm on the nightstand and had left a wake-up call request with the stewards as a backup. There were only a few hours until then, but a few hours were better than none. Even so, his body didn't want to comply. He wondered if maybe he should have accepted the bottle of bourbon from Nicholas after all.

He was used to going to bed with a lot more alcohol in his system and it took forever to fall asleep. But once he did, he couldn't stay asleep—at least not for long.

He tossed and turned until the sun began to rise and then gave up. Dressing in the workout gear from his wardrobe, he decided to go for a run.

Unlike Key West, the morning air was cool and crisp. He wanted to clear the cobwebs and burn off any residual booze in his system.

He pushed himself hard—harder than most mornings. By the time he was done with his run and back at the cabin, he was drenched with sweat. He had been out longer than he had planned and so took a quick shower, shaved, and found something to wear.

At seven a.m., sharp, he opened the door to Hickory Lodge and strode into the restaurant. He was completely unprepared for who he saw sitting with Nicholas.

Judging by the plates of half-eaten food and half-empty coffee mugs, the duo had been there for a while. He could only imagine what they had been talking about, though in all honesty, he had a pretty good idea.

The man sitting across from Nicholas was an accomplished warrior and intelligence operative. He had been based in Berlin during the Cold War, tasked with recruiting foreign intelligence assets. He not only spoke Russian, he had also killed a lot of them.

After the Wall had fallen, he had left U.S. Army Intelligence and gone to work for the FBI, rising to Deputy Director. Later in life, the President had tapped him to run a covert program parked at the Department of Homeland Security called the Office of International Investigative Assistance or OIIA for short. It was as head of OIIA that he had been Harvath's boss.

Their relationship, though, went back much further. Gary Lawlor had been best friends with Harvath's dad, Michael. He had stepped in when Michael had been killed and had become a de facto father to him, making sure he and his mother never wanted for anything. He had also pushed Harvath to become the absolute best in whatever he did. They hadn't seen each other since the funerals for Lara, Lydia, and Reed.

Walking over to him, Scot extended his hand. "It's good to see you."

Lawlor stood up, put his arms around him, and pulled him in for a bear hug. He was very fit for a man of his age. "You doing okay?" he asked, quietly enough so no one could hear.

Harvath swallowed hard and nodded. It was the only response he was capable of giving. He didn't know what would happen if he tried to verbalize what he was really feeling. He was proud and didn't want to come apart in the middle of such a public place.

Lawlor held him there for an extra moment. He could practically feel the weight of all the sorrow hanging from Harvath's body, like heavy, iron chains, crushing him. It was a feeling he knew all too well. His wife, though long ago, had been taken from him in a similar fashion.

"It gets better," he promised.

They were the same words he had given him, months ago. Harvath was still waiting for things to "get better." Once again, all he could muster in response was a nod.

Patting him on the back, Lawlor broke off the hug and pushed him out to arm's length. "You're looking a little on the slim side," he said, studying him. "How about some breakfast?"

"Sure," Harvath replied, helping himself to a chair. As he sat down, he looked at Nicholas and asked, "You couldn't have told me?"

"I didn't want to spoil the surprise," the little man responded.

"You and I are going to have a talk later about surprises."

Nicholas shrugged as Lawlor waved over the server. "Coffee?"

Harvath nodded.

"Anything else?"

"Sure. Eggs, scrambled, crispy bacon, wheat toast, and ice water—lots of it, please."

The server took the order and once he had left for the kitchen, Lawlor continued catching up, "How's your mom?"

"She's good," he replied. "Nice apartment, great view of the ocean."

"How often do you get out to see her?"

"Probably not as often as I should."

When Reed Carlton was diagnosed with Alzheimer's, Harvath had started paying more attention to his mother's lapses in memory. He eventually grew concerned enough to have her tested. The news wasn't good. She had dementia.

He knew how fiercely independent she was and had offered to hire someone to come in and check on her. To his surprise, she was interested in a local senior living development on Coronado Island. Several of her friends were there and loved it. She could still be independent, but as she needed more care, it could be added on.

While Scot was sorry to see her sell the home he had grown up in, he knew it was time. The best part of the move, though, was how much happier she was in her new place. "All's well that ends well," Lara had said. And she had been right. He just wished that they could have gotten to know each other better before Lara had been taken from him.

"I'm sure she understands," said Gary.

Harvath was going to respond, but stopped as the server returned with a pot of hot coffee and filled all of their mugs.

By the time the man had left the table, Nicholas had changed the subject.

"I've got some good news," he stated. "Gary has done a little digging into what happened down in Key West and—"

"Hold on," Harvath interrupted. "Gary's been read into what happened down in Key West?"

"Yes he has. And before you push back, know this. You made your position crystal clear. You didn't want to run this business. That was fine while Lydia was here, because she was willing to do it. But when she was killed, we had to make new plans. You were MIA, so we did it without you. Gary's the best person for the job and you know it."

He did know it, and he couldn't argue.

"Scot, this has all been moving fast," said Lawlor. "Nicholas and I have been huddled with Bob McGee since the funerals. Everyone wanted to give you space—including me. But you have to understand, that's over. The fight's here and the fight's now. I said yes to this job because I know that I'm needed and, frankly, because I wanted to work with you again. But all that matters at this point is if you want to work with me. And, of course, if you're *still* in the fight."

Part of Harvath wanted to stand up, walk out, and go back to drinking in Key West, but he couldn't do that. Lawlor had called him out and no Tier One operator, no American war fighter was *ever* out of the fight. As long as the country needed them, they would keep going no matter what toll it took.

Even so, Harvath was careful not to knee-jerk himself into a commitment. As much as he loved the Old Man, Carlton had been a master manipulator and had taught him a lot about his gut and people who tried to appeal to him through it.

Instead of answering right away, he circled back to the information Gary uncovered. "What did you find regarding Key West?"

Lawlor removed a folder and slid it across the table. Harvath opened it and, sipping his coffee, scanned the pages as Lawlor narrated.

"The chief in Key West is a graduate of the FBI's National Executive Institute, and we happen to know each other. His officers showed up moments after you left. The two heavies you laid out both had outstanding warrants, so after they got some much needed medical attention, they were taken into custody. After our initial conversation, the chief made a call to the Florida Attorney General. In exchange for dropping some low-level beefs, they were able to get the suspects to cooperate.

"The bottom line is that someone they don't know paid them five hundred bucks to get you outside and beat the crap out of you."

"After which, I was supposed to get a bullet in the head," said Harvath.

"They claim to have no knowledge of anything else."

"But they knew enough to remove their jewelry and buy new long-sleeve shirts and boots in order to help avoid identification."

Lawlor nodded. "From what the Key West chief says, it wasn't their first rodeo."

"How far did the chief get read in?"

"Not far at all. The two goons were still unconscious when the cops got there, so they didn't see anything. No one but us knows about the would-be shooter."

It was good intel. Lawlor had come through for them and he had done it quickly.

Harvath turned to Nicholas. "Have we identified the corpse?"

"Not yet," the little man answered, "but his weapon was pretty interesting. Glock 43. Single stack magazine. Nine-millimeter. It was modified with a switch that stops the slide from cycling. Not only does it make it quieter, but it prevents the brass from being ejected. The suppressor appears to have been 3D-printed. Perfect for a professional, one-and-done assignment."

"What'd you do with the body?"

"It's someplace safe, on ice for the time being."

"What's next?"

"*Next*," said Lawlor, as he saw the server approaching, "is you eat breakfast. Then, assuming you're in, we're going to go over everything you know about Pedersen and develop a plan."

There was no question in Harvath's mind. Based on their intel, he was being hunted. He wasn't wired to sit and wait this sort of thing out; to play defense instead of offense. "I'm in," he stated. "*All* in."

It sounded nice to think that he was doing it for his teammates, or for The Carlton Group, or the Old Man's legacy, or even for the country. But deep down, down near that flickering flame of his humanity, he knew his reasons weren't nearly so noble. It was because the rage was still there.

And as the realization swept over him, he was reminded of a quote about the dangers of hunting monsters. If you weren't careful, Nietzsche had warned, you became what you hunted. "When you gaze long into the abyss," he had said, "the abyss gazes also into you."

But no sooner had that quote entered his mind than it was expelled by another, one sent from deep down near his anger: "Fate whispers to the warrior, '*You cannot withstand the storm.*' The warrior whispers back, '*I am the storm.*'"

As the server set down his meal, Harvath forced himself to concentrate and begin forging a mental path toward the person who had betrayed Carl Pedersen.

CHAPTER 11

L
ong before Paul Aubertin had killed his first police officer, he had been a lover of all things French.

Born Michael Collins McElhone to a Catholic family in West Belfast, he was a teenager during the ongoing, partisan "Troubles" of Northern Ireland in the 1990s. France, with its "Liberté, égalité, fraternité," couldn't have seemed farther away.

With a passion for its history, its language, its culture, its politics, and its gastronomy, the young Francophile had hoped to study in Montpellier, Lyon, or maybe even Paris one day.

It was a lofty goal for a working-class boy whose parents were constantly late on their rent and struggled to put food on the table.

Nevertheless, he had clung tightly to his dream. Until, one day, his entire life had been shattered.

His father, a deliveryman who supported a unified and independent Ireland, had been beaten to death by members of a paramilitary group that preyed on civilians called the Loyalist Volunteer Force, or LVF for short.

Despite their absolutely heinous actions, they had been able to evade anything resembling accountability or prosecution. So emboldened were they by their apparent untouchable status, that they even developed their own Hitler Youth–style offshoot called the Young Loyalist Volunteers.

He was sixteen and had thought about joining, working his way up the organization from inside, and killing all those responsible. He had seen similar things done in the movies and for a moment felt it was a solid plan.

But then, he had applied a little more brainpower. The LVF was based only a half hour away in Portadown. They would have access to any number of people in Belfast who could check his background. There was no way he could pretend to be a motivated Protestant, looking to join the fight. And the minute they realized he was the son of a man the LVF had murdered, it would be all over for him. He couldn't do that to his mother. He would have to be more covert.

With his father gone, so too was his family's income. He had no choice but to drop out of school and work full-time to make up for the shortfall and help take care of his family.

But while he had no choice but to work, he did have a choice *where* to work. His maternal uncle was whispered to be a member of the Irish Republican Army and worked in the construction industry, which hired lots of workers off the books in order to skirt taxes, trade unions, and National Insurance contributions. That's who he went to see. And that's where he found employment.

Most of the men on the job sites were "doing the double"—collecting welfare checks while getting paid under the table for construction work. The money wasn't very good, but it was better than nothing. His sickly mother, as much as she hated his missing school, was grateful.

"I'll find a better job soon, Michael," she had told him. "Then you can go back to school and everything will be fine. You'll see."

But a better job never materialized. His income was critical to their family, and so he worked twice as hard as any of the adults around him in an effort to make himself indispensable.

The labor was strenuous, but it served to build his muscles. At night, he made sure to read in order to build his mind. The books were always about France and he devoured them.

When he wasn't working, or reading, he would accompany his uncle and some of the men from work to the pub. He was too young to drink, but the Irish had practically invented the policy of "don't ask, don't tell"— especially when it came to underage drinking in working-class pubs.

As long as the boy didn't make an ass of himself, no one cared. And the boy made sure not to make an ass of himself. He was there to listen, learn about the IRA and, more importantly, about its enemies—especially the Loyalist Volunteer Force.

His uncle, though, wasn't stupid. The few times he had tried to broach the subject, his uncle had shut it down—immediately. The boy was far too young to be thinking about revenge. "The day will come," he said. "Trust me, it'll come."

But just like his mother's "better" job, it didn't come—and he eventually grew sick of waiting for it. Then, one day, while going up to the bar for another round, God placed someone in his path.

"Your uncle tells me you have a lot of questions about the LVF," the man said.

He was a regular in the pub, but Paul had never seen his uncle nor any of the other men they drank with speak to him. As such, he was wary of talking to him.

"I am sorry for your father's death, as well as what it has done to your family. A boy your age should be in school."

"Well, I'm not. Am I?"

The anger, while misplaced, was genuine. The boy had idolized his father. With each day since his murder, the pain of losing him had only become more acute and more ingrained in his soul.

That said, he had been raised better than to be disrespectful to his elders—even ones who were complete strangers. "I'm sorry," he said. "Thank you for your condolences."

"There's nothing you need to be sorry for," the man replied. "Your father was a good man."

"Did you know him?"

"No, but I have asked around. He took care of his family. He attended church. And he was on the right side of this fight. So, out of respect for your father, I am here to answer your questions."

The boy was confused. "I don't even know who you are."

"Your uncle knows who I am. That's all that matters. Now, what can I tell you?"

"Who killed my father?"

"The Loyalist Volunteer Force," the man said.

"I want their names."

"With all due respect, you're a sixteen-year-old boy. What would you even do with those names if I gave them to you?"

"I'd take my revenge."

The man made a face and took a sip of his beer. "What if there was a better way to hurt them? To really make them feel pain? Would you be interested in being a part of that?"

The boy didn't even need to ponder his answer. "Absolutely," he replied.

"Don't you even want to know what would be asked of you?"

"I don't care. I'll do it. Whatever it is."

"Good boy," the man said, as he finished his beer and stood up from his stool. "I'll be in touch."

The way to hurt the LVF turned out to be by appearing at a day of youth soccer it had organized near Portadown. It was a propaganda event for the Young Loyalist Volunteers, disguised to look like a violence mitigation effort. There was zero vetting at this stage. The boy had been signed up under the name Terrance Macaulay.

He had told his mother he had to work and would be leaving early that Saturday morning. Three blocks from his house, the man from the pub picked him up in his car and began the short drive to Portadown.

As they drove, he explained to the boy who his target was and why he was being given this assignment. The LVF had been able to escape culpability for their actions because they had a very powerful patron— a high-ranking police inspector who had repeatedly made evidence and witnesses disappear.

"If he is allowed to live," the man said, "there will never be justice for your father. Do you understand what you need to do?"

The boy nodded.

"Good," the man replied. Nodding toward the glove box, he said, "Open it."

The boy did. Inside was a small, hammerless revolver, its grip wrapped with tape.

"Have you ever fired a gun before?"

The boy shook his head.

"It's just like you have seen on TV. You point it where you want the bullet to go and you squeeze the trigger. You'll be fine."

And he had been fine. He had gotten to the pitch early, before any of the other children had arrived. The police inspector was not hard to find. He was a large man with a shock of white hair and a big, bulbous red nose. He looked exactly as he had been described.

Even so, the man from the bar had insisted that the boy have the inspector identify himself. The LVF might embrace random violence, but that was not how the IRA acted, at least not this wing of it. Part of the terror their division struck into the hearts of their enemies was based on their unfailing precision. They were legendary, known for being able to hunt anyone, anywhere. The boy had no idea what he had been drawn into, but he would soon find out.

The key to their success was the amount of research they put into their kills. They were patient, almost glacial in their movements. Revenge was indeed, in their book, a dish best served cold. Ice cold.

The police inspector was an incredibly guarded, quietly whispered about pedophile. The boy had heard about pedophiles, but to the best of his knowledge had never met one. That was about to change.

After introducing himself, the man asked where his parents were. The boy explained that they had to work and had dropped him off early. The inspector was almost salivating.

He enlisted the boy's help in setting up the nets, bringing out all the balls, and placing cones for various drills they would begin with. Then, he asked the boy to follow him into the field house.

It was cold and damp inside. The only light came from the windows set into the eaves high above. The man didn't bother turning on any lights. He preferred what he did to be kept in the darkness. Reaching out, he touched the clothing over the boy's genitals.

As instructed, the boy had kept the pistol hidden for the first shot and had fired it from inside his jacket pocket. The round struck the police inspector straight in the gut and tore its way in.

When the man grabbed his belly in shock and unbelievable pain, the boy withdrew the pistol and fired two more times—hitting him once in his chest and once in his face.

He then wiped the pistol off, dropped it next to the body, and walked out of the field house—just like he had been told to do. Ditching the jacket, he found the man from the pub waiting, his engine running, a block away.

"How did it go?" he asked as the boy got into the car.

"He's dead."

"You did a good thing. Your father would be proud of you. I'm proud of you."

The boy didn't know what to feel. He had taken a life. Based on everything the church had taught him, he should have felt remorseful. Yet, he didn't. He felt nothing, really.

They didn't return to Belfast. At least not right away. The man from the pub drove for quite some time. During the trip, they didn't speak. That was fine with the boy. He didn't feel like talking.

In a small village in the middle of nowhere, they parked behind a nondescript building and knocked on a thick, secure door. A pair of eyes looked out through a slot. Words were exchanged. Then the door was opened.

It was a social club of sorts. One he would get to know well over the next couple of years. The men inside would become his comrades in arms. He would drink there, laugh there, plan there, and even mourn the loss of some of those very same men there.

On this first visit, his new IRA handler had only one mission—to get him a bit drunk and to celebrate his first kill. It was a rite of passage.

Big men, important men he would later learn, came by the table to shake his hand and congratulate him. They were also "proud" of him, they said.

He drank three bottles of cider before his handler looked at his watch and said that it was time for them to be getting back to Belfast.

The boy was still not interested in chatting, so like the ride from Portadown, they made this last leg of their journey in silence.

When they rolled to a stop several blocks from his home, his handler gave him a final talking-to. It went without saying that he shouldn't tell anyone what had happened—not his mother, not his uncle, not his priest—no one. Not even his mates. If he did, there'd be hell to pay and his handler made it quite clear that he'd be the one delivering the bill.

After giving him an alibi and explaining what he should say and do in the unlikely event the police came around asking questions, he handed him an envelope.

"What's this?" the boy asked.

"Open it."

He did. Inside was several hundred pounds sterling.

"You're one of us now," his handler said. "We take care of our own. You've earned that."

It was his first, rudimentary taste of the dark arts. Like losing one's virginity, it had been quick, anxiety-inducing, and somewhat clumsy. But it had been successful. He had gotten the job done—which was all that mattered.

The boy didn't know it at that moment, but he had just been introduced to a profession he would show an incredible aptitude for and grow quite comfortable in.

His handler had run the best assassins the IRA had ever fielded. The boy, in time, would surpass them all.

The British would both hunt and fear him. They would publicly declare him a savage, but privately marvel at his abilities. His kills would be the subject of lengthy newspaper and magazine articles. Then, one day, he would simply vanish.

It was Christmas 1999. The Good Friday Agreement had been signed, voted on by the citizens, and put into effect. The Troubles, for the most part, were finished. The demand, locally, for men of his vocation had practically collapsed overnight.

There was also a rumor that he remained at the top of a very secret "most wanted" list. With the ground shifting under Northern Ireland, new political parties and new allegiances were being forged. There was a dirty, ignoble scramble for power that would have made the ancient Romans blush. The knives were out. It was only a matter of time before someone turned on him.

With his mother already two years in the grave from a heart attack and his siblings old enough to take care of themselves, there was no reason for him to remain. He could go wherever he wanted. And where he wanted to go, was France.

Through an IRA contact in Dublin, he was able to change his identity and get a Republic of Ireland passport. Michael McElhone became Paul Aubertin and he never looked back.

After traveling through France, seeing all the sights he had always dreamed of, he applied to join and was accepted into the French Foreign Legion.

His plan was to serve for three years and then take advantage of the opportunity to apply for French citizenship. Two years in, on a mission in Kosovo, he was wounded and rotated back to France for a series of lengthy surgeries.

Per a provision in French law, any soldier of the Foreign Legion who gets injured in battle can immediately apply to become *Français par le sang versé*—"French by spilled blood." A social worker helped him fill out the application from his hospital bed.

By the time his physical therapy was complete, his application had been approved.

After his naturalization ceremony in Paris, he decided to stay for a while. He took extension classes at the Sorbonne, immersed himself in the city's museums, and devoured every history book he could find from the stalls along the Seine near Notre-Dame, as well as the Abbey and Shakespeare and Company bookstores of the Latin Quarter.

The more he read, the more he fell in love with the Normandy region to the north. That was where his truest passion lay—Deauville, Rouen, the beaches of D-Day, and the most mesmerizing abbey he had ever seen, Mont-Saint-Michel.

The dramatic medieval monastery and fairy-tale village sat on a fortified island in the middle of a tidal basin at the coast—abutted by the mouth of the Couesnon River.

It was a UNESCO World Heritage Site that looked like it had been torn out of a Harry Potter movie. Attracting over three million people a year, it was considered one of the most awe-inspiring attractions in all of

Europe. With all the books he had read about it and all the pictures he had seen over the years, nothing compared to viewing it in person.

According to legend, the original site had been founded by an Irish hermit. Then, in the eighth century, the archangel Michael had appeared to Aubert, the bishop of Avranches, and told him to build a church on the island. It was why Michael McElhone had taken the name "Aubertin." He had always felt a special kinship with Mont-Saint-Michel. The fact that it had been founded by an Irishman only made that kinship stronger.

After visiting a couple of times while still living in Paris, he realized this was where he belonged. Packing up his meager belongings, he moved to Normandy.

He survived on a small pension from the Foreign Legion, which he augmented by working as a private tour guide for wealthy tourists. The business, though, was spotty—and he had his eyes set on a beautiful house with a view of the ocean. So, to pump up his bank account, he fell back on what he did best—killing.

Being a tour guide was a great cover, and he actually enjoyed it. The challenge was saying no to wet work contracts during tourist season.

None of the other guides disappeared during the spring and summer. That was bread-and-butter time. They normally bumped into each other several times a week, if not a day, making the rounds at the same sights. Often, when things got really booked up, they even referred clients to each other.

Dropping off the grid would have been highly unusual, and something he wouldn't have been predisposed to do. But then, Lieu Van Trang had contacted him.

For lack of a better term, Trang was his business manager. On those off-season occasions when he did take contracts, that's who they came from. This time, though, he had offered something quite different. He wasn't operating as his business manager, but rather he wanted to be partners.

The eccentric and notoriously security-conscious Vietnamese would only discuss the deal face-to-face. He had family in Paris and would use the opportunity to see them as cover for their meeting. It was only a train ride for Aubertin and so he had agreed.

Because of its colonial past, Paris was home to the oldest Vietnamese community in the Western world. There were said to be, at any given time, more than 100,000 people of Vietnamese descent within the city limits. Unlike the Chinese or North Africans, they weren't congregated in one particular neighborhood. Instead, they were spread out, many of them having even married into traditional French families.

Trang had access to a Buddhist temple in the 17th arrondissement and had suggested they meet there. It was safe and no one would bother them. Aubertin, though, didn't like it—for the same reason he would never take a meeting in a French mosque.

The security services in France were granted a lot of latitude when it came to bugging and surveilling houses of worship. Perhaps they weren't interested in anyone at Trang's temple, but he wasn't willing to roll the dice. He told him to find another location.

Trang came back to him with a restaurant owned by one of his cousins. It was a much better idea. Unlike Buddhist temples, fair-skinned, blue-eyed Westerners walked into Asian restaurants all the time in Paris.

They had met in a private room in the back. Trang had been in high spirits. In fact, Aubertin didn't know that he had ever seen him like that. After ordering food and drinks, Trang had gotten down to business.

He had just been assigned the largest contract killing in history—one hundred million dollars. The target was an American intelligence operative. He had no idea who the client was. It had been arranged by a middleman, someone Trang had worked with before.

Allegedly, the client was so eager for the contract to be filled, the middleman had instructed Trang to put it out to a select pool of assassins, simultaneously. Whoever killed the intel operative first would receive the money. Trang, though, had his own idea.

He would make it look like he had followed all of the instructions, but in reality he and Aubertin would take the money for themselves and split it fifty-fifty.

"You should never steal from the people you work for."

"It's not stealing if the job gets done," Trang had said. And then, he had laid out his plan.

It was a bold collection of double crosses. Not only would the client's wishes be ignored, but the assassin who bagged Scot Harvath would end up getting a bullet in the head.

Aubertin would be a fool not to wonder whether Trang had a final double cross prepared for him. If he chose to follow this path, he would have to tread very carefully. With a potential fifty-million-dollar payday, how could he not?

In order to insulate himself, Trang wanted Aubertin to run everything—the selecting and tasking of the assassins, all of it.

Then, when the successful assassin came to collect his pay, Aubertin would debrief him, kill him, and use the information to collect the bounty for himself—splitting it later with Trang.

"It's all upside," the Vietnamese had said. "You're not labor on this one, you're management."

The offer was incredible—one he knew he would never see the likes of again.

"I get to do it my way, with the people I want?" said Aubertin. "No strings attached?"

"No strings attached," Trang had replied.

For the next twenty minutes they talked. Finally, with all of their issues resolved, they clinked glasses, and sealed their deal.

CHAPTER 12

The Thief Hotel was one of the coolest, most opulent hotels in the world. It took its name from its location—Tjuvholmen, or Thief Islet. Once known as a haven for bandits, pirates, and prostitutes, today it was a trendy waterfront neighborhood jutting out into the Oslo Fjord filled with restaurants, yacht harbors, condos, and office buildings.

Built by a Norwegian billionaire and adjacent to the Astrup Fearnley Museum of Modern Art, the chic, splashy hotel functioned like a swanky additional wing. It displayed a rotating array of the museum's most impressive contemporary pieces. But the art was nothing compared to The Thief's guest list.

The six-star property, famed for "treating rock stars as guests and guests as rock stars," attracted a powerhouse, international clientele, as well as the crème de la crème of Oslo's cultural, financial, and political elite. It also had a kickass rooftop bar and restaurant, which was why Sølvi Kolstad had chosen it for her rendezvous.

She had loved The Thief since before it had even opened. As part of the waterfront renovation, it was an ambitious urban-renewal project and she was proud of what it said about Oslo's commitment to always move forward.

The whole area, packed with financial, advertising, and media executives, dripped with money and was incredibly glamorous. In fact, she had suggested to Gunnar that this was where they should live, but he had brushed it off. He wanted to be in one of the older, more established quarters of the city—like Briskeby with its shops and luxury apartment blocks, or leafy, park-studded Bygdøy.

It was too bad. Had he jumped in when she had suggested, they probably would have doubled their money by the time they divorced.

None of that mattered now. Or maybe it did still matter, a little, but she knew better than to dwell on it. Nothing good would come from thinking about Gunnar and what could have been. It only served to upset her.

Parking in the underground garage, she came up to the street level, walked to the bridge in front of the hotel, and peered over the railing. There were always beautiful boats moored along the dock below. Today was no exception.

An exquisite Riva bobbed against its fenders in the sparkling water. She had to be almost fifteen meters long. The sparkling, silver paint job stood in perfect harmony with the caramel-colored teak decking and highly polished chrome railings, cleats, and assorted fixtures.

Sølvi loved boats and loved getting out on the water. Despite everything else they had in common, the fact that Gunnar didn't, should have been a sign.

Entering The Thief through its massive, automated revolving door, she breathed in the delicious, rarefied air. Simply walking into the lobby, she felt like a VIP. Crossing to the elevators, she took it all in, the art, the décor, the staff—there was no other way to phrase it, the whole place was just so damn sexy. It only got better once she got to the roof.

Walking down a narrow hallway, she stepped out onto the deck and into the open-air restaurant. The young manager greeted her with a bright smile and treated her as if she was a regular. She gave the man her name, he consulted his tablet, and then, picking up two menus, led her to the exact table she had requested.

As she walked, she could feel the eyes of most of the male, as well as the female customers on her. It was a sensation that used to make her uncomfortable and self-conscious. But if anything good had come from her otherwise disastrous time abroad as a model, it was getting used to people noticing her.

In the intelligence game, one normally didn't want to be noticed. To put it more succinctly, one especially didn't want to be remembered. She had ways of downplaying everything, including her height. When she wanted to slip by unnoticed, she wasn't half bad. On the occasions when she wanted to catch someone's attention and stand out, she was exceptional.

Her table was in the back corner. It had both privacy and amazing views. The glass doors had all been retracted, lanai style, as had the long fabric awnings above. Planter boxes filled with herbs and wildflowers ran along the edges of the roof and provided a riot of color as well as a sweet perfume.

After she had sat down, the manager unfolded her napkin and handed it to her, followed by a menu and a wine list. Before he had even finished wishing her a good lunch, her waiter had appeared, but stood a respectful distance away. Once the manager had departed, he stepped forward and introduced himself.

They chatted pleasantly, Sølvi ordered a kokekaffe, and the man disappeared to place her order. Norwegians were the second largest consumers of coffee in the world—imbibing over twenty-one pounds per capita annually. Only the Finns drank more. And when it came to how Norwegians liked their favorite caffeinated beverage prepared, they were rabidly passionate.

Kokekaffe was one of the most popular methods and came from coarsely ground beans steeped in boiling water. Because it used a lighter roast, it produced a lighter coffee than most of the world was used to, but Norway's citizens loved it.

As she waited, Sølvi looked out over the fjord. Weekends were always the busiest, especially when the weather was nice. Sailboats, with their bright white sails, tacked back and forth as gleaming motorboats and large passenger ferries pushed through the light chop. If she had to be stuck on land, she couldn't think of a better place with a better view in which to be stuck.

When the waiter returned with her coffee, she thanked him, took the porcelain cup in both hands, and continued looking out over the water. It was a good thing, she mused, that her office was surrounded by trees. If she could look at boats all day, she probably wouldn't get any work done.

As much as she enjoyed taking in the fjord, she was still a professional intelligence officer who had been trained to maintain her situational awareness. Therefore, she made sure to keep one eye on her surroundings.

A few minutes after her coffee arrived, she saw her guest step out onto the deck and approach the host stand. Catching her CIA colleague's eye, she waved. Her old friend waved back and, thanking the manager, headed her way.

Sølvi sat up straighter. She was nervous and suddenly wished she had ordered something alcoholic. As she watched her colleague getting closer, she knew it was too late. The moment of truth had arrived.

CHAPTER 13

Holidae H. Hayes was who Sølvi Kolstadt wanted to be. The raven-haired CIA Oslo station chief was not only exceedingly attractive, but she was also whip-smart, highly respected, and, after the next American election, was actually being considered for an ambassadorial post. Langley's loss would be the State Department's gain—and it was the right move.

"Triple H," or "H3" as she was known, was eminently qualified. She had paid her dues in some of the best, as well as some of the worst postings around the world. She had steered ambassadors with half her intelligence and a fraction of her experience through moments of great crisis, never once taking credit, nor asking for any recognition. All that had ever mattered was the mission as she zealously served the United States abroad. She was a legend in D.C. and the President had taken notice.

Sølvi had no idea how much she had missed her until she walked up to the table, opened her arms, and said, "Carl was one of a kind. I am so sorry for your loss."

Without giving it another thought, Sølvi stood and embraced her friend. She thought, alone in the privacy of her office, that she had exhausted herself of tears, but there were still a few more left. Quietly, she let them out.

They stood there together for several moments, not caring what anyone else thought. Then, it was Sølvi who stepped back and invited her friend to sit.

As they did, she touched her napkin to the corners of her eyes, drying the remaining tears, just as the waiter walked up.

"Can I get you ladies something to drink?"

Sølvi looked at her colleague. "The usual?"

"Are you okay with that?"

It was a well-intentioned question. Sølvi's weakness had never been alcohol. It had always been drugs. And while alcohol could loosen one's inhibitions, it would take a lot more than a couple glasses of champagne to push her back into that dark world.

Nodding, Sølvi looked at the waiter and said, "We'll take a bottle of the Ruinart Blanc de Blancs and a dozen oysters."

She was delighted to hear that they had just received a shipment of fresh oysters from near Sarpsborg, where she was from. "We'll take those, please," she replied.

As soon as the waiter had left the table, it was time to start rebuilding bridges. To her surprise, though, Holidae went first. "I can't tell you how happy I was to get your email. I didn't know if you were ever going to speak to me again. I've missed you."

"I've missed you too," Sølvi replied.

"I can't imagine what you're going through. What can I do for you? Better yet, how are you?"

"Still in shock, to be honest. Carl's death was quite gruesome."

"I spoke with the head of NIS and I'm not going to lie, I agree. It sounded terrible. I'm so sorry."

"We're beside ourselves. And I'm sure you can understand, that as an organization, this is a priority. But for me personally . . ."

Holidae jumped in as her friend's voice trailed off. "Of course. Carl was your mentor. I've got to imagine you want to get to the bottom of this more than anyone else."

"I do. Thank you."

"So," said Holidae as the waiter appeared for a moment, set down an ice bucket, and left again. "Is that why I'm here?"

Sølvi nodded. "But first I want to apologize."

"For what?"

"For the fact that we haven't spoken."

"You know I only went to Carl—"

"Because you were concerned about me," Sølvi interrupted, finishing her friend's sentence for her. "I know that. It was a very difficult time for me."

"I can't even begin to imagine," stated Holidae. "But let's just pretend, for a moment, that I have. Suffice it to say, I have zero doubt that we could snuff that d-bag, ex-husband of yours, dump the body, and be drinking Chablis an hour later without anybody ever being the wiser."

Sølvi smiled. She knew her friend was kidding, but at the same time she didn't doubt that she was capable of it. "You're a good friend. Thank you. Right now, though, I have my mind set on a different man."

"Scot Harvath?"

The Norwegian nodded.

"I thought that's where this might be headed," said Holidae.

"What can you tell me about him?"

Hayes smiled. "First thing's first. How is it that you got reinstated at NIS? I found drug paraphernalia in your apartment."

"Which was part of a case I was working."

"Okay," said the American. "But how do you explain your behavior?"

"The divorce was very hard on me."

Hayes smiled again. "I love you, Sølvi, I really do. But you were always Carl's favorite. If I had to guess, I'd wager that he cooked up some sort of story that saved you from losing your job. And now, instead of being honest with me, you expect me to believe it too."

"You can believe what you want. I'm telling you the truth," Sølvi insisted. It was a lie, but one which Carl had stressed was necessary if she was to keep going in the espionage business.

It would hurt to tell it, he had said, especially to colleagues and close friends, but it was necessary. Without the lie, she was done for. Her career was over.

"I'm not asking you for state secrets," she continued.

"Actually, that's exactly what you're asking for," Hayes replied.

"My God, Holidae. What does a friend have to do to get a favor?"

"Simple. A *friend*, needs to tell the truth. Come clean."

"I'm desperate," said Sølvi.

"I knew that when I received your email. I haven't heard from you since I told Carl I thought you had a problem. After that, you went completely off the grid. Even when you came back to work, though, you didn't reach out to me. I got the message loud and clear. It took Carl being killed for you to reestablish contact."

"Don't make it sound like—"

"Like what?"

"Like I froze you out."

"But that's exactly what you did," said Hayes. "And you know what? If you did have a substance abuse problem, and if going to ground was what it took to get everything straightened out, as your friend, I'm okay with that."

Sølvi was about to protest, when the waiter returned, set two glasses on the table, and then presented her with the bottle of champagne.

She nodded, but remained quiet as he removed the foil and the cage. Releasing the cork, there was only the faintest hiss. *Like a lover's sigh*, as they used to say in France.

He poured, she tasted, and then nodded again. Once their glasses were filled and he had left the table, she raised hers in a toast. "To Carl," she said.

"*To Carl*," Hayes replied.

They clinked glasses and took a long sip of champagne. It was cold and popped on their tongues. Not too sweet, not too dry. In fact, it was as it had always been—perfect.

How many times had they gone through this ritual? How many lunches, or brunches, or nights had they gotten together after work to split a bottle, or just grab a glass because they were racing to something else?

As NATO allies, they were expected to work together, but their friendship had gone beyond a work relationship. They enjoyed being together. Jogging, working out, movies, shopping, they had been tight. Very tight.

It was all the more reason that Holidae going to Carl with suspicions over her drug use had felt like such a betrayal. Friends didn't turn each other in.

In fairness—and if pressed—Sølvi would likely be forced to admit that friends also didn't sit idly by and watch their friends descend into a narcotic pit there was little hope of climbing out of.

Nonetheless, Holidae could have come to her first. She didn't need to go over her head to her boss. It was something, right or wrong, she still was struggling to forgive.

It felt as if they'd had this great friendship, but the moment something had gone wrong, something that potentially could have impacted work, Holidae had been all business.

It had made their friendship feel false, hollow. It had also made Sølvi feel betrayed. Having just lost her husband, the betrayal of such a close friend had been even more bitter and difficult to absorb.

"What is it you say in English?" Sølvi inquired. "I'd like us to bury the hatchet?"

Hayes smiled. "Interesting choice of idioms. I didn't know we had been at war. I thought we just weren't on speaking terms."

The Norwegian smiled back. "I'm a Viking. *Å grave ned stridsøksen* is what we say. I think burying war axes sounds better than offering olive branches. Peace?"

The CIA operative raised her glass. "To peace."

CHAPTER 14

"So," said Hayes, once their oysters had arrived, "you want me to tell you what I can about Scot Harvath."

Sølvi smiled and, after setting an empty shell down on the platter, replied, "Actually, I want you to tell me what you *can't*."

"Can't or *shouldn't*?"

"It's the same thing in English, isn't it?"

Hayes nodded. "Usually. But why are you asking me? I told Ivar everything we know."

"Ivar Stang. The NIS Director?"

Hayes nodded. "When Harvath's name was discovered in the searches on Carl's devices, he asked me to come in and meet with him."

"And?"

"And I spoke to Langley. Out of a spirit of cooperation, they prepped a presentation, which I gave in Ivar's office."

"Who else was there?" asked Sølvi.

"Ivar's number two, Norvik."

"Lars Norvik."

"Yes," said Hayes. "And then someone I had not previously met before. A woman named Holst."

"*Hella* Holst?"

"She didn't give a first name."

"Heavyset woman?" Sølvi asked. "Late fifties? Short brown hair?

Greenish eyes that bulge out just enough to make you wonder if she has a thyroid condition?"

Hayes tapped her index finger against the tip of her nose and then pointed it at her friend. "Maybe we can help each other. Tell me about Holst and I'll share a couple of things about Harvath that weren't in my presentation. Deal?"

Sølvi nodded. "Hella heads a new division at NIS. In English, it roughly translates to *Strategy Section*."

"What's it responsible for?"

"As you know, when it comes to population, Norway is a relatively small country. We have less than five and a half million citizens. But despite our size, bureaucracy is a growing problem—as it is for most advanced Western nations.

"Like a person with heart disease, the arteries of our agencies are calcifying, making it impossible for blood to efficiently flow. In the case of the NIS, our blood flow is information. Cut it off, or even reduce it partially, and not only does our agency risk atrophy and even death, but our greater body, the country of Norway, is susceptible as well. Does this make sense?"

"Of course," said Hayes.

"Good, because now it gets tricky. Strategy Section," Sølvi continued, "was designed, in part, as a heart bypass, if you will. If NIS was ever severely compromised, or shut down—say in the case of an invasion or a massive terrorist attack—Strategy Section's job is to make sure that critical information is still pumped to all the vital organs of state."

"So it's a continuity-of-government program. In essence, a backup. A fail-safe."

The Norwegian nodded. "The ultimate fail-safe. In case of national emergency, it would be largely immune from oversight by Parliament. The thought was, if a patient has had a heart attack and needs to be rushed to the hospital for surgery, should politicians be slowing things down arguing about speed limits, or should those most intimately involved with the patient, the actual people in the ambulance, be making the calls?"

"Interesting. But that doesn't explain why Holst was in the briefing. What involvement, if any, would she have regarding the death of Carl Pedersen?"

"Strategy Section was Carl's idea."

"Do you think it might be connected to his murder?" Hayes asked.

"Ivar is a careful man. It was likely just out of an abundance of caution that Holst was there. Strategy Section is a bit like your Red Cell teams. Part of their job is to think outside the box—to look for connections no one else is seeing."

"Are you a member of it?"

"No," said Sølvi. "At least not officially. Carl told me that my name's on a list of intelligence officers who might be tapped in an emergency. My day-to-day portfolio, though, is outside of what they do."

"How big a program is it? Approximately. How many people work there full-time?"

Sølvi smiled, pulled the champagne out of the bucket, and topped off both of their glasses. "I've probably already said too much. Besides, I believe you were about to tell me about Scot Harvath."

Hayes smiled back. While they had been good friends, they still worked for allied yet *separate* intelligence organizations. As such, there had always been a good-natured push/pull between them. If, in the course of their friendship, one of them picked up something of benefit for her country, then so be it. That was icing on the cake. It wasn't the primary reason they had become friends. They had become friends because they had liked and respected each other.

"Okay," said the American, taking a sip of her champagne. "I'll tell you what I told your colleagues at the briefing. Then, if you want to ask me questions, feel free."

Sølvi got comfortable in her chair, took a sip of champagne, and nodded for her friend to begin.

"You've never met Harvath, have you?"

The Norwegian shook her head.

"I only met him once," Hayes recounted. "Years ago. In Turkey. He was part of a SEAL team that conducted a hostage rescue operation. He was handsome. *Really* handsome. But cocky as hell. He single-handedly killed the hostage-takers and got the hostage out alive. I can't go into operational specifics, but let's just say that the equipment he was using was meant for very limited target engagement.

"His teammates were floored when they made entry and all the tangos were down. In my opinion, he got lucky. But as they say, it's often better to be lucky than good.

"Fast-forward a couple of years, and he distinguishes himself while helping secure a maritime location for a U.S. presidential visit. To this day, I still don't have the requisite 'need to know' as to what the threat was that Harvath uncovered, or how he diffused it.

"Suffice it to say that he impressed a lot of people, including the United States Secret Service—who brought him on board to help bolster their counterterrorism expertise at the White House. You heard about our previous President, Jack Rutledge, and his ill-fated ski trip to Park City, Utah?"

"Where all those agents were killed and he was kidnapped?" said Sølvi. "Of course."

"Well, Harvath not only saved the President's daughter, but he figured out who had taken the President, tracked him down, and took him back. One would think that would be the kind of guy you'd want to keep on your protective detail, but that wasn't how President Rutledge saw it. Instead, Harvath was put back in the field, tasked with various nondisclosed covert activities from that point forward."

"Black work?"

Hayes shrugged. "Could be, but again, I'm not in that loop. What I do know is that he eventually ended up at CIA doing contract assignments, before going to work for a good friend of Carl's, who had established the Agency's Counterterrorism Center, named—"

"Reed Carlton," the Norwegian said, finishing her friend's sentence for her.

"Exactly."

"Carl liked to talk about them—a lot. He was fond of both Reed and Harvath."

"Then you know," Hayes continued, "how far back Reed and Carl went. All the way back to the Cold War."

"Yes, they not only conducted multiple ops together, they were also good friends."

"Do you know how they met?"

The Norwegian nodded. "While training the CIA-initiated 'stay behind' teams meant to conduct guerrilla warfare if the Soviets ever invaded Norway. According to Carl, part of his inspiration for Strategy Section came from his conversations with Reed."

"I'm not surprised," Hayes replied. "Having known them both, I can say those two were cut from the same cloth. They had similar views of where the world had been and where it was headed. And while many in Oslo and D.C. were looking in their rearview mirrors, expecting the next war to look like the last, these two were trying to wake people up and get them prepared. They were real visionaries."

"Agreed. So what else did they have in common? What would have gotten both of them killed? And why does Harvath seem to be next on someone's list?"

"We're not sure they're connected," the CIA operative replied.

"Come on, Holidae. I know Carl was up to something with Harvath. He told me."

"What, specifically, did he tell you?"

"A couple of months ago, when an anti-NATO terrorist group was carrying out attacks in Europe, Harvath had tracked a cell to Norway. Along with a Norwegian Police Security Service assault team, backed up by Norwegian Special Forces, he had gone in to take them down, but there had been an ambush. Several officers and soldiers were killed, and many more were gravely injured.

"Following a firefight, Harvath had chased down the surviving cell member. There had been another gunfight, Harvath had killed the guy, and had recovered valuable intelligence from the backpack he had been carrying. That intelligence had then been used to unravel a larger plot sponsored by the Russians."

Hayes's brow furrowed slightly, but only for a fraction of a second. "Was this in Carl's reports?" she asked. "Or did he tell you privately?"

"He told me privately," said Sølvi, who had noticed the change in her companion's expression. "There's not much in his reports—and I've read *all* of them. That means that whatever they were doing, he had been keeping most, if not all of it off-book. Normally when he did that, it was so that if anything went sideways, Russia couldn't draw a straight line back to Norway."

"A sound policy."

"Carl was always three steps ahead."

An awkward silence fell over the table. Hayes knew she owed her friend more and remained quiet as she debated what she had been authorized to reveal.

Per her training, Sølvi knew to wait and not to fill such pauses with talk.

Finally, Hayes broke the stalemate. "Suppose," the CIA operative offered, "I do know what Carl had been up to with Harvath. If I gave you that information, what would you do with it?"

"What do you *think* I'd do with it? I'd use it to get to the bottom of who murdered him."

"And once you got to the bottom? Then what?"

"I'd do my job."

"What does that mean?"

"It *means*," replied Sølvi, playing to Hayes's rule-following nature, "that I'd turn it over to my superiors."

The CIA operative leaned back in her chair, raised her champagne glass, and said, "Then I can't help you," as she took a long sip.

"Wait. What?" The Norwegian was confused.

"Sølvi, I know you. You want to avenge your mentor. My government wants to protect a valuable intelligence officer. Our goals are aligned."

"Then what's the problem?"

"Once Carl's killer has been identified, the United States wants that intelligence first. If you hand it over to NIS, they're going to sit on it. I know it and *you* know it. We have a mandate from the White House to put the pedal to the metal right now."

"Why now? Why all of a sudden?"

"It's complicated," said Hayes.

"Is it ever *not* complicated in our business? Try me."

"We no longer have the confidence that if a hostile nation moved on

Norway, our citizens, much less our politicians, would support honoring our commitments under Article 5 of the NATO treaty. Americans are tired of war."

Sølvi was stunned. "You're saying that if we were invaded, the United States might stand back and do nothing? No 'an attack on one NATO member is an attack on all NATO members'?"

"Believe me, I find it distasteful, but it's possible."

"It's also pretty damn hypocritical," she said, growing angry. "Since NATO's founding in 1949, the Article 5 mutual defense pact has only been triggered once. One *fucking* time."

"I know," Hayes replied.

"By whom?" Sølvi demanded. "Who cried out, 'We've been attacked and now NATO must come to our aid'?"

Hayes looked her in the eyes and answered, "America. Right after 9/11."

"Exactly," the Norwegian stated. "Three thousand people died. It was a horrible attack. The civilized world was sickened. And you know what? Norway was proud to fight alongside its American ally.

"Yet you're telling me now—despite the Norwegian lives lost and blood spilled post-9/11—that if our country was invaded; if we had foreign soldiers in our streets, taking over our homes, burning our businesses, and usurping our government, that America 'might not' come to Norway's aid?"

"Yes," Hayes responded. "As terrible as that sounds, that's what I'm saying. We're in uncharted political waters. All of us. You know that. So we can either ignore reality, or deal with the facts as they are. The United States has chosen to deal with the facts as they are.

"America is willing to do whatever it takes to make sure none of us get dragged into war."

"What precisely does that mean?"

"It means that we don't let boils fester. When we find one, we go in and we lance it. We're of the mind that an ounce of prevention costs a lot less than a pound of cure. This is what the new Cold War looks like."

Sølvi took it all in. The world was changing, rapidly. Hayes had that right. Some of it was organic—a reaction to rapid advancements in technology and globalization. But some of it, because Norway had seen it firsthand, was the product of bad actors, skilled in propaganda and information warfare. They exploited divisions within countries, turning citizens against each other, against their government, and against their institutions. They were hell-bent on sowing chaos, distrust, and discord wherever they could.

One of the worst actors was Russia. And the only thing Russia hated as much as the United States was NATO. It saw each as a threat to its very existence and worked to undermine them both every day.

"And it's only going to get more brutal," the CIA operative added. "If Norway is going to survive, it needs a lot more Carl Pedersens—operatives willing to do whatever it takes to succeed. But those operatives will need to find ways to give Oslo plausible deniability because there are many things Norway would *like* to do, but strategically it just can't. That goes double for punching back at Russia, *if* that's who's behind this."

"So that's what you're offering me? Plausible deniability?"

"I'm offering you a chance to hunt down Carl's killer. That's what you want, isn't it? All I am asking in return is that you give us a head start on whatever you uncover. Quid pro quo. I don't care what you share with NIS, as long as my agency gets it first. Fair?"

Sølvi was being co-opted. If she said yes to this deal, she'd be placing the CIA ahead of her own organization—completely contrary to her oath.

By the same token, she was intrigued. She had no idea what information Hayes had, nor whether any of it would be helpful. The proof would be in the pudding.

"Okay," she said, refilling their glasses and signaling the waiter to bring another bottle. "I'll bite. What have you got?"

Taking a sip, the CIA operative scanned the patrons around them to make sure no one was listening. Once Hayes was confident that it was safe to speak, she said, "What I'm about to tell you goes no further. If you ever mention my name in connection with this intel, I'll deny this conversation ever took place. Are we clear?"

Slowly, Sølvi nodded.

CHAPTER 15

O kay," Lawlor said. "Walk me through it. Everything that had to do with Pedersen—and anyone who knew you were connected."

Nicholas had turned the Laurel cabin, which was where most of Camp David's official meetings took place, into a makeshift operations center. It had three conference rooms, a kitchen, a dining room, and a small presidential office.

Though the structure had been built under President Nixon in 1972, the main conference room boasted technology on par with the Situation Room back at the White House. There were not only multiple flat-panel monitors, capable of broadcasting television and live encrypted video feeds, but also large glass screens, which could display visuals such as maps or satellite imagery and be annotated by touch.

The glass screens were on tracks and could be slid in either direction, revealing a huge whiteboard bolted to the wall. Though Lawlor appreciated all the tech, he preferred the whiteboard—especially when brainstorming.

Nearby, a sideboard had been loaded with soft drinks, bottled water, a samovar of coffee, and an array of snacks.

As Harvath talked, Lawlor paced. In one hand he carried a green dry-erase marker, and in the other a mug of coffee. When a new name was mentioned, he added it to the whiteboard.

Once Harvath had finished speaking, Lawlor stood back, and looked at their list. He read it aloud, hoping that they had missed someone.

"Admiral David Proctor—NATO's Supreme Allied Commander Europe, Monika Jasinski of Polish Military Intelligence, and Filip Landsbergis of the VSD—Lithuania's State Security Department. That's it? That's the entire cast of characters?"

"That's it," Harvath responded. "Those are all the people who knew about the op Carl and I ran."

Lawlor referred to a file on the table. "Proctor is a distinguished graduate of the U.S. Naval Academy and, among his many achievements, he has commanded Destroyer Squadron 21, as well as the Enterprise Carrier Strike Group, has served as a special assistant to the Secretary of Defense and the Chairman of the Joint Chiefs, and ended up heading the Special Operations Command before taking over at U.S. Central Command. He was nominated for the SACEUR position by President Porter two years ago, and was unanimously confirmed by the U.S. Senate. Impressive résumé."

Harvath agreed. "I knew him back when he was at SOCOM. He's solid. President Porter spoke to him once. After that, only I spoke with the Admiral. No staff were allowed to listen in, nor were any brought into the loop."

"Did Carl's name come up?"

"Once or twice, but solely in the context of the mission."

"Any chance that–"

Harvath held his hand up and cut him off. "Zero. The man is a bank vault."

"Vaults can be cracked."

"Not this one, and especially not over the name of an allied Intelligence officer. The Admiral was a fanatic about operational security. You can ask anyone he worked with at SOCOM or CENTCOM. He oversaw some of the biggest post-9/11 ops we have undertaken. Not a word ever leaked to the press or to our enemies. Like I said, he's *solid*. Full stop."

"And he recommended Jasinski?"

"Correct," said Harvath. "She had been billeted to NATO's terror-

ism intelligence cell in Belgium. Admiral Proctor had tapped her personally. She legitimized my cover so I could be part of the raid on the cell in
Norway. Afterward, Jasinski and I met up with Carl at Værnes Air Station
in Stjørdal and debriefed him on the operation. There were some things
with the cops and the Norwegian military that needed to be mopped up,
but Carl told us he'd take care of them."

"Do you think he may have mentioned you to them by name?" Lawlor asked.

"Carl? Not a chance. I was traveling under an alias and it had been
provided to him. He wouldn't have given me away."

"What about once he returned to Oslo? Do you think he told anyone
at NIS?"

"The Norwegian Intelligence Service knew better than to ask Carl too
many questions—especially ones they didn't want the answers to."

"That's not what I asked you," said Lawlor. "Do you think he revealed
your presence in Norway to anyone at NIS?"

"Officially?" Harvath replied. "No."

"What about *unofficially*?"

"Unofficially, he could have been running an all-male review out of
the NIS parking lot. The point is that the Old Man trusted him and so
did I. Carl understood that our relationship functioned best as long as
knowledge of it was kept limited. If he brought someone into his confidence, I have no reason to doubt his judgment. More importantly, if the
killer we're looking for came from inside NIS, why would they need to
torture Carl in order to access his files, his phone, and the NIS database?"

It was a sensible argument and though Lawlor could come up with
some thin reasoning as to why someone might, it would have been a waste
of their time to pursue. So, he moved on. "Okay, let's focus on Jasinski
then," he stated. "Do you think she spoke to anyone about you or Carl?"

"No."

"Why not?"

"Because," Harvath replied, "she was working on direct, classified orders from the SACEUR himself. Admiral Proctor had directed her not
to discuss the operation with anyone else, not even her colleagues back at
Polish Military Intelligence."

"And you trust her?"

"Fully."

"Based on what? A couple of operations in the field with her?"

Harvath shook his head. "She hates Russia with a passion. Her number one pastime at NATO headquarters has been rooting out their spies. It's personal for her."

"Why is it personal?"

"Because the Russians killed her husband."

Harvath let his words hang there, knowing the effect they would have. Decades ago, Lawlor's wife, Heide, had been killed by the Russians in Berlin. Scot, Gary, and Monika had all been dragged, unwillingly, into a horrific club.

"I'm happy to send someone to question her," Harvath finally offered, "but I'm telling you, she didn't give up Carl."

Temporarily unable to speak, Lawlor waved the offer away. It wouldn't be necessary.

It may get better, Harvath thought, watching the older man and replaying his words in his head. *But the pain, obviously, will never, ever be gone. It was always going to be there, right under the surface.* He was certain of it.

Harvath hadn't had a drink since sitting on the porch with Nicholas. He was beginning to want one again, badly, and tried to ignore the urge.

"For what it's worth," he said, focusing on Lawlor and hoping to ease the man's mind regarding Jasinski, "Monika had a special affinity for Carl. As Poland borders Kaliningrad, they're in a similar situation vis-à-vis Norway and its border with Russia. She appreciated what he was willing to do for his country and there's much of it she wants to emulate on behalf of Poland."

Composing himself, Lawlor said, "Then that leaves us with Landsbergis of the Lithuanian VSD. Tell me about him."

Now they were getting into dangerous, highly classified waters. Harvath wasn't sure they should be headed in this direction.

Sensing his reluctance, Nicholas spoke up. "Gary's clearances are all up to date. The President has authorized him to have full access to anything The Carlton Group has worked on. Nothing is off limits. You can tell him everything."

It wasn't until that moment that Harvath understood how much had been decided in his absence. It didn't feel like he had been gone long, but he had been gone long enough. The world *had* continued to spin without him. But slowly, its gravitational pull was drawing him back.

"So, you want me to talk about the op?"

Nicholas nodded.

CHAPTER 16

As Harvath prepared to speak about the op, Nicholas activated one of the screens and pulled up a map of the Russian exclave of Kaliningrad.

A spoil from World War II along the Baltic Sea, it was geographically cut off from Russia, pinched between NATO members Lithuania to the north and Poland to the south.

Much as it had been during the Cold War, Kaliningrad had remained a serious militarized threat, capable of hitting Scandinavia and Central Europe at a moment's notice. It was heavily armed with air-defense missiles, antiship missiles, and surface-to-surface missiles, which enabled the Russians to engage NATO air, sea, and ground forces for hundreds of miles in all directions.

Approaching the touch panel, Harvath drew a circle around Kaliningrad with his finger. "All of the anti-NATO terror cells were being run from here by a high-ranking GRU operative. His name was Colonel Oleg Tretyakov."

Lawlor knew the area well. "Kaliningrad. Not an easy spot to get into or out of."

Harvath agreed. "No, it isn't."

"What was the op?"

"Get in, grab Tretyakov, and get back out."

"How'd you do it?"

"Because Kaliningrad is such a heavily guarded territory, we knew normal ports of entry were off-limits, especially for me. The Russians had been given CCTV footage of me and we were certain that I'd be nailed the minute we attempted a normal border crossing. So, we decided to parachute in.

"We flew the company jet into Šiauliai International Airport in Lithuania. Carl met us there and introduced us to Landsbergis, who was his primary contact in Lithuanian State Security.

"Landsbergis runs agents into Kaliningrad on a regular basis. He not only paved the way for a U.S. Super Hercules full of gear to land at Šiauliai, but he also helped select our drop zone and arrange for a Lithuanian truck driver who moves in and out of the exclave to pick us up, get us into the capital, and then transport us back out again."

"Did you exfil back across the border via the truck?" asked Lawlor.

Harvath shook his head. "It's a long story, but no. We didn't go out via Lithuania. Part of the border between Kaliningrad and Poland runs through a lake. That's how we got out."

"*Barely* got out," Nicholas clarified.

"Yeah. It turned ugly fast. We made it, though."

"*Barely*," Nicholas added once more.

"All right," said Lawlor, trying to get them to focus. "If you don't think Jasinski would have given up Carl, what about this Landsbergis guy? Someone must have connected Carl to you. Of the three possible, Landsbergis is the one you're least able to vouch for."

"I only spent a few hours with him," Harvath admitted, "but he seemed reliable. Without his help, we never would have been able to get into Kaliningrad, much less snatch Tretyakov and get back out. He was critical."

"Do we know of anyone he might have spoken with? Colleagues at the VSD?"

"Landsbergis said one of the recurring problems Lithuania faced was penetration by Russian spies. Like the Norwegians, he didn't want Moscow to know his country was helping us. In order to do that, he claimed that he limited any knowledge of the operation to just himself. And even then, just to be safe, he insisted on not knowing all of the details."

"That's admirable, but he would have needed to involve other Lithuanians. You landed a giant C-130 right at one of their air bases."

"Thankfully," said Harvath, "Šiauliai is where the air policing for NATO's Baltic member states is based. U.S. planes go in and out of there all the time. One more probably wasn't going to raise a lot of eyebrows—especially a transport aircraft—but, again, it was Landsbergis who got it cleared. He basically hid the plane in plain sight."

Nicholas raised his coffee mug. "Here's to Landsbergis and hiding in plain sight."

Harvath understood what his colleague was trying to say, but the way Nicholas had said it gave him pause and raised a question in his mind.

Lawlor recognized the look on Harvath's face. "What is it? What are you thinking?" he asked.

"I'm wondering, if the situation were reversed, how would we piece together what had happened?"

"I can tell you exactly what we'd do," said Nicholas. "When the Russians took you, we vacuumed up every piece of evidence, kicked over every rock, and broke every rule until we found you and figured out how to get you back."

"So do you think that's what this is all about?" asked Lawlor. "Them trying to get Tretyakov back?"

Harvath shook his head. "If that were the case, if they wanted to extract information from me, they would've sent in a team, not a lone hitter. The shooter in Key West wasn't there to interrogate me. He was there to kill me."

"You seem pretty certain."

"I could hear the police cars getting closer. Believe me, he didn't have time to ask questions."

"Let's go back to Kaliningrad then," said Lawlor, tapping the cap of his green dry-erase marker against his chin. "You said it 'turned ugly fast.' What did you mean?"

"The only thing that went correctly," Harvath replied, "was our insertion. We managed to breach their airspace without being detected. We landed in a farmer's field, spent the night in a barn, and the Lithuanian truck driver met us along a nearby road the next morning."

Lawlor made a note on the whiteboard. "The drop zone had been selected with assistance from Landsbergis, correct?"

Harvath nodded.

"Presumably, if he had been working for the Russians, this would have been the perfect time to roll up you and your team?"

Again, Harvath nodded.

"Keep going."

"The truck driver was hauling a load of fruits and vegetables in a refrigerated trailer. He had blankets stacked up in back for us and we all piled in. When we arrived in the city, he dropped us off, handed us four public transportation tickets, and we didn't see him again until our exfiltration."

"And then what happened?"

"We set up surveillance on Tretyakov's apartment. We knew where he lived, where he worked, and a small park he occasionally went to. That was it. There was no intel about any girlfriends, boyfriends, bars, restaurants, or hobbies. We had very little to work with and knew we were going to have to improvise. Which is exactly what I did when we saw him leave his apartment. Instead of getting inside and wiring the place, I decided to follow him."

"Why?" asked Lawlor.

"Call it a hunch."

Nicholas hopped off his chair ostensibly to get some more coffee, but more to walk off a wave of nervous energy. What had happened following Harvath's "hunch" still bothered him. Harvath had acted with incredible recklessness.

"What would you call it?" Lawlor asked the little man, sensing this had been an inflection point in the operation.

Nicholas didn't even bother to turn around. Stepping onto a footstool to get more coffee he answered, "I don't second-guess people in the field."

Loyalty. Lawlor liked that. He pressed on.

"What was your hunch?"

"That it was time to grab him."

Lawlor looked at him. "Right there? On the street in front of his apartment?"

Harvath shook his head. "In the park. If that's where he was headed."

"And was it?"

"It was *exactly* where he was headed," Nicholas replied, topping off his mug and turning off the spigot with a little too much flourish.

There was tension between these two. Lawlor wanted to know why.

"Let's skip ahead to where it started getting ugly."

Nicholas expelled a burst of air through his nostrils and shook his head as he climbed down from the footstool and returned to his seat at the conference table.

"I found Tretyakov sitting on a bench," said Harvath. "I thought I had the drop on him. In reality, he had the drop on me."

"He knew you were coming."

"Yes. It was an ambush. I walked right into it."

"How did he know?"

"We had cracked the Norway cell and not long after, the cell on Gotland Island," said Harvath. "Gotland was not just another cell, it was his most *important* cell. Their job was to help defeat the Swedish garrison and hold off reinforcements until Russia could take complete control. Once they had their missile batteries in place, they would have been in a position to prevent any ships from entering the Baltic. That was the final domino they needed to fall before invading Latvia, Lithuania, and Estonia. By taking down that cell, we denied the Russians the strategic advantage they needed to carry out their plan."

"But it didn't end there, did it?"

Harvath shook his head. "We didn't know what Plan B was, much less whether they had a Plan C, D, or E. Without Tretyakov, we couldn't be totally sure we had scuttled the invasion. We had no choice but to go into Kaliningrad and pull him out."

"Again, how would he have known you were coming?"

"I think he was also playing a hunch. Two of his cells got taken down, right in a row. The leader of the Gotland cell was a colleague of his— someone who knew where he lived and where he worked. Tretyakov had to have known it was only a matter of time before we got to him."

"So he sets a trap and waits for whoever shows up."

"Exactly."

Lawlor looked at him. "When the Russians grabbed you, did they ask about Tretyakov?"

"They asked me a lot of things."

"I'm sure they did. You've been a thorn in their side for a long time. But what about Tretyakov?"

"They asked," Harvath replied, "about him and a bunch of other Russians we had gone after over the years."

"The important thing," Nicholas offered, "is that Scot didn't tell them anything."

"Nothing of value, at least," Harvath clarified. "I gave them a lot of disinformation—stuff I knew was going to be hard to source—in order to buy myself time. Had I not escaped when I did, I don't know what would have happened."

"I can tell you what would have happened," said Lawlor. "It would have gotten worse. Beyond your imagination *worse*. They know what we know—everyone breaks, eventually."

Harvath, his expression grim, nodded in response.

"All right, then. Let's say this isn't about Tretyakov—not directly. This is, though, about you. And, let's say the Russian President *is* behind it. This time, instead of taking you alive so he can interrogate you and eventually put a bullet in your head, he's skipping right to the bullet part. But to do that, he needs to find you. How'd he do it the first time?"

"I led him right to me."

"I don't understand. How?"

"Matterhorn," Nicholas interjected.

"What's Matterhorn?"

"Not *what*," the little man replied. "Who. He's a European intelligence officer who had been doubled back on his home country by the Russians. When the Old Man figured it out, he decided that instead of exposing him, he'd play dumb and draw the man, whom he had become friends with, even deeper into his confidence. From time to time, he provided the Russian spy with high-level intelligence."

Lawlor didn't know how to take that. "He did? Why?"

"So that when he fed him bogus intel, the European not only bought it, he ran with it straight to Moscow."

Harvath, who felt compelled to defend his mentor, added, "Reed only handed over intel that we believed the Russians already had, would eventually have, or that we felt was worth surrendering. For our disinformation to continue to be pumped straight into the Kremlin, we needed to make Matterhorn appear to be a superstar."

"I assume the Russians gobbled it up."

"Hook, line, and sinker."

"What does Matterhorn have to do with leading them to you?"

"Not long after the Old Man was diagnosed with Alzheimer's, his brakes started failing. He started regaling his caretakers with tales of derring-do, chock-full of classified, national security information. We likened the situation to a loose nuke. If the enemy got a hold of him, there was no telling what damage it might do.

"Word of his illness had begun to spread and so I made the decision to move him. He had spent summers as a boy at his grandparents' cottage on Lake Winnipesaukee in New Hampshire. As the oldest memories tended to be the last to fade, we thought that he might enjoy returning. I rented a place for him up there and the President okayed a request for a team of Navy corpsmen to rotate shifts around the clock. They all had security clearance, so he got the care he needed and, no matter what he might say, we knew nothing would go beyond the cottage."

"Good plan," said Lawlor.

"That's what we thought," Harvath replied. "Under the guise of having been 'friends' for such a long time, Matterhorn had been pressing to see him."

"Do you think it was genuine?"

"Maybe. I also think Moscow was pushing for Matterhorn to do an assessment and report back. Both reasons served my purposes, so I agreed."

"Served your purposes how?"

"Matterhorn was still useful to us. It had been the Old Man's intention that he become my asset and that I start running him. Allowing him to say a final goodbye was a good way to build rapport. I also hoped that if he could see for himself how far gone Reed was, that the Russians would write Reed off and not attempt to get to him."

"So you set up a meeting."

"I did," said Harvath. "Short of throwing a bag over his head, I took as many safeguards as I thought were warranted. Not until now would I have believed the Russians could pull together the hit murdering Lara, Lydia, and Reed that quickly. It happened in a matter of hours."

"Have you talked to this Matterhorn since then?" Lawlor asked.

"No."

"Did he speak with anyone who would have known you were in Key West?"

"No," Harvath repeated.

"Did he know about your relationship with Carl Pedersen?"

"No."

Lawlor pulled the cap off the green marker and wrote the codename Matterhorn on the whiteboard, only to draw a line through it.

"Okay," Lawlor continued, "for the moment, let's take him off our list of active suspects and go back to something Nicholas was just talking about. If you were the Russians, how would you go about reverse engineering what happened to Tretyakov?"

"I'd go back to CCTV footage. I'd want it from any cameras that may have picked up something—cameras around his apartment, his office, and the park where he was abducted."

"Were there any?"

"Not any that caught our team."

"You're sure?"

"Positive," Harvath replied.

"So then what would you do?" asked Lawlor.

"I'd widen the net. I'd review all footage from all ports of entry in the days leading up to his disappearance. Examine everybody and everything coming into Kaliningrad. Every bus, train, car, boat, and truck."

"Same for vehicles leaving the exclave immediately after Tretyakov's abduction?"

"It depends on how smart the Russians are," said Harvath. "We had a major shootout with their soldiers leading up to our exfil. Those who survived saw us pile into a boat and race off across the lake into Poland. We didn't hide our method of extraction."

"But the Lithuanian truck driver helped get you close to the lake, correct?"

Harvath nodded.

"Where was he headed after he dropped you?"

"He said he was going home."

"Back to Lithuania?" Lawlor asked, just to be clear.

Harvath again nodded.

"It's a pretty big haystack—vehicles that entered and left Kaliningrad around Tretyakov's disappearance—but if they looked at vehicles crossing back into Lithuania near the time you conducted your exfil, it narrows the field considerably."

Nicholas, who had been clicking away on his laptop, asked, "What kind of details can you give me about the driver and his truck?"

"The truck was a Swedish make," said Harvath, pulling up a picture in his mind. "Scania. It was old. Nineteen-nineties, maybe. Manual transmission."

"Color?"

"Blue."

"Did you get a number plate?"

Harvath shook his head.

"Tell me about the driver," Nicholas continued.

"Caucasian. Gray hair. About five-foot-seven. Forty-five to fifty pounds overweight. Somewhere in his sixties. According to Landsbergis, the man came from proud stock. His father, grandfather, and two uncles were Forest Brothers—Baltic partisans who waged guerrilla warfare against the Soviets during and after World War II."

"You've got exceptional recall. How about a name?"

Harvath knew this was the logical next question. "We were never given his name. That was part of protecting him."

Nicholas consulted his notes. "So, overweight, mid-sixties, Lithuanian driver of a blue 1990s Scania whose ancestors harassed the Red Army. That's all we have? Nothing else? Nothing at all?"

"In his defense," stated Lawlor, "you don't get to see a lot from inside a refrigerated trailer."

"Except I wasn't inside the trailer," Harvath replied, searching his memory. "Not on the exfil."

"You weren't?"

"No. The entire op had gone sideways. Everyone was looking for us.

We were hiding out in an old, broken-down car wash. A couple of Kaliningrad cops had shown up and Chase had been left with no choice but to take them both out. It had been hard on all of us. Regardless, in the midst of all that heat, I didn't want to be in the back, blind, and so had told the driver I would be riding up front with him in the cab."

"Did you see anything there that might help?"

Ever the detail guy, Harvath strained to remember something of value. The Lithuanian had been partial to new-car-smell air fresheners, which was humorous, considering how old his truck was.

He remembered the pieces of duct tape covering the cracks in the truck's faded dashboard. He also remembered the practically vintage, removable, orange-buttoned Alpine radio. But there was something else. Harvath remembered seeing some paperwork.

The driver had been taken aback when he had insisted on riding shotgun. Nevertheless, the Lithuanian had relented. When Harvath had climbed in, there were several documents laid out in the cab. As the driver was on his way back across the border, Harvath figured they must have been transit documents.

"I think I saw a name," he said.

Nicholas looked up, over the top of his laptop.

"Lukas," said Harvath, not really trusting his mind after all the drinking. "No, wait," he corrected. "It wasn't Lukas. It was *Luksa*. Spelled L-u-k-š-a."

"First or last?"

"Last name. I think. There were only bits and pieces of papers visible."

"Like I said," Nicholas repeated, "Your recall is exceptional. Anything else?"

"Yeah. The guy was wearing a knockoff Members Only jacket and smelled like Drakkar Noir. That's it."

The little man chuckled. "I don't know how useful that last bit is," he said as he went back to his computer, "but it paints a definite picture."

Harvath's life sucked. His body ached, his heart was smashed in pieces, and he was dying for a drink, but the graveyard humor in him refused to die. The truck driver had actually been wearing a threadbare sweater and had smelled like garlic. It felt good to make his friend smile.

It was the first time he had felt anything other than rage or despair in a while.

"So where does all this leave us?" he asked.

Lawlor shook his head. "I don't know that it leaves us any better than when we started. Despite your feelings regarding Jasinski, I think someone should speak with her, just to make sure she hasn't talked to anyone about Pedersen. Same thing for Proctor. Landsbergis too. I don't think we should take anything for granted."

"And what am I supposed to do while all of this is going on? Lawn darts? Horseback riding?"

"Actually," said Nicholas, checking the clock on his computer, "you've got a tee time."

"A what?"

"Someone's expecting you at the golf course."

"Who?" he asked, knowing it couldn't be the President. Had POTUS been at Camp David, there would have been a palpable buzz and a heck of a lot more activity.

"Don't worry," said Lawlor. "Just go. It's important. We'll be here when you get back."

CHAPTER 17

The minute Harvath saw who was standing at the second tee, he regretted having made the walk over.

"It's no Burning Tree," the man said, referring to the exclusive golf club in Bethesda that was allegedly a design inspiration. "But how many people can say they've played the President's personal course?"

Dr. Joseph "Joe" Levi was the CIA's top psychiatrist. When Harvath had escaped Russia and had been delivered back home, he had spent four days in a safe house on the Eastern Shore of Maryland being debriefed by Levi and CIA Director McGee.

It was standard operating procedure. Harvath had been held captive and tortured by a hostile foreign intelligence service. His debrief focused on three elements—what information the Russians had tried to extract from him, what information, if any, he had given up, and how the interrogations were carried out. Harvath had no doubt that his experience would be a case taught to future American intelligence operatives.

Once McGee was confident that the Russians hadn't had Harvath long enough to break him, and that the handful of tiny things he had offered up were small potatoes, he had removed himself from the debrief and had let Levi conduct a more personal review. The moment the shrink had begun asking about Harvath's feelings over losing his wife, Harvath had colorfully instructed him to take one very large step back.

He wasn't interested in having his feelings explored. What's more, he worked for The Carlton Group, not the CIA. Levi, beyond the national security implications of his capture, didn't have the standing to analyze him. He wasn't applying for a job with the CIA. If and when he ever did, they could run him through the psychological wringer then.

Levi was an interesting duck. In a clinical, debrief setting, he was all business—super professional, attuned to every detail. Nothing escaped him and he took copious notes. But when you caught him in a more relaxed setting, he seemed able to only speak one of two languages—cars or golf.

Dressed in a polo shirt and madras Bermuda shorts, he leaned nonchalantly on his graphite club, pulling a glove onto his right hand. "A hundred bucks says I'm in the cup in two."

This fucking guy, Harvath thought. This was a part of the modern intelligence world that he really disliked. Access to mental health professionals was a good thing. Having them forced upon you, though—no matter how casual the setting—was something entirely different.

The last time Levi had tried to crawl inside his head, he had been sitting on the dock of the aforementioned safe house, minding his own business, when the shrink had materialized, dragging a cooler full of booze. It had been his attempt at bonding, in the hopes that Harvath would open up. But after a couple of drinks, Levi had left, disappointed.

Harvath just wasn't a talker—especially about his feelings. What he was, was a survivor. And in his line of work, you survived by being able to wall yourself off from your feelings; to put unpleasant or uncomfortable things in a box and lock them away. Feelings were distractions and being distracted could get you, or worse, others, killed.

Just off the tee were two golf bags. One was very high-end and obviously belonged to Levi. The other was one of the "loaners" Camp David kept for visiting dignitaries. The fact that the doc had not only had the foresight, but also the self-assuredness, to bring along his own sticks said a lot about him.

His glove in place, Levi leaned over, pressed a tee into the ground, and placed a ball atop it. Straightening up, he gestured toward the guest bag and said, "I thought we'd get a little exercise and have a chat."

In Harvath's world, golf wasn't "exercise." It wasn't even close, and especially not on a one-hole course. "How about we go for a run instead?" he offered, knowing the shrink wouldn't bite. Levi was more of the "gentleman's triathlon" type—sauna, steam, and then shower.

"Didn't bring my running gear," the man replied. "Go grab a club. We'll see who gets closest to the pin."

Harvath wasn't interested. "I'm good," he said. "You go ahead."

Levi shrugged and, after taking a couple practice swings, asked, "You know what the difference between golf and government is?"

"No. What is it?"

"In government, you can always improve your lie."

Harvath smiled. It was funny, even more so coming from someone who worked for the government and whose job it was to get to the truth.

"Now watch this drive," said Levi, quoting an infamous line George W. Bush had given right after delivering a serious statement to the press on terrorism.

Drawing the club back, he swung straight down and through the ball. There was a resounding *thwack* and the ball went sailing into the air. The two men then watched as it dropped three feet from the hole.

"Drive for show," said Levi, "and putt for dough. Let me switch clubs and we'll walk to the green."

"Is this the exercise part? Because maybe I should stretch first," Harvath deadpanned. The green was only 140 yards away.

Levi looked at him and then, removing a pencil and scorecard from his bag, pretended to make a note on the back. "Subject's sense of humor appears intact," he said to himself, but loud enough so that Harvath could hear.

"What are you doing here, Joe?"

"Working on my game."

Harvath smiled. "I think you're here to work on my game."

"That depends," Levi replied, smiling back, as he tucked the card and pencil into his pocket. "Does your game need work?"

"Nope."

"Good. Then we're just two guys out strolling the world's most exclusive golf course."

Slipping his driver back into the bag, Levi selected his putter and headed for the green. Harvath accompanied him.

"I understand you were down in Florida for a while," the doctor said. "How was it?"

"Warm."

"I heard you got kicked out of a hotel for slugging a guest in the bar. Would you like to talk about that?"

"Not really."

"How about when your team found you? You were outside another bar, this time fighting with not one, but *two* men. Why don't we talk about that?"

"Sorry, Joe, I'm not interested."

"In talking about Florida?"

"In talking about anything," said Harvath.

Levi changed direction. "What do you think about McLarens?"

"The sports cars?"

"Yeah, particularly the 720S Spider."

"Why?"

"Because I'm thinking about getting one."

Harvath didn't want to laugh, but he couldn't hold it in. "You're a psychiatrist employed by the CIA. Those cars cost hundreds of thousands of dollars."

"And?"

"*And*, I think if you rolled up to Langley driving one of those, they'd think you were crazy, on the take, or maybe both."

"So not a good idea?" the doctor asked.

Harvath shook his head, the smile lingering on his face. "There'd be an investigation opened before you even reached the lobby."

"Lower my sights then?"

"Just a little."

Levi nodded as he pretended to reflect upon Harvath's advice and they walked on.

A few moments later, he asked, "Do you remember the last time we saw each other?"

This time it was Harvath who nodded. "On the Eastern Shore. Right after I got back."

"Correct. Do you remember what I said to you?"

"We were in that safe house for days. A lot was said."

Levi shook his head. "No. Out on the dock. Right before I left."

"Not really."

It was a lie, but Harvath had meant it when he had said he didn't feel like talking.

"I spoke about the trauma you had been through. Not just the physical, but the emotional and psychological trauma as well. Those were what I was most worried about—and I told you that, in my experience, people who had suffered like you went in one of two directions. They either allowed themselves to grieve and heal, thereby coming out stronger, or they gave up, turned to substance abuse, and often ended up committing suicide."

It was now Harvath's turn to pretend as if he were reflecting. Finally, he said, "Don't remember that part."

Levi knew that was a lie. He also knew, just by looking at him, that Harvath knew it as well.

"The last thing I said to you," the shrink stated, "was that I was positive you could come back stronger, but that it had to be your choice. You had to want it badly enough to do the work."

"Maybe I don't want it badly enough."

"I don't believe that."

"Believe whatever you want," said Harvath. "It's not my problem."

They were now halfway to the green and Levi stopped. "Tell me what happened in Florida."

He was pissing Harvath off. "For fuck's sake," he replied. "Let it go."

"You know I can't do that."

"What I know, is that you work for the CIA and I don't. Therefore, you have no authority over me."

"Scot—"

Harvath held up his hand and cut him off. "This isn't happening. I'm not interested in being analyzed."

Levi was about to respond when a golf cart pulled off the path and sped toward them. Harvath recognized Lance Corporal Garcia behind the wheel.

"You're wanted back at Laurel," she said, coming to a stop next to him.

"Now?"

"Right away."

Harvath looked at Levi as he climbed into the cart. "A hundred bucks says you miss that putt."

Feigning disapproval, the doctor removed the scorecard and pencil from his pocket, and pretended to make another note. "Since last session, subject also seems to have developed a distinctly sadistic streak."

Harvath made a finger gun, pretended to shoot the doc in each knee, and then gestured for Garcia to move out.

CHAPTER 18

Nicholas was where Harvath had left him, sitting behind his laptop in the conference room. Lawlor was nowhere to be seen.

As the dogs rose to greet him, Harvath showed them a little attention and then asked, "What do you have?"

"I think I found your truck driver."

"The Lithuanian?"

Nicholas nodded. "Apparently, he had a somewhat nasty accident. Except nobody thinks it was an accident."

"Is he dead?"

"No, he's alive, but pretty banged up."

The little man turned his laptop around so Harvath could get a look at the screen. It showed a man with two black eyes, a fat lip, and a nose that appeared as if it had been broken. "Is this your guy?"

"Yeah, that's him," Harvath replied. "What happened? Where'd you get that photo?"

"The Lithuanian state health database. All medical records in the country are electronic. According to his file, two weeks ago Mr. Antanas Lukša said he had been in a car accident."

"He looks like he went through the windshield."

"In addition to his facial injuries, he had four broken ribs, and his right hand and left knee had been shattered."

Harvath watched as Nicholas scrolled through the rest of the injury photos. When he was done, Harvath asked, "What did you mean by *no-body thinks it was an accident?*"

"Mr. Lukša changed his story to the doctor. First, he said he had been driving his truck when it happened. Then, when the doctor told him he would need verification from his employer for a work-related injury, he said he had actually been driving his personal vehicle at the time."

"That's weird."

"It gets weirder," Nicholas continued. "I've managed to track down both vehicles, but I can't find any police or insurance reports dealing with the alleged accident."

"The guy was a smuggler. We couldn't have been the first load of cargo he had ever helped sneak into or out of Kaliningrad. Maybe something happened and he didn't want his legit employer to know. If he damaged his boss's truck, maybe he paid in cash to get it fixed and keep it quiet."

"Whatever it was, he definitely wanted to keep it quiet."

"What do you mean?" asked Harvath.

"If I'm translating the file correctly, before he went to the hospital for treatment, Mrs. Lukša had reached out to their general practice doctor. She didn't mention any car accident. Instead, she claimed that he'd had a fall, but was okay and merely in pain. She wanted the doctor to prescribe painkillers. But because it was a weekend and his office was closed, the doc recommended he go to the emergency room."

"Interesting."

"There's more. Not only did Mr. Lukša change his story with the ER physician, he was also evasive when it came to providing details. The physician said the whole visit was 'suspicious.' In fact, he wrote in his notes that it looked like Mr. Lukša had been beaten up. Drawing attention to his patient's shattered right hand and left knee, he indicated that it looked like Mr. Lukša had been struck, repeatedly, with a blunt instrument—most likely a hammer."

"And like I told you," said Harvath, "his truck was a manual. It's one thing to beat a guy up, but if you break his right hand and left knee, he's not going to be working the stick and the clutch for a while."

"If that was someone's goal, that means they knew what kind of equipment he operated. Do you know if he had any enemies?"

"He wasn't much of a talker."

"What if," Nicholas responded, scrolling back through the photos, "this wasn't about settling a score?"

"What do you mean?"

"Let's say this wasn't about some angry border guards not getting their monthly payoff. What if the Russians did exactly what we were talking about? What if they went back and reviewed all their CCTV footage from ports of entry, made a list, and Lukša was on it? What if they then decided to pay him a visit? And during that visit, the Russians decided they've got the right guy and put the screws—or in this case—the hammer to him?"

"And he gives up that he was working for Lithuanian Intelligence?"

Nicholas shook his head. "It wouldn't be a straight line, they understand proper tradecraft, there'd be cutouts along the way. But the Russians are smart—smart enough to reverse engineer it. All Lukša would have had to do was admit that he picked up a team of Americans and they'd be off to the races."

He had a point. A good one. Once the Russians started pulling on that thread, it wasn't impossible to believe that they could unravel the entire thing—right up to Landsbergis at Lithuania's State Security Department.

"I need to get to Vilnius," said Harvath.

"Lithuania? Are you kidding me?" Nicholas replied. "When you very well may have a one-hundred-million-dollar bounty on your head? Are you insane? No way."

"I want to speak to Landsbergis myself. I want to look him in the face."

"Negative. We can send the Ghost."

The Ghost was a deep-cover operative who had been brought over to The Carlton Group from CIA. His real name was Steve Kost. Because his last name rhymed perfectly with "ghost," the call sign had practically selected itself.

"And what do you expect me to do?" asked Harvath.

Nicholas threw up his hands. "I don't know. Stay here? Survive? Take up a hobby. I don't really care. All I know is that you're not leaving."

Harvath was nothing if not obstinate. The surest way to get him to do something was to tell him he couldn't. Nicholas knew that, yet he had still dropped the hammer on him.

"Listen," said Harvath, "if you needed to insert someone over there for a long-term reconnaissance, or to build an extensive human network, Kost would be one of the top people on my list. Sending him over to do an interrogation? That's like asking Rembrandt to do welding."

Nicholas chuckled. "I'm writing that down. I don't think I've ever heard anyone pay Kost that high a compliment."

"Come on, Nick. You know I'm right. He's not an interrogator. That's not what he does."

"Maybe not, but he's good at reading people."

"What he's good at is building rapport. All of his assets would go to the ends of the earth for him. They love the guy. And they love him because they know he has their back. That's not what this is about. If Landsbergis did give up Pedersen to the Russians, whoever confronts him is going to have to be ready to do anything to pry that information out of him."

The little man thought for a moment and said, "I'll send Preisler with him."

"Wait," said Harvath, recognizing the name. "Peter Preisler is an Agency guy. Ground Branch. He was part of McGee's protective detail when I was at their safe house."

"He's with us now."

Nicholas might have been better at running The Carlton Group than he himself believed. Harvath had taken to Preisler. Not only was he squared away with an impressive Special Operations pedigree, but he had also been one hell of a cook. He had taken responsibility for most of the meals while they had been holed up on the Eastern Shore.

"You're going to put something this big on a guy you just hired?"

"Fine," Nicholas responded, "I'll send Johnson."

Harvath's eyes went wide. "You send Kenneth Johnson and he'll kill him. I guarantee it."

"You're being overdramatic. We haven't had a problem with Johnson for some time."

"No? How about Beirut?"

"That was an accident."

"Okay," said Harvath. "What about Bangkok?"

"Also an accident."

"And Auckland?"

Nicholas paused. "Auckland," he conceded, "wasn't an accident. Not even close."

"Listen, I get it. Everybody loves Johnson. But you have to let him do what he does best. And it isn't interrogations. They're like heart surgery. They're delicate and can get very messy very quickly."

"Then who? Haney? Staelin? Who am I supposed to send?"

"Me," Harvath declared. "If Landsbergis gave up Carl to the Russians, the moment he sees me, it'll be written all over his face. I won't even need to interrogate him."

Nicholas had heard Harvath go on ad nauseam about microexpressions, the barely perceptible tells subjects gave off when they were lying and under stress. The U.S. Secret Service, as well as Harvath, swore by them.

Nicholas, though, wasn't the best reader of human emotions, much less facial cues. He preferred cold, hard data. There was no gray in data. Only black and white.

"Even if you were the best person to send," the little man asserted, "there's still the problem of the contract out on you."

"*Alleged* contract."

Nicholas shook his head. "I love you, like a brother, but you're an idiot. A well-meaning, driven, highly determined idiot. The answer is no, so stop asking me. You're not going."

Harvath didn't want to lock horns with Nicholas, but as far as he saw it, they had two choices. They could sit around hoping to get another piece of actionable intel, or they could act on this one. "What if *I* didn't go?"

The way he said "*I*" caught Nicholas off guard. "What do you mean?"

"I operate under an alias. I don't travel as Scot Harvath."

The little man shook his head. "If it were twenty years ago . . . hell, if it were only ten years ago, that might have worked. With all the retinal scans and facial recognition technology these days, it's impossible to get into or out of a country as anything else but who you are."

"So we skirt the borders," Harvath replied. "We slip in and out at the edges. Take advantage of those gray areas that are under-monitored or not monitored at all."

Nicholas again shook his head. "Not worth it. It's too risky."

"Risk is exactly why The Carlton Group exists. The Old Man established this organization precisely because the CIA was shying away from risk."

"We don't do suicide missions."

"Agreed, but we also don't say no just because something is complicated or difficult. We do our research, we plan, we take as much risk out of the equation as possible, but danger and the unexpected are always going to be there. We can't insulate against Murphy's Law. Besides, if the assignments were easy, why would anyone need us?"

"You're changing the subject," Nicholas countered. "The Old Man said you were too valuable to keep going into the field. He wanted you back here, permanently. But for some reason you couldn't do that. And like an overindulgent parent, he caved. He let you keep conducting ops. If you go back out now, we can't protect you. You'll be exposed."

"So what's new?"

The little man smiled. "You're committed to ignoring God only knows how many professional assassins, all competing to be the first to kill you in order to bag a once-in-a-lifetime, one-hundred-million-dollar prize."

Suddenly an idea began to form in Harvath's mind. Smiling even more broadly, he asked, "What if we didn't ignore it?"

"Excuse me?"

"What if we leaned into it? Better yet, what if we actively encouraged it?"

"I'd say you need to be locked in a room with Dr. Levi."

"Where's Lawlor?" Harvath asked, changing the subject back.

"He had to make a call to Langley. Why?"

"Once he's off, let's get him back in here," said Harvath. "I think I've got a plan."

CHAPTER 19

Nikolai Nekrasov, the billionaire owner of the Hôtel du Cap-Eden-Roc in Antibes, told his driver, Valery, to pull over. Nekrasov had grown up on the rough streets of Moscow and still enjoyed a good brawl.

"A thousand euros on the Arab," he said, pointing to a group of teens that had gathered in a trash-strewn vacant lot.

The only thing Nekrasov liked more than watching a fight, was betting on its outcome. He had an uncanny ability to assess a conflict and immediately know who was going to win. It was a skill that had served him well—not only recreationally, but also as he had scaled the sharp heights of one of Russia's deadliest crime syndicates.

And while it was his gifted mind for strategy that had gotten him to the top, it was his unflinching willingness to resort to absolute brutality that had kept him there—and for far longer than anyone would have ever imagined possible.

Of course, if you had asked Nekrasov the true secret to his success, his sophistic response would have been that he placed loyalty—particularly to friends and family—above all else.

It would be a bullshit answer, but in addition to overflowing with money, the man was also overflowing with bravado. No matter how far he had risen above the gutter into which he'd been born, he still maintained a cavernous insecurity over who he was and where he had come from.

That insecurity drove him to put forth a façade that even the most decent, upstanding Russian couldn't compete with. For instance, wanting to appear ever the perfect family man, Nekrasov would have others believe he had left his hotel on a busy workday to meet his wife at the Centre Antoine Lacassagne—a leading cancer research institute in Nice—in order to discuss her oncologist's plan for her ongoing treatment. But nothing could have been further from the truth. Nekrasov was going along for one reason and one reason only.

Believing her breast implants were the source of her illness, Eva wanted them removed. Nekrasov had made it clear, though, that the only way that was happening was over his dead body. He had spent good money getting her tits absolutely perfect and he would be damned if she was going to have some French doctor cast the deciding vote for having them yanked out.

What's more, after several years of marriage and a couple of kids, it was about the only part of her that he still found attractive.

Eva drank like a fish, smoked like factory chimney, and ate whatever the hell she pleased. Early in their marriage, she had been stunning—the toast of Moscow. The Russian President himself, Nikolai's best friend since childhood, had not so subtly hinted that if not for their friendship, he would have wooed her as his mistress. But then, suddenly, she had just given up.

Perhaps it was the stress of motherhood. But as Nikolai had looked around, he had seen plenty of his contemporaries' wives taking exceptional care of themselves. They had armies of nutritionists, private chefs, personal trainers, and plastic surgeons. As they dieted, worked out, coolsculpted, and Botoxed themselves without end, they seemed to not only hold aging at bay, but in some cases to reverse the process altogether. Not Eva, though.

Even before her cancer diagnosis, she had been slipping. It was sad to watch. No matter how much he had tried to encourage her, she hadn't been interested in taking care of herself. Her health and her appearance had taken an obvious turn for the worse. Now, she wanted to get rid of the implants.

Nekrasov supposed he loved his wife. She was the mother of his children after all, but in addition to her appearance going downhill, so had their sex life. They used to make incredible, passionate, swing-from-the-chandelier love. In the early days, they would make so much noise the neighbors would call the police. Those were good times. Those times, though, were gone. Long gone.

Her breasts, on the rare occasions that they made love, were the only part of their marriage that he still felt passionate about.

In fact, despite his well-crafted image, he had recently begun toying with the idea of getting a divorce. Then, Eva's cancer diagnosis had arrived.

He couldn't leave her in light of such news. That wasn't the kind of man he wanted others to see him as. So, he had stayed.

And now here he was—late to his wife's oncology appointment, double-parked in a shitty part of Nice, a part the tourists and wealthy residents rarely saw, waiting for a street fight to take place.

"Are you in?" he asked again. "One thousand euros on the Arab."

Valery, the driver, counted the number of young Frenchmen arrayed against the skinny Arab. He couldn't understand why his boss was backing such a hopeless cause. But he had been working for Nekrasov long enough to know he was never wrong in these matters. "I know better than to bet against you, boss."

"For Christ's sake, Valery. Come on. It's five to one. Even you have to like those odds."

Putting the pearl-white, bullet-proof Bentley Mulsanne in Park, the beefy driver turned to face his boss. "In my heart, I *love* those odds. Even in my gut, I know there's no way he can win. But in my head—"

"In your head, *what*?" Nekrasov prodded.

"In my head, I know you're like an old witch. You see things before they happen. Somehow, you know. You *always* know. So, I'm not betting. Not on this."

Nikolai enjoyed the compliment, but at the same time he was disappointed that his driver had refused to bite. As much of a dumb beast as he understood Valery to be, perhaps, in the end, there was a little wisdom hiding inside the man.

Depressing the button for the refrigerator behind his armrest, he removed two chilled shot glasses and a small bottle of exquisite Polish vodka. Though it was considered a sacrilege to drink anything but Russian vodka, he and Valery had an understanding—what no one else knew wouldn't hurt them. Pouring one for himself, he handed the other forward. The two men clinked glasses, then settled back in their seats to watch the fight. Things didn't take long to kick off.

Normally in these situations, there was a lot of posturing—taunts, a bit of shoving, and a wait for an antagonist to identify himself as the chief aggressor against the victim, who in this case was the Arab.

Unlike the French, Nekrasov didn't look down his nose at the country's Arabs. Most of them were descendants of Arabs from the French colonies of North Africa who had come over in the 1960s and 70s looking for better lives for themselves and their families. They had worked in the most thankless, most menial jobs imaginable, hoping their kids would have it better. But even their children, who had been born and raised in France, were never accepted by the French as full French men and women.

Nekrasov loved France and loved all of its people. He didn't give a damn what color or what religion they were. If you could hold your own, you were worth giving a shit about. It was why he wanted to watch this fight.

The Arab couldn't have been more than fifteen. The other boys gathered around him were about the same age, but Nekrasov couldn't be sure. A couple of them looked like they might have been a year or two older.

It didn't make a difference. What mattered was that the Arab was outnumbered five to one. You never would have known it looking at him. He stood in front of the French teens, his birdlike chest puffed out, defiant.

He didn't stare at the ground, eyes downcast, already beaten; hoping they'd take pity on him. He glared at all of them, his face a stony mask, giving nothing away. His confidence radiated all the way into the plush interior of the armor-plated Bentley. This young man was something special.

Nekrasov couldn't wait to see him fight. If his fists were anything like his attitude, he was going to be a full-on force of nature. It didn't take long to find out.

Like most mobs, a member of the pack, emboldened by the presence of his comrades, eventually develops enough confidence to step forward and act. When it happened, the skinny Arab was ready and knocked him out cold.

For a moment, the rest of pack was stunned, unsure of what to do. But the moment quickly passed and they set upon the young man en masse.

He seemed to be expecting it, because out of a pocket of his jeans, he produced a straight razor and as the pack attacked him, he slashed back and forth.

It was bloody. It was barbaric. And Nikolai Nekrasov *loved* it.

It was like watching some crazy form of ballet. He had never seen anyone move like this kid. He parried and pirouetted—moving from one attacker to the next as if he was some master swordsman, marking his hapless opponents with whatever cuts he saw fit to deliver.

Nekrasov chuckled. No matter how pissed Eva might end up being with his tardiness, this was worth it. Totally worth it.

He had known the young Arab had something up his sleeve. He could tell just by watching him.

To be honest, he had figured there were seven or more Arabs just around the corner, waiting for their signal to pop out and overwhelm the French teens in support of their buddy. But that wasn't what happened.

The fact that the lone teen had stood up to such a larger force and was prevailing, impressed the hell out of the Russian billionaire. This kid, properly mentored, would go places.

Pouring another shot of vodka for himself and his driver, Nekrasov continued to enjoy the display.

The French teens were pissing their pants with fear. They had all been slashed, though not as bad as the Arab probably could have delivered. They were also shocked. They had the greater force and should have already won this fight. Their egos had gotten the better of them—and were continuing to do so. Self-preservation dictated that they disengage, but they were young and stupid and had apparently not yet endured enough punishment.

Scouring the lot for weapons, the French teens picked up whatever they could find—rocks, sticks, broken bottles, even broken pieces of concrete—and dabbed at their bloody wounds with dirty hands and tee-shirts as they prepared to finish off their victim.

Standing his ground, the young Arab smiled and beckoned them forward with his razor.

The leader of the mob had been cut badly enough that he had dropped back. Now, a new leader had taken over. After giving his colleagues a few instructions, he turned to face their opponent.

If the skinny, brown-skinned teen was frightened, he gave no indication. His face retained its inscrutable visage. His apparent calm must have been terrifying for his enemies.

Nevertheless, the French teens mustered their courage and came at him from multiple angles.

Once more, the Arab spun and slipped their strikes, like an experienced surfer allowing a wave to pass overhead. What he didn't do this time, though, was strike back. He allowed them all to pass by unscathed. Nekrasov sat riveted, fascinated by the spectacle of it all.

The young Arab had them exactly where he wanted them. He could have ended the fight right there, but instead he had danced away from their attack and had allowed them all to move right by without consequence.

The only explanation was that he enjoyed toying with them; that he enjoyed flaunting his superior skills.

At some point, though, he was going to have to bring things to a close. That's what Nikolai wanted to watch. Unfortunately, it never came.

From a building nearby, an old woman leaned out her third-story window and shouted that she had called the police. The French teens froze. The threat, if real, presented a problem. It also presented an opportunity.

Judging by the looks of them, these were neither local honor students nor altar boys. These were rough young men. It was likely they'd all had run-ins with law enforcement—possibly multiple times. If the cops were on their way and they didn't disperse, who knew what kind of trouble they could be in. This was the "problem" part.

The "opportunity" part was that they had been handed an excuse to flee, before the Arab could finish them off. Later, they could buck themselves up and soothe their wounded egos by claiming that if it wasn't for the old lady calling the cops, they would have finished off the Arab and left him in a bloody heap.

And so, like a murmuration of starlings, they turned together and fled down a narrow alley.

Discretion being the better part of valor, the Arab turned in the opposite direction, and ran as well.

To Nikolai's amusement, he was headed right toward him. Rolling down the Bentley's window, the Russian beckoned the boy over.

Wary of the myriad of wealthy sexual predators who trolled the Riviera, the teen approached the expensive car cautiously.

"That was quite impressive," said Nekrasov. "Where'd you learn to fight like that?"

"From my brother," the young Arab said, the pride evident in his voice.

"Sounds like someone I might be interested in hiring. Where can I find him?"

"Clairvaux."

Nekrasov knew the high-security prison well. Russian anarchist Peter Kropotkin—who had helped to establish socialism in France—had been housed there, as well as the international terrorist Carlos the Jackal. It was not a nice place and was reserved for some of the most serious criminals in France.

"What does your father do?" the Russian asked.

"He's dead."

"Your mother?"

"She cleans the houses of rich people like you."

Nekrasov smiled. The boy was fearless and also highly intelligent. He reminded him of himself at that age.

"Do you work? Go to school?"

The teen shrugged. "Work, yes. School, sometimes."

"Do you want a better job?" the Russian asked.

"You don't even know what I do."

"I don't care. I'm giving you one chance. Take it or leave it. Do you want a better job?"

The young man nodded.

Removing his business card, Nekrasov wrote something on the back. "What's your name?"

"Beni."

"Come by the hotel Friday," he said as he handed the card out the window. "You're not a guest, so make sure to use the service entrance."

It wasn't meant as an insult and Beni didn't take it as such. Rich people, in his experience, were simply direct.

Pocketing the card, he stepped back as the man gave a command in Russian and the driver pulled away from the curb.

He stood watching until the huge car turned a corner and disappeared from view. Then he did the same, calmly making his way down the nearest side street. He doubted the cops were coming. If they had actually been on their way, he would have already begun hearing the staccato, high-pitched wail of their klaxons. Besides, they had better things to do than break up groups of teenagers fighting. Nice was awash in drugs, gambling, human trafficking, and organized crime—industries he suspected his new benefactor was all too familiar with.

In the back of the Bentley, Nekrasov's thoughts should have returned to Eva and her oncology appointment. But they didn't. Instead, his mind was focused on a bigger problem.

He had fronted one hundred million dollars to activate the most lucrative murder-for-hire contract in history. His assumption had been that by opening it up to multiple assassins, the rush would be on to kill the target as quickly as possible and be the first to claim the prize.

The contract, though, was still open. The target had yet to be taken out. He was not happy. In fact, the more he thought about it, the angrier he became.

By the time Valery had brought the Bentley to a stop in front of the Centre Antoine Lacassagne, Nekrasov knew what he had to do.

It was time to start letting people know what would happen if he didn't soon see results.

CHAPTER 20

Sølvi Kolstad hadn't been to the Baltics in a long time—and for good reason. The last time she'd run an operation here, she had almost been killed.

It should have been easy. A foreign diplomat, with information valuable to Norway, wanted to make a trade. In exchange for a list of Norwegian diplomats who were actively being recruited by his government's intelligence service, the man wanted to be smuggled out of Lithuania, along with his family, and given a new life in Norway.

Carl Pedersen had put Sølvi in charge. It had been her first major operation and from the word go, everything had gone wrong.

For starters, the diplomat was a sexist. He had refused to work with a woman, especially one who, at the time, appeared so young and inexperienced. As soon as Sølvi was introduced as his handler, he had threatened to call off the deal.

"You dictate the terms of the relationship," Carl had instructed her, "or they do. You never want it to be them. *Always* make sure it's you."

She tried everything she could think of, but nothing would change the diplomat's mind. Finally, Carl had encouraged her to call the man's bluff and cut off all contact.

The gambit worked. Within only a couple of days, the man finally came around. Multiple hurdles, though, had still remained.

One of the biggest sticking points was whether the diplomat's intelligence was authentic. His story jibed with bits and pieces of information the NIS had picked up over the prior year, but the man refused to say how he had come across it. What's worse, he refused to provide any solid evidence of his claim, nor a plan for how he would secure a copy of the list. Everything, he stated, would be handed over, once he and his family were safely in Norway.

Sølvi didn't need to be told that it was a lousy deal. Instead, unauthorized, she had gone out on a limb and had made a counteroffer. Once he had provided evidence of his claim, she would get the diplomat's family to Norway. Then, once he had produced the actual list, she would arrange for him to follow.

When she reported back to Carl the new agreement, he had done two things. First, he had complimented her. Then, he asked how she planned on getting the diplomat's family out of Lithuania. To her credit, she had come up with an excellent ruse. Norway would invite a range of diplomats and their families, from several of the embassies in Lithuania, on an all-expense-paid energy, tourism, and climate delegation.

As part of the arrangement, the diplomat's family would leave Vilnius with the rest of the guests. It would be up to him to come up with a legitimate excuse as to why he would be a day late in joining the delegation. If he tried to show up at the airport with his family having not honored his end of the agreement, a problem with his passport would materialize in order to bar his travel. Sølvi, though, didn't think it would come to that. The diplomat was desperate to leave his country and start over in Norway.

It took some arm-twisting, but the Norwegian government eventually came around and agreed not only to host, but more importantly to pay for the delegation and the visit around the north of Norway.

On the appointed day, the diplomat drove his family to the airport and saw them off. Later that night, he met with Sølvi and presented both the list and the underlying intelligence files for each person on it—all of which she copied and transmitted to Carl for verification.

When word came back that everything was in order, Sølvi informed the diplomat that he had been cleared to travel to Norway and join his family. The man was overjoyed.

After entreating him to act normal and get a good night's sleep, she wished him safe travels.

"You're not taking me to the plane tomorrow?" he had asked.

"Absolutely not," she had replied. "You delayed a trip with your wife and kids. The last thing you want is to be seen with some strange woman. That goes double if anyone from your intelligence service is watching you."

"Watching me? Why would they be watching me?"

She had been speaking candidly, but it had spooked him. It was important to calm him down. "You have nothing to worry about. Nobody is watching you. Everything's going to be okay."

"How could you possibly know that?" he asked, growing more tense with each passing exchange.

"Think of Norway," she replied, trying to soothe him. "You and your family are going to have a wonderful life there. Keep your mind focused on that and everything will be okay."

"How do you know we'll be safe?" he asked, his anxiety still getting the better of him.

"We talked about this. No one will know you are in Norway. A trail of evidence will show that you had arranged for a car to meet you at the delegation hotel and that it drove you and your family to a private airfield. There, a private jet was waiting, which flew all of you to South Africa. Outside Cape Town your trail will go cold, except for a few conflicting rumors that a foreign family was trying to figure out how to quietly get to Botswana. Or was it Namibia? No, wait. I think the family was trying to get into Zimbabwe."

It had taken a *lot* of handholding, but she felt she had gotten him to the right point. All he had to do was get through the night and get to the airport the next morning.

When the time came for him to leave his apartment building, she was sitting in her car, watching, from a half block down. He never appeared.

A million things raced through her mind. *Had he overslept? Was he sick? Hungover? Had he suffered a heart attack? A stroke?* What the hell was going on?

She waited for as long as she could and then gave in to the character trait that killed the cat. She had to know why the diplomat hadn't left.

Locking her car, she walked casually up the street, pretending to be engrossed in her phone.

They had established a way to signal each other through Instagram. Based on what she could see, he hadn't been active since they had spoken yesterday. Something was definitely up. He should have logged onto his account before doing anything else this morning. He hadn't.

Walking past the apartment building, she kept a casual watch for anything out of the ordinary—stray figures in doorways, occupied parked cars, or anything else that might signal some sort of surveillance. She didn't see anything. As far as she could tell, the street was clean.

Against her better instincts, and with no team to back her up, she had decided to check out his apartment.

It was an old building. It wouldn't have been hard for her to break into. As it turned out, that hadn't been necessary.

In their push to get to work, a stream of residents had been pouring out. None of them even bothered looking behind them to make sure the lobby door had closed and locked shut. All Sølvi had to do was stand nearby and wait. When the next person exited, she slipped inside.

The diplomat lived on the third floor. Shunning the elevator, she took the stairs, making sure to be as quiet as possible.

She could hear the sounds of a struggle coming from inside the apartment before she had even arrived at the door at the end of the hall.

While the NIS had issued her a firearm, Carl had told her to leave it in Oslo. Any weapon she carried abroad should never be traceable—and whenever possible, should always be standard issue of a foreign, hostile government. For her work in the Baltics, he had recommended several types of pistols. He had then handed her an envelope with a thousand U.S. dollars and the name of a black-market arms dealer he trusted.

Based on what the man had available at the time, she had selected a Russian-made Pistolet Besshumnyy, which translated to "Pistol Silent" in English, and was also known as a "PB" for short.

A Soviet design from the late 1960s, it was still in service and manufactured by Kalashnikov—Russia's largest arms manufacturer. Built for the 9x18mm Makarov round, it used an integral suppressor, which consisted of two parts. This meant that the PB could be easily concealed. The pistol, with half its suppressor already attached, could be placed in one coat pocket—the remaining half in another.

It took minimal training to become adept at rapidly drawing, assembling, and firing the weapon. Sølvi had practiced the routine so many times that she could do it in her sleep. By the time she was halfway down the hall, she had already put it together.

She had never been inside the diplomat's apartment. The handful of times they had met, it had always been in an NIS safe house on the outskirts of the Lithuanian capital. She had no way of knowing how it was laid out. If it was like most of the other apartments of its age she had seen in Vilnius, the door would open onto a corridor leading to a living room, dining room, and kitchen. Along the way, there'd be a bathroom and, likely, two bedrooms.

Stopping at the door, she steadied her breathing and listened. All she could hear were thuds and angry, muffled voices.

She would have given a year's pay for a sack full of flashbangs. Making entry without some sort of distraction device was doubling the danger she was about to encounter. The only way this could possibly work was if she maintained the element of surprise.

Reaching down, she tried the door handle. It was locked.

Think, she said to herself.

All the old buildings, at least the nice ones like this, had an on-site superintendent. Such a person would have keys to each apartment. But by the time she found the superintendent, it could be too late. She needed to get inside that unit *now*. The only question was how.

If her diplomat was being beaten, the people doing the beating were going to be on edge—suspicious of every sound they heard—even a simple knock at the door.

That gave her an idea. The key was to be anything *but* simple.

CHAPTER 21

When foreign missions selected residences for their diplomats, they did so with the cooperation of the host country. In addition to the quality of the dwelling and the safety of the neighborhood, one of the biggest considerations was the ability for local police, fire, and EMS to quickly respond to any calls. All diplomats and their addresses would be flagged in the emergency response database.

What Sølvi wanted to do was to pound on the door like an angry neighbor, demanding to know what all the noise was about. But that would have destroyed her element of surprise. Whoever was inside could go silent and just choose to ignore her, hoping she'd go away.

She could have called in a robbery, a fire, or a medical event, but if Vilnius first responders were like those in most major European cities, they were seven to ten minutes away. If she wanted to waste that kind of time, she would have already begun looking for the superintendent. Besides, there was no guarantee that if she sent the cops or fire department in, that she'd be able to peel her diplomat away.

She needed to stack the odds in her favor. Looking at the solid wooden door and its carved iron lock once more, that's when it had hit her.

The building reminded her of the one in which she had lived in Paris as an au pair. From its façade, to the cage elevator, marble staircase, and hallways they were practically identical. She hoped the attic space was as well.

Measuring her paces back down the hall, she found a utility door, and was able to open it with a single kick. Behind it, was a set of wooden "servant's stairs" that led up to the attic area under the roof.

It was dusty, scattered with boxes and other junk that must have belonged to the superintendent or the property owner, and ran the length of the building—just like the one she knew from Paris. From the north end of the building to the south, a plank walkway traversed the exposed, hand-hewn joists.

Retracing her steps, she picked up things along the way she thought might be helpful and kept moving until she was standing right above where the diplomat's apartment should be.

There, careful not to cause anything to creak, she knelt down and listened. Lowering her head between two of the beams she was able to pick up the same muffled noises she had heard downstairs in the hallway. All she needed to do now was to zero in on her entry point.

Between two different sets of joists, spaced many meters apart, she located the mounting hardware for two separate chandeliers. *Living room* and *dining room*, she figured.

Straight back from the living room she found another. *Entry hall*. What she was looking for now was one additional set of hardware, just off that axis. Moments later, she found it. *Master bedroom*.

Unlike the French, who turned their attics into tiny living spaces for their maids, many Eastern European buildings had unfinished attics. Thankfully, this was one of them. That meant Sølvi didn't have to deal with pulling up a subfloor. She could go right to work on the plaster and lath between the two joists she had selected.

Using the chandelier hardware as her "zero," which she figured would be centered over the master bedroom, she had kept going until she assumed she was over the bed. Then, with the tools she had gathered, she went to work making a hole.

Had she been overly ambitious, she could have jumped straight through, hoping for the best, but she knew that posh, top-floor luxury apartments could have ceilings up to fifteen feet high. Even with all her experience jumping out of airplanes, if she didn't nail the landing, she could be looking at a broken ankle, broken leg, or worse.

It was like a punching through spring ice on a shallow pond. She made a little hole at first so she could see where she was. To her credit, she was right above the bed. Widening the hole a bit further, and peeling out the chunks of plaster and stucco, she could see that the master door was shut.

A few more whacks and she had enough space to slide between the joists. Taking one final look to make sure the room was empty, she slid into the hole, feet first, and dropped athletically onto the bed below.

She landed hard, concerned that the bed frame might give way and crash onto the floor. It didn't.

Even so, it had still created some noise. If not for the door being closed, she would have given herself away.

Raising her weapon, she hopped off the bed and hurried across the room. As best she could tell, the voices were coming from what she assumed to be the dining room area—out the door, at the end of the hall, and to the right.

Pressing herself against the wall, she reached for the door and slowly depressed the handle. When she felt the lock release, she drew the door back. It glided soundlessly on well-oiled hinges.

She peered into the hall, weapon up and at the ready—first right and then left. There were no targets in sight.

Moving toward the living room, she kept her pistol in tight, yet ready to engage. The closer she got, the better she could discern the different voices.

There was her guy—the diplomat, as well as two other men. They were all three arguing in what she assumed was their native language.

At the end of the hall, she pulled up short. She still had the element of surprise. As soon as she stepped into the living room, though, it would be gone and all bets would be off.

She didn't want to go in blind, but she didn't have any alternative. She couldn't see anyone from where she had taken her position. Best-case scenario, the men—whom she assumed were armed—didn't have their weapons drawn.

Applying pressure to her trigger, she took a deep breath, and button-hooked into the living room.

As soon as she did, she could see everything. In the dining room, her diplomat had been bound, hands behind his back, to the thick pull handle of the swinging door into the kitchen. He was being assaulted by two very large men. She had to stop herself from firing. All of it was being played out in the reflection of a large mirror at the boundary between the two rooms.

Without her even being conscious of it, Sølvi's mind did the calculations, reversing everything she was seeing, in order to tell where the bad guys actually were. Adjusting her pistol, she aimed as best she could and began firing through the wall.

The closest of the two men dropped instantly. She had drilled two rounds through his head. The second man had only been grazed and a fraction of a second later returned fire.

He seemed to be using the mirror too because as Sølvi dove for cover, he was able to pinpoint her location and fire three times.

Two of his shots went wide, but one found its target. It went through her abdomen, near her right hip, and out through her lower back.

The pain was sharper than anything she had ever felt, but she had to push it down, ignore it as she had been trained. Which is exactly what she did.

She tried to use the mirror again, but she could only see a sliver of her opponent. The man had scrambled under the dining room table and was barely visible. Nevertheless, she aimed for what she could see and let the rounds fly as she rushed for a better position.

The man cried out as she shot him in his right foot, the round going through the sole of his boot and out the top.

She looked down at her own wound and saw that she was bleeding. She needed to put pressure on the wound, but first she had to finish this guy off.

Getting one more look at the mirror to see where he was, she fired at it, and shattered its glass, so that he couldn't track her. Moving to a new position, she ejected her nearly spent magazine and slammed home a fresh one.

Whoever this guy was, she didn't want to give him time to regroup, much less to crawl over to the diplomat, grab on to him like a shield, and place his gun to his head in order to use him as a bargaining chip. It was time to act.

Reversing course, she returned to where she had previously been, dropped to the floor, and began firing low, through the wall, toward the base of the dining room table.

The room was already thick with gun smoke, and grew thicker still. Chips of paint, pieces of drywall, and splinters of wood went flying everywhere.

She heard the man cry out in pain twice more. He fired three rounds in her general direction, but then he and his weapon fell silent.

"Help me!" the diplomat yelled.

"Are they dead?" she shouted back, her ears ringing from the booming cracks of her opponents' weapons.

"Yes," he shouted.

"*Both* of them?"

"The one nearest me is definitely dead," the diplomat replied. "The other crawled out from under the table and has collapsed in the corner of the room. Near the window. He isn't moving."

Sølvi swapped out her current magazine with a new one, struggled to the far side of the living room, and then slowly moved behind the furniture toward the side with the windows.

Once she was confident that she'd be able to get a good line of sight into the dining room, she readied her pistol and risked a look.

The man was propped up in the corner, right where the diplomat had said he was. His shirt and his trousers were covered with blood. There was also a trickle dripping from his mouth. His hand, still wrapped around the butt of his gun, lay in his lap. His eyes were wide open and he was staring right at her—as if he knew exactly where she was going to reappear.

Pressing her trigger, she fired in two controlled pairs—two shots to his head, two shots to his chest.

Blood, skull fragments, and bits of brain splattered on the wall behind him. The gun fell from his hand. Slowly, his heavy body, slick with blood, tilted to the left and slid along the wallpaper until he landed on the floor with a thud.

Getting cautiously to her feet, Sølvi scanned for additional threats. As the ringing in her ears started to recede, she thought she could hear the wail of police klaxons.

"Is there anyone else here?" she asked.

The diplomat shook his head. "Only them. Untie me. Please."

Motioning for him to be quiet as she slipped into the dining room, she checked the assailants and kicked their weapons away. They were both dead.

Cutting the diplomat loose, she gestured for him to stay put and stay quiet. Opening the kitchen door, she made sure no one else was hiding nearby. She then did the same thing with the bathrooms, the closets, and the children's room.

Returning to the diplomat, she asked. "Are you injured?"

The man shook his head. "No."

"Can you move?"

He nodded and Sølvi helped get him to his feet.

"You've been shot," he said, eyeballing the dark spread of crimson across her midsection.

"I'll be okay. Do you have any bandages?"

The man nodded again.

"Go grab them. And then we need to get the hell out of here."

As the man went to do as she had instructed, Sølvi patted down the corpses. There was nothing on them—no passports, no wallets, no cell phones. Nothing.

When the diplomat came back into the dining room, Sølvi had trouble standing up and he had to assist her. "Are you sure you're going to be okay?"

"I'm fine," she lied. "Let's go."

Buttoning her jacket to hide the blood, Sølvi checked the hallway first before signaling to the diplomat that it was safe to follow.

Taking the stairs down to the ground level in her condition was out of the question, so she, the diplomat, and the one suitcase she had told him he could bring when they had originally hatched their plan, all crammed into the little cage elevator and headed down.

She kept her weapon handy in case any more assailants might be waiting, but the lobby was empty. Plenty of neighbors had heard the gunfire and many could be seen peeking out of doorways and peering over the stairwell railing.

Outside on the street, she guided the diplomat to her vehicle and reluctantly agreed to let him drive. After getting her into the passenger seat, he threw his bag in back and they took off for the airport.

"Slow down," she admonished, as she kept one eye on her side mirror while bandaging her wound. "Everything's going to be okay."

"Are you sure? It looks bad."

"I've seen worse. Just get us to the airport in one piece and you'll be back with your family before you know it."

Once the bandage was in place, she took out her cell phone and sent Pedersen an encrypted message. She had been shot and had lost a lot of blood. She was now traveling with the diplomat and they were on the way to the private aviation side of the airport. She needed a doctor.

Pedersen had only one thing to say in response—**I'll take care of it.**

And that's exactly what he had done. It wasn't until days later, recuperating in a private hospital in Oslo, that she learned how he had made it happen.

Carl had reached out to his number one contact in Lithuanian Intelligence—Filip Landsbergis of the VSD.

It was Landsbergis who had rushed a trauma physician to the jet Carl had chartered for her to fly home on. Without that doctor's expert care, she wouldn't have survived. She owed Landsbergis her life.

But based on what Holidae Hayes had told her, specifically that Harvath and Carl had been recently involved in an operation in Lithuania, that made Landsbergis a suspect in her book.

If he had compromised Carl, or had played any role whatsoever in his murder—she didn't give a damn if the man had helped save her life. He was going to die. That's why she had come back to Lithuania, all these years later.

According to Hayes, Carl had helped pave the way for two aircraft to secretly land at an air base in Lithuania. One was a private jet from

Scot Harvath's company, The Carlton Group. The other, which arrived shortly thereafter, belonged to the U.S. military. Whatever they had been up to, the entire mission had been highly classified.

Sølvi knew that there was only one person Carl would have trusted enough to put something like that together—Filip Landsbergis.

She needed to see him, to look him in the eye and put the question directly to him about Carl's murder. Only then would she be satisfied. Only then could she know what her next move would be.

CHAPTER 22

A ge hadn't softened Gary Lawlor. In fact, if anything, it had made him more of a pain in the ass.

He had hated Harvath's plan—had hated it with a passion. The symphony of profanity he had composed upon hearing it would have shamed the hardest of hard-core sailors. The more Lawlor had raged against it, though, the more Harvath knew he was right on the money.

Nicholas, on the other hand, liked it, but wasn't convinced it could be pulled off in time. There were a ton of hurdles that would need to be surmounted, all of them by him. It was a technological nightmare and would take days, if not weeks, to pull together.

Similar to the military's use of chaff to distract radar-guided missiles, Harvath wanted to flood the zone with disinformation. Using deepfake technology, he wanted to be "seen" on CCTV cameras at multiple airports and train stations around the world.

To make it look like the same person traveling under different identities, he also wanted Nicholas to insert his legit biometric information into each corresponding port of entry computer system, but always attached to a different, fake passport.

Any professional worth their salt would eventually uncover the breadcrumb trail. And, if The Carlton Group played their cards right, they could funnel one, if not more, of the assassins into a trap. Meanwhile, Harvath would be freed up to pursue his own, parallel agenda.

The plan was classic Harvath—audacious, difficult to implement, and likely to change a million times once under way. He had an undeniable talent for getting out ahead of the curve, though. Often, his genius didn't fully reveal itself until the battle was on and the chess pieces had begun to fall. The big question now was—could he stay ahead of the curve?

Like Nicholas, Lawlor appreciated Harvath's capabilities. But he also knew that, right now, Harvath was far from being one hundred percent. He was physically, emotionally, and mentally ground down. And on top of that, he had developed one hell of a drinking problem. In short, the guy was a mess.

Only a fool would have sent him out into the field. Only a fool like Lawlor.

He knew that at 65 or even as low as 45 percent, Harvath was still better than almost any other operative on the planet. It didn't mean, however, that he didn't have his reservations. Lawlor had plenty of them. Harvath was a nuclear reactor of rage. He could see it just by looking at him. The clenching of his hands into and out of fists, the tightening and releasing of his jaw, the grinding of his teeth—Harvath was a hate-filled wreck and his intentions were clear.

Everyone at The Carlton Group wanted Carl Pedersen's killer to get what was coming to him. But could Harvath be depended upon to get the job done? Lawlor was having his doubts.

No matter what he said, though, Harvath was going to do what he wanted to do. If Lawlor knew nothing about him, he knew that much, which was why—in the end—he had agreed to set him loose.

Harvath thrived on adversity. The worse his circumstances, the deeper he drew from himself and the greater his performance. He would turn everything that had happened into fuel, boosting his chances for success. Lawlor was certain of it.

In any other organization, a man that damaged would have been sent home, checked into a hospital, or nailed to a desk. But not at The Carlton Group. Their entire raison d'être was risk-taking. *Calculated* risk-taking, but risk-taking nonetheless.

Putting Harvath in the field was like dropping a malfunctioning nuclear weapon over an enemy city—depending on how the stars were aligned, it could all go stunningly right or spectacularly wrong. And until you had your answer, the wait would be excruciating.

Harvath's plan involved leap-frogging his way into Europe and killing three birds with one stone. A Black Hawk would return him to Andrews where he'd hop a private jet from the U.S. Air Force fleet. The jet would fly him to Chièvres Air Base in Belgium—a short drive from NATO's Supreme Headquarters Allied Powers Europe.

There'd he'd meet privately with Admiral David Proctor as well as Monika Jasinski—just to reassure himself, as well as everyone back at The Carlton Group, that neither of them had sold out Carl Pedersen.

Then, he'd climb aboard an 86th Airlift Wing flight for Šiauliai International Airport in Lithuania and NATO's Baltic Air Policing mission—pick up a car, and make the two-and-a-half-hour drive into Vilnius to accost Landsbergis.

He'd be traveling under an assumed name with fake documents. By using NATO-supported air bases, he would avoid normal ports of entry with their CCTV cameras and biometric scanners. The only people in Europe who would know that he was there would be Proctor and Jasinski, and for them, not until he showed up. It was a risk Harvath, Lawlor, and Nicholas were all willing to take.

In addition, there was also a backup plan he wanted to run—an insurance policy of sorts. If someone was willing to murder Carl to get to him, they'd likely be willing to go after other people close to Harvath. He wanted to make sure certain people were protected.

Once everything was settled, Lance Corporal Garcia picked him up and drove him down to the helipad to meet his ride.

The Black Hawk made the trip from Camp David in just over a half hour. By the time Harvath touched down at Andrews, everything he had asked for was waiting for him. All of it, including the fake documents, were handed over to him in person by CIA Director Bob McGee.

A modified Gulfstream 550 jet—owned and operated by the U.S. Air Force and referred to as a C-37B—was fueled and standing by to make the trip to Belgium. On board were the pilot, copilot, crew chief, and a flight attendant.

The C-37B's primary function was to provide worldwide airlift for senior American leadership and dignitaries. It was an all-weather, long-range aircraft capable of high-speed, nonstop flights. Its elegant interior was designed with comfort in mind and its crew was extensively trained in catering to VIP passengers.

After spending forty-five minutes in the hangar reviewing everything and getting a briefing from McGee, Harvath had boarded the aircraft, kicked off his shoes, and asked for a drink.

The flight attendant brought him a bourbon, handed over a printed menu card, and asked what his preferences were and when he would like his meals to be served. When she spoke, she addressed Scot as "Mr. Brenner." "Donovan Reed Brenner" was the name that had been created for him on his fake documents. McGee had chosen it himself.

Donovan was a nod to Wild Bill Donovan, founder of the CIA's precursor, the OSS. Brenner was a reference to the Brenner assignment—the most daring spy mission undertaken in World War II. McGee knew that the book by the same name was one of Harvath's favorites. And also because he was one of Harvath's favorite people, the name Reed had been chosen as a homage to the Old Man.

None of the names served any strategic purpose, they were merely symbolic, but as Harvath had learned while fighting for his life in the subzero wilderness of Russia, the smallest of things could often supply the most inspiration.

Considering some of the lousy names he had been given to work with over the years, he appreciated McGee putting so much thought into it.

After committing his false identity and background, or "legend" as it was known in the espionage business, to memory, he asked the flight attendant for another bourbon. He didn't intend to pass the flight stupid drunk, but he sure as hell wasn't going to pass it stupid sober either.

Airplanes were weird spaces. Private planes were even weirder—especially if you were traveling alone. Perhaps it was the quiet speed with which they moved, or maybe the soft cocoon of luxury that gave them an unusual, contemplative pull. You couldn't help but be sucked in, to be lulled by the steady hum of the engines, into an almost trancelike state.

Alone, tens of thousands of feet up in the air, knifing through the sky, your mind could open and swallow you alive.

Harvath wasn't ready for his mind to open. He wanted it to remain closed. And the only way to guarantee that was to drink. Because if he allowed himself to feel the true degree of his pain—how bitter and deep and raw it was, he would have to face it, deal with it. He wasn't ready for that. Not now. Maybe not ever. And so, he drank.

The drinking allowed him to be a bystander, to stand on the rim of his soul and peer over the edge. The alcohol allowed him to take measure of his personal landscape, to stare at it good and long and unflinchingly. It was as if he was sitting on a jury, visiting dispassionate judgment on a total stranger. The verdict—*guilty*.

Guilty of every sin imaginable. His list of offenses was long and, in some cases, quite shocking. While the worst had been visited upon him, so too had he visited the worst upon others.

Of course, he had justified those actions by blaming the conduct of his victims. They were "bad men"—his shorthand for those who had earned the retribution he had meted out to them. He had accepted every one of his assignments willingly and, more often than not, had been the chief architect of the punishments that had been delivered.

He had taken more than a professional interest in the details. His desire to see justice done had usually bordered on the obsessive. Good didn't need to just triumph over evil in his mind, it needed to make evil pay—dearly. That was the crux of his job and who he was. That was why he had continued to go into the field, had continued to take the most dangerous assignments.

Evil so offended him that he didn't trust anyone else to teach it the lesson it so rightly deserved. No one was willing to inflict the pain that he was more than capable of delivering. Maybe that was why he was so screwed up. The most incredible evil possible had been done to him and despite the vengeance he had wreaked, he still didn't feel like the debt had been fully paid.

Maybe that was why he had agreed to leave the bars of Key West and hunt down Carl Pedersen's killer. It certainly wasn't out of self-preservation. They could send an army of assassins after him. He didn't care. It was when people harmed others—those he saw as innocents, or those undeserving of their fates, that he was most offended by and most wanted to make evil pay the steepest price he could exact.

He could sense that he had tipped over the rim, that he was falling into the blackness of the abyss.

When the flight attendant arrived with his meal, it was a welcome and much needed interruption, a respite from the storm-tossed sea of his unchecked thoughts.

He switched from bourbon to red wine and tried to focus on the flavors of the food. It had been a while since he had eaten this well. There was a tender, lean filet of beef, roasted potatoes, and thin, sautéed French green beans. The roll was crispy and warm. The butter soft, salty. Even the salad was exceptional.

The only other time he had eaten this well on a government aircraft was aboard Air Force One. Considering the level of passengers who were flown on C-37Bs, he wouldn't have been surprised to learn that the same culinary team was involved in planning the dishes.

But as much as he enjoyed the food, his mind was eventually pulled back to the same place it always was—Lara.

Part of the curse of being a detail guy was that he could remember everything about her. He remembered the beautiful way she had smelled. He remembered the way her body had felt in his arms. He remembered the sensation of her hair brushing across his chest and the sensation of her lips on his mouth. He remembered all of it and it drove him crazy.

Signaling the flight attendant for another glass of wine, he tried to think of something less devastating. Something good. Something pure.

His mind went to Lara's beautiful son, Marco. They would have made such a wonderful family together.

They had all needed each other. But when Lara had been taken, it had all fallen apart.

The last time Harvath had seen Marco was the day of Lara's funeral. He had taken the little boy out to eat, then to the Lego store, and finally to a spot on the Charles River in Boston where he liked to feed the ducks.

It had been heart-wrenching for him, but also heartwarming as there was a wonderful spark of Lara that lived on inside Marco. Lara's aging parents were taking care of him.

During a couple of alcohol-fueled episodes, Harvath had reached for his phone, intending to call his in-laws and tell them that he wanted to adopt Marco and raise him himself.

It was, of course, totally insane. Harvath couldn't even take care of himself, much less a four-year-old boy. Nevertheless, it had felt like the right thing to do and something he wanted.

As the flight attendant refilled his glass and cleared the dishes, he settled back in his seat and closed his eyes. He was remembering the first vacation he and Lara and Marco had taken together. It had been to Cape Cod and they had spent every waking hour on the beach, riding bikes, or eating ice cream.

The trip had been cut short by work. A crisis had popped up and Harvath had to leave. Lara, though, had understood. She had been grateful for their time together and she had assured him that there'd be many more vacations to come. And he, because he loved her and her little boy so much, had believed her. If only, somehow, he could go back in time and warn himself.

But of course, he couldn't do that. All he could do was relive those wonderful moments in his mind. So that was exactly what he did.

He fell asleep, remembering one of the happier times in his life— having no idea of the incredible danger he was flying into.

CHAPTER 23

When the jet touched down at Chièvres, Harvath descended the air stairs and was met on the tarmac by Lieutenant Colonel James Mitchell, Commander of the 424th Air Base Squadron. The 424th was a geographically separated unit of the 86th Airlift Wing out of Ramstein Air Base in Germany. Mitchell was in charge of everything that happened at Chièvres.

As Harvath had been identified as a Department of Defense adviser and was dressed as a civilian, Mitchell greeted him with a firm handshake, saying, "Welcome to Belgium, Mr. Brenner."

"Thank you, Colonel," he replied.

"I understand you won't be with us long."

"Just a quick meeting and then I'm on my way to Šiauliai." Nodding toward a waiting car and driver, he asked, "Is that for us?"

"I thought you might want to get cleaned up before your meeting," the Base Commander said. "We've got a VIP lounge, complete with shower, set aside for you. Airman Williams can take you over and then bring you back to my office whenever you're ready. You'll be using our secure conference facility."

Lawlor had gone directly to the President with Harvath's request. The President had then put Lawlor in touch with the Secretary of Defense, who had set everything up. He had definitely instructed Mitchell to pull out all the stops. This was first-class treatment.

Looking at his watch, Harvath rubbed the stubble on his cheeks. He had more than enough time for a hot shower and a shave before his meeting with Proctor and Jasinski.

"That sounds excellent," he responded. "Thank you."

Airman Williams helped transfer Harvath's gear from the jet to his vehicle while Harvath thanked the flight crew. They planned on spending the night in Belgium and flying back to the States in the morning. He wished them safe travels, thanked Mitchell again, and hopped into the passenger seat of the car.

Williams was a courteous, professional young man originally from the Florida Panhandle near Destin. The building they were headed for was so close, they barely had any time for small talk.

Parking out front, Williams popped the trunk and insisted on carrying Harvath's personal bag inside.

"Not necessary, Airman," Harvath replied. "But thank you. All I need is for you to make sure the rest of my gear is here when I come out."

"Yes, sir. It will be," said the airman. "I promise."

Williams walked Harvath up to the door and swiped his keycard through the electronic reader. "Down the hall, first door on your left. Take all the time you need. I'll be here."

Harvath thanked him and headed inside.

The space looked like it might have been an officer's club at one point. The walls were paneled with wood and there were plenty of framed photos and pieces of art depicting military aviation.

The furnishings, while tasteful, were several decades old. It had the same industrial cleaning supplies smell that most U.S. installations had—probably because Uncle Sam bought those supplies in bulk.

Walking down the hall, Harvath found the door he had been told to look for and stepped inside.

The lounge was about the size of a small studio apartment. There was a sitting area complete with TV, a desk, a snack station cum kitchenette with a minifridge, coffeemaker, and a microwave, as well as a small bathroom with a shower.

In addition to sourcing gear for Harvath, McGee had been kind enough to have someone pack him a go-bag with clothes and toiletries. It was all comfortable, middle-of-the-road casual stuff. Nothing that would make him stick out and get noticed.

He laid out a few things, turned on the hot water in the shower, and crossed over to the kitchenette. Opening the fridge, he checked out the contents.

It had been stocked just like a hotel minibar. There were waters, soft drinks, juices, beer, and mini-bottles of hard liquor. The Maker's Mark bourbon, with its signature cap dipped in red wax, immediately caught his attention.

"Just one," he said to himself as he pulled it out, kneed the fridge shut, and searched the cabinets for a glass.

The glasses were all the way to the right, along with the coffee cups. Taking one down, he opened the bourbon, and poured.

He knew it was a bad idea the same way he knew it wouldn't be "just one." It'd be one now, then another when he got out of the shower. He'd try to cover up the odor of alcohol by brushing his teeth, gargling with mouthwash, and taking a strong, black coffee to go.

No sooner had he raised the glass to his lips than his conscience got the better of him. He couldn't let his demons hold sway over him like that. He was working, for God's sake. The President had personally signed off on this operation and had set all the wheels in motion. The last thing he needed—no matter how good he thought he might be at hiding it—was for Proctor to report back to the Secretary of Defense that he had shown up with booze on his breath.

Setting the glass down, he fired up the coffeemaker, grabbed a mug, and inserted a pod.

As the machine brewed his coffee, he carried his glass of bourbon into the bathroom and dumped it down the sink. There'd be plenty of time for drinking later.

Retrieving his coffee, he carried it back to the bathroom and took off his clothes. Climbing into the shower, he let the hot water pound against his body. He let himself be in the present, appreciating the warmth. There was no telling how long it would be until he had another relaxing, unguarded moment.

Assignments had a way of going sideways in the blink of an eye, the tension spiking off the charts. He had learned a long time ago to appreciate the little things and take nothing for granted.

That sense of thankfulness seemed to always be heightened right before he underwent an operation. It was as if time slowed down and, as it did, his senses grew more acute. He could experience things in greater detail. Tastes, sounds, sensations—all of them were more richly available as they passed by in slow motion.

It was the exact opposite of what happened in the field, where everything sped up, and information—sights, sounds, movement—had to be rapidly processed and decisions made in a fraction of a second.

It was almost as if this was his mind's way of taking deep breaths and limbering up—like a sprinter, preparing to climb into the blocks. And as with a sprinter, it was always a gun that set everything off.

Throwing the temperature selector all the way to cold, he stood under the spray for as long as he could. Sometimes referred to as a "Scottish Shower," the shock of the freezing water sent a jolt through his body. It was like consuming a couple of espressos back-to-back. He felt energized, his mind sharpened.

Stepping out of the shower, he toweled off and shaved at the sink. When he was done, he polished off his coffee, brushed his teeth, and slowly got dressed.

Despite the jolt from the caffeine, as well as the cold water, he was dragging his feet. The meeting he faced wasn't going to be easy.

He had no clue whether Proctor and Jasinski had heard about Carl's death. He suspected, though, that they hadn't. The Norwegians had been keeping it quiet while they continued their investigation.

That meant he was going to have to read them in on all of it, including Carl's torture and the killer's search for information via all his devices and the NIS database. But as bad as that was going to be, it wasn't even the worst of it.

He had not seen Proctor, nor Jasinski since his torturous personal nightmare had begun. His wife, along with his colleague and mentor had all been murdered. The Russians had then dragged him back to Russia to interrogate and kill him.

They would begin by sharing their condolences, because that was what good, decent people did. Then, they would do the next thing good, decent people did—they would ask him how he was doing.

That was still the part he found the most painful. Not because it was offensive or overly intrusive, but because it asked him to look inward, to examine how he was feeling. He didn't know if he'd ever be able to do it.

Picking up his pace, he packed his bag and ignored the impulse to make a second coffee to go. He needed to get out of the building. He was starting to think twice about having poured that bourbon down the sink. He knew if he got anywhere near the coffeemaker, he was going to open the minifridge. And if that happened, he wouldn't be having just one.

He needed to keep himself together—compartmentalize. That used to be something he was good at. *Really* good.

He could put everything in an iron box, lock it shut, and hide it away in the furthest corners of his mind. It was he how he survived. It was what made him such an exceptional hunter of men—an apex predator. If he were to lose that ability, none of his other skills would matter. Like a sick animal on the edge of the herd, he'd be as good as dead. The lions would come for him first. He refused to let that happen.

Grabbing his bag, he pushed down his pain and headed out to meet Williams.

CHAPTER 24

Williams walked Harvath into the Base Commander's office, showed him where the secure conference room was, and asked him if he needed anything. Harvath thanked him and said that he was fine.

In addition to pens and pads of paper placed neatly upon leather blotters in front of each chair around the table, there were bottles of water, a large carafe of coffee, cream, sugar, mugs, and a tray of fresh fruit, cheese, and pastries. Colonel Mitchell was a thorough professional.

He was also a smart operator. It wasn't every day the Supreme Allied Commander of Europe showed up and needed to borrow your conference room for a private meeting put together by the Secretary of Defense. This was his opportunity to shine—and that was exactly what he was trying to do.

"All good?" Mitchell asked, sticking his head in.

Harvath flashed him the thumbs-up. "This is perfect. Thank you."

"I have my AV and IT people standing by if you need any help. The Wi-Fi password for the day is on the whiteboard."

"This is going to be pretty low-tech. In fact, it's going to be *no* tech."

The Base Commander shook his head. "A military meeting without a PowerPoint? I think that's a sign of the Apocalypse."

Harvath smiled. "PowerPoints are nothing more than silent screams for promotion."

"You're not interested in being promoted?"

"I'm unpromotable. Unless there's an opening on a pirate ship some-where, I'm going to have this job for as long I can hold on to it."

Mitchell smiled back. "Bottle of rum. A dead man's chest. If there's anything you need, just let me or Williams know. We'll get you squared away."

"Good copy," Harvath replied.

As the colonel disappeared into the hallway, Harvath checked his watch. Proctor and Jasinski would be arriving at any moment. Reaching for the coffee, he filled a mug and then selected a chair near the middle of the conference table and sat down.

His brain was doing that thing again. The mug felt warm in his hands. The coffee smelled delicious. He closed his eyes and breathed it in.

As he did, he wondered if he would ever conduct another operation after this. He had been content down in Key West. If you could call it that. Perhaps numb was a better word for it. He had surrendered himself to his fate. Whether it was the alcohol, or an assassin that took him out, it didn't seem to make much difference. But that was before Carl Pedersen had been murdered—*tortured* and murdered, because of him. It was still so hard to come to grips with.

Whether or not he returned to some bar at the southernmost point of the United States to drown himself was yet to be seen. What mattered at the moment was making sure that Proctor and Jasinski were exactly the people he believed them to be. Until he had that question answered, nothing could move forward.

A chorus of clocks ticked away upon the wall, marking the passage of time from different zones around the world. Harvath kept his eyes closed and listened, as he continued to drink his coffee. No matter what he did or didn't do, the world still kept turning.

There was a commotion from somewhere down the hall, a flurry of activity. "They're here," he said to himself, opening his eyes.

Standing up, he prepared to meet his guests. It was going to be an un-comfortable reunion.

David Proctor was the epitome of the Navy maxim "High speed, low drag." He had left his protective detail outside. They didn't even come in and do a sweep. He had no aides, no entourage. He came exactly as the President had asked, alone—except for Monika Jasinski. Colonel Mitchell showed them to the conference room.

They had not been told with whom they would be meeting. All they had been informed of was that it was in regard to their disruption of recent terror attacks against NATO diplomats.

The flashes of recognition on their faces were immediate. Harvath held out his hand and introduced himself before anyone could blow his cover. "Admiral Proctor, I'm Donovan Brenner. Thank you for agreeing to meet with me."

Harvath shook his hand and then turned to Jasinski and repeated the introduction.

The Base Commander pointed out where everything was, and made sure his guests knew to pick up the conference room phone and to personally contact him if they needed anything. Once he had exited and had shut the door behind him, the questions started. Jasinski spoke first.

"*Donovan Brenner*? You're not using that Stephen Hall, NATO alias anymore?"

"Not on this assignment. It all came together very fast. Everything had to be brand-new."

"*Assignment*?" said Proctor, drawing out the word. "What's with all the subterfuge? What's going on, Scot?"

So far, the read he was getting on each of them was good. Proctor and Jasinski had been surprised to see him. The surprise had melted into happiness, but had quickly turned to concern. He had already made up his mind to pull no punches and to drop the news as soon as he was comfortable that he had registered their baselines.

"Carl Pedersen was murdered."

"What?" responded Jasinski, shocked. "When?"

"A week ago. Maybe more. They found him at his weekend place outside Oslo."

"Who killed him?" Proctor asked, better at keeping his composure, but still obviously taken aback.

"Why don't you get some coffee and we'll all sit down."

Silence filled the room as they filled their mugs. Harvath hadn't been wrong. This was an uncomfortable reunion.

Someone needed to tear the bandage off. Admiral Proctor decided to be that someone.

"Scot," he said, "what you've been through is unspeakable. We just want you know that we are very sorry for your losses."

Jasinski nodded. "If there's anything we can do for you. All you have to do is say it."

"Thank you," Harvath responded.

He could feel the breath leaving his body, like water being sucked away from a beach before a tsunami. The anguish was building up inside him. He needed to shut it down.

"The best thing for me right now," he added, "is not to talk about it— *any* of it."

The Admiral was a compassionate man. "Understood," he said. And that was that. It wasn't spoken of again.

They gathered together at the head of the table, a sign of their friendliness for each other and solid relationship.

Once they were settled in and ready to restart the conversation, Harvath picked back up where he had left off.

"He was found by a neighbor. He had already been dead for several days. About four to be specific. But leading up to his murder, he had been tortured. When the killer finally finished him, it was with one round through his heart."

"Jesus," said Proctor, the word coming in a whisper.

Jasinski's hand covered her mouth.

"No physical evidence has been recovered," Harvath continued. "The Norwegians have been turning over every stone. They have no leads whatsoever. Except for one."

"What is it?" Jasinski asked.

Raising his right index finger, Harvath pointed at himself. "Me."

"You?" said Proctor. "I don't get it."

"During the time they believe Carl was being tortured, files were accessed not only on his phone and laptop, but also within the NIS database.

All of them had to do with me. They believe the killer was compiling a dossier."

"How many people even knew about your relationship with Pedersen?"

"Outside this room? Not many."

"Wait a second," Jasinski interjected. "You're not here because you think we had something to do with this, are you?"

"Does the President think we were involved?" Proctor added.

Harvath shook his head. "I made it crystal clear back home that neither of you would have ever been involved in something like this."

"Good."

"With that said, I need to know if either of you may have mentioned Carl to anyone. Did his name appear in any of your reporting? Anything like that?"

"*Reporting?*" said Jasinski. "What reporting? We didn't even take notes. And in case you don't remember, I had no idea what kind of operation I had been sent on when I linked up with you. I went because the Admiral told me to. I reported to him and him only. I didn't even tell my own government about it."

Harvath believed her. One hundred percent.

"Scot," Proctor assured him, "if someone linked you to Carl, it wasn't through us. We kept the entire operation locked down, airtight. If you've got a leak, it's someplace else."

Harvath believed the Admiral as well. Neither one of them had directly betrayed Carl, nor did it appear as if there was an ancillary contact he needed to track down and question.

Ever the perceptive intelligence officer, Jasinski sensed that Harvath was holding out on them. It was just a feeling, but it was pretty strong. There was something he wasn't telling them.

"Why would someone target Carl in order to build a dossier on you?" she asked.

"I'm not completely certain."

"Rarely is anyone in our line of work *completely* certain. But let's put that aside for a second. You're holding out on us. I'm more than sure. I'm positive. What's the rest of the story?"

She was really good—which was why he had enjoyed working with her. She had a solid moral compass, but wasn't afraid to get her hands dirty if she had to. Sometimes, in their line of work, the ends did justify the means. They were paid to save lives and protect their nations from foreign aggression. Occasionally, it was necessary for the bad guys to be shown what lengths they were prepared to go to in order to meet those goals.

"Three nights ago someone tried to kill me," stated Harvath.

Proctor's eyes widened. "The same person who killed Carl?"

"We're not sure. We don't even have a positive ID on the body."

"At least you got him before he could get you."

Harvath shook his head. "I shouldn't even be here. He had me. Dead to rights. The only thing that saved me was a warning from the Norwegians and my team finding me before he could pull the trigger."

Jasinski looked at him. "So if you didn't recognize him, someone must have sent him, right? And I can guess who."

"Who?"

She laughed, thinking that he was joking. "Well, it certainly wasn't the Tibetans. After all the damage you have done to the Russians? And I'm just talking about everything that happened before they kidnapped you. Then there was that cascade of mayhem that happened after and—"

"Cascade of mayhem?" Harvath interrupted.

"Come on, Scot. I read reports and connect dots. That's part of the job. A few weeks after you were rescued, key figures around the Russian President Peshkov began dropping dead—including his son."

"From what I read in the papers, his son overdosed."

"That's part of the job, right?" she countered. "To make it *look* like an accident. Except a bunch of connected 'accidents' quickly begin to look like an orchestrated campaign. It wasn't random. It wasn't dumb luck. And it wasn't a coincidence. It was *you*. I knew it then and I'm even more certain of it now. In fact, I'll go on record and say that I'm *completely* certain."

Resting her case, Jasinski leaned back in her chair, raised her mug, and took a sip of coffee.

Admiral Proctor didn't waste the moment. Looking at Harvath, he said, "You asked for our best person. Now you know why I sent Monika."

Harvath never doubted that she was their best person. He had known it from the beginning. He also knew that she was trustworthy. So was Proctor.

"Supposedly , there's a contract out on me. A big one," he confessed. "One hundred million dollars. To make it even more interesting, it wasn't just given to one assassin. It was offered to a pool. Whoever gets to me first, gets the prize money."

"And I thought *my* week was off to a bad start."

Jasinski not only had the natural talent for their line of work, but she also had the requisite sense of humor.

"So let me get this straight," said the Admiral. "You don't know who killed Carl. You don't know who tried to kill you. And behind all of this, there's allegedly a one-hundred-million-dollar contract. Does that about sum it up?"

"That about sums it up," said Harvath, nodding.

"What are you doing here? Why aren't you in a bunker somewhere? They can't kill you if they can't find you. Isn't there anyone else who can get to the bottom of this?"

It was the argument Gary Lawlor had made. That he was only making it easier on the people out there who were competing to kill him. And this was a key point upon which he had disagreed. The hardest target to hit was a *moving* target. It was the guy who sat still, the *stationary* target, who would be easier to pick off.

"I was the architect of everything that led up to Carl's murder," Harvath admitted. "That makes me responsible for what happened to him."

Proctor shook his head. "The person who killed him is responsible. Not you."

"With all due respect, Admiral, he was tortured by someone trying to get to me. The way I see it, if it hadn't been for me, he'd still be alive. That's why I'm here. I know every detail of what we did together. There isn't someone else we could have put in the field who would have been able to process and sort the information the way I can."

It wasn't an unreasonable argument. In fact, based on everything the Admiral knew about him, Harvath probably *was* the best person for the job. That didn't mean, though, that he wasn't concerned for him. If there really was a one-hundred-million-dollar bounty on his head people would be selling out their own family members to get to him.

"So," Proctor relented, "how can we help?"

"For right now, you've already done it. By clearing me to land here, arranging my flight to Lithuania, and having a car waiting—that's all the help I need."

"I did that, though, because I had orders from the SecDef. I didn't know 'Brenner' was actually you."

"And as long as we keep that a secret amongst us, everything else will be fine."

"Are you sure?"

"I may need even more help, but it'll depend on how everything unfolds."

The Admiral smiled. "If it involves violating Russian airspace, providing close air support, or repositioning highly specialized aircraft to get you out, you know who to call."

"I do," said Harvath. "And by the way, I remain very grateful."

"Why the hell would you go back to Lithuania?" Jasinski asked, changing the subject. "What thread could be that important?"

"It was our launching point for Kaliningrad—and was the last place Carl and I ever saw each other. There are a couple of leads there I want to run down. If I'm right, I'll be on top of Carl's killer in the next twenty-four to forty-eight hours."

"And if you're wrong?"

Harvath looked at her. "Then we should say our goodbyes here, because that means he's going to be on top of me."

CHAPTER 25

After wrapping up his meeting, Harvath had Williams drive him to the Chièvres PX to pick up food for his flight to Šiauliai. Proctor and Jasinski had offered to take him out for a meal, but he declined. He wasn't in the mood to be social. His head was in the game, and that's where it needed to stay.

When the C-130 Hercules was ready for takeoff, Williams pulled up as close as he could to the enormous aircraft and helped Harvath transfer his gear.

Once everything was stowed, they shook hands, Harvath thanked him, and they wished each other well.

As he boarded and found a seat, an aircrew member handed Harvath a pack of foam earplugs. Normally on missions, he brought his own. This time, though, someone else had put together his kit and he had forgotten to ask for them. The noise level in the four-engine turboprop cargo plane could be quite high. Thankfully, this crew had thought ahead. That wasn't always the case. He had been on plenty of ops where if you weren't prepared, you were out of luck.

The nylon webbing seats bolted to the fuselage were a far cry from the plush leather seats of the C-37B he had crossed the Atlantic on, but all that mattered was the destination, not the journey.

He rolled his earplugs and stuck them in as the C-130 thundered down the runway and lifted off. Once it was level, he unpacked his lunch and ate. He had thought about picking up a six-pack to bring on board, but had decided against it. All he needed was some overzealous MP at Šiauliai smelling beer on his breath and preventing him from driving off the base. He had too much work to do and time was of the essence.

While Landsbergis was his ultimate target, he wanted to pay Lukša, the Lithuanian truck driver, a visit first. If he really had been beaten up by the Russians, Harvath wanted that intel straight from the horse's mouth. He wanted to confront Landsbergis having assembled as much information as possible.

Besides, going to speak with Lukša wasn't too much of a detour. According to Nicholas, he lived in a working-class suburb of the capital. And considering the extent of his injuries, Harvath felt relatively certain the man wouldn't be tough to track down. In fact, he would have been surprised if he wasn't laid up at home, watching TV, and being taken care of by his wife.

Landing at Šiauliai, he was met by an Air Force officer who checked his ID and handed him the keys to a black Toyota Land Cruiser, idling on the tarmac. No further words were exchanged. After Harvath had loaded his gear, he plugged Lukša's address into his GPS, headed for the nearest gate, and exited the base.

The first thing he noticed was a sign for a popular attraction called the Hill of Crosses, about twelve kilometers northeast of town. It had popped up when he had been online researching the best route to Vilnius. From what he understood, it was a small hill covered by a vast collection of over 200,000 wooden crosses. Like the Lithuanians themselves, some were plain, some were very ornate. A pilgrimage site dating back to the nineteenth century, it was meant to symbolize resistance to Russian rule.

It was a noble part of the country's heritage—a solid, passionate part of its DNA. But like the human body, sometimes DNA could become corrupted and that corruption could bring forth incredible sickness, even death.

Heading southeast of town, Harvath made himself and Šiauliai a promise. He already knew what he was going to do to every person he tracked down who was responsible for Carl's death. In addition to putting each of them in the ground, no matter where in the world he was, he would send Šiauliai a cross to place upon its hill.

In a warped, messed-up way, he'd at least be leaving something behind—a legacy of sorts—his own little family of wooden crosses.

• • •

Like a lot of espionage work, the drive to Vilnius was dull and uneventful. Halfway there, he noticed a farmer's market, and pulled off the highway.

Lithuania might no longer be part of Russia and the old Soviet Union, but Russia and the old Soviet Union were still very much a part of Lithuania. Neighbors still took an unhealthy interest in what other neighbors were doing, strangers were regarded with suspicion, and gossip spread faster than a fire in dry grass.

Harvath knew that the moment he appeared in the truck driver's neighborhood, tongues were going to wag. He couldn't control that. What he could control was what the neighbors were whispering. That was why he didn't intend to hide his presence. In fact, he wanted to be as obvious as possible about why he was there and who he was going to see.

Just like a private investigator throwing on a utility worker's reflective vest to get a closer look at a house, Harvath figured—human nature being what it was—that he could run a version of the same ruse; give the neighbors something *not* to be suspicious of.

He paid for his purchase, returned to the Land Cruiser, and got back on the highway. There was still over an hour left to go.

With the endless road unfolding in front of him, he could sense his jet lag trying to kick in. Rolling down the window, he turned on the radio to help him focus and stay awake.

Sandwiched between countless Europop offerings and local folk music channels, he found one playing American classic rock—on vinyl, no less, with all of the original hisses and pops.

He tuned in just as the needle was dropped on "Sympathy for the Devil" by the Rolling Stones.

If you paid attention to the lyrics, it was an incredibly dark song. If you tuned them out, it was—as Mick Jagger stated—one hell of a hypnotic groove, a samba that doesn't speed up or slow down—just a sinister constant, which was what Harvath needed at the moment.

And the DJ didn't let up. After the Stones, there were high-energy songs by The James Gang, Eric Clapton, Jefferson Airplane, Aerosmith, and even KISS. The next hour passed without his eyelids getting any heavier, or his mind wandering to things he didn't want to think about.

By the time his exit came up, he was looking forward to getting out of the car. The sooner he could question Lukša, the sooner he could get the answers he had come here for.

Checking his GPS, he found a gas station a bit off the beaten path. There, wearing a baseball cap he had pulled from his bag and keeping his head down to avoid any CCTV cameras, he refilled his tank and bought an energy drink.

He cracked it as he pulled back out into traffic and slowly snaked his way toward the truck driver's home.

The outskirts of Vilnius were like any other major Baltic city he'd ever visited—industrial, rough, and very poor. This was definitely where the have-nots lived.

Graffiti was everywhere. The streets were dirty. Weeds sprouted up from the cracked sidewalks. Steel shutters and bars over windows spoke to a high level of crime. This was not a good place to live.

As he got closer in, the neighborhoods began to get nicer, but only by a degree. They were still poor, but the properties were better kept. Graffiti was no longer evident. Many homes had modest landscaping. And while some had bars over the windows, many did not.

This was a buffer zone—the working-class ring that surrounded Vilnius's more affluent neighborhoods and its bustling city center. This was where Mr. and Mrs. Lukša lived.

Seeing the truck driver's home now clearly marked on his GPS, Harvath did a wide reconnaissance sweep of the surrounding area. His eyes took in everything.

He wanted to know what businesses there were, if any. What about police or fire stations? If something went wrong and he had to flee on foot, what direction would he run and where might he hide out?

All of it was necessary, pre-approach surveillance. If anything went sideways, no one was coming to save him. He was on his own. The better he knew the lay of the land, the better he could handle any problems that might pop up. And knowing what he knew about field operations, problems were almost a sure thing.

He drove in ever tightening circles, until it was finally time to drive down Lukša's street. One pass was all he'd be able to make. Anything more than that was asking for trouble.

Not only would he be given one shot to study the truck driver's house, but simultaneously he'd need to figure out where to park the Land Cruiser.

His preference was to stash it someplace out of sight and walk up to the house. That said, he didn't want to leave it anyplace that might be tempting for thieves to break into. He had too much stuff in the cargo area that he didn't want to lose.

In the end, as was so often the case, fate handed him his answer. One of the side streets was involved in a public works project and was off-limits. That had pushed cars onto the next side street, where they were parked along the curb almost bumper to bumper. The only open parking was on Lukša's street and based on the posted signs, it was permit-only. Harvath found an empty spot at the beginning of the block and pulled in. Now, he had a decision to make.

Murphy's Law being what it was, he felt certain that the moment he stepped out of his vehicle and walked away, a cop or a parking enforcement officer would come by and notice the infraction. Not knowing what kind of sticklers they were for enforcement, at best he was looking at a ticket, at worst—getting towed. Either way, there would be a record of his vehicle being in the area.

Depending on how his meeting with the truck driver went, that might not be a problem. But his job was to prepare for the worst. And there was actually something worse than getting towed. If the cops forced their way into his vehicle and went through his gear, it would no longer be a parking enforcement issue. It would become much more serious.

His other option was to find a car that was unlocked and steal that person's parking permit. That was asking for just as much trouble. There was no telling how many pairs of eyes were looking out from behind curtains and upstairs bedroom windows. It would only take one person to call the authorities and all the aforementioned problems would come crashing down on top of him.

Picking up his encrypted phone, he texted Nicholas a request. As he waited for the answer to come back, he pulled a piece of blank paper and a Sharpie from his laptop bag.

Two minutes later, he had his response. Zooming in on the picture Nicholas had sent, Harvath copied the sentences exactly as they had been written in Lithuanian. *This vehicle belongs to a home healthcare nurse. I am visiting a patient. I will return shortly. Thank you for your understanding.*

From the armrest, he retrieved the Sig Sauer P226 9mm pistol McGee had given him, as well as two of the additional magazines. Removing it from its Sticky holster, he did a press check to make sure a round was in the chamber. Then he returned it to its holster and placed it inside his waistband at the small of his back. The mags went into his pocket.

Placing the note on the dashboard, he knew it was contradictory to the image he was about to present the neighbors. Hopefully, he could get in and out before anyone noticed.

Leaning back, he grabbed his purchase from the farmer's market and then unlocked the Land Cruiser's door.

Stepping onto the street, he looked slowly around and didn't see anyone. Because it was a weekday, most of the residents were likely at work.

Shutting the door, he armed the vehicle's alarm system, and headed toward Lukša's home. He didn't like the fact that he was going to have to confront the man while his wife was there. He liked even less what he might have to do—to both of them.

Nevertheless, there was no way around it. The ball was in the truck driver's court. How the game played out would be entirely dependent upon what happened the moment Harvath rang his bell.

CHAPTER 26

Taking his time, Harvath walked up the street toward the narrow, two-story home. It was a warm day and the windows facing the street were open. There was a light breeze and, when it picked up, striped yellow curtains could be seen billowing in and out.

As he got closer, he could hear a television on inside. It sounded like someone was watching sports. Based on the enthusiasm of the broadcaster, he assumed it was soccer.

Approaching the front door, he peeked in one of the windows and saw Lukša—one leg propped up, lying on the couch. He was indeed watching sports, but it wasn't soccer. It was rugby.

He positioned himself so that the truck driver couldn't see his face and then rang the bell. As he heard Mrs. Lukša come near, he held up the bouquet of flowers he had bought at the farmer's market. Upon opening the door, it was the first thing she saw.

Harvath smiled as she said something to him in Lithuanian. He assumed she was asking who he was.

"I'm an old friend of your husband's," he replied, in English. Not knowing and, actually, not caring if he had gotten the question right. Already, he had placed his foot inside the door frame so she couldn't close it.

The shift in his body frightened her and the color drained from her face. The truck driver yelled something from their living room.

Mrs. Lukša's words again were in Lithuanian, but this time Harvath understood one of them—*"Amerikietis." American.*

In any other situation, Harvath might have been worried about his subject bolting out the back, but based on his injuries Mr. Lukša wasn't running anywhere.

"You should put these in some water," said Harvath, offering the lady of the house the flowers and gently pushing past her.

When he entered the living room, the truck driver had already picked up his crutch and was struggling to get off the couch.

He was wearing a stained tank top and brown cargo pants. His left knee was in a brace, his right hand in a cast. His hair was matted and it looked like he hadn't shaved in a while. Movement was probably quite painful for him.

Harvath told him to sit back down and the man obeyed.

In addition to the TV remote, some magazines, and two empty bottles of beer, there was a plate of half-eaten food on the coffee table along with several bottles of prescription medication. The house, even with all of its windows open, smelled like fried fish.

"What the hell are you doing here?" Lukša demanded.

"I heard you were in a car accident. I wanted to make sure you're okay."

"I'm fine. Now you can go. Same way you came in."

Harvath smiled. The man was just as gruff as he had been on their operation in Kaliningrad.

There was something else about him, though. Once he had recognized Harvath, he had stopped looking him in the eye. At first he thought it was guilt, but then he realized it was something even more intense—shame.

Harvath studied him, allowing several moments to pass, which only added to the man's discomfort. "Do you want to tell me what really happened?" he finally asked.

"Like you said, *car accident.*"

The doctor had been right. Lukša was lying. Harvath was positive. Like any good smuggler, he was good at hiding his lies, but he wasn't perfect—

at least not when it came to hiding them from Harvath. There was a subtle microexpression—a twitch near his left temple—that gave him away.

"Antanas," Harvath replied, using the man's first name to further unsettle him, "you have a pretty good idea of who I am or, at the very least, the kinds of things I do for a living. Which means you know I didn't come all this way to be lied to. So, in order to save us both a lot of time, I'm going to give you a choice. You either tell me the truth, or I'm going to drag your wife in here by the hair and make her pay for your lies. What's it going to be?"

The truck driver glared at him. Involving his wife was beyond the pale. "I didn't think Americans played so dirty."

Harvath smiled again, but there was no mirth in it. "You have no idea *how* dirty."

He waited for Lukša to say something and when he didn't, asked, "Who did this to you? And for the record, before you answer and I have to go fetch Mrs. Lukša, no one believes you were in a car accident. I'd be willing to bet that she doesn't even believe that. Now, tell me what happened."

The truck driver exhaled a long breath of air and his tense body sank into the couch cushions. His eyes looked up at the ceiling. The fight had gone out of him. He wasn't going to put his wife through any sort of pain—not even the threat of it.

"A couple of weeks ago, men came."

"What kind of men?"

"Big men," said Lukša. "Russians."

"They came here? To your house?"

The truck driver nodded.

"What did they want?"

"*You.*"

The response was what Harvath had feared. Russian intelligence had reverse engineered—at least partially—his assignment in Kaliningrad.

"What did you tell them?" he asked.

"At first, nothing," said the truck driver. "That's when they started beating me. Two of them held me down—the two biggest ones—while a third man, with a shaved head and a thick red beard, did his worst to me. Yet, I still said nothing. Then he broke my hand. Next, my knee."

Though he kept a stoic expression, Harvath felt terrible. He had been the source of so much pain and so much death for so many people. Looking at Lukša, he said the only thing he could say, "I'm very sorry that happened to you."

The Lithuanian grew terse. "What you should be sorry about is coming to my house with your threats and disrespecting not only me, but also my wife."

Harvath understood the man's anger. "You're right. I apologize. To you and your wife."

The response seemed to mollify the man, at least a little bit, and he went from staring daggers at Harvath to once again studying his ceiling.

"I'm sorry to have to ask you this, but I need to know what you told them."

Lukša took his time gathering his thoughts. Finally, he said, "Even when they were beating me, breaking my bones, I tried to lie. Then the man asking the questions removed a phone and showed me a video."

"What kind of video?"

"It was a video of me, buying the public transportation tickets I gave you."

The Russians really had done their research. Not only had they identified Lukša as a potential suspect, they had gone through all of their CCTV footage, looking for corroborating evidence. And they had found it.

"The man asking the questions, what did he look like?"

"Big like the others, but slimmer. He had black hair, like a raven, and a mustache with a small beard that wasn't connected."

"A Vandyke?" Harvath asked, pantomiming on his own face what one looked like.

Lukša nodded and Harvath encouraged him to continue. "What happened after the man with the black hair showed you the video?"

"He knew my wife was away, visiting her sister in the countryside. If

I didn't tell him what he wanted to know, he threatened to wait for her to come back and do horrible things to her."

Harvath now felt even worse for threatening the man's wife.

"So you told them. Everything."

"Wouldn't you?" Lukša asked. "If it had been your wife?"

"They never gave me that choice," Harvath admitted, seeing an opportunity—through his pain—to hopefully secure more cooperation from the man. "They murdered my wife right in front of me and forced me to watch."

The truck driver became indignant. "Animals," he spat. "You see why we hate them? They have always been like this. They are absolute animals."

Harvath appreciated the man's fury. He needed the rest of the story, though. "What, specifically, did they ask you, Antanas—and what exactly did you tell them?"

"As you said, I told them everything. Where I picked you up. Where I dropped you off. How many of you there were. What, if any, equipment I could identify. How we communicated. What, if any, discussions of yours I overheard. And then, where I picked you up later that night and where I dropped you off before I left Kaliningrad and crossed back into Lithuania."

"I assume they also asked how we were even connected in the first place."

The truck driver nodded. "The man had lots of questions about that. He accused me, repeatedly, of working for the CIA. This was after I had told him everything else about that day. No matter what I said, he still wasn't satisfied. He started talking about my wife again, explaining in disgusting detail what they were going to do to her. He even threatened to go after my grandchildren. Animals."

"So, what did you tell him?"

"The truth. That I was working for the VSD."

"Did you tell him who, at State Security you were working for?"

"Of course," Lukša replied. "He demanded it. I had no choice."

"I understand," Harvath said, and he meant it. "What name did you give him?"

"The only name I had—Filip Landsbergis."

"Did you tell Landsbergis about what happened?"

The truck driver lowered his eyes. "No."

"Why not?" asked Harvath.

"Because they told me that if I did, they would kill my entire family and his."

CHAPTER 27

Restaurant La Promenade was a short drive from Paul Aubertin's house and had a fabulous view. From it, he could look out onto the Granville rocks and the Chausey archipelago.

La Promenade was a wonderful family restaurant with a *menu du marché* that changed daily. Today, they were offering pan-fried solettes with mashed potatoes, basil, and asparagus. Aubertin ordered a bottle of Sancerre to go along with it and as he basked in the 1930s Belle Epoque setting, he tried to make sense of his project.

True to his word, Trang had allowed him to run everything the way he had wanted, and with no strings attached.

As he had been taught back in Belfast, he had taken his time and had done his research.

He hadn't planned on getting his hands dirty on this one, at least not right out of the gate, but his trip to Norway had been unavoidable. It was too good a lead, too rich with potential intelligence to leave to anyone else.

He had seen some tough, crusty old bastards in his day, but Carl Pedersen of the Norwegian Intelligence Service took the prize. Jesus, could he withstand a beating. And to be fair, not just a beating, but some of the worst torture Aubertin could put on him. Whoever this Scot Harvath was, he hoped he knew what a loyal friend he'd had in Pedersen. Right until the end.

But as nobly as the Norwegian had resisted, as bitterly as he had fought back the pain, it was all for naught. No one came to rescue him and Aubertin got what he wanted eventually. Though he had told the NIS man repeatedly that it would be easier if he would just cooperate, Pedersen had been quite stubborn.

With the information he had accessed, Aubertin had put together a dossier and then had gone searching for Harvath.

Aubertin didn't like operating in America—not if he didn't have to. Their relationship with Great Britain's law enforcement and intelligence agencies was too tight. Instead, he had hoped to pick up a lead on Harvath from Europe. The information broker he went to for these things hadn't disappointed him. Though it had cost a small fortune, the investment had been worth it.

From what he got from Pedersen, it was a quick jump to the next rung on the ladder. As soon as his information broker secured Harvath's credit card information, Aubertin began tracking all of it, along with his cell phone.

The usage was spotty, but it had put him squarely in the Florida Keys—first at an exclusive resort called Little Palm Island and then in Key West.

Aubertin had compiled a list of accomplished contract killers. The decision he needed to make was who to set loose first. More important, who could get the job done and not be a pain in the ass to kill once it was all over.

He had decided to offer it to a Belgian he had worked with in the Foreign Legion. The man was very competent. But more important, Aubertin knew what his weak points were, knew where he lived, and knew how to get to him after the job was complete.

The man had been given a handful of days to conduct his surveillance and decide on the time and place to eliminate the target.

Based on their communications, it should have happened three days ago. There had been no word from the Belgian since. Considering the dangers inherent in their line of work, Aubertin had to assume the worst.

This put him in a very difficult situation. He'd had a solid lead and now it had been lost. Harvath had not turned his phone back on, had not used a credit or ATM card, nor had his passport been used to exit the United States and enter another country. Yet, his source could no longer find him in Key West. The same went for all of the known aliases he had been able to come up with.

The Belgian must have spooked him and Harvath had gone to ground. It was now going to be a much bigger challenge to track him down.

The problem with a man like Harvath was that he had experience finding people who didn't want to be found. He likely had a whole bag of tricks to keep him off the radar.

At some point, though, he was going to need help. That was the key. If Aubertin could figure out to whom he would turn, then he might be able to pick up his trail.

To do that, he would have to map out all the important people in Harvath's life—all of the people he might go to. It was a Herculean task. And if Harvath was smart, which Aubertin knew he was, he'd avoid the most obvious ones. In fact, there was a good chance he might go to an enemy—someone no one would ever think he would turn to.

Aubertin's head hurt. The double and triple crosses that existed in this game could be madness-inducing. It was like standing in a funhouse hall of mirrors trying to discern reflection versus reality.

There was also the problem of Trang's client—the person who had ultimately put up the money and had ordered the contract. Apparently, they were growing angry with how long the operation was taking.

Whoever this person was, they were threatening to pull the contract if results didn't happen soon. What's more, they had also hinted at serious, physical reprisals.

Trang, already nervous because of the double crosses they had planned, decided to extend his stay in Paris. Returning to his home in Vietnam—the spot where Andre Weber had opened the contract and had paid him his fee, didn't seem like a great idea right now.

Aubertin needed to get results. To do that, he'd have to clear his mind. That's why he had come to La Promenade. If he didn't come up with a plan by the time lunch was over, he'd take a walk along Jullouville's beach. Sometimes, he did his best thinking when he wasn't thinking.

He was already on his second glass of wine when the waiter brought out his entrée. The baby Dover sole looked, and smelled, delicious.

It struck him that he had never asked how the local fishermen caught them. He assumed it was with a net, but he was more interested in what artistry, what skill was necessary to trap these highly prized specimens.

Did you have to go deep? Or were they closer to the surface? Near shore? Or far out into the English Channel? It was almost laughable how little he understood about a simple subject and a food he so regularly enjoyed.

But thinking about it had the effect of focusing his mind even more keenly on Harvath.

He didn't realize that's what had happened until he was preparing to pay his bill.

That was when it hit him. That was when he knew how he was going to flush Harvath out into the open.

CHAPTER 28

Harvath had spent the next twenty minutes talking with the truck driver. Initially, he had been stunned that a seasoned intelligence operative like Landsbergis hadn't been using a cutout to run Lukša. But when the truck driver explained their relationship, it made sense.

Lukša had been friends with Landsbergis's uncle and the pair had been smuggling contraband for decades.

Not wanting to involve a family member, especially one as unreliable as his alcoholic uncle, Landsbergis had first recruited Lukša for a small operation. It was a trial run of sorts and had gone off without a hitch. From then on, Landsbergis called whenever he needed something. He always paid in cash and the truck driver only dealt with him. He had never met nor had he interacted with anyone else at the VSD.

The more Lukša spoke of what a good man Landsbergis was, the harder it was to reconcile the fact that he was the one who had sold Carl out. He was the only other person in the loop, though, and despite having had an excellent initial introduction to the Lithuanian intelligence operative, Harvath steeled himself for what had to happen now.

After collecting some more information, he left the truck driver's house and headed back to where he had parked his Land Cruiser.

Nearby, an old woman was walking a small, mixed breed dog. It looked like a little white dachshund with a Labrador face and spotted ears.

Harvath had never seen anything like it and he did something he never should have done—he smiled.

What he should have done was ignored the woman, kept his head down, and kept moving. The moment he smiled, the woman started speaking to him in Lithuanian—peppering him with questions. When she pointed at his SUV and the note he had left on the dashboard, he began to get the gist of what she might be asking. She was one of the neighborhood busybodies and was curious who he had been to see.

As Russian was one of Lithuania's three official languages, Harvath mumbled a couple of barely passable phrases and pointed to his watch, signaling he was late, as he kept moving toward his vehicle.

Whether the woman bought it or not, he didn't care. He just wanted to get out of there without creating a scene.

Arriving at the Land Cruiser, he opened the door via its keyless entry feature and slid into the driver's seat. After texting Nicholas a quick, encrypted update, he entered the address he'd been given into his GPS and fired up the vehicle.

Putting it in gear, he engaged his turn signal and checked his mirrors. As he was pulling out, he caught a glimpse of the old woman. She was walking away, but appeared to have been writing something. He couldn't be certain. When he turned to look over his shoulder, she was no longer visible.

Had she made a note about him? Had she taken down his license plate number? Even if she had, what was she going to do with the information? Call the police and rat him out for parking on a permit-only street without a permit? Maybe she wanted to have his vehicle "on file" in the event she saw it parked illegally again and wanted to make a federal case out of it.

Whatever it might be, he didn't see the harm. The cops had better things to do, and he didn't plan on ever coming back. Besides, according to his GPS, it was a twenty-four-minute drive to Landsbergis's house. he wanted to be there long before the man got off work and returned home.

In a perfect world, Harvath would have had the complete element of surprise. This, though, wasn't a perfect world.

He felt certain that the moment he walked out the door the truck driver was going to call Landsbergis. He would inform him that Harvath was in Lithuania and had been to see him. Everything that they had talked about would be relayed to the VSD man. At that point, Landsbergis would have a choice to make. He could either face Harvath or he could run.

What the intelligence operative chose to do would dictate what plan Harvath put into action.

On the list of things he had asked Nicholas to do, at the very top was to lay down a series of digital tripwires. If Landsbergis chose to run, Harvath wanted to know. And not only did he want to know, but he wanted to be able to follow him—to track his every move. That way, he could choose the exact time and the exact place to confront him and carry out his revenge.

•   •   •

Landsbergis lived in a sleek modern house in a trendy gated community known as Laurai. The security was more show than anything else.

Surrounded by forest, Harvath had already identified an old logging road where he could park the Land Cruiser and hike in on foot.

Once he got to where he wanted to be, he pulled off into the woods. Climbing out of the SUV, he took in a deep breath of the fresh, pine-scented air. It reminded him of the time he and Lara had spent in the wilds of Alaska.

He closed his eyes and allowed himself to linger for a moment in the memory, to feel her—as if she was right there next to him.

Exhaling, he put her back in the iron box, shoved it to a far corner of his mind, and began unpacking his equipment.

Though it was still daylight, the first thing that went into the top section of his backpack were a pair of night vision goggles. He had no idea what time Landsbergis would be home, nor what time he would be returning to the Land Cruiser. As far as he was concerned, the night vision equipment was a must.

Also a must was the extremely compact SIG MCX Rattler. When its minimalist stock was folded against the short-barreled rifle's frame, the weapon was only twenty three inches long. The pack had a hidden sleeve with a magnetic closure that allowed rapid deployment of the Rattler if the situation warranted.

Into the main compartment and some of the side pockets, he placed extra magazines, a small medical kit, one of his Tasers, zip-tie-style flex cuffs , and several other odds and ends. The backpack wasn't exactly light, but considering the amount of gear he was transporting, it was reasonable. In his SEAL days, he had rucked much heavier loads. This was nothing.

Cinching the pack tight, he set it down in the cargo area of the SUV and opened a small black Storm case. Nestled in the Pick N Pluck foam inside was a compact drone. Harvath took it out and, as he expanded its arms, walked with it back to the road.

Powering it up, he synced it to his phone and brought up the precise coordinates for Landsbergis's house. After selecting from a drop-down menu what he wanted the drone to do, he set it on the road, took a step back, and pushed the button on his phone to activate its mission.

While he was a firm believer in the maxim that nothing could beat old-school tradecraft, he loved how rapidly technology had advanced. The tiny, autonomous drone could do everything except provide him with close air support. And even that was a feature he was sure was on its way in the not too distant future.

What surprised him the most was how whisper-quiet the geeks at DARPA had been able to make it. Gone was the loud, distinct buzz so common in the early versions operators had taken into the field. This model you could barely hear unless you were standing right underneath it, which could be easily corrected by taking it to a higher altitude or positioning it off at an angle.

Having his own "eye in the sky" was an incredible advantage. As he picked his way through the woods toward the house, the drone would be monitoring the entire area for any sign of movement. And with its infrared camera, it would allow him to pick up any heat signatures that might suggest hostile actors lying in wait.

Walking back to the Land Cruiser, he shouldered his pack, and locked the SUV up tight. Then, after checking the video feed from the drone, he struck off again for the house.

As he walked, he thought about the different approaches he might take with Landsbergis. There was a lot he didn't know about the man—and that put him at a disadvantage. He was likely going to have to wing it and go with his gut. And while he had a good gut, he didn't like being relegated to that as his only option.

When you didn't know much about a subject, a proper interrogation could take time, lots of it.

Lukša, the truck driver, was less difficult because he had already been broken. Thanks to the interrogation the Russians had subjected him to, he had no desire for a repeat. He had put up very little resistance and had cooperated quickly. Landsbergis, on the other hand, might be something else entirely.

What confused Harvath about this whole thing was that Carl had trusted the Lithuanian. *Really* trusted him. Pedersen knew, going in, how dangerous it could be for Norway if the Russians discovered what he had done. Helping Harvath get in and out of Kaliningrad to snatch one of their top people was a big deal. And it was just as big a deal for Landsbergis and Lithuania.

Yet both men had gone along with the plot. They had supposedly taken great care to make sure that their involvement, and thereby the involvement of their nations, wasn't discovered. But in the end, just as with the truck driver, perhaps the Russians had gotten to Landsbergis. Maybe they had found a pressure point so excruciating that he had broken.

Outside of morbid curiosity, it really didn't matter to Harvath what that pressure point was. Granted, it was important that if Landsbergis was the leak, he answer for what he had done and reveal what was so important that it was worth trading Carl's life for.

He doubted it would be anything too sophisticated. In the end, the Russians weren't subtle when it came to this stuff. They were brutish thugs and their default setting was to resort to brutish tactics. Taking the time to develop a menu of clever extortion options wasn't really part of how they did business anymore. There were exceptions, of course, but that took higher-level thinking, something very much in short supply in post-Soviet Russia. The Great Game, as it was once known, had ended at about the same time the Wall had come down.

It was now a different age with different players and much different rules. These days, it was less high-stakes chess, and more short-term checkers. A crude, even simplistic analogy to be sure—but probably one that was overly generous to the Russians. After all, even checkers demands obedience to a set of rules and, at the most basic level, appreciation for strategy.

Harvath's own strategy was simple. He planned to confront Landsbergis and ferret out what he knew about Carl's death. If he had been the one who gave him up, Harvath would extract the details, and then put a bullet in him. If everything went according to plan, he'd be done and on his way out of the country by midnight.

Checking the drone feed, he pressed on toward the house, choosing his steps carefully, just as he had been trained. The gated community wouldn't have gone to the effort to place sensors, or worse, in the woods, but there was no telling what Landsbergis might have done.

Two hundred meters from the property, Harvath pulled his phone back out and retasked the drone.

It had been flying high overhead, looking for heat signatures and any signs of motion. He now wanted it to look directly inside the house. Because it was a big glass box, the assignment was a piece of cake.

None of the window treatments had been drawn and the drone was able to peer into multiple rooms on every side. There was no sign of life.

Harvath increased the drone's altitude and placed it back into surveillance mode. Then, he inserted an earbud and called Nicholas.

Their conversation, like their texts, was encrypted and, via an added layer of security, their voices were also distorted. It gave a weird, otherworldly feeling to their back-and-forth. They sounded like a couple of robot hostage-takers discussing a ransom. While the drone technology may have come a long way, the communications technology Nicholas was using left a bit to be desired.

"How's your view?" he asked when the little man answered.

"Not bad," said Nicholas, watching the drone footage back in the United States. "Nice place our guy has."

"Maybe crime *does* pay," Harvath replied. "We'll find out. In the meantime, what about the alarm company?"

"The whole community uses the same one. It's the Lithuanian version of ADT. I've already accessed his account. When you're ready to make entry, let me know."

"Roger that. Stand by."

He didn't believe anyone was home, but out of an abundance of caution double-checked his pistol and then unslung his pack and removed the Taser, so that he could have it handy.

Taking another deep breath, he reshouldered his pack and crept forward.

When he got to his next waypoint, he announced, "One hundred meters out."

"Good copy," Nicholas responded. "Norseman, one hundred meters out."

Norseman had been the call sign given to Harvath as a SEAL. Like most military call signs, there was a funny story behind it.

With his blue eyes and sandy-brown hair, Harvath looked more Germanic than Nordic. The nickname hadn't come from any special attachment he'd had to the Vikings, but rather his penchant for dating Scandinavian flight attendants who flew in and out of LAX.

Norwegians, Swedes, and Danes—they'd all been gorgeous. Something else, though, about them had been rather telling. None of them had been U.S.-based. They had all been based back in Scandinavia. Like him, they were unavailable, except for short, carefree bursts. It was only as he had gotten older and more mature, that he had begun to realize the futility of dating women so geographically unavailable.

It didn't mean that he had lost his appreciation for Scandinavian women—not by a long shot. He had always found them incredibly sexy, incredibly confident, and tantalizingly independent. There was no drama and no bullshit with them. They told you how it was, one hundred percent of the time. And when it came to sex, they were amazing—no guilt, no inhibitions, and no problems communicating what they enjoyed.

Every one of the women he had dated had been smarter than him—and he was pretty sharp. As much as they had loved the United States, they all knew better than to trade their careers for some cocky young SEAL, off to God only knew where for God only knew how long.

Not that Harvath had ever admitted to being a SEAL. That wasn't something you were supposed to do in casual relationships. Had he hinted at it, especially when he was trying to bed a gorgeous Scandinavian flight attendant? Though he would have denied it in a court of law, it "may" have happened. As the old saying in the Special Operations community went—if you weren't cheating, you weren't really trying. Tier One guys were not selected because they were experts at following rules. They were selected because they did whatever it took to get the job done.

"Property line," Harvath said as he neared the edge of the woods. "Fifty meters out."

"Good copy," Nicholas replied. "Norseman, fifty meters out."

Harvath checked the drone feed once more. Everything looked good. There was no one near the house—no neighbors trimming rosebushes or walking dogs, no landscapers mowing lawns, no children kicking soccer balls or riding bikes. He was good to go.

He took a moment, unslung his pack, and waited. Crouching down behind the last copse of trees, he waited.

It wasn't that he didn't trust what the drone was showing, he simply trusted his instincts and his own eyes more.

Pulling his earbud out, he closed his eyes and listened. The easiest thing to hear was the wind blowing through the trees around him. Beyond that, he could make out the tumble of water from the fountain in Landsbergis's expansive backyard. From somewhere else came the high-pitched notes of a metal wind chime.

They all came together to form the soundtrack of an affluent suburb. The only threat here appeared to be Harvath. And that was exactly how he preferred it.

"Breaking property line," he stated, having reinserted his earbud. "Norseman inbound."

CHAPTER 29

Harvath quickly made his way across the manicured lawn and came to a stop with his back against the side of the house.

Studying the door, he noticed a metal strip, lined with buttons, about three inches high and an inch wide embedded in the frame.

"In addition to standard locks, I also see a keypad here. Do we have an entry code?" he asked.

"Negative. There doesn't appear to be one in the file."

That wasn't unusual. The alarm company's job was to monitor for break-ins and dispatch a response if one took place. They didn't need a set of keys or an entry code to carry out that job.

"Roger that," said Harvath, as he fished the lockpick gun out of his pack. "What about the alarm panel location and passcode?"

"From where you are making entry, go left into the dining room and back through the kitchen. There's a panel in the hallway behind the refrigerator."

"Good copy. Panel in the hallway behind the refrigerator."

"Passcode one, one, seven, six, two, zero. Repeat one, one, seven, six, two, zero."

"Roger that. Confirming passcode one, one, seven, six, two, zero."

"Affirmative," said Nicholas.

"Zero comms," Harvath directed, requesting radio silence. "Unless and until you see movement."

"Roger that. Zero comms."

Sliding over to the door, Harvath gave it a quick once-over before inserting the lockpick gun and opening it.

The moment he entered the house, the alarm started beeping.

Per Nicholas's instructions, he went left into the dining room, traversed the kitchen, and emerged into the hallway. There on the wall, in a mudroom-style area, was the alarm panel.

Harvath punched in the code: *one, one, seven, six, two, zero*. The beeping stopped and the alarm panel fell silent. He was in.

There were no children's or women's items in the mudroom. The only clothing he saw appeared to belong to Landsbergis, including the Barbour jacket he'd been wearing the one and only time he and Harvath had met.

Returning to the kitchen, Harvath quickly searched for any signs someone might have recently been in the house. The espresso machine, oven, and stovetop were all cold. There was nothing unusual in the garbage or the microwave either. All good signs.

Making his way back to the hallway, he wanted to check the rest of the rooms before resetting the alarm and picking a place to await the intelligence officer.

But no sooner had he turned the corner and stepped into the hall than he discovered a pistol pointed at his face.

He recognized the weapon immediately. With its two-piece suppressor, it wasn't one you saw every day—at least not outside Russia. The would-be shooter, though, was a complete stranger to him.

"Drop the backpack," the figure said. "*Slowly.*"

Harvath did as the woman instructed. Had Landsbergis sent her to intercept him? She spoke English with a slight accent, but it wasn't Lithuanian.

"Hands up."

Again, he did as she ordered.

"If you lower your hands, even a millimeter, I'll shoot you. Is that clear?"

"Crystal," said Harvath, beginning to zero in on the accent. She was tall, blond, and even with her hair pulled back and barely any makeup on, she was attractive. He didn't see a ring. "Who are you?" he asked, buying time. "The girlfriend?"

"You ask too many questions for a man on the wrong end of a gun. Turn around so I can see your back."

He obeyed.

"Now," she instructed, "touch your hands to your shoulders, pinch the fabric of your shirt, and lift it up so I can see your waistband."

As Harvath did, he revealed the pistol tucked at the small of his back. She then had him turn all the way around, which exposed a smaller pistol—a Sig Sauer P365—he was carrying as a backup, the top of the Taser he had slipped into one of his pockets, as well as a folding knife. After checking the tops of his boots, she had him slowly discard everything and put his hands back up in the air.

"Based on all of that," she continued, alluding to the pile of gear, "it's obvious you didn't come to cut the grass. So who are you and what are you doing here?"

Good-looking *and* a smartass. If she hadn't been pointing a gun at him, he might have liked her. "I came to have a chat with Landsbergis."

"About what?"

"It's private."

The woman smiled—two rows of perfectly straight white teeth. Adjusting her aim, she said, "I think we're beyond keeping secrets at this point."

"Can I put my hands down?"

"No. Answer my question. What did you come to *chat* about?"

Finally, Harvath had pegged the accent and decided to give the truth. "I came to find out whether or not he killed a friend of mine."

Sølvi Kolstad looked at him. "And who was this friend?"

"I don't think it's an accident that we're both here at the same time. I actually think you know who I'm talking about."

"Say his name."

Harvath met her gaze as he stated, "Carl Pedersen."

A flash of grief rippled across the woman's face. Whether she couldn't hide it, or didn't bother to, Harvath wasn't able to ascertain. All he knew was that as quickly as the emotion had appeared, it was gone.

"I know who you are," he said. "At least I think I do."

"Really?" she responded. "Who am I?"

"Turn around and I'll tell you."

Considering the power dynamics of the situation, it was a ridiculous request and Sølvi couldn't help but chuckle. "Would you be willing to hold my gun while I do?"

She was growing on him. "You'll have to hold it yourself," he said, indicating the position he was being made to stand in. "My arms are starting to get tired."

"Why do you want me to turn around?"

"Because, if I'm right, you have some sort of a tattoo down your back. A quote from Rousseau, if my memory serves."

"It's Sartre," she said, correcting him.

Harvath smiled. He had been testing her. "It could have been from Ibsen and Carl still would have hated the idea of anyone working for him, much less his protégé, being inked."

During her recovery, she had started jogging again. On one particularly nice day, Carl had shown up to check on her just as she was returning. She had been wearing a sports bra and he had not only noticed the tattoo, but he had also given her hell for it.

He hated tattoos because they were a visible identifier, and identifiers were deadly for spooks.

Making matters worse, unlike a man with a limp or a man with a facial scar, hers—a woman with the tattoo along her spine—was a self-imposed vulnerability.

He had chalked it up to her descent into drug-induced darkness, but there was one other thing about it that pissed him off. Of all the quotes she could have chosen, she had chosen Sartre. That probably bothered him the most. He didn't see Sartre as a brilliant philosopher or existentialist, Carl viewed him—as he viewed everything—through politics. Sartre had been a Marxist and that had made him Pedersen's enemy.

On every complaint about the tattoo, she had humbly acknowledged his points. The Marxism stuff was just stupid and she had told him as much. Politics had nothing at all to do with why she had chosen it and she informed him that they were done discussing it. *Permanently*.

Carl apparently, though, hadn't seen it that way.

"I'm surprised he told you," she said.

"I'm surprised I still have my hands up," replied Harvath. "Can I put them down, please?"

Sølvi nodded.

"Thank you," he said, lowering his arms. "And for the record, Carl never told me about your tattoo. He mentioned it to my boss, who said something to me."

"Your *boss* being Reed Carlton."

"Yes," replied Harvath, extending his hand. "Scot Harvath."

Sølvi lowered her pistol, stepped forward, and they shook hands. "Sølvi Kolstad."

"I'm sorry for your loss. Carl was a very good man."

"And I'm sorry for yours," she offered. "I heard you also lost your wife and a colleague in addition to Reed."

Harvath nodded and changed the subject. "How long have you been here?"

"A while."

"How'd you get around the alarm system?"

"I have my ways," she replied.

He didn't doubt it. "I think we should get some things straight before Landsbergis gets home."

"Agreed."

"First, I'd like to do a sweep for weapons."

"Already done," said Sølvi. "There was a nine-millimeter Beretta in a holster mounted under the entry hall table. Behind one of the pillows on the couch in the living room was a Glock 17. I found a CZ-75 in the kitchen and a Browning Hi-Power in the nightstand upstairs."

He was impressed. "What did you do with them?"

"I unloaded all of them, reset the triggers and put them back where I found them."

"I guess I can scratch that off my list then."

Sølvi smiled. "He carries a Glock 19. So be aware that he'll be walking in already armed."

Harvath had figured as much. What he couldn't figure out was how she knew, down to the precise make and model. "How do you know what kind of weapon he'll have on him?"

"In some cases, Carl left behind very detailed notes. In others, such as what you and Reed were doing with him here in Lithuania, there are no notes at all."

"Which is why I want us to talk before he arrives. I don't know how much time we're going to have."

The Norwegian slid the phone out of her pocket, activated its screen, and held it out so Harvath could see it.

It looked like a version of Google Maps in dark mode. On it, was a flashing dot slowly making its way north out of Vilnius.

"As long as he doesn't stop on the way home from the office," she informed him, "we have approximately twenty-seven minutes."

"You have a tracker on his car?"

"Carl *may* have put some software on his phone."

Typical spymaster, thought Harvath, shaking his head. "So Carl didn't trust him."

"What was it your President Reagan said?" she asked. "Trust, but verify?"

"But Reagan was talking about the Russians."

"And this is Lithuania, which means—like it or not—that we're *also* talking about the Russians."

It begged an important question. "With Landsbergis's help, we mounted a pretty big operation against the Russians. Why would he have agreed to help us, to have helped Carl, if he was a Russian asset?"

"I'm not saying he was. In fact, if Carl involved him in something that sensitive, I'd say he did it with full confidence that he was in the correct camp. You need to understand that Carl did a lot of things that pushed the envelope, including—when he could—putting software on his assets' phones. Just because Landsbergis was on our side one day doesn't mean he might not be on Russia's the next. Part of what made Carl *Carl* was that he was always thinking ahead."

She could have been describing Harvath's very own mentor. Reed Carlton had a gift for peering over the horizon, recognizing an approaching problem, and coming up with solutions before anyone else knew what was going on.

With Carl's protégé here, Harvath's operation just got more complicated. He needed some more information from her. But, his jet lag kicking back in, he first wanted some more caffeine. He suggested they step into the kitchen.

CHAPTER 30

I n the cupboard next to the fridge, Harvath had discovered an exceptional bottle of whiskey. He had found it while looking for where Landsbergis kept his coffee. If nothing else, the man had good taste. Setting it on the counter, he kept searching until he uncovered the coffee.

"Tough day?" Sølvi asked, nodding at the bottle.

"Tough year," Harvath replied, as he took down two cups.

"Do you normally drink on the job?"

"Nothing I do feels normal anymore."

"Well, just so we're clear, I'd prefer not to get shot. You can have a drink or your gun. It's up to you."

She was right, of course. As much as he wanted to numb himself, and as much as he figured he could still function with a small amount of booze in his system, there was too much risk. He couldn't afford deadening his senses and possibly making a serious mistake—one that might get either, or both, of them killed.

He decided against an Irish coffee, returned the bottle to the cupboard, and got to work preparing two espressos.

"We still doing okay on time?" he asked.

Sølvi checked her phone. "Yes."

Removing his phone, he activated the screen and propped it up on the counter where they could both see it. After their exchange in the hallway, he had given Nicholas the "safe word," as they jokingly referred to it, and had let him know everything was okay before disconnecting the call.

"Where's this feed coming from?" she asked.

"I brought a small drone with me," he replied as he went back to making their coffees. "This way, we'll be able to make sure he's alone."

"Why? Are you expecting him *not* to be alone?"

"I'm not taking any chances."

When the espressos were ready, he brought them over, they each pulled out a stool, and sat down.

"Who wants you bad enough to have tortured and killed Carl?" she asked, getting right to the point.

He couldn't blame her. It was the same question he had been puzzling over. "It's the Russians," he answered. "I'm just not sure *which* Russians. That's what I am here to find out."

"By talking to Landsbergis."

Harvath nodded. "I think he's the one who gave Carl to them."

"Why do you think that?"

"We have good contacts in a lot of places. Unfortunately, not the Baltics. When I told Carl about the op we wanted to run in Kaliningrad, he told me he had the perfect person to help us on the Lithuanian side."

"Filip Landsbergis."

"Correct," said Harvath. "It turns out that Landsbergis has an asset, a Lithuanian truck driver who smuggles things into and out of Kaliningrad. They were family friends. Allegedly, no one at the VSD knew about him—only Landsbergis. Carl set up the introduction and Landsbergis arranged for his truck driver to secretly move me and my team around Kaliningrad."

"So what led you to believe that Landsbergis gave Carl to the Russians?"

"Only a handful of people knew of my relationship with Carl. Even fewer knew about our operation. I tried to think like the Russians. How would they piece together what had happened? In doing that, I looked at anyone who could have been a link in the chain connecting me to Carl. That's when we got a hit.

"We learned that the truck driver had sought medical attention recently. His story kept changing, though, and his injuries suggested that maybe it hadn't been an accident. I decided to find out for myself.

"He lives on the outskirts of Vilnius. When I landed, I went straight to see him. It took some prodding, but he admitted that a couple of weeks ago a team of Russians had shown up on his doorstep."

"What did they want?" she asked.

"The security services in Kaliningrad had assembled enough evidence to suspect he was involved in our operation. They wanted to know what his role was and who he had been working for."

She looked at him. "And he gave it up? All of it? Including Landsbergis?"

"They didn't offer him a choice. They beat him pretty badly. They even threatened to go after his wife and grandchildren. He's a tough, proud man. But nobody holds out indefinitely."

"I can't believe the Russians let him live. Where is he now? You didn't let him go did you?"

"Of course, I let him go," he replied. "The guy has been through enough. He told me what I needed to know. I didn't have any reason to hold him."

"*That's* why you have a drone overhead. The minute you left the truck driver's house, you know he was on the phone to Landsbergis. That's why you're concerned he might not be coming home alone."

"He claims he didn't tell Landsbergis about the visit from the Russians."

"And you believe him?" she asked.

"He'll show up alone if he's not guilty. If he shows up with a protective detail or a SWAT team, we'll have our answer. Either way, I want to look him in the eyes when I ask him about Carl. Now, it's your turn. What are you doing here?"

"We've already established that," she stated. "I'm here for the same reason as you—to confront Landsbergis."

"But based on what? You said Carl didn't leave any notes, that you didn't know what we had been working on."

"I received a tip."

"A tip?" asked Harvath. "From whom?"

"The CIA's station chief in Oslo."

"Holidae Hayes."

"Yes," she replied. "You don't sound surprised."

He gestured at her phone. "How much time do we have?"

"Fifteen minutes. Give or take."

"What did Hayes say?"

"That you, Carl, and Reed had all been working on something linked to the Russian-sponsored attacks on NATO diplomats. It started with you coming to Norway to take down a cell and ended up with an operation launched from here in Lithuania."

"Did she tell you what that operation was?" Harvath asked.

"No, but as it had to do with the Russians, and as Lithuania borders Kaliningrad, it wasn't hard to imagine where the operation took place."

"Was this before or after Hayes gave her briefing to the NIS about me?"

"You know about that?"

Harvath nodded. "The CIA Director signed off on it. He briefed me before I left."

"That's why you weren't surprised when I mentioned her name."

"Correct."

"In exchange for the information she gave me, she made me promise that anything I developed, I would share it with her first—before I reported back to NIS. Was all of it just a ruse?"

"No, the Director gave her a wide scope. He wanted her to cooperate with your service, but he also wanted her to push the envelope, *fast*."

"Because whoever killed Carl was coming for you next."

"Someone *did* come for me."

This was the first time Sølvi had heard any of this. "When?"

"Three nights ago. A lone, unidentified assassin."

"Why didn't you share any of this with us?"

"We did. The CIA submitted prints, a retinal scan, and photos for facial recognition."

"That was Langley's high-priority John Doe?" she asked, remembering the submission. "All they said was that he *might* have a connection to Carl's murder and asked us to run him. There was nothing in the request about the subject being an assassin. Pretty important detail. Why leave it out?"

"Because if there *wasn't* a connection, we didn't want you to have already convinced yourselves that he was the guy you were looking for."

"Hold on," she stated. "Within hours of us notifying your government about how Carl's assassin was compiling information about you, an assassin shows up to kill you—and you don't think there's a connection?"

"We think there's a connection. We just don't know how direct it is."

"For someone who's supposed to be so good at this, you make no sense."

Harvath decided to let the other shoe drop. "We have reason to believe there's a contract out on me, one hundred million dollars, let to a pool of professional killers. Whoever gets me first, gets the money."

Sølvi didn't know where to begin. "*One hundred million?* What the hell did you do to the Russians?"

"It's a long story. Right now, I think we need to focus on how we're going to handle Landsbergis."

"You're right," she relented, checking her phone and noticing how close the VSD man was getting. "But after, we're going to finish this conversation."

She reminded him a lot of Carl—she was smart, intense, and totally direct when she needed to be. Yet, there was an underlying sense of humor, a willingness to smile or make a joke in a tough situation. In short, he liked that. More to the point, he liked her. And that scared the hell out of him.

CHAPTER 31

Filip Landsbergis arrived alone in a black 1980s Alfa Romeo Spider. When he rolled into his driveway, the soft canvas top was down, his suit jacket was off, and his briefcase was on the seat next to him.

Producing a remote from the center console, he opened the garage door. But instead of driving in, he parked several meters away, turned off the engine, and stepped out of his vehicle. Harvath, who was watching everything unfold via the drone, didn't like it.

First, only a fool—or someone extremely careless—drove with the top down and something valuable, like a briefcase, on the open seat next to them. In most places, it was an invitation to get robbed.

The other thing he didn't like, was that Landsbergis had opened the garage door, but hadn't proceeded in. The fact that he had his jacket off also gnawed at the edges of his mind. He looked for the Glock that the man was supposed to be carrying, or any weapon for that matter, but didn't see one. He looked way too relaxed, too casual. *Was it intentional? Did he know Harvath was there and was trying to put him at ease?*

Maybe his jacket was off because he was enjoying the warm weather on the drive home. Maybe crime between his office and his house didn't concern him. And maybe he had left the car in the driveway because he was going to wash it this evening. All of the behavior, while it felt odd to Harvath, was explainable.

When Landsbergis examined the edge of his driveway and began to pull some scattered weeds, Harvath's concern again ticked up. Was he stalling, waiting for men to get into position—men Harvath couldn't see? Or was Harvath just jumpy like he had been about the old woman outside Lukša's?

"As far as I can tell," said Sølvi, looking at the feed from the drone, "unless he's got someone stashed in his trunk, he's alone."

"He doesn't appear to be in any hurry to come inside."

"It's beautiful outside. Why would he?"

"I don't like it," he replied.

"Then what do you want to do?"

Harvath signaled for her to follow as he headed into the dining room. "We exit via the side door. I go around the front, meet him head-on in the driveway. You cut across the back and provide cover. Keep your eyes on his vehicle. If things go bad, flank him."

Sølvi nodded and hooked to her right the moment she stepped outside. Harvath hooked to his left and as he moved, called Nicholas.

"Landsbergis is back," he said, when the little man picked up. "I need you to be my eyes. We've gone out to confront him. I'm going around front and Carl's protégé is going around back. I've got an earbud in and am going to leave this call active. If you see something, say something."

"Good copy," Nicholas replied. "Roger that."

With his P226 tucked into his waistband and his encrypted cell phone returned to his back pocket, Harvath stepped out from behind the corner of the house and walked slowly across the front lawn.

His eyes scanned for threats, but didn't see any. When Landsbergis caught sight of him, Harvath locked eyes on the man and held his gaze as he closed the distance between them.

The VSD man was in his early forties, tall, with blond hair. "You," he said, surprised to see Harvath. "What are you doing here?"

"I'd prefer to talk inside," said Harvath.

"Is everything okay? What's going on?"

"Inside," Harvath repeated.

"No problem," Landsbergis responded, pointing toward the garage and indicating that his visitor should go first.

Harvath demurred and gestured for the Lithuanian to take the lead. There was no way he was going to turn his back on him.

When they entered the garage and were out of sight of any prying eyes, Harvath ordered him, "Stop and put your hands against the wall."

Landsbergis began to object, but as soon as he looked over his shoulder and saw the Sig Sauer in Harvath's hand, he did as he was told. "What the *hell* is going on?"

Harvath remained silent as he patted him down. Once confident that he was clean, he nudged him toward the door that led into the house. Sølvi was already waiting for them in the kitchen.

"The trunk was clean," she said. "I found this in his briefcase. Want to guess the make and model?"

Harvath didn't need to guess. He recognized the pistol from where he was standing. "Glock 19."

The Norwegian smiled.

"Who is she?" Landsbergis demanded. "And what are you two doing here?"

Harvath sat him down at the kitchen table and took the chair opposite. As he had with Proctor and Jasinski, he got right to the point. "Carl Pedersen is dead."

"He is? Oh my God. When?"

"We don't know. His body was discovered three days ago, but he had already been dead for a while."

"What happened?"

"He was murdered," said Sølvi. "*Tortured.* And then murdered."

"And you think I had something to do with it?" the VSD man asked. "Is that why you're here?"

"What did Lukša tell you?"

"Lukša? What does he have to do with any of this?"

"When was the last time you spoke with him?"

Landsbergis's eyes shifted to Sølvi and then back.

"She's okay," said Harvath. "You can speak freely in front of her. She worked for Carl."

"I saw Antanas after he got back from the operation. I paid him the rest of his money, and that was it."

"You haven't seen or spoken to him since?"

"No."

"But of course you heard about the *accident*?"

"What accident? What happened?"

Harvath studied him for several moments before responding. "He's fine. Or at least he's going to be fine." Looking at Sølvi, he then said, "He doesn't know anything."

"Obviously," the VSD man replied. "Would someone please explain to me what's going on?"

"Who else did you tell about the operation?" Harvath asked.

"No one."

"You told me, very specifically, that because the VSD has had a history of being penetrated by the Russians, you were keeping the entire operation to yourself."

"And I did. I swear."

Suddenly, there it was—just like the truck driver—a tiny facial tic that gave him away. Landsbergis wasn't telling the truth.

"You're lying to me, Filip," said Harvath, pulling himself in closer. "Believe me, you do not want to do that. Now, who did you tell?"

"No one. *I swear.*"

Without taking his eyes off Landsbergis he said to Sølvi, "This looks like it's going to get messy. Will you grab two pairs of restraints out of my bag? And I saw a roll of plastic sheeting in the garage. We'll need that too."

"What the hell?" the VSD man argued. "Are you insane?"

"At this point, I really couldn't tell you. I will say this, though. My guess is that no one is going to miss you until tomorrow morning, at the earliest. That means I have all night with you. I can take my time. Do you know how much time Carl's killer took in torturing him? At least two days. Two *entire* days. So, look on the bright side. It could be worse. I guess, in a way, you should consider yourself lucky."

"You can't do this."

Harvath smiled. "You just don't know me well enough. I appreciate the opportunity to earn your confidence."

"You *are* insane."

"It looks like we're about to find out."

Sølvi dropped a couple of pairs of plastic restraints on the table next to

Harvath and then went off toward the garage, presumably in search of the plastic sheeting he had asked for.

Landsbergis was visibly shaken by the sight of the restraints. The fact that Harvath had exhibited this level of forethought worried him that the American wasn't bluffing and would carry out his threat. "You don't have to do this."

"Apparently, I do," replied Harvath. "If you won't tell me the truth, this is the way it's going to have to be."

"There's something I don't understand," Landsbergis interjected, trying to forestall what now appeared inevitable. "What made you go see Lukša? How did you know he'd had an accident?"

Normally, Harvath didn't allow his interrogation subjects to ask their own questions, but the VSD man's query seemed legit. "Over the two days that Carl was tortured, his killer was accessing his devices to compile information on me. The only recent, large-scale operation he and I had done together was the Kaliningrad op with you. As we looked at all the loose ends, Lukša popped up.

"According to reports, he'd had an accident. His injuries, though, were more consistent with having been beaten or tortured. I wanted to see for myself, so I flew all the way here to see him. And do you know what he confessed to me?"

Landsbergis took a breath before answering. "That he had been tortured?"

Harvath nodded. "He claims it was a team of Russians. And not only had he been tortured, but he had been forced to admit his role in the operation, and give up the name of the person he had been working for. *You.*"

Landsbergis didn't believe him. "Now *you're* lying. Antanas Lukša is like family. There is no way he'd ever reveal my name—to anyone."

"We'll see how good you are under a similar scenario. Something tells me you won't find it so hard to believe once we get started."

"Is this what you wanted?" Sølvi asked, as she walked in with the roll of plastic sheeting.

Harvath nodded.

"Where should I set it up?"

"Let's do it in the dining room."

"Wait," offered Landsbergis. "If he really did reveal my name, why didn't anyone ever show up and pay me a visit?"

Harvath was watching him, intensely, as he spoke. There was no tell this time, no microexpression that gave away a lie. He appeared, at least on this, to be telling the truth.

"No one came to you? No one at all?"

Landsbergis shook his head. "No one."

"But you still told someone," said Harvath. "Who was it?"

The VSD man averted his eyes, just as the truck driver had before admitting what he had done.

A couple of seconds later, he asked, "When did Antanas get his visit?"

Harvath continued to indulge him. "A couple of weeks ago. Why?"

It was then that Landsbergis dropped a bombshell that Harvath had never imagined was coming. "I know who gave up Carl."

CHAPTER 32

As if on cue, Harvath's phone started beeping. The drone was almost out of power. He programmed it to land in the backyard and returned his attention to Landsbergis.

The VSD man laid out everything that had happened, answered every question Harvath had, and didn't hold back on any of the details. He was convinced the Lithuanian was telling him the truth. It was too big a story, too big an indictment not to have been.

Via Harvath's earbud and their encrypted call, Nicholas had heard the whole thing. To call it a bombshell was to put it mildly.

Leaving Sølvi to keep an eye on Landsbergis, Harvath stepped out of the kitchen to lay out what he wanted to do. Nicholas and Lawlor were going to have to get a buy-in from McGee and the President on his plan.

Once he had finished the call, he went outside and retrieved the drone. The charger for it was in its hard-sided case back in his Land Cruiser, along with another, smaller battery. It wasn't the optimal situation, but he'd have to deal with what he had been given.

Like Harvath, Sølvi had parked in the woods and hiked in. They decided to put Landsbergis's car in the garage and take him with them. It was as if they were reading each other's mind. Neither of them felt fully comfortable leaving the VSD man alone.

They arrived at Harvath's vehicle first. After swapping out the dead drone battery and putting it on its charger, he gave Sølvi a ride to her vehicle, which turned out to be a sleek Audi Q5.

"Not bad," said Harvath. "NIS must give you a hell of a per diem."

"Actually," she replied, hopping out of his Land Cruiser, "the moment they found out I'm Norwegian, they wanted to give me an upgrade."

"Right. I'm sure that's *exactly* what it was." Badass and smartass—he really did find that combination attractive.

Landsbergis had given them the address of his boss, which Harvath plugged into his GPS. Once Sølvi had pulled out onto the road behind him, he headed toward their destination.

It was located in the center of Vilnius, not far from the Old Town, at the top of Algirdo Street. The former embassy of a failed state, the building had three floors, a walled courtyard, underground parking, and multiple CCTV cameras.

For the rest of their ride, Harvath peppered Landsbergis with questions as he tried to come up with a plan. He also asked him about Carl—how they had met, what they had worked on together, and how much the Lithuanian government—in particular its State Security Department—knew about him.

Some of the discussion was uncomfortable, even painful—for both of them. It was clear that Landsbergis had not only appreciated Carl, but had also genuinely enjoyed working with him. Like Harvath, the VSD man felt guilty over having a role in the Norwegian intelligence operative's death. Carl brought out the best in everyone he worked with and inspired deep loyalty. His loss, especially in the midst of the ongoing battle against a revanchist Russia, was going to be felt by everyone who had ever worked and fought alongside him.

The longer they drove and the further they talked, the greater Harvath's confidence in Landsbergis grew. The man was not only intelligent, but humble. As information came in, he was able to quickly weigh, catalogue, and analyze it. When the time came to make an assessment, he did so dispassionately, without influence from his ego. He was guided by something much truer and much more valuable—his moral compass.

Bottom-line—Landsbergis was a guy who did the right thing. Which was why, when they arrived at the rendezvous point, two blocks from the target, Harvath handed him his Glock back.

"What's this?" the Lithuanian asked.

"What's it look like? Take it. Better to have it and not need it than to need it and not have it."

Landsbergis nodded in agreement and accepted the pistol. But then his face became solemn. "I have to ask you something."

Harvath had a feeling he knew where this was going, but he opened the barn door anyway. "Go ahead."

"Back at my house, were you really prepared to torture me?"

Harvath didn't flinch. "One hundred percent. And if the situation were reversed, Carl would have been too. As someone put it to me recently, the Russians are animals. Not the people, per se, but the people in power. And those who serve the people in power. You are on the front lines here. I'm sure you know that. And I'm sure that Carl told you that."

"Repeatedly," said the VSD man.

"You need to act like it. Every day. Every hour. Every moment. They're coming for your country. They will get to pick the time and the place. The only thing you get to pick is how well prepared you'll be. It sucks, and so is what we're about to do, but it is what it is. Sometimes, the fight chooses us."

Idling in the parking spot, he waited until Sølvi had pulled up, parked behind him, and joined them in the Land Cruiser.

The first thing she noticed was that Harvath had given Landsbergis his Glock back. "You two seem to be getting along well," she commented.

"We're all good here," Harvath replied. "Now, let's take a few minutes and discuss how this is going to go down."

For the next ten minutes, he went over his plan, as well as the contingencies they'd need to execute if anything went wrong. As seasoned intelligence operatives, all three of them understood the risks.

When they were done with their discussion, Harvath put the Land Cruiser in gear and eased out into traffic. He wanted to do another drive-by of their objective.

The sun was setting and lights were already coming on inside. Pedestrians moved up and down the sidewalk. What they could see of the inner courtyard through the wrought iron gates was empty. If there were any vehicles present, they must have been down in the underground parking structure.

For all intents and purposes, it was quiet—which was exactly how Harvath had hoped to find it.

Turning right at the next intersection, he followed the street until he could make another right, and then found a parking space halfway up the block. Before they did anything else, he wanted to deploy the drone.

Getting out of the Land Cruiser he walked back to the rear of the SUV and popped the hatch. Checking the main battery sitting in the charger, he was disappointed. He had hoped it would charge faster. In the time since they had left the woods near Landsbergis's house, only 12 percent of the power had been replenished. He was going to have to rely on the smaller battery.

Powering up the drone, he brought up its app on his phone and waited for the diagnostics to display. As soon as they did, he grew angry.

The smaller, backup battery only had 4 percent power. Whoever had used the drone last hadn't fully recharged it before turning it back in.

Ultimately, it was his fault. As a SEAL, he had been trained to check all of his equipment before taking it into the field. Just because the CIA Director had personally handed everything to him didn't mean Harvath was absolved of making sure each item was topped off and in perfect working order.

He was not going to be able to leave the drone on station overhead the way he had at Landsbergis's. There just wasn't enough power in either battery. He had just lost an incredibly valuable tool.

The best he was going to be able to do was to conduct an overflight now and hope to get a feel for the inner courtyard, as well as a look at the rooftop—along with the adjacent buildings—and maybe a peek in a few of the windows.

It would all be good reconnaissance material, more than he was normally used to having. But being blind while they were inside, just because the damn battery hadn't been charged, galled him. That was the kind of simple mistake that could end up getting people killed.

Launching the drone, he got back into the Land Cruiser so that they could all watch the feed together.

Nicholas was also watching from his perch back in the U.S. It was more out of loyalty to Harvath than anything else. He knew the drone didn't have enough juice to be part of the next phase, but on the off chance that he might notice something during the reconnaissance, he wanted to be there for his friend. Anything, no matter how small, that might lend Harvath an advantage was valuable.

The cameras around the building were way out of date—more for show than anything else. None of them had infrared capabilities. The only areas they'd be able to pick up were those that were strategically lit by security lamps bolted to the structure's façade. As long as the drone stayed out of the light, it would likely go undetected.

The small embassy compound, with its crumbling rooftop antenna array and rusted, oversized satellite dishes, looked like it had been frozen in time at the very height of the Cold War. If, at that moment, a couple of Soviet apparatchiks had stumbled into the courtyard for a smoke and a hit from a bottle of vodka hidden in the bushes, it would have looked absolutely normal.

Instead, all they saw were cobblestones, chipped plaster, and peeling paint. If real estate was all about location, location, location—that was definitely all that this place was about.

Harvath had the drone increase its altitude so they could get a better look at the roof. Beyond the aforementioned radio antennas and satellite dishes, there wasn't much to see.

The adjacent rooftops were steep and clad with smooth red-clay tiles. If things went wrong and that was their only means of escape, they were going to be in a lot of trouble.

Carefully directing the drone, he had it begin peeking in the windows. All of them, though, were covered—either by aluminum blinds in the office areas or shades or draperies in the residential portions. There was nothing left to see and so he recalled it.

The drone set down in the middle of the street, just next to the Land Cruiser. Harvath hopped out, repacked it in its case, and secured it in the cargo area.

Closing the hatch, he looked up at the sky that only minutes ago had been a deep purple. Much like his mood, it was transitioning rapidly from dark blue to black. This wasn't going to be an easy night. There was a lot they were about to do that he didn't like.

For starters, both the CIA Director and the President had told him—
in no uncertain terms—that he was absolutely forbidden from doing it.
Lawlor, whose call he had ignored because he was too busy talking with
Landsbergis on the drive in, had also sent him a series of angry texts telling him to stand down. Only Nicholas had been on board.

Getting back into the driver's seat, Harvath looked at Sølvi, then
Landsbergis, and said, "Let's go over the plan one last time."

CHAPTER 33

Harvath didn't need to speak Lithuanian to understand that Andriejus Simulik was pissed off. *Really* pissed off.

As Director of the VSD, he expected all of his people—even one as high-ranking as Landsbergis—to strictly follow agency protocols and, at the very least, to practice *basic* tradecraft. Bringing an American intelligence operative, unannounced and uninvited, to his home violated every rule in the book.

Bring him to the office, bring him to a restaurant, use a safe house—hell, set up the meeting at a fucking park bench, he didn't care. Revealing where he lived, though, and not giving him time to prepare was unforgivable.

Nevertheless, he buzzed them in and, as the gates swung open, ordered them to leave the vehicle in the underground parking area.

Harvath wasn't crazy about the idea. He had planned for Sølvi to remain with the Land Cruiser in the courtyard. Without the drone, they needed an extra set of eyes outside. He was also worried that if Simulik was guilty, having a member of the Norwegian Intelligence Service suddenly turn up was only going to spook him. There was no telling what he might do.

Harvath's presence wasn't that much better, but at least he was a known commodity to the VSD Director. And that had figured heavily into his plan.

He hadn't wanted to wait until tomorrow to set up a meeting someplace else. All that would have done was give Simulik a chance to plot against him. He needed to take him by surprise and catch him off balance. To do that he needed a pretext for why it had to be tonight and had to be at the Director's house. He needed to dangle something so valuable that the man would take the bait, agree to a meeting, and buzz them in. He decided to play one of the best and most authentic cards he had.

It told him a lot that after beating the information about Kaliningrad out of Lukša, the Russians hadn't gone to Landsbergis. They had gone to his boss. In Harvath's mind, that could only mean one thing—the VSD Director was already compromised.

The Russians didn't need to waste any time leaning on Landsbergis. They told Simulik to get them the information they wanted and he had done it.

According to Landsbergis, on what he now understood to be the day after Lukša had been beaten, his boss had called him into his office at the State Security Department for a chat.

There were rumors that Lithuania had assisted in a foreign operation that had taken place in Kaliningrad. The President wanted a full briefing on it. If Landsbergis knew anything about it, said Simulik, now was the time to come clean. If he didn't tell him everything he knew, the VSD Director wasn't going to be able to protect him.

At the time, Landsbergis explained to Harvath, it had seemed odd that Simulik had focused in on him. Only with knowledge that the Russians had tortured Lukša did things make sense.

Simulik had a pretty good understanding of what had taken place, which obviously had been provided to him by the Russians, and Landsbergis had come clean—giving him the rest. After that, his boss never mentioned it again.

What Landsbergis didn't know was who the target of Harvath's snatch-and-grab operation in Kaliningrad had been. That was the bait that had been dangled to get the VSD Director to open up his gates.

The Russians were desperate for any information about Oleg Tretyakov, their head of covert activities for Eastern Europe. Moscow wanted to know if he was still alive, where the Americans had been keeping him, and how much he had revealed.

When Landsbergis explained that not only was Harvath in the car, but that he also had information gleaned from the recent operation vital to Lithuanian national security, there was no way Simulik could resist the meeting.

Harvath had put his plan together on the fly, but it had worked. They were inside the compound. The rest, he hoped, would be even easier now.

According to Landsbergis, Simulik lived in the home alone—his wife having left him several years ago. There were no security guards and the VSD Director did not have an overnight personal protection detail.

Pulling into the garage, Harvath took note of the cameras. "If he has no on-site staff, who watches all of these?" he asked.

"The interior cameras are either broken or disconnected," said Landsbergis. "The few outside that function feed into a screen in his study."

There were two cars parked in the garage—a Mercedes sedan and a BMW convertible, as well as a Harley-Davidson motorcycle, all of which, per Landsbergis, belonged to Simulik.

Harvath parked near the stairwell door that led up into the building. Sølvi, who had been lying down, out of sight, on the backseat, sat up.

"I think we need to rethink your plan," she said. "I'm not going to sit down here and watch a garage while you're upstairs with the guy who got Carl killed."

"The pin has already been pulled from the grenade."

"Then put it back in. I'm going with you."

"Listen," Harvath replied, "I promise you that if he's guilty, I'll give you a chance to confront him. We both want the same thing. I know what I'm doing. Let me go do it."

Sølvi wanted to be there. She wanted to watch the entire thing unfold. She understood, though, why Harvath wanted to handle it the way he did. "As soon as you have something, I want to know."

"Understood," he said. "And if you see anything at all that doesn't look right, I want to know. Okay?"

The Norwegian nodded and Harvath signaled for Landsbergis that it was time to go.

Climbing out of the Land Cruiser, Harvath let the Lithuanian lead the way. They had been over this part of the plan several times. Everything had to go perfectly. If any part went wrong, Harvath was screwed.

By just making contact with the VSD Director, he was in direct contradiction of a presidential order. Not only was he told not to make contact, he was also told that under no circumstances was he to lay a hand on Simulik.

In for a penny, in for a pound, he figured. And, as he had told Sølvi, the pin had already been pulled. Full steam ahead.

Once the door into the stairwell was buzzed open, they went up to the second floor. The place was an absolute dump. The VSD Director must have been putting every paycheck, along with any payoffs he was getting from the Russians, into his mortgage, car, and motorcycle payments. He certainly wasn't spending any money on housekeepers or interior decorators.

Apparently, it was a fixer-upper and Simulik was doing all the fixing himself. Here and there, Harvath could see places where the man had replaced a window or a run of crown molding, the new pieces waiting to be primed and painted.

It wasn't living in squalor—Harvath had seen worse—but if this was Simulik's weekend gig, the job was going to take him two lifetimes. He had definitely bitten off more than he could chew.

All things being equal, though, his remodeling problems were the least of his worries. He was about to come face-to-face with the one person even the Grim Reaper didn't want to see at the other end of a dark alley.

At the end of the dimly lit, stained, carpeted hallway, light spilled from an open doorway. That's where they were headed.

Harvath had never met Andriejus Simulik, but he had heard about him. Carl didn't think the guy was worth two bits. Lithuania, in Pedersen's estimation, deserved much better. That was why he had chosen to work with Landsbergis. Someday, he had hoped that the younger Lithuanian would ascend to the directorship of the VSD. Anyone would be better than Simulik. Landsbergis in his estimation would be exceptional. Just based on the little bit of him Harvath had seen, he agreed.

As they approached Simulik's study, Landsbergis didn't break stride.

There was an air of resolute determination to him as he led the way. So much so, that Harvath couldn't help but wonder if Landsbergis had been harboring suspicions about his boss long before this night.

Just before the doorway, the VSD man slowed, composed himself, and then stepped inside. Harvath, right on his six, stepped into the room behind him.

CHAPTER 34

Andriejus Simulik was a thick man who sat behind an even thicker desk. He was still dressed in his suit from his day at the office. His flabby jowls hung over his buttoned collar as well as the sloppy knot of his red silk tie.

His gray hair was longer than it should have been for a civil servant, not to mention a man of his age. Flakes of dandruff peppered the shoulders of his jacket.

Atop the credenza behind him, a martini station was on display. Judging by the half-empty pitcher, cocktail hour was already in full swing.

"Right there," the VSD Director ordered, pointing his guests as they entered to the two worn, antique velvet chairs in front of his desk.

Once they were seated, he said, "After everything that has happened, you've got a lot of nerve coming back to our country. We should have sent a démarche to your ambassador."

A démarche was the diplomatic community's equivalent of a harshly worded letter, usually protesting or objecting to something another government had done.

In this case, though, there hadn't been a démarche. Simulik—likely at the request of the Russians—hadn't said or written a damn thing. In fact, Harvath was fairly certain that Landsbergis and his director were the only two people at the VSD who knew anything about the operation in Kaliningrad and Lithuania's involvement. Simulik was all talk.

He was also twitchy, or possibly paranoid, as hell. He couldn't keep his eyes from flicking to the large computer monitor on his desk. Though Harvath couldn't see what he was looking at, he assumed it was the feeds from his CCTV cameras.

Carl was right about this guy. Harvath had been in the room less than a minute and he already despised him.

He would need to keep reminding himself, though, that if it came to it, he had promised not to kill him before Sølvi had been allowed a crack at him. A promise, after all, was a promise.

"So why am I talking with you, Mr. Harvath? Why are you here?"

"Recently, I paid the Russians a visit in Kaliningrad. When I left, I took something that belongs to them."

Simulik raised an eyebrow. "Took something or took *someone*."

Harvath smiled. "You're familiar with the operation, then."

"Nothing happens in my corner of the world without me knowing about it."

This guy was so full of shit, it was unbelievable. Not only was he full of it, he was also proud of it. Harvath was willing to bet he didn't know a quarter of what was going on in his "corner of the world."

"Two weeks ago, a team of Russians—one with a fancy Vandyke—paid a visit to a Lithuanian citizen named—"

Harvath stopped speaking mid-sentence. A distinct change had come over both men. Simulik's eyes had stopped shifting to his computer monitor, while off to his right, Landsbergis had stiffened.

"Black hair and a Vandyke?" the younger VSD man asked.

Harvath nodded. "Sounds like you know him."

"Sergei Guryev. Russian Military Intelligence. Works out of their embassy here in Vilnius."

"How about one of his colleagues—large man, shaved head, big red beard?"

"Alexander Kovalyov. Also GRU from the embassy."

"I'm going to assume that the other two leg-breakers who were with them are similarly employed."

"That's probably a safe bet."

"What does any of this have to do with information critical to Lithuanian national security?" Simulik interrupted, growing annoyed. "After all, that's why you're here, *isn't* it?"

"It definitely is," said Harvath. "You see, right after this GRU team beat and tortured a Lithuanian truck driver named Antanas Lukša for information, that should have led them to Filip. Instead, they came to you. And the reason they came to you was because they already *had* you. You were already compromised.

"Why should they waste any time in breaking Filip, when you could get them the intelligence they wanted? And that's what you did. Filip told you about Carl Pedersen, you told the Russians, and the Russians had Carl killed."

"Pedersen is dead?" the VSD Director asked, his face pale, his arrogance gone.

Harvath glared at him. "What did you think the Russians were going to do with the information? Send him flowers?"

Like the coward he was, Simulik's shock quickly began giving way to something else: self-preservation. "I couldn't have known what they would do with the information."

"Norway is an ally, and a fellow member of NATO."

"So is the United States," he snapped. "Yet you used our air base to launch a hostile, unsanctioned action against a foreign nation. Your operation could have dragged all of us into war."

The VSD Director had no idea what he was talking about. Harvath's operation had saved them from war. The Russians had already set the wheels in motion for an invasion—and not just of Lithuania, but of Estonia, Latvia, and a portion of Sweden as well.

As much as he hated the Russians, their plan had been brilliant. By overrunning the tiny garrison on the Swedish island of Gotland, they would have been able to install their mobile missile batteries and close off the entire Baltic Sea. From Kaliningrad, their air defense systems, along with legions of their fighter jets, would control the skies. The only way for NATO to resupply their tiny partners and pump soldiers and equipment into the area would be via trains out of Poland.

There was just one problem—the gauge of the railroad tracks changed at the Polish-Lithuanian border and everything had to be transferred onto new trains. These transfer points were predesignated for sabotage.

No matter how many times the Pentagon had run the simulation, no matter how many times they had brought in new and even more brilliant strategists, the Russians always won the conflict—and a new world war broke out as a result.

Harvath's Kaliningrad operation—the risking of a handful of American lives in order to remove one Russian from the game and therefore avoiding World War III—had been considered worth it.

What hadn't been considered was how many others would die as a result of Harvath's actions. If he had known his wife would be slaughtered, along with Lydia Ryan, the Old Man, and Carl Pedersen, would he have still gone through with it? It was a question he didn't have the courage or emotional strength to ask himself. Not at this point. Not yet. Maybe not ever.

Simulik, growing in confidence over the cover story he was constructing, kept on talking. "You Americans think you can go anywhere and do anything you want. Well, you know what? You can't.

"If Lithuania chooses to share intelligence with Russia, we are within our rights. And there's nothing America can do about it. We decide how our nation survives. Not you."

It was a real stemwinder he was getting himself into. As the self-righteous indignation built, little flecks of spittle—as white as his dandruff—formed at the corners of his mouth. The color had returned to his face and the anger radiating from him was almost palpable.

Harvath was starting to get the impression that Simulik didn't care for the United States and had probably felt this way for a long time. There were plenty of older people in the former Soviet satellites, as well as Russia itself, who still pined for the "good old days" of communism. Harvath was always tempted to ask them what they missed the most—the breadlines or the gulags.

Simulik could call what he was doing, assuring the "survival of Lithuania," but the truth was that the only survival he was interested in was his own. Harvath figured that over a single lunch hour he could probably uncover enough banking irregularities to show that the VSD Director was dirty. He made a mental note to encourage Landsbergis to do just that. He might even rope in Nicholas. This guy needed to be ousted.

He was about to lay into him, when the man turned to vent his rage on his deputy in Lithuanian.

"You lied to me. You knew he was coming here to accuse me of this. You are actively conspiring with the Americans against your own country. This will not be allowed to stand. You are finished. Do you hear me? *Finished.*"

For Harvath's benefit, Landsbergis addressed his boss in English. "You're the one who is finished, Andriejus. You sided with the Russians and sold out an ally. That will not play well. Not with our government and not with our people."

"And you contributed material support, *Lithuanian* support, to a rogue operation against the Russians, which they could use as a justification for war against us."

"I say we take our arguments to the Parliament and let the chips fall where they may."

"Thankfully, that is not going to be necessary," said a new voice in the room.

Harvath and Landsbergis spun to see a man with jet-black hair and a perfectly pruned Vandyke standing in the doorway.

Sergei Guryev had joined the conversation.

CHAPTER 35

With Guryev was the aforementioned red-bearded thug Kovalyov, as well as the other two goons who had presumably held Lukša down while he was being tortured. All of them had weapons, and all of their weapons were pointed at Harvath and Landsbergis.

"Hands," said the Russian, in perfect English. "Let me see those hands. Nice and high."

Harvath and Landsbergis did as he commanded while his men streamed into the room and disarmed them.

"You took your time getting here," Simulik complained.

"Quiet, Andriejus," Guryev shot back. "Don't forget, you work for me—not the other way around."

Harvath was glad to have the confirmation, but it came with a downside. Admitting that the VSD Director worked for them meant that Guryev and his crew weren't about to let him go.

If anything, they were going to take him back to Russia and finish the job that had been started before he had escaped. Unless, of course, he was worth more to them dead than alive. If that was the case, he could be seconds away from being executed.

"I cannot tell you what a strange and unexpected pleasure this is," Guryev said, turning his attention to Harvath. "You killed several friends of mine back in Russia. I am looking forward to returning the favor."

"I killed a *lot* of Russians while I was there," he replied. "So you'll forgive me if I don't remember them."

"Americans—always making jokes."

"I wasn't joking."

Harvath knew he was in trouble and shouldn't have been kicking the hornet's nest.

His opponents were not typical Russian muscle—the sides of beef normally seen rolling with Moscow gangsters. He could tell by their eyes that these men were not only intelligent, but also switched on. They were probably ex-military, possibly even ex–Special Forces operatives, Spetsnaz.

He needed to come up with a way out of this. Quickly. *Think*, he exhorted himself.

Scanning the room, he looked for any advantage. He and Landsbergis had been positioned up against the wall—there was no cover or concealment. There were, though, multiple items he could turn into weapons.

From the highly polished pair of scissors or the brass inkwell on the desk, to the martini pitcher and nickel-plated cocktail picks behind it, his choices were broad. The challenge was getting to just one of them without being riddled with bullets. What he needed was a distraction.

But when Guryev next spoke, he realized that wasn't going to happen. "My President wants you dead or alive. He prefers alive, of course, because you killed his son and he'd like the pleasure of killing you himself.

"Escaping from Russia, as I said, you killed several of my friends. These men were highly skilled, which tells me I need to be very careful with you. So, while I'd like to deliver you to my President alive, I think dead is a much safer option."

Harvath smiled. "Then you're even more arrogant than Director Simulik."

The Russian smiled back. "That's a very high bar. You'll forgive me if I disagree."

"If your President had wanted me dead, he could have killed me when he murdered my wife and my colleagues. Instead, he brought me all the way to Russia. Why do you think that was?"

"I cannot possibly know the President's mind."

"Exactly. Which is why you'd be a fool to assume you can now."

Guryev's smile broadened. "Does banter like this normally work for you, Mr. Harvath?"

"Only with less intelligent people," he replied.

For a moment, the Russian was unsure of whether he had been complimented or insulted.

"I have a lot of information that your President wants. Believe me, your reward is going to be a lot bigger if you bring me in alive."

"You sound to me," the Russian responded, "like a man who is trying to buy time. I'm sorry, though, Mr. Harvath. There is no more time. I'm not taking you in alive."

"In that case," said Harvath, "let me show you my shocked face."

As he opened his mouth, plugged his fingers in his ears, and closed his eyes, a pair of flashbang grenades were tossed into the room.

When they detonated, they did so with ear-splitting, 180-decibel bangs accompanied by blinding flashes of over one million candela.

Their purpose was to throw an enemy into confusion and disorientation while interrupting their balance and coordination.

Distracted and temporarily incapacitated, it was impossible for them to adequately respond.

Having prepared himself for the explosion, Harvath was able to spring into action.

The two Russian operatives nearest him received the brunt of his response. These were the men who had pinned Lukša down and held him while he was being tortured.

Snatching the heavy brass inkwell off the desk, he swung it like a mace, striking each of the men in the head and knocking them unconscious.

Grabbing one of their guns, he spun to face the others, but the task had already been completed. Sølvi had used the two Tasers from his bag in the Land Cruiser—the same bag in which she had found the flashbangs—to drop Guryev and Kovalyov to the floor.

The effect wouldn't last long, though. They didn't call it the "ride for five" for nothing. The jolt of electricity bought you only a handful of seconds.

"Did you bring any restraints?" Harvath asked.

"I brought the whole bag," she replied. "It's out in the hallway."

As Harvath hurried to grab it, Sølvi noticed Guryev and Kovalyov coming around. Pressing the triggers of the Tasers, she let them ride the lightning again.

Fishing out a handful of flex cuffs, Harvath came back into the room and restrained all of the Russians. He also cuffed Simulik.

Once everyone had been patted down and their weapons taken away, it was time to get some answers. Harvath started with Guryev. Sølvi and Landsbergis, pistols in hand, kept everyone covered.

"What do you know about Carl Pedersen?"

"Fuck you," the Russian replied.

Harvath was about to give him a warning when Sølvi lowered her suppressed pistol, pointed it at the man's right knee, and pulled the trigger.

Guryev howled in pain.

"Answer the question," the Norwegian demanded. "Or your right knee will be next."

"Fuck you," he repeated, this time at her.

Sølvi adjusted her aim and fired at his other knee.

The Russian screamed even louder.

Harvath looked at her. There was no emotion on her face. She was all business. As cold as ice.

"You've run out of knees," said Harvath, turning his attention back to Guryev. "You'd better answer my question, before she finds a new body part to target."

The man barely managed to mumble "Fuck. *You*," from behind his gritted teeth, when Sølvi shot him again, this time in his left shoulder.

It was followed by another wave of screaming.

"What do you know about Carl Pedersen?" Harvath asked again.

"Norwegian Intelligence," came the reply, but not from Guryev. It had come from Kovalyov.

Harvath shot him a glance.

His boss told to him to shut up in Russian and they began arguing, before Sølvi put a round past each one of their heads and they instantly fell silent.

"What do you know about him?" Harvath repeated. "Besides the fact that he was Norwegian Intelligence."

"He introduced you to Landsbergis and Landsbergis helped facilitate your operation into Kaliningrad."

"Was Landsbergis next?"

The bearded man looked at Harvath confused. "*Next?*"

"All Carl did was make the introduction. Landsbergis was responsible for much more. If you were willing to torture and murder Carl over an introduction, I can only imagine what Moscow was planning for Landsbergis."

Kovalyov was even more confused. "Torture? Murder?" he said, before addressing his boss again in Russian.

Sølvi fired another round, intentionally missing his knee, but not by much. It was enough to get his attention. "English only," she ordered, as she ejected her magazine and inserted a fresh one. "No more Russian."

"We didn't know Pedersen was dead."

"Bullshit," Harvath replied.

Sølvi adjusted her aim and prepared to not miss his knee this time, but the bearded man begged her not to fire.

"If he was killed, it wasn't by us."

"He *was* killed and it *was* by you," she spat back. "Maybe the assassin wasn't GRU. Maybe the killer was FSB. The orders, though, came from Moscow."

"Think about it," Guryev managed with a grimace as pain radiated throughout his body. "If someone on our side was angry enough to kill Pedersen for his involvement, then Landsbergis would have been killed too. And I would have been tasked with carrying it out."

"And you never received any such tasking?" Landsbergis demanded.

"No," the Russian replied. "We didn't even know Pedersen was dead. Our job was to unravel how the operation took place and report back anything we learned. When the truck driver was identified, we were sent to interrogate him. And, if we discovered he was involved, we had orders to hurt him so that he couldn't work. But we were never told to kill him."

Harvath didn't want to say it, but the man's argument made sense. If Carl's involvement had merited killing, then certainly Landsbergis's did, and so too did Lukša's. It would have settled the score and sent a strong message—*Cross Moscow at your peril. If you do, you'll pay the ultimate price.* But that was looking less and less like what was going on here.

While Harvath appeared to be the reason Carl had been killed, perhaps it was possible that Moscow wasn't behind it. If it wasn't Moscow, though, who was it?

"I don't buy any of this," said Harvath. "Shoot him again."

"No!" Kovalyov shouted, sticking up for his boss. "There may be another reason."

Harvath waited for him to elaborate. When he didn't, he nodded at Sølvi. As she pointed her pistol at the bearded man's crotch, the Russian exclaimed, "Montecalvo!"

"What is 'Montecalvo'? she demanded, applying pressure to her trigger.

"She's a person," Kovalyov clarified. "A broker of information."

"What does she have to do with Carl's murder?"

"I gave her Pedersen's name."

"You did what?" Guryev grunted.

"Don't worry about it."

"What did you do?" the Russian GRU boss demanded.

"I sold a small piece of information."

"About one of our operations?"

"Only *after* the report had been filed," the bearded man said in an attempt to justify his actions. "Why should our superiors be the only ones getting rich off of our work?"

"Alexander, you have betrayed us."

"I have only done what is done every single day in Moscow. They use the information from our intelligence operations to steal intellectual property and to take advantage of the stock market. Why should we not do the same? Especially when we are the ones out in the field taking all of the risks?"

Guryev was in too much pain to even shake his head. All he could do to show his disappointment was to close his eyes for a moment.

When he opened them, he said, "Tell them how to find Montecalvo. If you don't, they're going to kill us."

CHAPTER 36

From the moment he was wheels down at Logan International, the Ghost did what he did best—he began to build a human network.

His cab driver, as most cab drivers tended to be, was a font of information. He not only knew a lot about the neighborhood the Ghost would be staying in, but he also had a friend whose sister-in-law owned a local business.

The business, it turned out, was a small grocery store, two blocks away from the three-flat owned by Harvath's deceased wife. Across the street was a playground.

The store was the nerve-center of the neighborhood and the collection point for every piece of gossip, rumor, and innuendo for ten blocks in any direction.

The Ghost had the cab driver stop and introduce him. He did some quick shopping, endearing himself to the owner, and then headed to his Airbnb nearby.

Over the course of the next two days, he popped in and out of the little store. He billed himself as a New York City photographer and videographer who was compiling a living history of the neighborhoods of Boston. The goal of his "project" was to capture the soul of each neighborhood—the day-to-day things that made them tick, as well as their eccentric and unusual characters.

The shopkeeper thought it was a wonderful idea. The store had been

in her family for three generations. She had grown up in the neighborhood and knew everyone. And so, his human network had begun to
grow.

Meanwhile, Johnson and Preisler had begun to build out the tactical
side of the operation. Based on their experience, and the limited amount
of time they had spent with Lara's parents, the most likely place for an attack was either at the house or somewhere between the house and the
playground. Thankfully, Marco wasn't in school at the moment, so that
took some of the logistical headaches out of the equation. Nevertheless,
they still were going to have their hands full. Harvath had been right to
send them to Boston.

And if it hadn't been for Harvath, Lara's parents never would have
cooperated with such a plan. Left to their own devices, they would have
retreated to the familiar.

They would have gathered up Marco and hopped a plane to Brazil.
There, in Providência—the notorious Rio de Janeiro favela where they
themselves grew up—they would have hoped to hide and ride out the
storm.

But with a possible one-hundred-million-dollar bounty on Harvath's
head and Marco as an irresistible piece of bait, there would have been no
place they'd ever be truly safe. This was the best way to handle it. Hope
for the best, prepare for the worst, and keep Marco's life as "normal" as
possible.

Unlike many of their friends, they didn't blame Scot for Lara's death.
Both their homicide detective daughter and their intelligence operative
son-in-law had difficult, dangerous jobs. More importantly, they knew
that Scot had loved Lara. They also knew that he still loved Marco. He
would never intentionally do anything to compromise them.

Which was why, when Nicholas had reached out, they had agreed to
go along with Scot's request. Even with their daughter gone, Scot was still
part of their family. They not only loved him, they trusted him.

They had put their lives in his hands and Harvath had treated that responsibility with the utmost seriousness. He knew Preisler, Johnson, and
Kost would fight to the death to keep them safe. That was why he had
asked Nicholas to send them. Marco was an obvious choice.

The men were also smart as hell. If something was afoot, not only would they pick it up quickly, but they'd put a knife in it so fast, lightning would be envious.

And that had been Harvath's concern at Camp David—that an assassin might use a family member to flush him out. He had worried that whoever had killed Carl would either try to get to Marco, as well as Lara's parents, or maybe even his own mother out in California.

Already, a team had moved her out of her senior community and over to Naval Base Coronado.

With such an alleged bounty in play, even a U.S. Navy base might not be perfectly safe, but Sloane Ashby and Chase Palmer, the two operatives Harvath had asked to watch over his mom, liked their odds. So too did the horde of U.S. Navy SEALs who had taken up residence around Mrs. Harvath. She was part of their family and there was no way they were going to let anything happen to her.

The remaining core of Harvath's team—Haney and Staelin, along with former Force Recon Marine Matt Morrison, ex–Green Beret Jack Gage, and ex-SEAL Tim Barton—stood ready as a Quick Reaction Force, prepared to deploy from Joint Base Andrews to anywhere in the world he might need them.

In the meantime, back in Boston, the Ghost continued to study Lara's neighborhood, developing a feel for its residents and rhythms.

In the apartment, Preisler and Johnson tried to stay in the background, out of the family's hair—something easier said than done.

Not only was it uncomfortable having two intense, flinty, well-armed men constantly nearby, but then there were the logistics. Lara's apartment was on the second floor and her parents lived above. The apartment on the ground floor was for rent, but currently vacant. The running up and down stairs, especially by Lara's mother, was an ongoing problem. Every time she went to fetch something, one of the men needed to be with her. Finally, it was Preisler who made a command decision. He was tired of all the back-and-forth.

Grabbing three empty laundry baskets, he accompanied Lara's mother upstairs, and told her to pack. Spices, books, clothes—he didn't care. She could fill the baskets with whatever she wanted. They just couldn't keep running up and down stairs. It was too dangerous. The only way Preisler and Johnson could really protect them was if they all stayed together.

Once Lara's mother had complied, Preisler took a break while Johnson accompanied Lara's father to gather three baskets' worth of stuff. In typical "guy" fashion, the man did it all in one basket. He only wanted his books, his "Brazilian rum" aka Cachaça, and a few changes of clothes.

With the crazy upstairs-downstairs portion of their program complete, they could refocus on simply being a heavily guarded family and trying to create some semblance of everyday, little-boy-life for Marco.

That meant that Marco needed to be allowed outside to run around and do all the crazy things a precocious four-year-old did. And the best place for a precocious four-year-old to *be* a precocious four-year-old was the playground down the street.

Protecting a little boy—especially when he was the primary—was a weird gig for Preisler and Johnson. Their previous protection details had been for diplomats in war zones, or in highly dangerous, cartel-controlled areas like Mexico, Central or South America. Guarding the life of a preschooler in Boston was a bit surreal.

Nevertheless, they were professionals and took it every bit as seriously as they did any of their previous assignments. There was no way they were going to let anything happen to Marco. The hardest part about the assignment, though, was that they weren't allowed to hunt. Only the Ghost, roaming free somewhere out there in the neighborhood, was authorized.

As sheepdogs, Preisler and Johnson instinctively knew their job—to protect Marco, and Lara's parents, at all costs. Per their training, they operated under the assumption that somewhere, unseen, a wolf was stalking their protectees. That wolf could be around the next corner or even standing right next to them. No matter where he was, he was always watching. They could take nothing for granted.

Because the wolf would decide when and where to attack, the wolf had the advantage. All the men could do was be ready to react. And when they did react, they reserved the right to visit overwhelming violence on the wolf.

Harvath had agreed and had insisted that they be kitted out with the best weapons and equipment available. If anyone came after Lara's parents or her son, he wanted the response to be "biblical."

Nicholas had arranged everything. The men were packing serious firepower, but moving in a civilian environment, especially a city like Boston, it had to be kept concealed.

They were all carrying short-barrel rifles. Preisler and Johnson had Kriss Vectors in custom messenger bags, while Kost sported a suppressed Honey Badger in a modified camera equipment bag.

For pistols, Preisler and Johnson had 1911s and Kost carried a Sig. They were all exceptionally proficient shooters with thousands of hours under their belts. It was not only their commitment to training, but in the cases of Preisler and Johnson, their years of active military experience that made them the best. Preisler had been with 7th Special Forces Group, and Johnson with 10th Group. Kost had entered the CIA immediately after college and had trained with multiple top tier military units—as well as with the DEA, who were some of the best gunfighters on the planet.

Harvath had handpicked the team for this mission. The only question was whether a wolf would show. Then, suddenly, one did.

Via his new relationship with the grocery store owner, the Ghost had learned of an overly ambitious apartment renovation that had run out of money. All work had stopped, the bank was moving to foreclose, and the owners had walked away. The situation couldn't have been better for the team, nor could the view.

It was on the building's top floor and provided not only an excellent overwatch of the playground, but also the surrounding streets. Getting in had been a piece of cake. Setting up his cameras was even easier.

He was using a telephoto lens, which allowed him to capture excellent details. That was how he had spotted the wolf. It was the same man he had bumped into the day before at the grocery store.

Kost had been on his way in as the man had been exiting. He was a Caucasian male in his early fifties and had been dressed similarly to how he was now—jeans, tee-shirt, gold chain, and white basketball shoes. The shopkeeper hadn't liked him.

"Shanty Irish," she had said. "That's what my grandmother used to call them."

Shanty, versus "lace curtain" Irish, was meant to catalogue an Irish person as being of low class.

When pressed, she explained that he had spoken with an Irish accent and had been gruff and rude. He had complained about her prices, before finally giving in and paying for the large energy drink he had pulled from the cooler. Asking if he wanted a receipt, he had ignored her and walked out.

He had brushed past Kost, who had held the door open for him, without saying anything. In addition to the man's poor manners, Kost got a really bad vibe off the guy.

The shopkeeper said he was definitely not from the neighborhood. She mused that he probably worked in construction and explained that there were lots of Irish who came to places like Boston and New York, overstayed their tourist visas, and illegally worked for cash.

While that might have been true, the man hadn't looked like a laborer to him—at least not one on his way to or from a job site. His jeans were clean; pressed even. He was wearing an expensive chain and his shoes were also pricey. The guy looked more like a middle-aged drug dealer than a construction worker.

Seeing him again had set off Kost's alarm bells. After taking a few more photos of him, he scanned the area. It appeared that Shanty might not be alone.

A block away, two similarly dressed men had just gotten out of a blue Hyundai Sonata. The driver had remained with the vehicle, and was slowly following them. It was time to officially raise the alarm.

"Heads up," he said over their comms link. "Possible hostile. Inbound on foot from the north. One block out. Fifties. Light hair. Jeans. Tee-shirt. Two more, same costumes, on foot, from the south. Two blocks out. Being trailed by a late-model blue Sonata. All headed toward you. Stay frosty."

"Roger that," Preisler and Johnson both replied.

With two entrances to the fenced playground, they had taken up opposite positions at each. They had unobstructed lines of sight, could react quickly if they needed to, and it allowed the family some breathing room.

Lara's father, who was a solid guy, always kept his eyes peeled while his wife played with Marco. When Preisler signaled to him that it was time to go, he immediately went over to his wife and calmly told her in Portuguese. She then informed their grandson that they were leaving. Preisler appreciated how seriously they took this. It made his role easier.

In the end, he had been sent to Boston with only two jobs. Number one, protect Marco and his grandparents at all costs. Number two, make sure Johnson didn't kill a metric shit ton of people. At this moment, though, all that mattered was job number one.

Adjusting his messenger bag, he moved to the family, making sure to smile as he did so as to not unnecessarily upset the boy. This could, after all, turn out to be nothing.

Johnson joined them as they approached the east gate of the playground. In studying the neighborhood, he and Preisler had developed multiple exfil plans.

One of the things they had agreed upon from the start, was that if there was an assault involving a vehicle, they'd use one of Boston's biggest pains-in-the-ass to their advantage—its one-way streets.

Exiting the playground, they turned to the right and walked toward the building Kost was in.

At the corner, they turned right again heading west. The traffic on the street was going in the opposite direction, which meant the Sonata couldn't follow them. The men on foot, though, could and did.

There was an alley coming up. That was their destination. Marco's grandfather encouraged him to move a little faster. He didn't know what was going on, but he could sense the tension in the adults. Coupled with the abrupt departure from the playground, he was starting to get frightened.

Preisler scooped the boy up and hurried their party forward while Johnson kept an eye on their six.

Once they ducked into the alley, Preisler found them cover and stayed with them while Johnson took up a concealed position out on the street from which to engage.

"Gun," said Kost, over the radio. "The pair of tangos coming up your side of the street. Looks like pistols."

"You're sure?" asked Preisler.

"Positive."

"Splash them," Johnson interjected. "I have my eye on the third tango coming up the other side of the street. Do it now."

"I can't see the third tango," said Kost. "He's under my window."

"Don't worry about him," said Preisler. "Get the two you've got in your sights. You're cleared hot."

"Roger that."

Moments later, there were two muffled cracks from outside on the street followed by a SITREP. "Tangos down," said Kost. "I repeat, tangos down."

"Blue Sonata inbound hot," Johnson warned from his vantage point out on the street. The driver had already looped around and was trying to get to their location. "Fifty meters out."

"Good copy," said Kost, as he leaned out the window and looked for Shanty Irish, as well as the vehicle. "Blue Sonata. I see it."

There was suddenly the sound of gunfire from down on the street.

"Tango down," said Johnson, who had killed the third man on foot.

When the blue Sonata was in range of his Honey Badger, Kost fired multiple rounds into the windshield. The vehicle swerved wildly, bashing into parked cars on both sides of the narrow street.

Johnson drilled a racing stripe down the side as it passed. The heavy 45 ACP rounds from his Kriss Vector tore through both the door and the driver.

The Sonata, its driver dead, began to slow, but didn't stop. Rolling through the red light at the intersection, it was T-boned by a Chevy Suburban, ironically plastered with Boston Celtics and "Luck of the Irish" stickers.

After helping Lara's parents to their feet, Preisler once again scooped Marco into his arms. "Time to go," he said.

CHAPTER 37

The transport plane, per Admiral Proctor's promise, had been fueled and waiting for them when they arrived at Šiauliai.

After swinging by Sølvi's vehicle to grab her gear, they had hit the road in Harvath's Land Cruiser. With all of the texts and emails that he had to deal with, she had graciously offered to drive. There was no classic rock and Rolling Stones for him on this return leg.

Nicholas had been quick to get to two pieces of bad news. The first was a rundown of what had happened in Boston.

They didn't know who was responsible, although they had plenty of photos of the perpetrators. One of the men was apparently off-the-boat Irish, and two others had extensive police records tied to Irish organized crime in Boston. The fourth perpetrator, the team's driver, had an Irish surname and a rap sheet filled with petty crimes. The working theory was that he was either a low-level initiate or had been hired just for this job.

The fact that the attack had been foiled, and all of the offenders were dead, was a testament to the skill of the team that Harvath had sent in. They had done exactly what he had assigned them to do. Marco and Lara's parents were safe. And now that they had been confirmed as active targets, he was having them moved to a new location.

While there were four fewer bad guys in the world, the flip side of all of the offenders being dead was that there was nobody to interrogate. It was a price he was willing to pay.

After filling in a couple more details, Nicholas then moved on to his second piece of bad news.

The deepfake software was turning out to be impossible to work with. Unless you had a subject sitting still and speaking directly to the camera, the superimposing of another face just wasn't convincing. You couldn't yet take a random person walking through an airport, bus, or train station and make it look like somebody else. They had thought they could do it, but it just didn't work.

The little man did have an alternative suggestion. Despite their age difference, Chase was a close enough match to Harvath that they could send him through the ports of entry and then reverse hack the customs and immigrations systems, replacing his passport with the fake identities Harvath had wanted to spread along his route. If Chase was careful not to look directly into one of the CCTV cameras and if he kept his head down—the way a smart fugitive would—it *might* be believable.

This meant, of course, that they would have to pull Chase off the protective detail for Harvath's mom. Nicholas didn't think it unreasonable, especially considering the highly secure bubble she'd been placed in. Harvath didn't agree.

Boston proved that they needed to be on their toes. His remaining loved ones were all potential targets. The teams stayed as they were, where they were. Politics, as well as one-hundred-million-dollar bounties, could make for strange bedfellows. There was no knowing who was hiring whom to do what.

At least they had a lead—Tatiana Montecalvo, or as Nicholas had called her, the "Contessa."

She wasn't a Contessa at all, but that had never stopped her from calling herself one. Born in Sicily to a Russian mother and an Italian father, her family moved to Rome, where she barely finished high school. Possessed of a voluptuous body, she worked as an artist's model at several of the city's art schools. Tired of taking her clothes off for such meager wages, she soon found other ways to do it for lots more money.

But as the youth that had made her so alluring began to disappear, so too did the men willing to pay to be with her. There was only one truly marketable skill she had left—her languages.

The Russian embassy had lost three members of its secretarial pool in the space of a week. One had left to have a baby, one had fallen off a table drunk while dancing in a bar and had broken both wrists, and another had fallen in love with a local and refused to come back. The embassy was in desperate straits.

She found a friend who quickly taught her basic skills such as typing, taking dictation, and running a desktop computer. A relative helped her phony up a résumé with a couple of sources back in Sicily who would vouch for her if the embassy ever called. After a cursory background check, she was invited in for an interview and hired on the spot.

It was obvious from the beginning that Montecalvo had zero experience and Mila, an older but very attractive member of the secretarial pool, took her under her wing. The two quickly became close friends—taking meals together, going out on the weekends, even setting each other up on dates.

What eventually became clear was that there were all sorts of people who took their clothes off for money. Mila was sleeping with various embassy employees, picking up bits and pieces of sensitive information—either through pillow talk or going through their pockets and briefcases after they fell asleep. She would then sell the information via a tidy little network she had built.

Most of it went to Western intelligence agencies based out of other embassies. Sometimes, it went to the Cosa Nostra. It had all sounded dangerous and very appealing, not to mention lucrative. Soon enough, Montecalvo was working for Mila. And when Mila returned to Russia, Montecalvo took over—and then some.

She upped her collection of information, using bolder and more sophisticated techniques. But soon, things got too hot to handle. Moscow was concerned that they had a mole in their midst in Rome.

Luckily for Montecalvo, she picked up this piece of intelligence just as the hunt was about to get started, and was able to quietly wind down her operation.

In the end, it turned out that there actually was a mole. A Russian military attaché had been recruited by British intelligence. Moscow had laid a trap and he had walked right into it. He was recalled to Russia and never seen nor heard from again.

It was enough to sour Montecalvo on being based inside the embassy. It was too dangerous. With her expertise, she figured she could be just as successful, if not more, by going private.

So after a reasonable amount of time had passed, she tendered her resignation and began her new career.

She plumbed the shadows of the sex work trade and hired a selection of attractive young girls, and boys, which she set loose on the diplomatic, political, and private industry sectors of Italy. She was both madame and spymaster. And, in addition to collecting sensitive intelligence, she also began collecting compromising intelligence.

Many of the trysts she helped orchestrate had ended up being quite valuable. Even in a country known for being the home of amore, it was amazing what powerful figures would agree to do, trade, or pay to keep their indiscretions hidden.

One thing was clear, Montecalvo was absolutely ruthless. She had been a competitor of Nicholas's back in the day. He had done business with her a handful of times. He did not care for her at all. In fact, he had suggested the "o" in *Contessa* should be replaced by another vowel, which would render a much more appropriate title.

Nicholas promised to put together a file on her and have it ready by morning. They debriefed for a few more minutes and then ended their call.

When Harvath got off the phone, even in the dimly lit Land Cruiser, Sølvi could see that he was wiped out.

"If you want to get some sleep, go ahead. I've got this," she said. "Norwegian women are usually very good drivers."

Harvath smiled. He knew she had heard the entire call with Nicholas, and yet she had chosen to make a joke—right out of the gate.

Her twisted sense of humor was a sign of high intellect. That was a good thing. Harvath had always been attracted to smart women.

Lara had been smart, brilliant even. She could give as good as she got and they used to constantly make jokes back and forth with each other.

That was one of the things he missed the most about her. He missed the joy she brought him.

To have that much laughter ripped from your life was like having a limb shorn off. It was probably a heavily contributing factor as to why he had fallen into such deep despair. Lara had "gotten" him.

She had understood him—not only who he was as a man and as a professional, but also what made him smile. Inside and out, she understood him better than anyone he had ever been with. It had been a phenomenon he'd never thought possible. And once he had lost it, believed it could never be possible again.

"Thanks," he replied. "But I need to stay awake and make sure you do everything right. How's our speed?"

Sølvi smiled. He was an incredible smartass. She liked that. "I keep trying to set the cruise control, but every time I do, liquid splashes the windscreen."

"Tell me about your tattoo," said Harvath. "The Rousseau quote."

"*Sartre.*"

"Right. Sartre. What does it say?"

"None of your business," she answered.

"Interesting. Does it say that in the original French, or did you have it translated into Norwegian?"

"As if either would make a difference for you."

"What are you saying? That I can't appreciate nuances between French and Norwegian?"

"We have a joke in my country," she began, stifling another smile.

"I can't wait for this. Go ahead."

"What do you call someone who speaks three languages?"

"Trilingual," Harvath replied.

"Very good. How about someone who speaks two languages?"

"Bilingual."

"And someone who only speaks one language."

"I give up."

As the smile broke out and spread across her face she said, "American."

It was a good joke. Not completely accurate, but a good joke nonetheless.

"*Du er søt,*" he responded, in his limited Norwegian, "*men du skal ikke skue hunden på hårene.*" *You're cute, but you shouldn't judge a book by its cover.*

"Well, look who speaks Norwegian. What else can you say?"

He knew only a handful of words and phrases. Some of them were absolutely useless.

"*Å stå med skjegget I postkassa,*" he replied. The rough translation was *standing with your beard in the postbox.* It usually referred to ending up in a dumb situation that you had cheated or snuck your way into.

"*Å stå med skjegget I postkassa?*" she repeated, with a laugh. "Not bad. I'm glad to see at least one SAS flight attendant taught you something."

Harvath looked at her.

She glanced back at him with a glint in her eye before returning her attention to the road. "Carl may have told Reed about my tattoo," she responded, "but you should know that Reed told Carl some personal things about you too. Remind me, where does the call sign Norseman come from?"

Touché, thought Harvath. She knew exactly where it had come from. "Why do you think they never introduced us?"

It was a good question, but one for which she really didn't have an answer. "I'm not sure," she said. "Carl was protective. He had a thing about compartmentalization."

Maybe, thought Harvath. But he had a growing feeling that it might have been something else.

Maybe their mentors knew their protégés all too well. Maybe they knew that once they had been introduced, they wouldn't be able to pry them apart.

They chatted the rest of the way to Šiauliai, asking lots of questions, but being careful not to go too deep or too personal. Each wanted to know more about the other, but instinctively they knew there was pain on the other side and they moved cautiously.

At the air base, they unloaded their gear, grabbed something to eat, and stepped aboard their plane. This time, there weren't any earplugs. The ride was loud and cold. Even Harvath, who was a pro at falling asleep anywhere, failed to get much shut-eye.

When the C-130 touched down at the NATO air base at Aviano in northern Italy, both Harvath and Sølvi were exhausted. A vehicle was waiting for them, and though they had been offered showers and a hot meal, Harvath wanted to get moving. Sølvi had agreed.

Hopping into their boxy brown Jeep Renegade, they had gotten on the road. It was a three-plus-hour drive to Lake Garda and Montecalvo the "information broker" Kovalyov had confessed to working with. Returning the favor from earlier, Harvath had taken the wheel.

There was no small talk, no witty back-and-forth during this drive. No sooner had they loaded the Jeep and discreetly rolled off the base than Sølvi was asleep in the passenger seat.

She had turned onto her right side, facing the window. He kept stealing glances at her, though knowing he needed to pay attention to his driving.

As his eyelids got heavier, he cracked his window and turned on the radio—not too loud, just loud enough that he could hear the music in order to help himself stay awake.

Nicholas had made a reservation for them at a hotel in Sirmione overlooking the lake. Judging by all of the cars, he hadn't been kidding when he had said he had found them the last room in town. Tourist season was in full swing.

Lake Garda was the largest lake in Italy and Sirmione was a narrow promontory that jutted two miles out into the crystal-blue water from the lake's southern shore. It was known for the thirteenth-century castle and winding cobblestone streets of its Old Town. It had been a refuge of tranquility for opera singer Maria Callas decades ago, before it had become such a mega destination.

As he eased to a stop in front of the hotel, Sølvi slowly opened her eyes and asked, "Are we here?"

"We're here," said Harvath.

She wanted to help him with his gear, but he told her not to worry. Checking in, he accompanied her to the room to make sure everything was okay, then came back downstairs, found a luggage cart, and, after parking, unloaded all his stuff, and headed back up to the room.

He had been gone only ten minutes, but she was already in bed, sound asleep. Grabbing the spare pillow and blanket from the closet, he made himself comfortable on the couch.

He texted Nicholas to give him a SITREP, then plugged his phone into its charger. Lying back on the pillow, he closed his eyes. Moments later, he was asleep as well.

CHAPTER 38

Harvath awoke to the sound of the doorbell ringing. Sitting up, he looked at the time. It was after nine a.m.

Wearing a white bathrobe, her hair still wet from a shower, Sølvi had stepped out of the bathroom and had already answered the door.

A room service waiter in a white jacket and black tie was standing in the hall next to a cart adorned with silver cloches, baskets of bread and pastries, a carafe of ice water and one of juice, a large pot of coffee, glasses, cups, linens, and other assorted breakfast accoutrements.

The waiter thanked Sølvi for opening the door, and with a polite bow offered for her to go first, and stated that he would follow her into the living room.

Once inside, he asked where she wanted breakfast set up. "How about on the balcony?"

"*Perfetto*," the waiter replied. *Perfect*.

While they prepped everything outside, Harvath slipped into the bathroom, splashed some water on his face, and brushed his teeth.

By the time he rejoined Sølvi, the waiter had already gone.

"Coffee?" she asked as he stepped onto the balcony and pulled out his chair.

"Yes, please."

Sitting down, he put his napkin in his lap and lifted up his cloche.

"I tried to get you the most American breakfast they had," she said.

"Scrambled eggs, bacon, roasted potatoes. No Texas toast, though. Sorry."

Harvath smiled and accepted the cup of coffee she had poured for him. "Thank you. And not just for the coffee. Thank you for everything back in Vilnius—with Simulik and the Russians. I should have said something last night."

"It's okay. You're welcome."

"When did you order all of this?"

"After I got back from my run."

"You've already been on a run?"

She smiled. "You looked so *søt* while you were sleeping. I didn't have the heart to wake you. I figured you needed the rest."

"You're like a Norwegian ninja. I didn't hear anything."

"That's a Norwegian woman for you. Silent *and* deadly. Make sure you take care."

Harvath smiled back and after a sip of coffee began his to eat his breakfast. "How was your run?"

"Educational. You'll never imagine whose villa I ran past."

"So many possibilities. Let me guess. The Contessa's?"

"Exactly. She has a very nice home, by the way."

"How's the security?"

"Better than we've seen with either Landsbergis or Simulik."

"Meaning?" he asked.

"She lives in Old Town, close to the castle. There are a lot of architectural restrictions. The cameras she has placed are subtle. You almost don't even notice them if you're not sure what to look for.

"In addition to the cameras, there are passive measures like walls, landscaping deterrents, and lighting. She's actually done a good job. Her villa is low-profile, *for a villa*, but highly secure."

"Guards? Dogs?"

"None that I saw or heard."

"I'd like to get the drone up to do a little more reconnaissance," said Harvath. "Does that seem doable?"

"There were a couple of guys flying drones out over the water. I asked them what the rules were and if they'd had any pushback from locals.

They said per Italian regulations, it's supposed to be line of sight and no higher than seventy meters.

"They admitted, though, that they've been flying up and down the peninsula—out of sight and up over one hundred meters—and nobody has complained. People just seem to have gotten used to drones being in all the tourist spots. And, with everyone on their phones, it's practically impossible to tell who's flying versus just scrolling."

Harvath liked that. They'd be able to hide their drone right in plain sight. That brought him back to the Contessa's security system.

"What else would you need to see in order to make a final assessment of the security system?"

Sølvi thought about it for a moment. "Ideally, I'd like to know what all the measures are, where the sensors are placed, if the property is being monitored remotely, if so by whom, are there human eyeballs—if any at all—on those cameras or is it AI, how does the feed go to the alarm company—hardwired, cellular, or both, if an alarm is triggered is it silent, and finally, who responds—private security or police, and what's the response time? And that's just for starters."

"Did you have all that intel when you broke into Landsbergis's house?"

"No, but his system was much less sophisticated."

"Okay," said Harvath as he excused himself from the table, went inside to grab his phone, and came back onto the balcony.

Thumbing out a text to Nicholas, he listed everything Sølvi had just asked for. Then, looking up at her, he asked, "What if we don't take her in the house?"

The Norwegian shook her head. "You can't take her in town. There's too many tourists. Even on my run, first thing in the morning, I had to weave in and out of people. Maybe if we came back in February."

"We're not coming back in February. This is happening now."

"I know. I was being sarcastic."

Harvath smiled and took another bite of food. "Let's pull the lens back a bit. What are our specific goals?"

"Simple," said Sølvi. "We know Kovalyov sold the Contessa information about Carl and his involvement with you in the Kaliningrad operation. The question is what she did with that information. Did she reveal it or sell it to anyone? If so, who?"

That was it in a nutshell. And, if the Contessa was anything like Nicholas, he knew she was going to be obsessed with not only her personal security, but also the security of her data. People in their line of work made some serious enemies. They also took some serious measures to protect themselves. Harvath didn't want to stumble into an Indiana Jones–style situation where if he stepped on the wrong floor tile in the entry hall, he got a poisoned dart in the neck.

He doubted the Contessa had poisoned darts and a huge rolling boulder that would come chasing after him, but he also didn't want to find out what her version of those things might be.

Had they more time, he would have set up extensive surveillance, developed a list of possible characters, and then would have tried to turn someone like a housekeeper or a cook.

Unfortunately, they didn't have the luxury of time. It just wasn't in the cards for them. They needed to get to Montecalvo ASAP.

"What if there was a way to get her outside the villa and away from the Old Town?" he asked.

The Norwegian thought about it for a few seconds. "And then what?"

"Then we grab her, put a bag over her head, and interrogate her."

"Where would we do that? A public park? An alley somewhere? Maybe a parking garage?"

Harvath looked out over the vast expanse of water and replied, "No. On a boat."

Sølvi followed his gaze. It was a bit half-baked, but not terrible. Once they had her out on the lake, they could keep moving. And with the roar of a motor, no one was ever going to hear her—even if she screamed her head off.

"Okay," the Norwegian said. "Tell me more."

"We work backward from heading out into the center of the lake. Where, onshore, do we load her onto a boat? Once we have that nailed down, we go backward even further and figure out where we intercept her."

"So we need someplace quiet, without a lot of witnesses."

"Exactly," replied Harvath, opening up a map of the area on his phone and turning it around so they both could study it. "Our best plan would be to do it in the evening."

"As in tonight?"

He checked his watch. "If we can get everything pulled together in time, yes."

"How do we know we'll even be able to get her out of the villa?"

"We're going to have someone she trusts make her an offer she can't refuse."

CHAPTER 39

After breakfast, Harvath showered and changed clothes. Then he went to scout locations with the drone while Sølvi handled renting the boat.

In the middle of the peninsula, there was a public park with access to a dock. If they waited until late enough in the evening, it would be empty. There was also a road that went almost to the water's edge. Once they were ready to move the Contessa from the boat back onto dry land, that was how they'd do it.

Harvath surveilled the entire property, looking for places someone might launch an ambush from. There were a few groves of olive trees, but not much else.

He next familiarized himself with the rest of the neighborhood, especially the various routes to the Contessa's villa. As a final checklist item, he did an overflight near her home, making sure not to appear that his drone was interested in anything at all to do with her.

With his surveillance complete, he texted Sølvi on the encrypted app they were using and asked her about the status of the boat.

His timing was perfect. She had just completed the paperwork. He told her where he was and that he'd wait for her on the end of the dock. It would be good for her to get in a practice run—especially as she was going to be the captain tonight.

It took her about twenty minutes to get there, but Harvath had filled the time with different texts and emails, as well as a call to Nicholas, who had been feeding *most* of the updates to Lawlor.

Harvath's visit to VSD Director Simulik's house hadn't been shared yet. He was saving that for when he got back to the States. He didn't need any grief from Lawlor right now. He needed to be left alone so that he could do his job. Nicholas understood and had promised to not say anything.

When he saw Sølvi approach, he couldn't believe the boat she had rented. The impressive Rivamare had to have cost a fortune.

The sleek, twin-engine craft was a work of art in gleaming black paint with teak decks the color of honey and railings that shone like polished silver. He put her length overall at about eleven meters.

"Let me guess," he said, as she brought it flawlessly up to the dock, threw the throttles into reverse, and spun the wheel like a pro. "You got an upgrade."

She smiled. "Everyone loves Norwegian girls, but the Italians *really* love us."

He put his foot out to help fend the boat off from the dock. "Do you want to tie up here and we can make a loop of the park? Just so you get the lay of the land?"

"Sure," she replied, killing the engines and getting out lines and bumpers.

There was a breeze, so in order to take advantage of it, they swung the craft around to the side of the dock. This way, the light wind would blow the boat away from the pier and prevent it from bumping against it.

Harvath gave her the quick, down-and-dirty tour. There wasn't much to see. He laid out what he thought their best course of action was and offered to show her the rest of the drone footage back at the hotel.

"How about lunch?" he had then asked. There was a nice trattoria with outdoor seating he had seen a couple of blocks up.

"What's wrong with you?" Sølvi replied, gesturing toward the water. "I could sit in a café anywhere in the world. How often do you get a chance to go out on a lake like Garda?"

He couldn't argue with her thinking. "You're right. We can eat later."

"Actually, we can do both. I picked up supplies while they were finishing the paperwork."

Like their room service waiter that morning, Harvath executed a bow and gestured for her to lead the way back to the boat.

As she fired up the engines, he untied the lines, shoved the Riva away from the dock, and hopped on board.

Ever the SEAL, he took care of the gear first—coiling and stowing the lines, along with the bumpers, followed by finding a secure spot for the drone, before joining her up front.

It was a beautiful day to be out on the water and the Riva's sharp hull sliced through it like a knife.

The air, moistened with occasional bursts of spray, smelled fresher out here. Commingled with the scent of olives were hints of cypress and lemon. Harvath had been to the more famous Lake Como multiple times, but he couldn't believe he had never been to Garda. It was incredible.

They did two tours of the peninsula, checking out the shoreline on both sides, before going off the clock for lunch. Heading out the approximate distance she thought they'd need to go with the Contessa, Sølvi then turned off the engines and allowed the Riva to just bob in the water.

"Where'd you learn to handle a boat like that?" he asked, as she pulled out the bag of food she had purchased.

"There's a lot of shoreline in Norway. Almost everyone, by definition, grows up near the sea. In my case, we had a house right on the coast. And a boat. That was my happy place. I love boats and being near the water.

"In fact, remember when we were talking about my getting a tip from Holidae Hayes?"

Harvath nodded as he helped her unwrap the food.

"We were at one of my favorite places in Oslo at the time," she continued, handing him napkins and plastic utensils. "It's a hotel called The Thief. Moored outside is an incredible Riva. Bigger than this one. Up on the roof of the hotel is a gorgeous restaurant which overlooks the water. You can see for kilometers. And if the weather is nice, there are so many boats. It's heaven."

Then, correcting herself, she said, "Actually, being on one of those boats is heaven. Eating on the rooftop of The Thief is the next best thing."

"Is that why you found us a Riva?"

"That, and I knew my rich Uncle Sam was going to reimburse the NIS. Right?"

Harvath popped the lid off a plastic container filled with olives and smiled. "I'll put in the good word."

Sølvi used one of the forks to spear an olive and smiled bigger than he had ever seen her do so to this point. It was dazzling.

"I love this," she said, beaming. "I could do this all the time. There is something about being out on the water that's just so wonderful."

Harvath smiled back at her. "Maybe you should have been a sailor instead of joining the Norwegian Army."

"Is there anything Carl didn't tell you about me?"

"He was proud of you. There was absolutely no doubt about it."

"Thank you," she said, uncomfortable with the conversation, her smile gone. "We should eat."

"I hope I didn't offend you."

"No. You didn't. It's just hard to have him gone."

"I can understand. We've both been through a lot."

"Hopefully, though," she replied as she ate her olive and unwrapped a block of cheese, "we're close to getting some answers."

"Whatever Contessa Montecalvo has, we'll get it from her. Trust me."

"I do," she replied.

Harvath looked at her and she looked back. They held each other's gaze for a fraction of a second, possibly for even a beat too long, and then broke it off—both at the same time.

They were in tune and it spoke to a deepening, potentially dangerous attraction. You couldn't work with someone, particularly not in an environment as deadly as theirs, when emotions were likely to cloud judgment. It was a recipe for disaster.

Harvath tried to compose himself. There was a lot to like, maybe even love, about the Norwegian ninja, but Lara's memory was still so fresh, so painful. Besides, they had a job to do. He needed to reassert his professionalism.

"The only thing this picnic is missing," said Sølvi, interrupting his thoughts, "is a great bottle of wine."

"Probably for the best," he responded. "I haven't exactly been the picture of responsible alcohol consumption lately."

She looked at him again, her face softer. Kinder. Empathetic. "Because of losing your wife?"

It was a topic she had wanted to raise while they were driving, but hadn't out of fear of ripping open what she knew was a very raw wound.

Harvath looked at what she had purchased for them to drink. "Mineral water?"

She nodded and joked, "After paying for the boat, it's all I could afford."

He smiled. "Let's open it."

She did, and after retrieving two glasses from the Riva's galley, poured.

"Cheers," said Sølvi, raising her glass. "To those we've lost."

"To those we've lost," Harvath replied, clinking glasses.

As he took a sip, he wondered if he would have said no to some wine. Here he was at Lake Garda, on a boat that had to have cost at least half a million dollars, and in the presence of a woman who, on a scale of one to ten, was a fourteen. Not many drinkers who stepped off the wagon did so under such unique circumstances.

"I remember you getting out the whiskey at Landsbergis's. How bad is your drinking?" she asked, gently. "Is it a problem?"

"Is it a problem? No," he admitted, appreciating her perceptiveness. "Is it too heavy, too often, and too much? Probably."

"So what are you going to do about it?"

Jesus, she was direct. Maybe that was the Scandinavian in her, but it was uncomfortable to have it put to him so bluntly like that. Nevertheless, he appreciated her honesty and attempted a smile. "I'm going to enjoy this nice, full-bodied mineral water and then focus on business."

"Good," she responded, taking a sip of hers. "Just know that I've been on the other side. Not alcohol, but similar things. If you ever want to talk, I'm here."

He wouldn't have guessed by looking at her that she'd had a substance abuse problem—or any kind of problem for that matter. Because of her looks, he wanted to graft a perfect story, a fairy tale onto her. He knew that was wrong. He knew that everyone you met was grappling with something—maybe not as rough as a drug problem, but *something*.

We all have our crosses to bear. What's more, we wouldn't trade ours for someone else's. If you and ten other people walked into a room and all laid their crosses on the table, everyone would be walking out with the same cross they walked in with.

He supposed that was because we got used to ours, but it was more than that. Our cross, we realize, helps define who we are. How we wrestled with our problems, how we battled the demons that often accompanied them, was what built character. And as much as her straightforwardness had unsettled him, it was good to have that reminder.

She was a good person. The world was full of people who would tell you what you wanted to hear. The valuable ones—the people worth holding on to—were those who told you what you *needed* to hear.

There was a lot to this Norwegian ninja. Still fjords, apparently, ran quite deep. On the list of things he found attractive, he had never really considered wisdom. Not, at least, until now.

She appeared to have taken a lot from her experiences. It added something to her, made her even more interesting. He wanted to know where she had been, what she had seen, and the lessons she had learned. But now wasn't the time.

Now, they needed to focus on the Contessa. Because if they didn't get this right, nothing else was going to matter.

CHAPTER 40

Tatiana Montecalvo—the Contessa—had indeed been glad to hear from Alexander Kovalyov again—especially when she learned that he had additional intelligence on Scot Harvath. Specifically, he claimed to have signals intelligence pinpointing Harvath's exact current location. "If what you have is authentic," she had told him, "I am very interested."

They had haggled over the price first. She had warned him that pigs got fed and hogs got slaughtered. He suggested that maybe one of her competitors would be willing to pay his asking price. Someone, perhaps, like the Troll.

Even mention of the little man's name made her skin crawl. She despised him. He was a glutton filled with despicable appetites, adrift on a fiendish sea of never-ending pleasure-seeking, and to this day, she was still angry at herself for having played a part in filling his greedy, tiny little belly.

Knowing his predilections for exotic sex acts and women of a certain look, she had thought she could play him. Before the ubiquitous cloud, in the days of mainframe computing, her goal had been to send her smartest, best-trained girl to him in order to plant a virus. Anything that already existed on his hard drives, as well as anything that ever crossed his computer screen from that point forward, would belong to her.

Instead he had double-crossed her, sending the girl back with a Trojan horse virus of his own. Once it had been uploaded to her system, he had cleaned her out and had set her operation back years.

It was a painful lesson in the art of war; one which she had never forgotten. When she took her shots these days, she took them with much more precision. And one of the easiest shots was outbidding a competitor before they even knew there was a contest.

This wasn't information she would have to shop. She had a buyer already interested in Harvath. He would pay three times what Kovalyov was asking. It would be very nice to get such an easy payday, and to do it while shutting out the Troll would make it even nicer.

So, she had agreed to the man's price—*if* the information could be authenticated. That's when the second round of haggling had started.

He wouldn't transmit any of what he had electronically. Once she had the treasure map, why should he expect her to pay for it? No, this was going to have to be done in person. The Contessa, not seeing she had a choice, agreed.

Then came the next point. Kovalyov was concerned that his absence from the embassy in Vilnius would be noticed. He would send a courier instead—someone he trusted. A woman. Once the Contessa had authenticated the intelligence, there would be an immediate transfer of funds into his account, and he would okay the courier to hand everything over to her.

While she didn't like working with a middleman or, in this case, a middle*woman*, she didn't want to be so difficult that she nuked their deal. Once again, she agreed to his demands. All that was left were the details of the meeting.

After he had laid out how he wanted it to go down, she had to give him credit—he had done his homework. He was a clever, resourceful man. She was glad to have him in her pocket. There was no telling what other valuable intelligence he might bring her in the future. If he kept going in this direction, they stood to make lots of money together.

What she didn't know was that Alexander Kovalyov would never contact her again. He was sitting in a former U.S. black site in Lithuania and had made a deal with the new acting Director of the VSD, Filip Landsbergis.

In agreeing to communicate with the Contessa, based on a script Harvath and Nicholas had put together, Kovalyov had been able to secure certain assurances from the Lithuanian government. If he continued to cooperate, his boss would continue to receive medical care, and their entire four-man team would eventually be allowed to leave and return to Russia.

If he didn't cooperate, Harvath and the Norwegian woman would be back, the Lithuanians would step aside, and the Russians would be at their mercy. There was only one smart path out of this and Kovalyov had taken it. So far, it appeared to be working.

With the meeting set, the biggest question was how far Harvath was willing to push things with the Contessa.

"Have you ever tortured a woman?" Sølvi had asked.

"Interrogated, yes. Tortured, no."

"It's different with women. What frightens them. What they respond to. The pressure points are not always the same as with men."

"You can be the captain, not just of the boat, but of the entire interrogation," he had said with a smile. "I look forward to watching you work."

"Speaking of which," he added. "Just going on what I saw in Vilnius, bullet holes in the Contessa could very quickly end up being bullet holes in the boat. Just going to throw that out there. I'm not a very good swimmer."

"I have always heard that about America's Navy SEALs. Good with flight attendants. Bad with swimming."

She was fun to spar with, but they had still had a lot of work to do. In addition to going over the drone footage and charging its batteries, he had come up with a different approach to the Contessa's interrogation—one that, if they were lucky, wouldn't have to involve getting rough with her.

"I'm all ears," Sølvi had said. "What are you suggesting?"

"It has already worked once. How about we make her another offer that she can't refuse?"

The NIS operative listened as Harvath had laid out his thinking, and she agreed that it was worth a try. They could always revert to harsh interrogation methods, and if needed, even worse.

The ball was going to be in the Contessa's court. How things unfolded would be completely up to her.

If she was intelligent, which by all accounts she was, hopefully she would do the right thing. Under pressure, though, sometimes people made very bad, very dangerous decisions. They would have to wait and see where the Contessa took them.

The one thing Harvath knew was that if she took them down the danger road, if she imperiled him or Sølvi, *he'd* put a bullet in her without thinking twice.

CHAPTER 41

At the appointed time, everything appeared to be in place. The boat was bobbing in the water, Sølvi was behind the wheel, the drone was floating in the air, and Harvath was in his hide site. All they needed now was the Contessa.

When she did show up, Harvath and Sølvi would see her before she saw them. There was no question.

Out on the lake, the Riva drifted with its engines and running lights off. Harvath watched the park and the dock via the drone's night vision camera. Sølvi surveilled the shoreline through the night vision goggles he had given her.

She picked up on the headlights before Harvath did. "Vehicle approaching," she said. "Southwest corner of the park."

"Roger that," said Harvath. "I see it. Our guest of honor has just pulled in, or a drug deal is getting ready to go down."

Moments later, another car pulled up, parked alongside, and it did actually look, via the drone, like a drug deal.

When the cars departed a minute later, they were back to waiting for the Contessa.

Then, Harvath noticed something. "Inbound. Lone figure. Northwest gate."

This time, things looked a bit more promising. While the Contessa could have driven to the park, it was within walking distance of her villa. That wasn't enough to determine if it was her, but it was a start.

The figure strode down the park path, not too fast, not too slow, and headed toward the dock.

"This is her," Harvath said, convinced.

"Roger that," Sølvi replied. "Any tail-gunners?" she asked, using a term sometimes applied to criminal accomplices who lagged behind, out of sight, waiting to strike if a job went south.

"Negative," said Harvath. "I don't see anyone. It appears she's on her own."

"What do you want me to do?"

"Wait until she's at the end of the dock and gives you the signal. Then you can come in."

"Roger that," Sølvi said. "Standing by."

The figure walked down to the end of the dock, pulled out her cell phone, and turned the flashlight feature on and off three times.

Harvath didn't need to say anything. This was the part where Sølvi took over. Starting up the engines, she put the Riva in gear and headed in toward the shore.

As she piloted the craft, she did everything via the night vision goggles, never activating the running lights, thereby denying an advantage to any ambush that might lie in wait.

Pulling into the shore, there was enough ambient light that her night vision goggles were no longer necessary. She peeled them off and tucked them into the compartment next to her as she blinked her eyes, adjusting to the new situation.

It took only a moment to see the lone figure at the end of the dock. Sølvi agreed with Harvath that this was most likely her, but until she had full confirmation, she wasn't going to relax.

They were operating off an old Italian Intelligence photo of Tatiana Montecalvo, from when she had worked at the Russian embassy in Rome. It had to have been twenty years old—if not older. There was no telling how much she had changed in the meantime, nor how much plastic surgery she may have had done.

As Sølvi got closer to the pier, she could see that the woman had had a little work done, but nothing so dramatic that she was unrecognizable.

She was older, a bit softer, and appeared more tired, but she was still Tatiana Montecalvo. This was their target.

Sølvi swung the boat in and sidled it up against the pier the same way she had with Harvath earlier in the day. That was when the Contessa pulled her gun.

"Shut the engines down," she ordered, pointing a Beretta pistol at Sølvi.

The NIS operative did as she had been commanded. Turning off the engines, she raised her hands.

"Open the door to the cabin and turn on the lights down there," the Contessa ordered, waving her Beretta.

Once more, Sølvi did as she was instructed. Then, with the lights on and the door open, she stepped to the side so Montecalvo could take a look for herself.

"It's just me," said the Norwegian. "Nobody else."

Withdrawing a powerful pocket flashlight, the Contessa flashed a burst of its high-intensity light into Sølvi's face, ruining her sight and temporarily causing her to see spots.

Tightening her grip on the weapon, Montecalvo demanded, "On your stomach. Now."

The Norwegian didn't like taking orders from this woman, but she did as she had been told.

As she lay facedown, the Contessa climbed aboard. She wanted to make sure the boat was safe before she got down to business. That meant making sure no one was hiding in back, or up front in the cabin.

She took a moment to pat Sølvi down and check the seat pockets, cushions, and various cubbies. Confident as she could be that the woman wasn't carrying a weapon, nor had one too close at hand, she backed away toward the cabin.

There were three steps leading down into the luxurious below-deck space. The Contessa took them slowly, shifting her eyes back and forth from the cabin to the woman who was facedown outside.

She checked the galley, the bathroom, and the sleeping area—none of which revealed any stowaways.

Satisfied, she started up the stairs and told Sølvi to get up. As she stepped through the hatchway, about to explain that they could get under way, or discuss their business right there, she noticed water on the deck. *Someone had gotten on the boat.*

But before she could raise her pistol, Harvath pressed his Sig Sauer against the side of her head and told her to drop it. She complied.

"The flashlight too," he ordered.

Again, she did as he told her.

Sølvi picked up the Beretta, released the magazine, ejected the round from the chamber and tossed all of it into the lake.

Then retrieving her own weapon, she kept the Contessa covered while Harvath—who had been floating under the dock and had crept up onto the boat via its swim platform—went back for his gear.

Everything was in a drybag stashed under the dock. He had been watching the drone footage through a waterproof phone pouch he had purchased, along with the drybag and a swimsuit, in town.

Climbing back aboard the boat, he used his last set of restraints to zip-tie the Contessa's hands behind her back. After a quick trip to the cabin to towel off and get dressed, he nodded to Sølvi that he was ready to go.

Firing up the engines, she pushed the throttles forward and plotted a course for the center of the lake. All the while, Harvath kept an eye on the Contessa.

Once they were far enough out, Sølvi put the engines in neutral and let the boat drift. Overhead, the drone was keeping watch. There were several other craft out and about, but nothing particularly close. As a result, they decided to keep their running lights off.

Harvath looked at the Contessa. "Do you know who I am?"

The woman nodded.

"Then you know why I'm here."

"I know that someone *really* wants you dead, but I'm guessing that you don't know who it is. That's why you're here. You're hoping to extract information that can help you, which means you'll be playing bad cop." Then, looking at Sølvi, she said, "And that makes you the—"

"Worse cop," the Norwegian intelligence operative responded, cutting her off. "Let me explain how this is going to go. I'm not a fan of waterboarding or pulling out fingernails. I prefer a much more direct route.

"I am going to ask you a series of questions. If you lie to me, I will shoot you in very painful, very specific parts of your body. If I even think you are lying, I will shoot you. If you hesitate, I will conclude that you're about to lie, and I will shoot you. Have I made myself clear?"

The Contessa had no idea how serious the threat was, but nodded, erring on the side of caution. "Is that what happened to Kovalyov?" she asked. "Did you shoot him? Is he dead?"

Sølvi shook her head. "I shot his boss, repeatedly. Kovalyov was next. He decided to cooperate. We made a deal. And we'd like to make a deal with you. If you agree to—"

"Not interested," the Contessa broke in.

"Either way, we are going to get the information we want out of you. You are choosing to make this much harder than it has to be."

"Go to hell," the woman sneered.

"You don't even want to hear the offer?"

"Not from you I don't."

"Well, how about from him?" Harvath asked as he activated a video call on his app and held out his phone so she could see it.

When the call connected, on the other side was Nicholas.

The Contessa was already testy and angry, but once she recognized who it was, she became downright aggressive.

She let loose with a string of expletives in Russian, only a handful of which Harvath knew. The woman was so pissed off and spat words so fast at his phone that he couldn't keep up.

Nicholas, calm at the outset, also lost his cool—something Harvath had rarely ever seen. There was a lot of bad blood between these two. Buckets of it.

The arguing, threats, and name-calling continued at a furious pace. Back and forth they went, their faces flushed, the veins in their necks bulging.

It took quite some time, but eventually the Contessa's outbursts began to slow, and she dialed back her tone. Nicholas also applied some self-restraint and became more measured. It wasn't détente, but the temperature was definitely being turned down. They were now entering the critical phase of Harvath's plan.

Nicholas had been resistant at first. The Contessa had started this. She had been first to try to stick a knife in his back. He had simply dodged the blade and had inserted his own between her figurative shoulders. Theirs was a cutthroat business. The purchase and sale of black-market intelligence was incredibly dangerous. If you tried to take out a competitor and failed, you needed to be prepared for the consequences.

Nicholas, though, had largely left that world behind. He did still dabble, keeping his skills sharp and preying upon the most unscrupulous in their industry. But basically, he had retired. And while he despised Tatiana Montecalvo, Harvath was family and had asked him for a favor. A *big* one.

They continued to speak in Russian, taking long pauses as each pondered what the other had said. There were a couple of flare-ups, but nothing close to what had transpired at the outset of the call.

After a little while longer, the Contessa looked at Harvath and said, "We're done. He wants to talk to you."

Turning the phone around, he inserted an earbud and walked to the swim platform, leaving Sølvi to keep an eye on their prisoner.

"My God," said Nicholas. "I hate that woman. Completely and totally. She is unintelligent, uncivilized, vindictive, and avaricious."

Harvath didn't need to hear what Nicholas was going to say next. He already knew. It had worked.

CHAPTER 42

eturning to the dock, Harvath put out the bumpers and tied off the Riva. He then brought his drone in for a landing and packed everything up. Once they were ready, he and Sølvi unloaded the Contessa from the boat.

Nicholas had warned them not to take their eyes off her, and they were heeding his advice. They had absolutely no reason to trust her. In fact, if anything, they had plenty of reasons to believe she might attempt to double-cross them.

With Harvath hanging on to their prisoner, Sølvi retrieved the Jeep and drove down to the dock. After he and the Contessa climbed in, it was a quick drive to her villa.

They parked out on the street, fully aware that they were in plain view of her security cameras and were being recorded. Harvath dropped his head so as not to reveal his face.

"Don't worry," she offered. "I'll erase all the footage once we get inside."

He'd have to see it to believe it. For the moment, he simply nodded as he took her arm and led her forward. A sweater had been draped over her hands secured behind her back so as not to reveal the restraints.

Sølvi hung back a couple of feet, watching their six. She had her weapon drawn, but concealed—ready to engage if need be, but out of sight so as not to rouse any suspicion from any neighbors or passersby.

Pulling the keys from the Contessa's pocket, Harvath unlocked the heavy oak doors facing the street and they all stepped into a Moorish-style paved courtyard flanked by arched arcades and a splashing fountain in the center. From the second story, flower boxes overflowed with bright purple hibiscus and electric pink gardenias. Their scent filled the space. Nearby, an alarm panel had started beeping.

The Contessa directed Harvath to it. Then, indicating that she wanted to be cut loose, said, "I need to enter the code."

"I'll enter it," he replied. Adding, "Don't worry. You can change it after we're gone."

She gave him the sequence of numbers.

Before he plugged them in, he warned her that he had people watching for a response from her alarm company. If this was not a code that legitimately disarmed the alarm, but rather turned the alarm off while simultaneously sending a distress signal, there'd be hell to pay.

He searched her face, looking for any sign of a tell as the beeping increased in intensity.

"Is the code safe?" he demanded.

"You're running out of time. Yes," she replied. "It's safe."

He didn't see anything that suggested she was lying, but to be absolutely sure, he would have needed more time—something he was all but out of.

He decided to punch in the code. Instantly, the beeping stopped.

"We're in," he said, over his earbud to Nicholas. "No dogs. No guards. Nothing so far."

Once his colleague had acknowledged the transmission, Harvath had everyone stop while he pulled out the drone and launched it from the courtyard. This way, if and when trouble did show up, they'd have eyes on it.

Harvath relocked the oak doors and the Contessa directed her "guests" across the courtyard to an Arabesque entryway which gave way to the main portion of the villa. At a set of tall glass doors that looked to be hundreds of years old, Harvath found the corresponding key on her ring and opened them.

Entering the house, the woman nodded toward another alarm panel that was beeping. "Same code, but backwards," she said.

Harvath entered the digits and as the panel fell silent, he took a look at the place. Nicholas obviously had his reasons for disliking her, but it certainly couldn't have been because she lacked taste. Her home was quite stylish.

The décor looked like a cross between *Casablanca* and *Lawrence of Arabia*. There were low-slung couches covered with pillows in an array of colors and fronted by ornate, hand-carved, antique tables. Sheer white muslin draperies were offset by potted palms. Large lanterns made of hammered metal hung at different heights from the ceiling. Somewhere, deeper in the villa, came the sound of another fountain.

"My office is that way," said the Contessa, pointing with her chin down a long hallway to the right.

"In a minute," said Harvath, as he unslung his pack and transitioned to his short-barrel rifle. "I'm going to take a look around first."

Montecalvo looked like she was about to say something, but Sølvi cut her off. Gesturing with her pistol to a nearby chair, she said, "Take a seat." After which, she looked at Harvath and added, "Keep your eyes peeled for ninjas."

"Try not to shoot her while I'm gone," he quipped back before turning and disappearing down the hall.

The house, with all of its closets, nooks, crannies, and other potential hiding places, felt like it took forever to clear. Finally, after checking out the cellar, he returned to his Norwegian counterpart and gave her the all clear.

"Now we can go to your office," said Sølvi, gesturing with her pistol again.

The Contessa stood up and led the way. Sølvi followed her and Harvath brought up the rear, constantly checking their six.

He had already been inside the woman's office and had swept it for weapons and other potential hazards. There had been another Beretta, like the one she had brought to the boat, mounted under her desk, as well as a "baby" Glock 26 in a lower drawer.

On the off chance he had missed anything, he had rearranged her computer monitor, as well as her wireless mouse and keyboard, so that she'd have to work from the other side of the desk. If she had been contemplating something stupid, it would be a lot harder now.

Dragging over a side chair, he set it in front of the desk and told her to sit down. He then handed Sølvi his rifle and had her watch the hallway while he cut the Contessa loose and relayed to Nicholas that they were ready to go.

Back in the United States, the little man prepared to return to Montecalvo her most prized piece of intelligence—one of the gems that he had stolen from her.

Though Nicholas could have sold it for a fortune, he had kept it as an insurance policy. It was pure blackmail gold; an explosive Get Out of Jail Free card implicating some very powerful people in a serious scandal.

And while it had been worth more to him sitting in his digital vault than he ever could have cashed it in for, he owed Harvath his life. It was time to play this card.

To facilitate the exchange, they set up a virtual meeting on the Dark Web. There, they traded files and took time to authenticate what each had been sent.

Each file contained a fail-safe; a sort of digital self-destruct feature. Only when both had agreed that the deal was satisfactory, could they exit the meeting with what the other party had given them.

In exchange for the return of the prized piece of intelligence Nicholas had stolen from her, the Contessa had handed over what Harvath and Sølvi wanted—the file on the person who had purchased the information about Carl and Harvath. That was who they were looking for. That was their assassin. Harvath was certain of it.

"What she sent looks good," Nicholas said. "It will take me a little time to run it all down, but it appears authentic."

"Are you happy with what you received?" Harvath asked the Contessa.

"Yes," the woman replied.

"Okay, we're good on this end too," he stated over his earbud.

The next part of the puzzle, though, introduced a new problem—how to make sure that after they left, the Contessa didn't tip off her client.

Allegedly, she didn't even know who the client was. She had never met him and the encrypted means of communication he used were constantly changing. Normally, he contacted her when he wanted something. That was what he had done in regard to Harvath. In return, she had put the blanket word out to her "collectors" that she was looking for anything they had on the American. Kovalyov, it turned out, had something very valuable. And he had been paid well for that information, in no small part because she had been paid *extremely* well.

With each client, she had developed a unique follow-up protocol—a way she could alert them if anything else bubbled up that she thought they might find interesting. Because clients burned even encrypted email addresses after each transaction, she needed another way to ping them.

She used predetermined online auction sites, placing obscure items up for bid, which would trigger alerts to the client in question. It was the modern equivalent of old-school tradecraft, back when coded messages used to be placed in the classified sections of newspapers around the world. Even today, in the age of modern technology, the simplest solutions were often still the best.

That didn't change Harvath's problem, though. How could they know that she wasn't holding out on them? That she didn't have another way to reach the client? That she might send out a warning?

In short, there was no way they could know. Their only option was to lock her up—physically or professionally.

Physically meant exactly what it sounded like—they could tie her up, put a bag over her head, and stash her away until they nailed her client.

Professionally it meant offering her something so valuable that she wouldn't dare jeopardize it by sending out an alert.

Needless to say, Nicholas was an instant fan of operation "bag-over-the-head."

Harvath, though, didn't want to wait around for an extraction team to show up in order to move her to a safe house and sit on her. Depending on where they came from, that could take a while—even if they used The Carlton Group's Quick Reaction Force.

As soon as the information on the Contessa's client provided a lead, he wanted to be wheels up. Thankfully, back in the United States, Lawlor had agreed with him.

In fact, Lawlor had gone so far as to suggest calling in a favor from the Italians and to have them ready to raid her villa with a terrorism, espionage, or sex-trafficking warrant—anything that would allow Italy to cut her off and throw her in a hole for the next seventy-two hours.

With that said, nothing was supposed to happen until Harvath gave the green light. Which was why it was so startling to suddenly have four plainclothes gunmen in the hallway.

"Contact right!" Sølvi yelled as they began firing at her. "They're coming up from the cellar!"

One of the alarm codes *had* been a distress code. Cops or a security company would have come in through the front door, not up from the basement. In fact, he hadn't even seen an entrance down there. There had to have been some hidden door, which only reinforced that she had double-crossed them.

He was about to ask Nicholas if he knew what the hell was going on, when he saw the Contessa lunge for something. That something was yet another hidden pistol.

Harvath pulled his Sig and shot her twice.

"What are we going to do here?" Sølvi shouted from the door.

"Engage!" Harvath yelled back.

As he rushed to join her, he grabbed a flashbang from his pack, pulled the pin, and tossed it into the hall.

"Flashbang!" he yelled, as he and Sølvi pulled back to be protected from the flash, as well as the concussion wave.

Once the device detonated, they swung around the door frame and laid down fire—Sølvi high and Harvath low.

They drilled all four men, filling them with rounds.

Ducking back into the room, they dropped their mags. Harvath slammed home a fresh one, while Sølvi did the same after grabbing one from the pack.

Over his earbud, Nicholas was demanding to know what had just happened. Harvath told him to stand by.

First, they checked the Contessa. She was dead and already headed toward room temperature.

Cautiously, they swung into the hall and approached each of the gunmen. Harvath checked them for pulses, but they were dead too.

Studying them, it was obvious that these weren't cops or security guards sent by an alarm company. They were relatively well dressed, with expensive shoes and gold jewelry. They looked more like mafia, pulled from a party at a local nightclub. And based on Montecalvo's Sicilian roots, it wouldn't have surprised Harvath to learn that she had recruited her own militia—even if she'd had to import them from Sicily.

He gave Nicholas a quick SITREP and then repeated to Sølvi the words that had been said to him in Key West only days ago when his teammates had rescued him, "Time to go."

"Wait!" Nicholas said, over his earbud. "Check her computer screen. Is she still logged in?"

Harvath looked at it. "Yes."

"Okay, before you leave, I need you to do something."

CHAPTER 43

With five bodies stacked up at the Contessa's, Harvath wanted to put as much distance between them and Sirmione as quickly as possible. Sølvi concurred.

After setting Nicholas up so he could remotely delete the footage from the CCTV cameras, they picked up all of their brass, wiped down anything they may have touched, and returned to their hotel.

There, they packed their things, left a tip for the housekeeper, and, using the back stairs, disappeared.

They lingered in town only long enough for Sølvi to pilot the boat back to the marina, tie it up, and drop the keys in the mailbox of the charter office.

The return journey to Aviano was going to be a little over two and a half hours. And while it would have been a safe idea to go someplace new and unpredictable, the air base was the most secure. Sølvi offered to drive so that Harvath could work his phone.

His first call was to Admiral Proctor to arrange discreet access back onto the base, a place to hole up, and an aircraft once they knew where they were headed next. Proctor told him he would get it taken care of and ping him back as soon as he had everything set.

Harvath then reached out to Lawlor, who had asked for a debrief once he was on the road. Though they were using secure, encrypted communications, he was wiped out and kept it short. Lawlor understood and didn't give him any pushback.

After their call ended, he traded texts with Nicholas. While he was certain his colleague was taking total advantage of being inside the Contessa's system, grabbing everything he could find, he wanted to make sure he was focused on the big picture—identifying the assassin who had murdered Carl.

Nicholas assured him that was indeed the case and that they had already begun processing the information from the file. He promised to get back to him as soon as he had something. And with that, Harvath was officially in a holding pattern.

"I'm happy to take over driving if you'd like," he said.

"That's okay," she replied. "I'm good. Why don't you get some sleep? This may be your only chance for a bit."

A part of him wanted to chat and get to know her even better, but he really was exhausted—his jet lag still weighing on him. She was offering him a gift. He decided to take it. Leaning the seat back, he closed his eyes.

• • •

When he awoke to the sound of his phone, he thought he had been out for only a few minutes. Looking at the clock, he saw that he had been asleep for well over an hour.

It was Admiral Proctor, calling to give him the details of who would be meeting them and where, as well as what their aircraft options were and how best to lock that in once they knew their destination.

After everything had been explained, Harvath thanked him and disconnected the call.

Proctor would have a team meet them in the nearby town of Sacile, take care of the Jeep, and handle getting them onto the base.

With more than fifty nuclear weapons housed at Aviano, security was incredibly tight. But there was a reason Proctor had been so good at helming both SOCOM and CENTCOM. He had an excellent mind for clandestine operations.

Harvath plugged the new destination into his GPS and filled Sølvi in on the change of plan.

She had no problem with the detour. In fact, it made a lot of sense.

This was a NATO air base they were headed to, but it was under Italian jurisdiction. The Carabinieri, who were one of Italy's main law enforcement agencies, fell under Italy's Ministry of Defense. They had a wide purview and could cause a lot of trouble if police in Sirmione put out an alert and somehow their vehicle was reported as having been seen at Aviano.

There was no telling how long they'd have to be on the base. The best course of action was to adopt a low profile and not give the Carabinieri, or any other Italian authorities, a reason to come looking for them there.

Proctor's team met them in Sacile with a row of three SUVs. The team leader introduced himself and explained that Harvath and Sølvi had been cleared onto the base by Brigadier General Sandra Collins, commander of the 31st Fighter Wing. He explained their cover story, and asked for their passports, as well as the keys to the Jeep.

Like Harvath, Sølvi was also traveling under an assumed identity—one of the many Carl had created for her.

She and Harvath handed over their passports and, after transferring their gear into their SUV, the column got rolling.

They moved with the tight precision of a team that had repeatedly driven in combat. Even in their tiny cars, no Italian was going to be able to slide in between any of their vehicles.

It took just under fifteen minutes to make the drive from Sacile to Aviano. Bollards, chain link fencing, and razor wire surrounded the entire base. At the gate, they swung, en masse, into a lane reserved for VIPs.

The team leader handed over the passports for Harvath and Sølvi, while all the other team members presented their Installation Access Control System passes and ID cards.

While one guard used a handheld scanner to verify all the IACS documentation, another approached the center SUV with a clipboard to compare the names on it to the passports and faces of the two VIPs about to enter.

As the verification was being conducted, more guards, including two canine units, swept the vehicles, including their cargo areas.

Harvath knew that this was standard operating procedure. The dogs were searching for high-grade explosives, not small arms. He and Sølvi were being escorted by a protective detail. If the dogs were looking for guns, they'd be going crazy over this team. Every one of them was armed.

Almost as soon as the security screening had begun, the passports were handed back, and the gate guards were waving the column through.

They drove to an admin building with holding rooms similar to the one Harvath had been placed in at Chièvres Air Base, though nicer and much more modern.

The team helped unload their gear and get them checked in. The team leader provided them with his cell number and told them to reach out if they needed anything else. Harvath thanked everyone and said good night.

Sølvi had been assigned the room next to Harvath's. They agreed to try to get a few hours of sleep and then find breakfast.

After chugging a bottle of water and downing a couple of small packages of almonds, Harvath lay down on the couch in his room. He thought about brushing his teeth, but found he didn't even have the energy to get back up. All he cared about was getting some sleep.

Kicking off his boots, he adjusted the cushion under his head and closed his eyes. His thoughts, though, wouldn't let him rest.

He had heard it referred to as "monkey mind"—the way everything kept jumping around.

Normally when he closed his eyes, he saw Lara. That happened this time too, but then his mind switched to Marco and what the little boy had been through. Not only had his father died just before he was born, but he had also lost his mom and had been caught up in some sort of failed, violent attempted kidnapping, accompanied by plenty of gunfire.

Harvath couldn't even to begin to imagine what all the long-term impacts would be. How do you even begin to have a "normal" childhood, much less grow into a healthy, fully functioning adult with that kind of stuff in your past?

What worried Harvath even more was what was to come. Lara's parents were wonderful people, but they were much older. What would happen if one or, God forbid, both of them passed before Marco was old enough to be on his own? How much pain could a child take? Just thinking about it threatened to shatter his heart into a thousand more pieces.

He needed to put his thoughts about Marco and Lara in that iron box, weld it shut again, and shove it as far back into his mental attic as it would go. The pain only served to drain his energy and exhaust him further.

An unhealthy part of him suggested a nightcap would be worth getting up for and would quiet his mind. He knew, though, that it wouldn't end well. He shoved that thought down too.

Looking for anything else he could lose himself in, he allowed his mind to drift. It landed on the woman next door.

As he thought about Sølvi, their lunch on the boat, and how her smile had dazzled him, everything else slipped away and he slowly began to unwind.

Not long after, he drifted off, sleep having locked him firmly in its grasp.

It was dark and dreamless, like tumbling off a cliff into a bottomless, midnight pit. He slept hard and deep.

At some point, the brain needed to power down—if only for a little while. Shock, trauma, and constant threats created an environment where the central nervous system—without periods of rest—could begin to deteriorate. Sleep was the key to remaining sharp. And his ability to remain sharp—to function at his absolute optimal limit—was what gave him his edge.

Unlike in the Jeep, this time he was able to get several hours of shut-eye. But when he awoke, he thought he had overslept. It sounded like Sølvi was knocking on his door.

After a few moments, he realized that the sound he was hearing wasn't someone knocking at his door, but rather his cell phone vibrating atop the wooden coffee table next to him.

Reaching over, he picked it up and squinted at the caller ID. It was Nicholas. He couldn't imagine what time it was back in the States.

Activating the call, he said, "You must have something."

"I absolutely do," the little man replied.

"What is it?"

"I think I know who the assassin is."

Harvath sat up on the couch. "Talk to me."

"In order to catch Carl's killer, I thought maybe we should set loose the most terrifying organization the United States has ever created."

"Which is?" he replied, eyeing the coffee machine.

"The Internal Revenue Service."

He smiled. They certainly were disliked by a lot of people in the United States. That said, Harvath would have guessed that Nicholas would have taken a shot like that at his old nemesis, the National Security Agency.

Nevertheless, maybe the IRS did make sense. After all, the most relevant data in the Contessa's file had to do with financial transactions.

"So, lay it out for me. What's the connection?"

"Remember OAKSTAR?" Nicholas asked.

"The NSA's internet surveillance program that Snowden revealed?"

"Precisely. While everyone was freaking out about their Facebook posts, emails, and private messages being gobbled up by the government, there was a whole other vein the U.S. government was mining. Uncle Sam was tracking all senders and receivers of bitcoin—*around* the world.

"According to the documents Snowden released, it went deeper than just the records contained in the blockchain—the ledger where users are designated via 'anonymous' identifiers. The NSA had actually collected passwords, years' worth of internet activity, IP addresses, and unique device identification numbers also referred to as MAC addresses. In short, if you ever even googled the word *bitcoin*, chances were the NSA had targeted your computer and had sucked up all the data they could pull from it."

Harvath had dealt with the NSA on multiple occasions. They had always been super people to work with. That said, there were more than a few high-level executives there who gave him pause.

"Snowden's revelation," Nicholas continued, "spooked a lot of users and sent them scrambling for added layers of encryption and protection. That's where the IRS comes in.

"They had been working on something, a software program capable of tracking financial transactions that was light-years ahead of OAKSTAR. They just needed a partner with enough computing muscle and a network with an all-powerful, global reach."

"Enter the NSA."

"You got it," the little man replied. "It's a brilliant joint venture. Together, they can outthink, outsmart, and outreach even the best criminals."

"Which is how you got our assassin?"

"Sending you his picture now," said Nicholas, transmitting the photo. "Meet Paul Vincent Aubertin."

Harvath watched as the photo appeared on his phone.

"His financial transactions were super murky and very convoluted," the little man admitted. "But the IRS program loves those kinds of challenges. Eats them for breakfast. As soon as we fed it the information we got from the Contessa, it began to unspool every transaction.

"He was good. *Really* good. He used a combination of anonymous bank and cryptocurrency accounts, particularly bitcoin, to move money around and make payments. But deep in his banking history, he set up an account with a one-time transfer from another, rather interesting account."

"What made it so interesting?" Harvath asked.

"The account received a pension payment from the French Foreign Legion before the payment was directed somewhere else."

That wasn't something Harvath had seen coming. First, Irish mobsters in Boston and now the French Foreign Legion? What the hell was going on?

"That's how you sourced the name Paul Aubertin?"

"Correct," Nicholas replied. "I may have accessed a certain French military database, which is where I got the photo. But that's just the start. When I searched for a facial match to any photos online, I discovered a private, password-protected Foreign Legion website. In a group photo, you can see Aubertin. But three people to his left is someone else I think you might recognize. I'm sending it now."

Harvath waited for it to come through and when it did, he said, "The assassin who tried to kill me in Key West."

"His name is Didier Defraigne. He's Belgian. He and Aubertin served in the Foreign Legion at the same time."

"Is Aubertin also Belgian?" Harvath asked, backing up.

"No. Are you ready for this? He's actually Irish—at least that was what his passport said when he joined the Foreign Legion. He was injured in Kosovo and per French law, he was able to apply for and receive French citizenship."

"What do the Irish say about him?"

"According to Ireland's Directorate of Military Intelligence, there was a passport issued in that name at the end of 1999, but they have no record of any citizen named Paul Vincent Aubertin."

Harvath walked over to the coffeemaker and fired it up. He liked where all of this was going. "The attackers in Boston allegedly had ties to the local Irish mob. Three were Americans, but the fourth was believed to have actually been from Ireland. Did you run his name through?"

"We did," said Nicholas. "Desmond Oliver Cullen's Republic of Ireland passport was issued just a little bit after Aubertin's—early 2000. It turns out, Cullen is a ghost as well."

"Why was Ireland churning out ghosts in late 1999, early 2000?"

"It could be that with the Troubles winding down, someone was running an underground railroad for the IRA."

"But weren't there amnesties?" Harvath asked, putting coffee in the machine. "Wasn't that part of the peace process?"

"Lots of convicted criminals were given early release, but if you were an un-convicted criminal, meaning you hadn't yet been prosecuted, there was no amnesty. You were out of luck. Even worse, the British government was as determined as ever to go after the most violent in the IRA."

"So we think these guys may be ex–guerrilla fighters?"

"At best."

"And at worst?" Harvath asked.

"Ex–IRA hitters. Hard-core assassins with mountains of experience taking out political, military, civilian, and law enforcement targets. Not too far-fetched if you think about it.

"A truce has been signed, the walls were closing in, and there's nothing left for them in Northern Ireland. Someone in Dublin, a sympathizer, can get them clean passports, which will allow them to start over somewhere else. Cullen jumps at the chance and goes to Boston, where he puts his skills to work for the Irish mob. Aubertin goes to France and ends up with the Foreign Legion. Like I said, not too far-fetched."

It wasn't too far-fetched at all, thought Harvath. "Do we know where Paul Aubertin lives?"

"That, I'm still working on. He is, though, registered as a Licensed Guide of France and promoted by the Federation of Guides of Normandy."

"Wait. Our assassin is a *fucking* tour guide?"

"Unless he uses it as cover for something else, it would appear that way. His ratings are pretty solid. Four stars or above. Consistently."

"How do we find him?" Harvath asked, knocking on the shared door between their rooms to wake Sølvi up.

"NormandyGuides.com has a profile on him. Unfortunately, he's one of a handful of guides who never uploaded a personal photo."

Harvath wasn't surprised.

"There is, though, a contact feature. It looks like you can fill out a request and they'll forward it to him."

"Let's do that. Make it look like it's coming from anyplace other than the United States or Norway. Present it as a couple looking for a guide in the next day or two. Pick the tourism site he gets the best reviews for."

"His specialty appears to be the D-Day beaches of Normandy, particularly Omaha and Utah, or the abbey of Mont-Saint-Michel."

"Go with the D-Day beaches," said Harvath, partial to America's World War II connection to France. "Hopefully, he'll take the bait, we can hire him as a guide, and set up a time and a place to meet."

"And if he doesn't take the bait?" Nicholas asked.

"We'll need another way to find him, preferably a home address or a cell phone number. Get inside the NormandyGuides.com system and see what you can find."

"Consider it done. In the meantime, what are you going to do?"

Harvath looked at the time and decided he had a wake-up call of his own to deliver. "We've got a flight to catch."

CHAPTER 44

Paul Aubertin sipped his café au lait and tried to control his anger. The story had now been picked up by the French newspapers.

As he scanned the article in *Le Figaro*, it was apparent there wasn't any new information.

The "Boston Massacre," as Monday's gunfight was being called, was being blamed on warring organized crime factions. It had taken place in broad daylight and four men were dead, including the driver of the "getaway car," which had collided with another, unrelated vehicle. Police were continuing their investigation. No further details had been released.

It was the same reporting he had seen all over the internet yesterday. *The Boston Globe*, local neighborhood "crime watch" sites, Boston police scanner blogs . . . no matter where he tried to dig up more background on what had happened, he couldn't find a damn thing.

The fact that the name *Desmond Oliver Cullen* hadn't yet appeared in the press was no consolation. Didier Defraigne's name hadn't appeared either. In the Belgian's case, he had simply vanished.

How the hell had Harvath done it? How was he one step ahead every single time?

It was becoming exceedingly apparent why such an enormous bounty had been placed on him. He was nearly impossible to take down, directly or indirectly.

That said, the man was still mortal, which meant two things: he needed to sleep, and he was capable of making mistakes.

My God, thought Aubertin. *Is that what this had come to? Counting on Harvath to make a mistake? Was that the only way he was going to be able to get to him?*

Aubertin refused to believe that a man of his experience, of his skill, would have to pin his hopes of success on a target screwing up. If that's what things had come down to, then he needed to get out of the business.

Except, he wasn't ready to get out of the business. Not by a long shot. At least not without a massive payday—and half of one hundred million dollars was as massive as anyone had ever seen. If it took waiting for Harvath to screw up, or even killing him in his sleep, then that was just the way it was going to have to be.

To take advantage of Harvath letting his guard down, he needed to be able to pinpoint him. That's why Key West had been so perfect. He had served up the job to Didier on a silver platter. But somehow Harvath had managed to escape—unless he and the Belgian had fallen into a mangrove swamp and had been eaten by alligators.

Aubertin doubted it. Harvath was still definitely alive. The foiled kidnapping of his stepson in Boston was enough proof. He was still out there, somewhere. And Aubertin was right back to where he was before. He either needed to reacquire Harvath's location, or find a new way to flush him out into the open.

How to accomplish either of those was the question. He had been wracking his brain, but still had yet to come up with an answer.

One would come, it always did, but if he pushed too hard his mind would keep it at bay.

As was often the case, some of his best answers came when he stopped thinking about the question—which was why he was sitting in the salon of the Château de Chantore, having a morning coffee, and waiting for a New Zealander family from Wellington to come downstairs.

They were return clients, who had not only been delightful to work with last year, but had also tipped very well.

Until the contract on Harvath was closed out—and provided Trang didn't come up with some sort of plan to screw him—he still had bills to pay. The time to make hay was while the sun shined.

And if focusing on the history of Normandy helped him unlock what to do about Harvath, then all the better. His day with the Kiwis would be even sweeter.

He was about to take another sip of his café au lait when his phone chimed. Looking down, he saw a request from NormandyGuides.com.

High season was kicking into gear.

CHAPTER 45

The jet that touched down at Aviano to fly them to France was a variant of a Gulfstream IV, known in U.S. Air Force parlance as a C-20H. It was part of the 86th Airlift Wing, but for all intents and purposes—from crew uniforms to the aircraft's registration—it appeared to be a private civilian aircraft.

Harvath and Sølvi had had just enough time to grab a shower and scrounge something to eat before it was time to leave. Over microwaved breakfast burritos and coffee in Styrofoam to-go cups, he explained everything he had learned about their assassin. He also explained his decision not to involve French authorities.

He had multiple connections to get any help he needed. The American and French presidents had an excellent relationship. CIA Director McGee worked very well with the head of French Intelligence. Even Gary Lawlor had extremely solid connections throughout French law enforcement. In the end, though, Harvath had thought it best to operate under the radar.

There was no telling what kind of tripwires Aubertin had in place, nor whom he might have paid off and in what area of the government. One word that the Americans were looking for him and he would vanish. For the first time, Harvath felt like he had the advantage. He didn't intend to waste it.

When they landed at Dinard-Pleurtuit-Saint-Malo Airport, Nicholas

had bad news again. NormandyGuides.com did have a phone number
for Aubertin, but it was no longer in service. Strike one.

Though it was first thing in the morning, Aubertin had already responded through the website to their request for a guide. Unfortunately,
he explained, he was booked up and could not help them. Strike two.

He did, however, suggest a colleague whom he felt would take exceptional care of them and provide a terrific tour of the D-Day beaches
or any other sites in the Normandy area they might want to see. He included her name, cell phone number, and a link to her bio on Normandy
Guides.com.

It wasn't a home run, yet they hadn't struck out entirely. They were
still in the game, but now with a degree of separation between themselves
and their target. Until they developed a better lead, this new guide—
Dominique Loiseau—was the best shot they had.

While Sølvi deplaned and went into the private aviation building to
pick up their rental car, Harvath remained on board and wrapped up the
list of things he needed from Nicholas. Once it was complete, he disconnected the call and deplaned as well.

It was an absolutely perfect morning—sunny and warm. They were less
than ten kilometers away from the coast; close enough that he could smell
the salt of the ocean carried on the breeze. Along with it came the scent of
grasslands and apple orchards. There was a reason why Winston Churchill,
Picasso, and even T. E. Lawrence had so romanticized this part of France.

As the crew off-loaded the gear, Harvath stood on the tarmac and
turned his face up toward the sun. It felt good to be outside. It also felt
good to breathe.

He enjoyed the warmth of the sun and the smell of the ocean for as
long as he could. He didn't know when he'd get another chance to close
his eyes and simply be.

The moment didn't last long. A few seconds later, he heard a vehicle
approaching. Opening his eyes, he saw Sølvi drive up in a black Land
Rover Discovery.

"Don't even say the words *Norwegian girl* or *upgrade* to me," he stated
as she put the vehicle in Park and hopped out.

She winked at him and then gave him her thousand-megawatt smile of perfectly straight white teeth, before popping the rear hatch and showing the aircrew where to place everything. Harvath just shook his head.

After loading the gear, he climbed into the passenger seat and they left the airport.

"Where to?" Sølvi asked.

Harvath checked his watch. "Let's head toward Omaha Beach," he said, pulling up the vehicle's navigation system and selecting their destination. "I'll call the guide and see when she can meet us."

As soon as the GPS system had mapped out the two-hour-and-eleven-minute drive, Sølvi sped up and merged into traffic.

Looking at his messages, Harvath opened the recent email from Nicholas and downloaded the attachment.

He then opened WhatsApp, checked his new profile, and confirmed that it showed both the assumed name and alias phone number he had asked for.

On NormandyGuides.com, Dominique Loiseau had listed her cell phone number, email address, and had also advertised that she was available via WhatsApp. Entering her number in the app, Harvath gave her a call. She answered on the second ring.

"Madame Loiseau," he said. "My name is David Owen. Sorry to call you so early, but we wanted to catch you before the day got going. Monsieur Aubertin thought you might be able to be our guide for a tour of Utah and Omaha beaches?"

"Yes, he texted me that I might be hearing from you," she replied. "You and your wife are from Canada, correct?"

"We are. Ontario, to be exact. We were hoping that we could meet you at Omaha Beach in a couple of hours and start there. How does that sound?"

"Unfortunately," the woman replied, "I am already committed to a tour this afternoon at Mont-Saint-Michel. I couldn't do the beaches with you and still be back in time."

Damn it, thought Harvath.

"If, though," she added, "you would like to see Mont-Saint-Michel instead, I could take you on a private tour this morning and if I'm able to move some things around, we could do Omaha and Utah beaches tomorrow. Would that work for you?"

In the driver's seat, Sølvi was nodding.

Harvath smiled and said into his phone, "Is Mont-Saint-Michel worth a visit?"

He could almost see the guide rolling her eyes as she replied, "Trust me, it's worth it. If you don't agree, it's free. I won't charge you. How about that?"

"Can you hold a moment, please? I need to ask my wife."

Muting the phone, he looked at Sølvi and smiled again.

"You're terrible," she said.

"I don't want to seem too eager."

"You *seem* like an idiot. Thank her, accept her offer, and ask where she'd like to meet."

Harvath stifled a laugh and did as he was told.

After setting up their rendezvous with Dominique Loiseau, he hung up and plugged the new destination into the GPS system. Mont-Saint-Michel was less than an hour away.

CHAPTER 46

T he tidal island of Mont-Saint-Michel was connected to the mainland via a man-made causeway. The causeway, though, was closed to all but official traffic.

Visitors were required to leave their vehicles in one of the official parking areas and then were allowed to cross the causeway on foot, via a cart drawn by draft horses, or on a free shuttle bus known as a "Passeur."

Harvath didn't like being cut off from their SUV, but he didn't have a choice. Finding a spot for the Land Rover, they locked it and headed over to the nearby Tourist Information Center, hoping to gather some intelligence.

One of his biggest questions was what security would be like once they got out to the site. It didn't take long to get an answer.

According to a sign they passed, only purses and small backpacks were allowed on Mont-Saint-Michel. Before you could enter through the fortifications, there was an inspection station. All bags were subject to search.

There was no mention of wanding or any other body-scanning technology, though knives were listed as a prohibited item. Drones were also prohibited and a red circle on a map showed the large exclusion zone around the island where nothing was allowed to be flown.

The only things they'd be able to take along were those they could conceal beneath their clothing.

Harvath tried to console himself with the fact that this was a reconnaissance operation and not a tactical engagement. Even so, he had always believed that you could never be too prepared.

Back at the Land Rover, he and Sølvi took turns keeping watch while the other covertly geared up. When they were done, they once again locked the vehicle, and headed toward the shuttle bus.

Once the Passeur arrived, the ride out to the island only took a few minutes. The views were amazing. Of all of the places around the world he had been, and all of the things he had seen, Mont-Saint-Michel was one of the most beautiful and most dramatic. He could understand why it had been referred to as the Eighth Wonder of the World. If a company of knights had come thundering out of the gates, and had galloped past them across the marsh, it wouldn't have seemed odd at all.

When the bus came to a stop and they got off, Sølvi hustled Harvath to the side, before the other tourists got the same idea, and had him pose for a photo with her. Though not usually a selfie kind of guy, he indulged her. After all, they were supposed to be a married couple on vacation. The unobstructed view of the fortified medieval stone town with its soaring abbey atop the hill was breathtaking. She had a great eye.

As warned back on the mainland, there was indeed a bag check. There were so many people in line that it took longer to get through than the shuttle ride out.

Thankfully, there was no wanding or body scan of any kind. Had that been the case, he and Sølvi had agreed that she would feign having left something important in the Land Rover that they had to go back for.

Waiting just past the bag check, as promised, was Dominique Loiseau. She was a stylish, petite Frenchwoman in her sixties, with platinum hair and a red and gold scarf. The scarf, she had explained over the phone, was to help her clients identify her. Though Harvath would have recognized her anyway, it was probably a good idea. The profile photo she had posted on the website was at least twenty years out of date.

"Is that her?" Sølvi asked.

"That's her," said Harvath.

As soon as Sølvi waved, Loiseau smiled, waved back, and walked over to them. She couldn't have been a more delightful woman.

"Monsieur and Madame Owen," she said, extending her hand. "How lovely to meet you. *Bienvenue à Mont-Saint-Michel*."

"It's a pleasure to meet you," replied Sølvi, shaking hands.

"Madame Loiseau," said Harvath, taking her hand next. "Thank you for accommodating us on such short notice."

Her English was excellent. "It is my honor," she stated. "And please, Madame Loiseau was my grandmother. Call me Dominique."

She was a charmer, which was why Harvath instantly liked her. Charmers were some of the easiest people to build rapport with.

"Okay," she energetically continued. "Have either of you ever been to Mont-Saint-Michel before?"

Harvath and Sølvi shook their heads.

"How about Normandy?"

Again, they shook their heads.

"France?"

This time, both nodded.

"Okay," said Dominique, as she motioned for her clients to follow. "Why don't we start walking, I'll tell you a little bit about the region, and then we can begin to learn how Mont-Saint-Michel came to be."

Dominique Loiseau was an absolute pro. Having confirmed that her clients were indeed hungry, their tour ended two and a half hours later, on the dot, at Mont-Saint-Michel's La Mère Poulard hotel and restaurant.

As they entered the dining room, the manager was already standing at the door and whisked them off to one of the best tables in the house. It was so well choreographed that Harvath had to subtly tip his hat. He couldn't help but wonder what kind of a kickback she received for bringing in high-end patrons.

There was a pleasant back-and-forth between Dominique and the manager in French, before he handed Harvath the wine list and said, "Something to drink?"

"I'm driving, but what about you, darling?" he said to Sølvi.

Sølvi looked at Dominique. "You won't make me drink alone, will you?"

The Frenchwoman smiled. "My next tour starts here, so luckily, I'm not driving. Yes, I'll join you."

"Red or white?" asked Sølvi, as Harvath handed her the wine list.

"*C'est à vous.* It's your decision."

"Champagne then," she said, showing the manager which vintage she wanted before surrendering the wine list and watching him scurry off to fetch the bottle.

"It's good to be on holiday," said Dominique. "I like your style."

Sølvi smiled. "I'm a lucky woman. Thanks to my husband, we have a very rich uncle."

Harvath couldn't wait to get the bill for this operation from the Norwegians. It was going to be off the charts. And Lawlor was going to wring his neck.

But by using Sølvi's alias and her credit cards, she was helping to further insulate him from the one-hundred-million-dollar bounty on his head.

When the manager returned, he walked right up to Sølvi, bowed deeply, and presented a bottle with his apologies. "We are out of the 2011, but I would like to offer you a bottle of the 2009 for the same price. It is an exceptional vintage."

She looked at Harvath, mouthed the word *upgrade*, then turned back to the manager and replied, "That is so kind of you. Thank you. We'll take it."

"Our uncle will be so happy that you're happy," said Harvath.

Sølvi winked at him and then turned her attention to Dominique.

Despite how loquacious the guide had been, she hadn't wanted to talk about Aubertin at all. No matter how subtly Harvath and Sølvi had tried to bring him up, she had changed the subject. She wasn't just a charmer, she was also a hell of a saleswoman—and she wanted to keep these clients all to herself.

The consummate intelligence officer, Sølvi plied her with the expensive champagne, making sure her glass remained full. She also asked a bunch of personal questions, including requests to see pictures of the woman's grandchildren, her dog, and her last vacation.

Each time she did, she caught Harvath's attention and signaled with her eyes for him to pay attention as the woman entered the passcode into her iPhone.

At first, he didn't understand what Sølvi was asking him to do, but finally—feeling like an idiot—he got it. But what good was a passcode without the phone?

He was about to find out.

After having downed a couple of glasses of champagne, Sølvi suggested that she and Dominique visit the ladies' room. The lovely Frenchwoman agreed.

As they got up and slung their purses over their shoulders, Sølvi feigned having trouble with her balance, but Dominique saved her from an embarrassing tumble.

Thanking her, Sølvi remarked, "Apparently, the 2009 goes right to your legs."

"If only the 2009 could give me legs like yours," said the Frenchwoman, "I'd buy it by the vineyard."

Sølvi smiled. "My husband is going to give you a great tip. You know that, right?"

Dominique smiled back.

"Speaking of which," Sølvi added, as she came around the table and planted a kiss on Harvath. "Don't go falling in love with anyone else while I'm gone."

"Never," he said, a bit shocked. "Not unless the Norwegian women's volleyball team walks in."

"Norwegian girls," she replied, putting her arm around the Frenchwoman and walking toward the ladies' room. "He's obsessed. Sometimes, it seems that's all he ever talks about."

As they walked away, he looked down at what Sølvi had pressed into his hand while giving him that kiss. The Norwegian ninja had struck again. It was the cell phone she had lifted from Dominique's purse.

CHAPTER 47

By the time the ladies had returned to the table, a little man halfway around the world had been set loose on one of the most important missions of his life.

Ever the gentleman, Harvath stood up to pull out each of the women's chairs. As he helped the Frenchwoman to be seated, he asked, "Dominique, is that yours?"

Following his eyes, she saw her phone lying on the floor, under the table. Before she could pick it up, he had already bent down and retrieved it.

"My goodness," she said, as he handed it to her. "Thank you. I didn't even know I had dropped it. Perhaps, I've had too much champagne."

"You can never have too much champagne," Sølvi confided.

"You can if it's a workday," Dominique replied pleasantly, waving the manager over. "Shall we order some lunch?"

La Mère Poulard was known for making the most famous omelet in the world. The eggs were whipped in large, copper mixing bowls—the kitchen staff beating out a hypnotic rhythm with their whisks. They were then cooked over a wood fire. The recipe and method of cooking hadn't changed in more than 130 years.

The history of the establishment over that time was amazing. Guests included Teddy Roosevelt, Édith Piaf, Claude Monet, Picasso, Hemingway, Patton, Margaret Thatcher, Marlene Dietrich, emperors, kings, queens, princes, and princesses. The list went on and on. Each had been asked to leave something special, a memento, behind. The walls were covered with framed autographs, photographs, drawings, and sketches. It was like being in a museum dedicated to over a century of power and celebrity.

They made small talk as they ate, with Sølvi deftly handling an innocent, yet potentially troublesome question that popped up at one point. Dominique was interested in why neither of them were wearing wedding rings.

Harvath's mind raced for an answer, but before he could come up with one, Sølvi stepped up. Without missing a beat, she explained that after France, they were flying to Thailand and had decided not to bring any jewelry on this trip. It was a terrific response and he was in awe of how quickly she had arrived at it and how effortlessly it had been delivered— even after a couple of glasses of champagne. She really was talented.

At the end of the meal, the manager came over to see how their lunch had been. They complimented him on the food and then he leaned in and said something to Dominique in French.

Smiling, she then relayed the offer to her clients. "Where are you staying tonight?"

Sølvi looked at Harvath and then back at their guide. "We actually hadn't gotten that far. We were just going to drive around Normandy until we found something."

Dominique's smile broadened. "Well, now you don't have to worry. They just had a cancellation here, upstairs. It's only for one night, but it's yours if you want it."

Harvath hadn't planned that far ahead yet. Once Nicholas had pinpointed Aubertin, he wanted to be ready to roll. With that said, there was no telling how long it could take. In fact, Nicholas had warned him not to expect a quick fix. It could be hours, or it could be days.

The idea of getting back in the Land Rover just to go to another hotel didn't make much sense—not when they were already here.

"This is a once-in-a-lifetime experience," the guide continued. "Unbelievably romantic. More than half the tourists will be gone by five o'clock. I can meet you for another drink, we'll go listen to vespers in the abbey at six-thirty, then you two can have dinner and walk the ramparts together. After a good night's sleep and a hearty breakfast, we'll meet at Utah Beach. How does that sound?"

"It does sound appealing," Harvath admitted. "I'm still a little jet-lagged."

He was also holding out hope that spending more time with the woman might result in getting a little more information out of her.

At the moment, and until they had something solid from Nicholas, they had nothing to lose.

"I guess we'll do it," he announced, sealing their decision.

"Wonderful. You can check in and take a power nap, while Mrs. Owen does a little shopping?"

"Or," said Sølvi, "I can take the Passeur back to our car to grab our overnight bags."

"And when you get back, *then* you'll do some shopping."

Sølvi smiled, raised her champagne, and the two women clinked glasses.

Calling the manager back over, Dominique told him that they would take the room. She then looked at her watch and apologized, explaining that she was going to have to get going if she was to meet her next clients on time.

Harvath settled up with her, added a nice tip—as Sølvi had promised—and they made a rendezvous for drinks that evening.

After she had gone and they had paid for lunch, the manager accompanied them to the front desk, where he handed them off to a young desk clerk, before disappearing back into the restaurant.

Though they had been introduced as Mr. and Mrs. Owen, the clerk didn't bat an eye when they filled out the registration card with the names on their fake passports. Had the clerk questioned the discrepancy, a hint that they were both married to other people would have been all that was necessary. This was France after all. It wouldn't have been the first time paramours had tried to keep their identities secret while checking into a hotel.

Accepting two key cards, they went upstairs and checked out the room.

Dominique hadn't been kidding. It was romantic. Incredibly so.

The room maintained the overall La Mère Poulard color palette evident on the façade of the building, as well as throughout the restaurant. The draperies were gold, the chairs and carpet red, and the soft bed linens a crisp white.

None of it compared to the views over the water through the large, open French windows. For a moment, Harvath was almost able to forget that this was an assignment.

"Is this going to be okay?" Sølvi asked.

"It's great," he replied, still looking out.

"Hey," she chastised him, "I'm not talking about the view. I'm talking about this."

Harvath turned to see her pointing at the queen-sized bed. Unlike their room in Sirmione, here there was no couch.

"Setting aside for the moment that a *true* Norwegian girl would have gotten us upgraded to a suite, I guess I'll just have to trust you to respect me."

"Me?" she replied. "To respect *you*?"

"Yes. My modesty *and* my virtue."

She shook her head. "We're going to need to light a lot of candles at the abbey tonight."

"That's okay, I saw an ATM outside."

"Very funny. How did it go with her phone?"

"Perfect," said Harvath. "Remind me to start putting my wallet in my front pocket when you're around."

Sølvi smiled. "I'll take that as a compliment."

"It is, and you should."

"How long until your people have something?"

Harvath checked his phone to see if he had any messages from Nicholas. So far, there was nothing. "Tech is always unpredictable," he said. "Sometimes the hardest jobs are the easiest, and the jobs you think will be the easiest are the hardest."

"Well, you get your beauty sleep. I'm going to go get our bags."

"I'm happy to come along and help."

"Don't worry about it," she said. "You want me to grab your black one, right?"

"They're all black."

"I know. It was a joke."

Harvath smiled. "Just bring the one with the toothbrush, *not* the rifle."

"I'm going to try *really* hard to remember that, but," she said, pointing at her head, "you know, *blond*."

Harvath smiled again. "Something tells me that even if you bring the wrong bag back, you'll still find a way to get it past security."

Batting her eyelashes, she flashed him another smile and left the room.

As soon as she did, Harvath—who had been holding himself up tall and straight—allowed himself to slump. Pulling out the drawer of the nightstand near the window, he began dumping all the gear he was carrying.

Then, sitting on the edge of the bed, he untied his boots and kicked them off. It wasn't bad enough that he was operating on practically no sleep, but he had been on a two-and-a-half-hour walking tour, followed by a long, French lunch. He couldn't wait to put his head back and close his eyes.

Giving his phone one last check, he then set it on the nightstand and lay down on the bed.

When sleep came, it came like a speeding train, drawn to a passenger who had just stepped off the platform. It hit him. And he was out.

CHAPTER 48

S he could have slammed the door, kicked the edge of the bed, or done any number of things to wake him up. They were both ex-military. The obnoxious possibilities were endless.

Instead, she had chosen to be kind. Sitting on the edge of the bed, she had gently drawn him from his slumber. Placing a soft hand on his shoulder, she had woken him up.

"Time to go to work," she said, as he opened his eyes.

"How long was I out?"

"Long enough. I made you a coffee and there's a change of clothes hanging in the bathroom."

"How much time do we have?" he asked, sitting up.

"We meet Dominique for drinks in half an hour."

Harvath rubbed the sleep from his eyes and picked up his phone. There had been no updates from Nicholas.

"I had a dream about you," he said.

Sølvi laughed. "You were out so hard, you're lucky to have even gotten oxygen to your brain."

"Seriously," Harvath teased, a faint smile on his lips. "I saw a nice house in Norway. On the water. And a boat."

"Hmmm," Sølvi replied, indulging him. "A house and a boat. You nailed it. That's the whole package. Every Norwegian girl's dream."

He knew she was being facetious, but he was concerned that he had offended her. "Did I miss something?"

"There's a lot more to life than just a house and a boat," she said, turning toward the open windows and looking out over the water.

He was certain that he had touched a nerve. What it was, though, he didn't know, nor could he get to the bottom of it right now. Picking up his coffee, he headed into the bathroom.

There, he saw that Sølvi had not only brought his personal items back from the Land Rover, but had also set them out on the counter.

For as cold-blooded as she had proven herself to be, there was also a thoughtful kindness to her.

Harvath didn't need a shower, but he took one anyway. After rinsing off, he threw the temperature selector to cold and, as he had done countless times before, stood for as long as he could before turning off the water.

Toweling off, he got dressed, and joined Sølvi in the bedroom.

"You look like a new man," she said.

"Thank you," he replied, wondering if she was still upset.

"Gun up. I'll be waiting in the lobby."

And there, again, was her cold professionalism.

He thought he understood Nordic culture, or at the very least Scandinavian women, but she vexed the hell out of him.

All he had wanted to do was to mourn Lara, drink himself into oblivion, and let everything else just melt away.

Then, the girl with the Sartre tattoo had shown up and it had all been turned upside down.

Now, every time he looked at her, he felt guilty. It wasn't her fault. It was his. He felt like he was betraying Lara, and it hurt like hell.

Pulling himself together, he brushed his teeth, and tried to push all of it from his mind.

• • •

Walking downstairs, he found her. She was standing in silhouette, lit by the fading light from outside. He could have stood there watching her for hours.

They didn't have hours, but he did indulge himself in a few seconds. The spot Dominique had chosen for drinks wasn't that far of a walk.

Sølvi must have sensed him. Turning her head, she looked over her shoulder and smiled. He wished he'd had his phone out. It would have been a great photo.

At least she didn't seem upset with him. Crossing the lobby, he opened the door and held it for her.

When they stepped onto the narrow cobblestone street, it was like they were salmon swimming up a packed stream. The throng of departing tourists was massive. Dominique hadn't been kidding about Mont-Saint-Michel starting to empty out at five o'clock.

Despite the exodus, it hadn't turned into a medieval ghost town. There were still people around.

They met their guide at the Auberge Saint-Pierre, where she had secured an outdoor table in the tiny, courtyard garden.

Harvath opted for an espresso, while Sølvi had an Aperol Spritz, and Dominique—glad to be putting the workday behind her—ordered a Calvados.

She was even more chatty than she had been at lunch. Harvath wondered if maybe she had stopped for a drink with her other clients before arriving here.

There was a benefit to it, though. She seemed more comfortable around them and, without coaxing, she brought up Aubertin.

It was brief. She didn't know much about him. He spoke with an Irish accent and while polite, was exceedingly professional. So much so, that he wasn't known to socialize with any of the other guides. In fact, the only social situations Dominique had ever seen him in were when he was at a restaurant or a café with clients.

He was considered an excellent guide and had sent her some wonderful referrals over the years. "Present company very much included," she added.

She didn't know anything about his personal life and believed that he lived somewhere along the coast.

And as quickly as the subject had come up, she moved on to discussing something else.

If nothing else, the fact that he spoke with an Irish accent confirmed Nicholas's information. Aubertin was their assassin.

The piece about him living somewhere along the coast was interesting and might be helpful in their hunt for him.

After waiting a few minutes, Harvath stood up and excused himself from the table, telling the ladies that he would be back momentarily.

He walked back to the men's room, but it was occupied and so he stepped outside to compose a text to Nicholas.

Standing there, thumbing out the message, he shuddered. It was unlike any feeling he had ever experienced before. Immediately, he looked up, half expecting to see a tiger charging at him, or a meteor falling out of the sky. The best way he could have described the feeling was with a saying his grandmother used to use. *It was as if someone had walked across his grave.*

But, of course, as he looked around there was no tiger, no meteor. There were only tourists, a group of whom had just entered a shop across the lane.

Shaking it off, he finished his text, hit Send, and returned inside.

CHAPTER 49

When the ladies had finished their drinks and Harvath his espresso, they left the Auberge Saint-Pierre and headed off for evensong, or as it was referred to at Mont-Saint-Michel, vespers.

As with every Point A to Point B excursion on the island, there were inclines and stone steps—lots and lots of steps.

Dominique had assured them that she knew a shortcut and was shaving considerable difficulty off their walk. Harvath watched with interest as they passed a young couple, baby and stroller in tormented tow, arguing. Someone in that family—husband or wife—needed to get much better at pre-vacation reconnaissance. This was not a destination to which you brought babies or small children. It was physically strenuous, even for adults.

Its inaccessibility, though, was what had made it such a formidable stronghold for well over a thousand years. The more time Harvath spent walking its streets and ramparts, the more he grew to appreciate it. It spoke to the warrior in him.

True to her word, Dominique had indeed found them a shortcut to the abbey, and was able to get them in through a side door. She had already purchased entrance tickets, which she handed over to a church official standing just inside.

As she did, she directed Harvath's attention to an offering box bolted to a thick stone column and intimated that he might want to make an additional donation.

Seeing as how they had been allowed to use God's VIP entrance, the least they could do was to show their appreciation.

Harvath didn't have a problem with it at all. Even if they had been forced to queue up at the main entrance, he still would have donated a little extra.

Wherever he traveled, he loved seeing older houses of worship. They were always works of art, with incredible attention to detail. Helping keep such beauty alive was an honor.

Directed to a special set of pews, they took their seats. After a few minutes of requisite history from Dominique, the service began. And it was amazing.

Six monks and six nuns, shrouded in white, stood at the front of the ancient church with its soaring ceiling. As they sang, their hallowed voices reverberated off the centuries-old walls, and was one of the most beautiful things Harvath had ever heard.

It didn't even seem real. It sounded like a movie soundtrack. But considering the movie-set-like beauty of Mont-Saint-Michel, it was fitting. Sometimes, if you stopped to appreciate it, real life was often more beautiful than fantasy.

At the tree line of civilization, though, evil was always poised, ready to rush in.

Maybe that was why he felt such a special kinship with houses of worship. If there was one thing religion understood, it was evil. The fact that some officiants referred to their faithful as their "flock," also had a special resonance with him. The whole sheep/sheepdog, wolf/wolf hunter thing seemed to be especially clear when he was sitting in a church.

It was also a sanctuary, the one place he should be able to let his guard down and reflect—to think about who he was, what his place was in this world, and if what he was doing was a noble, virtuous, even moral thing.

As he allowed himself to slip into a contemplative frame of mind, dropping his guard just a fraction, lulled by the music, the shudder swept over him again.

Like someone had walked across his grave. And just as it had outside the Auberge Saint-Pierre, it shook him.

Moving his hand to his concealed pistol, he turned his head and swept as much of the church as he could with his eyes. All he could see were tourists, though. *Nothing but tourists.*

Yet if that was the case, why were his Spidey senses tingling off the charts? Was he getting jumpy again? Like he had when leaving the truck driver's house or when Landsbergis had lingered in his driveway and not come directly inside? Or was this something else?

As if he needed something to complicate matters further, his phone began to vibrate. Pulling it out he saw it was a call from Nicholas. He couldn't take it. Not here. Not during vespers. He sent a text back. **Can't talk now.** And slid the phone back into his pocket. As soon as he did, it started vibrating again.

Harvath pulled it out, silenced the call, and sent another text message. **I will call you ASAP.**

Almost instantly, a message came back. **We got a lock on his phone. We've located Aubertin.**

The people around Harvath were getting angry that he was on his phone and not respecting the mass. He understood where they were coming from, but this couldn't wait. It also would have been a hell of a lot more disruptive if he had stood up and walked out.

Where is he? Harvath texted.

He's there, Nicholas texted back. **At Mont-Saint-Michel.**

Where? Harvath asked, stunned. **Specifically?**

At the abbey. Where are you?

Taking one very slow, very long look around, Harvath texted back, **Also at the abbey.**

CHAPTER 50

The abbey was a collection of buildings and outdoor spaces—some of which were off-limits to the public. Aubertin could have been anywhere. Harvath, though, knew he wasn't just *anywhere*. He was close. He was *here*.

The reason he had recommended Dominique was because he was already booked for the day. If, as Nicholas had texted, he was at the abbey, it was because he had brought clients. And if they were on the premises at this time of the evening, it had to be because they were attending vespers in the church. The challenge for Harvath was to find him, without being seen.

As he took another look through the crowd, Sølvi leaned over and asked him what was going on. Handing her his phone, he let her read the texts.

The look on her face said it all. She couldn't believe it either.

"What do we do?" she whispered.

Harvath didn't have an answer—at least not a good one. They had been shoved down their pew to make room for a group of latecomers. It was going to be impossible to exit without crawling over people. And no matter how quiet or polite about it they were, it was going to draw attention.

While they had an excellent view of the service, when they were forced to slide farther down the pew, the view behind them became partially obstructed by a column. As a result, Harvath was unable to see a considerable slice of people. He was convinced that was why he hadn't yet been able to spot Aubertin.

But even if he had, what was he going to do about it? Pull out his pistol and yell for the man not to move? There were too many civilians. He needed to come up with a better plan.

With the tide coming in outside, there was only one way off the island—via the causeway. There were several ways, though, to exit the abbey and make it down to the main gate. He and Sølvi were going to have to split up. If he lost Aubertin up top, he would be counting on her to trap him at the bottom.

He emphasized the word *trap*, making sure to clearly distinguish it from the word *kill*. Aubertin was the next link in the chain. Without him, Harvath would be in the dark again, back at square one.

When the pair was done whispering, Sølvi leaned over to Dominique—who had been watching their exchange out of the corner of her eye—and gave her regrets. She explained that they had received bad news from Canada about a close friend and that she needed to return to the hotel.

Dominique explained that the service was almost over. Sølvi, insisting that she had to leave, thanked her and said goodbye.

Harvath told her he'd join her there shortly and stared straight ahead. Aubertin, as far as he knew, had no clue who Sølvi was. Even if he saw her get up and leave, it wouldn't have given him pause. Already, other tourists—prompted by their guides—were gathering their things and getting ready to be the first ones out the church doors in order to beat the rush.

He wished the tracking system Nicholas was using was more precise, but despite not knowing where Aubertin was sitting, he still had the ultimate advantage—the assassin had no idea he was there.

As the final, haunting note of the service reverberated through the church and faded away, Dominique tapped Harvath on the arm and said, "*C'est fini.*"

"This is for you," he replied, having pulled another generous tip from his pocket. "I need to join my wife. Thank you for everything."

Before the guide could respond, he was headed off in the opposite direction. Not toward the door by which they had entered, but rather deeper into the church.

Like a shark moving through the water, he slipped through the crowd. His senses were fully heightened, keen, and on alert. He kept his head down and his eyes up, sweeping back and forth, searching for his quarry.

As he moved, he expected the shudder to hit him again—for Aubertin to walk across his grave once more and announce that he was there. But the shudder didn't come.

Instead, a flash of something else caught his attention. Just off to his left—a polo shirt he had seen earlier. As if it were a drop of blood in the water, he swam toward it.

Getting closer, he noticed a familiar skirt. Then a blazer, a sundress, and a pair of sandals. He knew these details, these people. He had seen them before—outside the Auberge Saint-Pierre.

This was the family that had been entering the shop across the road when he had first felt the shudder. They appeared wealthy enough to hire a private guide. And if they had, he was willing to bet that he knew the guide's identity.

So where the hell was he?

Harvath continued scanning the people around them. Then, suddenly, he saw him. *Aubertin.*

The apex predator part of his brain took over and he went for his pistol. That was when all hell broke loose.

It was so out of context that Aubertin didn't immediately recognize him. His expression, though, was unmistakable. It had changed in an instant—like someone had thrown a switch. Only when he pulled his weapon out did he realize who he was looking at—Scot Harvath.

Aubertin drew his weapon but, unlike Harvath—who must have been concerned about the crowd—he didn't hesitate. He fired.

The bullet dropped a man who had inadvertently stepped in front of Harvath to take a photo.

At the sound of the gunshot, there was instant panic, along with a stampede. Terrified families and tour groups were torn apart as they scattered in different directions. Numerous people, including children, were trampled. It was pandemonium.

And it provided Aubertin with an opportunity—concealment.

Surging with the crowd toward the nearest exit, he kept his pistol low and out of sight. He had no idea how Harvath had found him, or how many men he might have brought with him. Right now, all that mattered was escape.

Outside, he snatched a baseball cap from a discarded backpack and kept on running. Wriggling out of his blazer, he wrapped the garment around his right hand to hide his weapon. His only hope was to get off the island before police locked down the causeway.

But, of course, that was exactly what they would be expecting him to do. That's where Harvath and his people would be waiting for him. They had him trapped—or at least, that's what they thought.

Aubertin, however, knew the island. And he had a different idea.

CHAPTER 51

A Good Samaritan leapt into action. Balling up someone's windbreaker, he applied a makeshift pressure bandage to the man who had been shot.

Harvath couldn't have done better himself. What's more, rule number one in a gunfight was to eliminate the threat. That was *his* job.

Charging out of the church, he gave chase.

"Talk to me," he said over his earbud. "Where is he?"

"He's on L'Abbaye Street," Nicholas replied, studying the map on his screen. "Moving away from the abbey."

Harvath was in a throng of tourists, all doing the same thing—getting away from where the gunfire had been.

"I think he's headed for the main gate," the little man added.

"He's trying to blend in. That's how he's going to escape, hiding in the crowd."

It was a smart move on Aubertin's part—sow total chaos and then use it to your advantage.

"The Logis Sainte-Catherine is up ahead on the left," said Nicholas. "There's a shortcut through there that pops out at La Mère Poulard. If he knows Mont-Saint-Michel, he'll know that's his fastest route to the exit."

"Tell me if he takes it," Harvath replied, pushing his way through the crush of people, trying to gain ground on the assassin.

Up ahead, he could see the building known as the Logis Sainte-Catherine. Maneuvering to his left, he prepared to charge the stairs leading to its flat, grass-covered common area. It was going to be his best chance to close the distance with Aubertin. Then came the news from Nicholas.

"He blew right past it," the little man reported. "He's still on L'Abbaye. Headed west."

What the hell was he up to?

Moments later, Nicholas believed he had it figured out. "I think he's going out the other gate. The one on Les Fanils."

Mont-Saint-Michel had two entrances, about fifty meters apart—the main gate and a secondary entrance near an administrative building.

"Ping Sølvi," said Harvath. "Let her know that we think he may be coming out the other gate. Have her move to the causeway and watch for him there."

"Roger that," Nicholas responded, keying out a quick text.

But no sooner had he sent it than Aubertin changed his route. "Heads up," he said to Harvath. "He just turned right."

"What do you mean, *he turned right*?"

"On Les Fanils. He should have turned left to get to the gate. He didn't. He turned right."

At a stand of trees, Harvath escaped the sea of frenzied people to check the map Dominique had given him earlier in the day. One glance told him all he needed to know. "He's headed to the beach."

"Is he crazy?" Nicholas asked. "The tide's coming in. He'll never make it to the mainland."

"I don't think he's headed for the mainland," Harvath replied, wishing that he had the drone overhead. "I think he's worried about the exits and is looking for someplace to hide, here on the island."

"If you're right, there are only two places I can see that he might be headed to. A pair of structures—the Chapelle Saint-Aubert, or just past it, something smaller called the Fontaine Saint-Aubert."

"It should be pretty easy for you to figure out which one. As soon as he stops you can relay the—"

"Hold on," Nicholas said, interrupting him. "We just lost the signal."

"What happened?"

"I don't know. It was there and then it wasn't. It's completely gone."

Harvath could see the tide coming in. "He ditched the phone."

"How do you know?"

"Because that's what I would have done."

"I'll pull Sølvi then and have her back you up."

"Negative," Harvath replied. "I want her to remain at the causeway. This could be a ruse."

"Okay," said Nicholas. "Good copy. Be careful."

• • •

The tide at Mont-Saint-Michel swept in so quickly, it was said to arrive as fast as a galloping horse.

Already, it was lapping up the deserted beach and splashing against the rocky promontory upon which the tiny stone Chapel of Saint-Aubert had been built.

Harvath moved rapidly, hugging the boulder-strewn hillside, hoping that if a gunfight did break out, there was enough cover to protect him.

Up ahead, a narrow set of steps had been carved out of the natural granite of the promontory and led up to the chapel. With high walls on both sides, it was a death chute. Anyone standing above could fire down and he wouldn't have a chance. Stepping into the rising water, he approached the structure from behind.

The sheer face of the promontory was slick with moisture, making it hard to get any purchase. But once he found a fissure he could wedge the toe of his boot into, he made quick work of it.

Halfway up, there was an old metal ladder bolted to the stone. Carefully, he tested his weight on it. Confident that it would hold, he used it to speed the rest of his climb.

The rear of the chapel, where the building faced the sea, had no windows whatsoever. On its east and west sides, beneath the slate-covered roof, the windows were too high to peer into and the stones too smooth to scale. Even if he could make it up that high, he didn't know how good his view through the leaded glass would be. Perhaps he could have detected a human form of some sort inside, but if Aubertin was sitting completely motionless it would have been tough. His only choice was going to be the lone entrance.

Creeping around the chapel, he climbed over its low wall, and arrived at a weathered gray door and an arrow-slit-style window. Drawing his pistol, he made sure not to cast a shadow.

He stood for several moments, watching for movement, and didn't see any. Approaching the old wooden door with its rusted iron rivets, he strained for any sound coming from inside. All he could hear was the wind and the rush of the tide. Making ready, he reached for the door handle.

CHAPTER 52

The door was locked. Whether it had been locked from the outside because Mont-Saint-Michel didn't want anyone in there at night, or whether the assassin had done it from within, he only had one way of knowing. Standing back, he raised his boot and slammed it home.

The wood splintered and the door flew open as Harvath spun and pressed himself up against the stone exterior outside. Standing in the doorway, he would have made an easy target.

As it was, no shots were fired. He risked a quick look inside. The chapel was empty. That left only one place Aubertin could be.

The beach was now gone, consumed by the rising tide. The shoreline that remained was nothing but jagged, sharply edged boulders, stretching from the chapel to the Fontaine Saint-Aubert. Soon, they'd be under water too.

Trying to climb across them was out of the question. He'd have to scramble through the trees and underbrush along the steep hillside instead. At least he'd be concealed.

It was about a hundred meters, but it was tough terrain. Not only did the vegetation snag his boots, but the angle was such that if you didn't place each step with precision, you could end up slipping and crashing headfirst down into the water and onto the rocks.

He also had to take care to be quiet. The wind and the tide could only mask so much. A snapped branch could give away his approach and bring a hail of gunfire down on top of him.

The assassin, if he was there, was cornered. He had his back to the sea. There was no escape. He'd be ruthless—and every option would be on the table. Not so for Harvath.

He needed him alive. He had come too far to have it all abruptly end with the assassin's death.

Aubertin had information that was critical. And until Harvath was in possession of that information, he was going to have to do everything he could to keep him breathing. Which, as black-and-white as that sounded, did leave a little bit of gray.

Arriving within sight of the ruins, he stopped and crouched down. The view, unfortunately, wasn't good.

The Fontaine Saint-Aubert dated from the eighth century. Supposedly, on that site, fresh water had sprung from a stone and supplied the monastery for the next seven hundred years.

With weeds and grasses growing from its pointed roof, it looked like a decrepit mausoleum. Carved from local stone, there were no windows—only a small opening, several feet off the ground. Iron stanchions and a rusted chain encircled the structure's base, meant to keep out the curious.

Even more than the drone, Harvath wished he still had a flashbang left. Dropping one through the opening would have rendered Aubertin an absolute wreck. Reaching in and snatching him would have been a piece of cake. But, as he didn't have a flashbang, he was going to have to come up with another plan. Something, hopefully, that would smoke the assassin out.

The moment the phrase popped into his head, as odd as it was, he knew that was exactly what he had to do.

Part of him found it hard to believe that he worked for a multimillion-dollar global business, and that he was now reduced to rubbing sticks together. But those were the kinds of skills he had been hired to deliver. Failure wasn't an option.

After gathering the materials he needed, he found a wide, thick piece of bark the size of a snow shovel head to help him deliver his surprise, and kept moving across the hillside. Just past the structure, he began his descent.

He worked fast, creating a makeshift basket filled with dried grasses, pine needles, and other highly flammable items, including powder he extracted from one of his pistol rounds. It was all about things that would burn hot, fast, and produce a lot of smoke.

Wading into the water, he positioned himself behind the building and pulled the cartridge out of his Taser. Depressing the trigger, he activated the electric arc between its poles and used it to ignite his homemade smoke grenade.

Once it was lit, he moved around toward the front of the structure and prepared to toss it into the opening.

To not tip his hand, he had to come from the downwind side. As he did, some of the smoke began to blow back on him, partially obscuring his vision.

Hurrying his pace, he tossed the burning mass through the opening and retreated, blinking his watering eyes repeatedly, trying to clear them. With his pistol raised, he took cover behind a slab of rock and waited for the assassin to show himself. It didn't take long.

The smoke quickly filled the small enclosed space, leaving no breathable air. Aubertin remained inside for as long as he could and then, hacking and coughing, climbed out.

"Drop your weapon!" Harvath yelled. "Do it now!"

The assassin tossed his gun, which clattered off a rock and splashed into the water.

"Come out slowly!" Harvath ordered.

Aubertin did as he commanded, rubbing his eyes and continuing to cough as he climbed down.

Harvath was feeling a range of emotions. He was thrilled to have caught the guy, but enraged that this was the man who had killed Carl and, very likely, had sent men after Marco. He was angry over all the trouble the assassin had caused, and remorseful for the role he himself had been forced to play.

While he was alert and on edge, having not yet restrained Aubertin, he was also feeling a sense of relief. This part of the hunt, at least, was over.

Even so, this was an impossible location in which to take someone into custody. Every rock, slick with moisture—as well as a thin cover of algae—was a potential hazard. He couldn't have the assassin lie facedown because there was no flat ground to put him on. He would have to get creative. That started with making sure Aubertin wasn't carrying any additional weapons.

"Lift up your shirt!" he ordered.

"Fuck you!" the man replied.

"Don't test me, Aubertin. You won't like how it ends."

"If you're going to shoot me, get it over with! Otherwise, fuck you!"

"Last chance," he warned.

When the Irishman gave him the middle finger, Harvath made good on his promise and gave *him* what he had asked for.

Applying pressure to the trigger, he fired his Sig and sent a round into the assassin's left leg.

Unlike in the movies, getting drilled with a nine-millimeter didn't send you flying dramatically backward. But, if you were precariously balanced on a pile of slippery rocks, knee-deep in water, when it happened, the chances were pretty good that you were going down. And that's what happened to Aubertin. The man lost his footing and went down hard.

There was a splash as he hit the water. Harvath waited for him to get up, but he didn't move.

Fuck, thought Harvath. If the assassin slammed his head against one of the rocks when he fell, they might be in real trouble. Getting this guy anything resembling medical attention wasn't part of his plan.

The other problem was the old mountain man rule about never firing your weapon twice in Indian country—at least not if you wanted to stay hidden.

Already, the gendarmes were swarming all over the abbey and throughout the village looking for a shooter. And now, thanks to him, a new shot had just rung out. It would be hard to pinpoint where it had come from—unless he was forced to fire again. At that point, the French police would be drawn to the beach and any hope he had of interrogating the assassin would be gone.

In reality, the clock was already ticking. It was only a matter of time before officers, just as a matter of course, came to check the structures along the beach. Holstering his weapon, he waded into the water after Aubertin.

As he got closer, he could see ribbons of blood staining the water near his thigh. Confirming his worst fear, there was also blood coming from a gash to the man's head. He had hit something on the way down. *Fuck*.

Kicking him with the toe of his boot, Harvath tested him for a reaction. He wasn't moving. He didn't look to be breathing either as the tide continued to come in and water washed over his face. He was going to have to try to resuscitate this guy. *Damn it.*

Not giving a rat's ass if the assassin had a cervical injury, Harvath reached down, grabbed him by the shirt, and dragged him out of the water, over the rocks to the base of the hill.

He was about to set him down when the man's eyes snapped open and Harvath felt a white-hot searing pain across his chest.

Looking down, he saw a small karambit—an Indonesian-style knife shaped like a claw, clutched in Aubertin's hand.

Though he had taken him by surprise, Harvath had no intention of giving the man the upper hand. He immediately dropped him, but instead of recoiling and clutching his wound, he brought his boot down hard to stomp Aubertin's face.

The Irishman must have known it was coming because the moment Harvath released him, he rolled to his left.

As he did, he lashed out once more with the blade, tearing through the right leg of Harvath's jeans, missing his skin by less than a millimeter.

With shades of the bar fight in Key West, Harvath knew he needed to end this now.

Backing away, he made sure he wasn't standing in any water as he pulled out his Taser, slammed the cartridge back in, and let the assassin ride the lightning.

Despite the injury to his thigh, the man's body went rigid from the shock and he arched his back off the rocks.

Once the effect had passed and his body had relaxed, just for good measure, Harvath hit him with another jolt.

And then, just because, he gave him one more.

When he finally stopped tasing him, Aubertin's eyes had rolled up into his head and his chin was covered with saliva.

Snatching up the karambit, Harvath tossed it into the water and waited for the man to come back around.

Finally, Aubertin's eyes began to focus. And when they did, the first thing they saw was Harvath's fist as it came down like a hammer onto the bridge of his nose. There was a spray of blood and the crack of cartilage as it shattered.

The man's instincts were to protect his face, but he couldn't raise his arms. Harvath had him pinned, and he beat him mercilessly.

He beat him for Carl, he beat him for Marco, and most importantly, he beat him for himself. He let the beast off the chain and let out all of his rage.

He broke the man's jaw, half of his ribs, and even one of his orbital sockets. But that was only the appetizer.

Standing up, his chest—and now his hands—bleeding, he dragged the Irishman back down into the brackish tidal water and pushed his head all the way under.

He felt the man thrashing beneath his grasp, struggling to surface so that he could breathe. Harvath kept him there, looking out over the water toward the sky. It was turning that deep shade of blue, which preceded the black of night.

Closing his eyes, he held the assassin there for as long as he dared and then yanked him back up. He wasn't done with him. Not just yet. He still needed him alive.

Aubertin simultaneously vomited and attempted to suck in huge hungry breaths of air.

"The contract," said Harvath. "Who hired you?"

"If you're going to kill me," he panted, "Just do it."

"I'll make you a deal. If you tell me what I want to know, I won't kill you."

Still gasping for air, he vomited once more and then said, "I don't believe you."

Grabbing the back of his neck, Harvath went to put the assassin's head back underwater again, when Aubertin yelled, "Stop! I'll tell you."

Harvath kept the man's neck painfully bent, his head hovering just above the surface of the water, as the waves splashed his face. "You've got three seconds," he said. "Make them count."

"His name is Lieu Van Trang," said Aubertin.

"Where is he?"

"In Paris."

"How do I find him?"

Harvath held the man there in the water until he had answered every one of his questions.

He was about to drag him back up onto the rocks, when he heard the unmistakable sound of a pistol hammer being cocked behind him.

"Did he tell you what you needed to know?" Sølvi asked.

Harvath nodded.

She gestured with her pistol for him to step away.

Harvath complied.

Straightening up, Aubertin turned to see who Harvath was talking to. He didn't know who she was, but he sensed something bad was about to happen. He watched as Harvath waded in toward shore and the woman pointed her suppressed weapon at him.

"We have a deal," the Irishman insisted. "I tell you what you want to know and I walk free."

Sølvi smiled. "That was your deal with him. Not me."

Pressing her trigger, she delivered a single shot—straight through his heart.

"That's for Carl Pedersen," she said as he fell into the water, dead.

CHAPTER 53

ONE WEEK LATER

T he slice across Harvath's chest was nothing to laugh at. But it also wasn't deep enough to have required a doctor. Sølvi had cleaned and dressed his wound, then waited with him until the Quick Reaction Force portion of his team arrived from Joint Base Andrews. Once they were there, she returned to Norway, her role in this assignment complete.

News of the shooting at Mont-Saint-Michel had been all over TV, the internet, and newspapers, especially in France. When the team found Lieu Van Trang, he had been moving from relative to relative, staying in a different house or apartment each night. Though the name of the tour guide shot and killed had not yet been released, he knew in his bones that it had to be Aubertin—and that he would be next. He had been right—on both counts.

His wound still fresh, Harvath was not able to get too physical with Trang. His teammates Haney and Staelin, on the other hand, were more than happy to step in.

With time, the Vietnamese man broke. He gave up all the details, including how he and Aubertin intended to keep the bounty for themselves. Most important, he gave up the name of the man who had opened the assassination contract on Harvath—Andre Weber.

With Morrison and Gage standing guard outside, and Barton warming up their SUV, Harvath asked Haney and Staelin to leave him alone with Trang.

Once they had exited the abandoned warehouse in the Parisian suburb of Clichy-sous-Bois, Harvath spent a few more moments speaking with Trang before making sure the man would never run another drug ring, sex ring, or assassination ring ever again.

It turned out that Andre Weber lived and worked in Basel, Switzerland, which was too bad for him because Harvath had a very good friend in the Swiss government who lived and worked just south of Basel in Bern.

When, as a Secret Service agent, he had been framed for the kidnapping of the U.S. President, Claudia Mueller had helped him get the President back and clear Harvath's name. They had been good together, and probably should have made a better go at carrying their relationship further. But things being what they were at the time, at least they had remained friends.

When he reached out to her, Claudia knew better than to ask too many questions. Trusting him, she quietly put a surveillance team on Weber, and arranged for a hangar and transport once The Carlton Group jet touched down.

She appeared only long enough to say hello and hand Harvath an address. Anything that happened after that, she made clear, she didn't want to know about. He was on his own in Switzerland.

As the Americans pulled up outside Weber's residence, Claudia's surveillance team drove away. The handoff was complete.

The home was located in one of the most exclusive areas of Basel: St. Alban-Vorstadt. On an enormous lot, bordered by trees and green space, there was no reason for them to spirit Weber away as they had Trang. His interrogation could happen in the luxurious comfort of his own home.

Harvath decided to allow Morrison and Barton, the youngest guys on the op, to handle subduing Weber when he walked in.

Back in the home's impressive kitchen, Gage brewed coffee while Haney and Staelin iced their knuckles from Paris, and Harvath sent an encrypted update to Nicholas. Finally, just after midnight, Weber got home.

Being somewhat of a gourmand, in addition to the hams, sausages, and salamis the man had hanging in his walk-in refrigerator, he owned a large stainless steel meat and cheese slicer like you might see in a deli. Morrison and Barton had both wanted to use it to "scare the fuck out of him."

Harvath explained that the threat was only as good as their willingness to carry it out. Could they put his hands in there and start slicing off the tips of his fingers? Had they weighed what he had done? Did it warrant that kind of response? It was important to get the younger guys thinking.

As it turned out, none of it was necessary.

Unlike Trang, the moment Weber saw Harvath—he knew he was screwed. It was game over and the only hope he had of getting out of this alive was to cooperate.

Weber claimed not to know who had put up the money for the contract, but he had no problem revealing who had paid him to fly all the way to Vietnam and bring it to Trang.

The use of cutouts didn't surprise Harvath. The name of this one, though, did. Harvath not only knew him, but had also dealt with him before. Years ago, he had been a middleman, charged with hiring an assassin to go after Nicholas.

As he had done at the end of Trang's interrogation, Harvath asked the team to wait for him outside.

He conversed with Weber for a few more minutes, told him a little about Carl Pedersen, and then, marching him back to the walk-in cooler, made him answer for what he had done.

En route to the Nice Côte d'Azur airport, Harvath called Nicholas and shared with him the next name on their list—Gaston Leveque. A concierge at the famous Hôtel du Cap-Eden-Roc, Leveque's considerably more lucrative job was as a fixer for wealthy Russians. Drugs, murder, children for sex, the more horrific it was, the deeper he trafficked in it. One of Harvath's deepest regrets was that he hadn't killed the man years ago when he'd had the chance. At the time, though, letting Leveque live was the only thing that had gotten Harvath out of the situation alive.

Upon hearing the man's name, Nicholas had gone ballistic—just like he had with the Contessa. They went back and forth for several minutes before ending their call. Nicholas let it be known that he trusted Harvath to do the right thing.

Though Leveque was a fixer for lots of wealthy Russians, there was one Harvath was particularly interested in—Nikolai Nekrasov, the billionaire owner of the Hôtel du Cap-Eden-Roc. Harvath had a history with him too.

When he had originally come for Leveque, he had done so at the hotel not knowing that all of the rooms were wired with microphones and hidden cameras. He had only begun to interrogate Leveque when an armed security team had entered and Harvath had been forced to shoot several of them, though none fatally.

On the way out of the hotel, by necessity he had to temporarily take a woman hostage. That woman had been Nekrasov's wife, Eva—and two things had immediately become apparent. One, she seriously disliked her husband, and two, she found Harvath very attractive.

She had certainly *not* resisted during the fifteen-minute kidnapping as they raced into Cannes in a stolen $400,000 sports car, and she had actively assisted him in escaping her husband and his band of men who were in hot pursuit. It was the most fun and excitement, she admitted, that she had had in years.

Yet winging a few security guards and taking a quick joyride with the man's wife hardly seemed worthy of a one-hundred-million-dollar bounty. Which was why getting to Leveque was so critical. Only he could reveal who had hired him, and hopefully why.

· · ·

On the west side of Antibes was the commune of Vallauris—best known for being home to Picasso from the late 1940s to the mid-1950s.

In its seaside town of Golfe-Juan, Gaston Leveque had a beautiful little bungalow. When he returned home from his shift at the Cap-Eden-Roc, Harvath was sitting on his patio, a glass of wine on the table, and his best, most-expensive Chablis in the ice bucket next to him.

"*Bonsoir,* Gaston," he said.

The man panicked and tried to run back into the house, but Haney and Staelin were waiting for him. Dragging him over to the table, they sat him down and flex-cuffed him to the chair.

After complimenting him on the wine, Harvath gave him a brief rundown on what had taken place, and then began asking questions. He was reticent at first, but Gage—who was eager to contribute to the information-gathering portion of their mission—was very persuasive.

Harvath thought he had seen it all, but what the man could do with off-the-shelf items, like a nasal spray bottle and lighter fluid, was quite inspired.

It wasn't something any of them reveled in. Leveque was a very, very bad man. Not just by way of all the murders he had facilitated, but just as equally all the sexual exploitation of women and children. The discomfort the man was feeling now paled in comparison to the physical, emotional, and psychological trauma he had caused countless others. He had racked up a huge bill and now karma, in the form of Harvath, had come to collect.

When Harvath left, his questions answered and the team out warming the car in the driveway, Harvath lingered only long enough to take a picture for Nicholas and grab the bottle of wine from the ice bucket. Not only was it one of the best he had ever tasted, he was going to be up late doing some serious thinking. There was one more move he needed to make, and he wanted to execute it perfectly.

CHAPTER 54

As soon as Nekrasov's driver, Valery, had put his boss into the elevator and the doors had closed, Staelin popped out from behind a parked car and hit him with the Taser.

"Coming up," he said over his earbud, as the big Russian fell to the floor of the garage.

"Good copy," Harvath replied.

Seconds later, on the building's third floor, the elevator chimed, its doors opened and Nekrasov stepped out.

He was in a foul mood. He didn't like being dragged back for a second opinion on whether his wife's implants should be removed. The only thing that made it worthwhile was that the facility had exceptionally attractive nurses. With what a headache Eva had been, he was tilting now, more than ever, toward taking a mistress. Maybe he would find one here.

Even though he was late, again, he spent a few minutes chatting up the nurses at the front desk before being directed back to his wife's room, where she was awaiting her exam.

When he entered the room, without knocking, a new doctor was already chatting with her. He stood in the doorway for a second, feeling the doctor was somehow familiar.

"Please close the door," the man in the white lab coat said, without fully turning around to face him.

Nekrasov did as he was asked.

Once he had closed the door, Harvath turned and pointed a suppressed Glock 43 pistol at him—just like the one the assassin sent to Key West had confronted him with.

"Hello, Nikolai," said Harvath. "Take a seat. We're going to have a chat."

"You," the Russian grumbled angrily. "You have the nerve to accost me in front of my wife. You have no—"

"Shut up," Eva interrupted her husband. "Do what he says. Sit down."

Nekrasov complied.

Harvath pulled out his phone, activated a banking app, and held it an inch away from the man's face. "Don't blink," he commanded. "Don't even fucking move."

There was a *click* and Harvath then swiped to another screen. Placing the suppressor against Nekrasov's forehead, he extended the phone again, this time saying, "Right thumbprint, in the red box. Do it now."

Nekrasov did as Harvath demanded, stating, "That boy you killed wasn't just President Peshkov's son; Misha was my godson."

"He was also a fucking psychopath," said Harvath. "You should have stayed out of it."

"I bet one hundred million dollars against you."

"And you lost."

"I never lose," said the Russian.

A moment later, Eva's phone chimed.

Harvath looked at her. "Everything good?"

She nodded.

"Are we happy?"

"Very," she replied.

Turning his attention back to Nekrasov, he stated, "You have no idea how lucky you are. Every single day when you wake up, you had better thank God for your wife and for your children. The day you stop thanking Him, is the day I'll be back."

With that, he turned and disappeared.

• • •

On their way back to the airport, Haney, who was riding shotgun, turned around to face Harvath. Holding out his phone, he showed him a website and asked, "That place in Lithuania, where you wanted me to send the wooden crosses, is the total still five?"

"No," Harvath replied. "For right now, it's only going to be four. But bookmark that page, just in case we ever have to come back."

CHAPTER 55

H olidae Hayes lifted her glass of champagne and said, "To the new Deputy Director of the NIS's Strategy Section."

Sølvi looked around to make sure no one was listening and then clinked glasses. It wasn't something they should be discussing out in public. "Thank you," she said as they both took a sip.

"And," Hayes continued, "I hear that Landsbergis is going to be promoted from acting head to official Director of VSD in Lithuania."

"We're hearing the same thing. I need to send him a thank-you note."

"Why? For helping you and Harvath?"

"I can't go too far into it, but a couple of years ago I was in Lithuania and needed medical attention. Diplomatically speaking, it was a sensitive situation. Carl reached out to him and Landsbergis provided a doctor, no questions asked."

"It sounds to me like we've got the right man in Vilnius."

Sølvi agreed and they clinked glasses again.

Hayes's phone chimed and she looked down. "You're going to hate me, but I've got to get going."

"What are you talking about? Landsbergis may get a thank-you note, but *you* get an entire thank-you lunch."

"I wish I could stay, I'm really sorry, but we've got a huge VIP in town. You wouldn't believe the list of things I have to tackle."

Sølvi wasn't happy. "Holidae, we just opened a wonderful bottle of champagne and the oysters haven't even arrived yet. You can't leave."

"You'll be fine," her friend assured her, standing up and giving her kisses on both cheeks. "Let's get together next week. Okay?"

The Norwegian smiled at her CIA counterpart and nodded. "I'd like that. Good luck with your VIP."

"Thank you," Hayes replied as she gathered her things and began walking away. "I'm going to need it."

Rearranging the cushions behind her, Sølvi turned to look out over the fjord. Kicking off her shoes, she put her feet on the bench and pulled her knees in close. She watched as the beautiful boats crossed back and forth. Taking a sip of champagne, she wished that she were on one.

Taking another sip of champagne, she wished that she was out there with Scot. He was the first man, since her divorce, and outside of Carl, whom she trusted.

Leaving him in France had been remarkably hard and it had freaked the hell out of her. She had worked with plenty of male agents, within Norway and elsewhere. Never had she ended an op feeling what she could only describe as being "heartsick." Who the hell was this American to have such a hold on her?

In all fairness, she had been scared by how she felt, and as soon as Harvath's team had arrived, she had run from France and Mont-Saint-Michel as fast as she could.

Now, she was back in her happy place—up on the roof of The Thief, wishing she was out on the water and trying not to think too hard about what the future might hold.

That was when someone stepped into the sunlight and cast a shadow across her table. She had always thought they should teach servers to avoid that.

But looking up, she saw that it wasn't a server.

Harvath was standing there in front of her with an empty champagne glass.

"May I join you?" he asked.

Sølvi smiled. "You two planned this, didn't you?"

Harvath smiled back and sat down. "All I know is that when a VIP like me comes to town, everything has got to be perfect."

"You know life isn't perfect, right?"

"For the moment," he said, "let's just pretend it is."

God, she was so gorgeous, he thought, as he helped himself to some champagne. She was wearing a simple sundress and she looked so beautiful.

Sølvi hated to ruin the moment. Nevertheless, she had to ask, "I'm assuming you got to the bottom of who took out the contract on you. Was it the Russians?"

"It was *a* Russian."

"President Peshkov?"

"No," Harvath replied, "but someone very close to him. A friend from childhood, Nikolai Nekrasov."

Her eyes widened. "The Russian mobster?"

"*Billionaire* Russian mobster," he clarified. "He was also the godfather of Peshkov's son."

"So this was about revenge."

"And now it's over."

Sølvi had a thousand more questions that she wanted to ask, but it was obvious he didn't want to discuss it. That was okay. Like he had said, it was over. And she was so glad to see him.

After a few moments, she noticed that his face had changed. It was softer somehow. "You're thinking about something," she said. "What is it?"

He decided not to beat around the bush.

"I like you," he replied. "And I've felt incredibly guilty about that. I didn't want to stop liking you, though. So, I asked Lara for a sign. It's crazy and I know it. I didn't remember right away that today was the anniversary of my first date with her. Then, in the flight lounge in France, waiting for the plane to get fueled to come up here, I saw a magazine. Its headline was about how Norway is the future. Under that, was an article about the immutable wisdom of Jean-Paul Sartre.

"I ended up reading the entire thing from cover to cover. But, as there was nothing about ninjas, I can't really say if it was a *definitive* sign."

Sølvi turned the dazzle up to 11 and smiled once more. "Stop talking," she said, as the waiter arrived. "We have oysters to eat."

They were wonderful and she explained that they were from the south of Norway where she was from.

When they placed the order for their main course, Harvath asked the waiter to please prepare it to go—and also to bring another bottle of champagne.

"What's going on?" Sølvi asked. "What are you up to?"

"You'll see."

Once everything was boxed up and placed in shopping bags, Harvath nodded toward the elevators and for Sølvi to lead the way.

After exiting on the lobby level, and pushing through The Thief's giant revolving doors and out into the motor court, Sølvi turned to Harvath. "Now what?"

Harvath had her follow him over to the railing that looked down onto a narrow channel where two boats were berthed.

"How about we go out on the water for a picnic?" he asked.

Looking at the little sailboat she was overjoyed. "I don't know how much wind there is today, but yes. I'd love to sail with you."

Harvath looked at the tiny sailboat she was looking at and smiled. Pulling a set of keys from his pocket, he pointed toward the splendid silver Riva she had talked about when they were on Lake Garda and said, "Someone heard I was going to take a cruise with a beautiful Norwegian girl. Naturally, they gave me an upgrade."

Sølvi could barely contain herself as they made their way down the steps. She had walked by this boat so many times, imagining the glamorous people who sailed on her. Now, she was one of those people.

"How were you able to afford this?" she asked. "The Carlton Group must have a hell of a per diem."

"A friend and I in the South of France just came into a little money. Call it a rich uncle. Welcome aboard."

After stowing their food and wine, she helped cast off and they cruised into the fjord.

Out on the open water, she looked back toward The Thief. The view from this perspective was every bit as good as she had always imagined it would be. She wanted to hug Harvath for giving her such a wonderful experience, but she also suspected that's exactly what he wanted her to do and so she held back.

They kept sailing, north from Oslo, as Harvath continued to consult the GPS system on his phone.

"Do we have a destination?" she asked.

"There are some houses I want to look at from the water," he replied.

"I see. Back to your dream from Mont-Saint-Michel. A house and a boat."

"Actually," said Harvath, "there's a little more to life than just a house and a boat. I was thinking Norway might be a nice place to spend the summer with Marco. What do you think?"

Sølvi smiled and wrapped her arms around him. Giving him a kiss, she said, "I think if you're serious about getting to know Norway, you're going to need a very special Norwegian ninja to keep an eye on both of you."

ACKNOWLEDGMENTS

I want to begin by thanking the most important people in the entire process— you, the magnificent **readers**.

This is my twentieth thriller and, whether you've read them all, or are just getting started, I want you to know how much I appreciate and value you.

Every year, I strive to set the bar higher for myself as a writer and to improve at my craft. I do it not only because it keeps my job interesting and challenging, but also because I owe it to *you*. I want to be the author you can always depend on for a thrilling escape.

If I meet that goal, then I have honored the faith you put in me. As I tell anyone who will listen, the readers are the people I work for—and you are the best bosses anyone could ever hope to have. When you recommend my books to friends, family, and coworkers, as well as when you leave great reviews online, I am humbled and filled with pride that my hard work all year has paid off. Thank you.

Here's to all of the fabulous **booksellers** who have introduced so many of their customers to my novels. Thank you for stocking, selling, and talking up my books over the (almost) past two decades. Booksellers are the on-ramp to adventure. You play a vital role in our society. Thank you for ALL that you do.

The very kind and generous **Holidae H. Hayes** made a lovely donation to a special charitable organization near and dear to my heart. I thank you for your generosity and hope you enjoy the character named in your honor.

With each thriller I write, I lean heavily upon the expertise of some incredible **military**, **intelligence**, and **law enforcement personnel**.

This space is always reserved to thank them together, because for their own security, I cannot thank them individually. To you ladies and gentlemen, please know how grateful I am. Thank you for what you have done for me, but more important, what you do every day for our country.

My three amigos—**Sean Fontaine**, **James Ryan**, and **Sidney Blair**—could not have been more helpful during the writing of *Near Dark*. There are times when I feel that they must be getting tired of questions from me, but they are always gracious and always encourage me to "Keep those questions coming, Thor!"—You gentlemen are the best. Thank you for everything.

My longtime friend **Steve Tuttle**–Principal, TASER CEWs & Founding Team Member of Axon, is absolutely fearless when it comes to taking my TASER questions. He doesn't just say "Yeah, I think that will work," he actually goes out and experiments until we get an answer. Thanks for helping me light things on fire!

One of the achievements I am most proud of is that all twenty of my novels have been with my wonderful family at **Simon & Schuster**. I cannot imagine working with a more talented, brilliant, kind, and professional team. It is an absolute joy to have brought to life so many books together. My deepest, heartfelt thanks to all of you.

With that heartfelt thanks, I have to admit that my heart is also broken, as this year we lost the amazing **Carolyn Reidy**, Simon & Schuster's President and CEO. Carolyn was an outstanding leader but an even more outstanding human being. I will miss her laughter, her fierce determination, and most of all, her friendship. Thank you, Carolyn, for every single thing you did for me.

While it is hard to lose someone who is so much a part of your career, it only makes you realize how fantastic and valuable all of the other pros are whom you work with.

Right at the top of that list, is my phenomenal publisher and editor, **Emily Bestler**. Emily and I have been together since the very beginning. After reading my first thriller, it was she who invited me to join the S&S family. One of the smartest things I ever did was saying yes. Since then, Emily has not only helped expertly guide me through the writing of twenty books, she has also become one of my dearest friends. Thank you for all of it, Emily, and for sprinkling in so much laughter and good humor along the way.

Along with Emily, the sensational **Lara Jones** and the rest of the **Emily Bestler Books team** are the absolute best of the best! Thank you, all.

Simon & Schuster's extraordinary President and Publisher, **Jon Karp**, is one of the nicest people I have ever met. He has had a monumental career, because he not only understands the publishing industry inside and out, but (as one himself) he also understands writers. Thank you for always being such a powerful advocate for me at S&S. I look forward to working together for many more years to come.

Remarkable people with superb ideas are the wellspring of success. I couldn't be happier than to have Atria publisher **Libby McGuire** and associate publisher **Suzanne Donahue** in my life. You two continue to be amazing, and I appreciate all that you have done for me. Thank you.

I also have to add the incomparable **Kristin Fassler** and **Dana Trocker** to the list of people I am so grateful for. You know you are working with confident, accomplished professionals when they refuse to rest on their laurels, are always looking for new ways to do things, and always want to go farther than last time. Thank you, both.

I don't get to thank the spectacular **Gary Urda** and **John Hardy** often enough. Having them on my side is like having my own Special Forces team inside Simon & Schuster. Every single day they are figuring out bold, new ways to advance, take ground, and achieve success. I am incredibly fortunate to know and to be working with them. Thank you, gentlemen.

While I'm doling out the praise, I want to give a big thank-you to the marvelous **Jen Long** and the outstanding team at **Pocket Books**. We have been putting some fantastic initiatives into play this year, and it is because of their creative genius. I really appreciate all of you. Thank you.

My awesome publicist, **David Brown**, continues to crush it, year in and year out. Always thinking, always adapting, and always coming up with new strategies, he is tireless in all that he does on my behalf. David, I'm the luckiest author on the planet. Thank you.

And, speaking of crushing it, I want to extend a huge thanks and my deepest appreciation to the superb **Atria**, **Emily Bestler Books**, and **Pocket Books sales teams**. If you're reading this, it's because they helped get it to the right bookseller. They are absolute pros, and I am so blessed to be working with them. Thank you, all.

Behind the scenes, the impressive **Colin Shields**, **Paula Amendolara**, **Janice Fryer**, **Adene Corns**, **Liz Perl**, and **Lisa Keim** continue to leap tall buildings on my behalf! You, along with the terrific **Gregory Hruska**, **Mark Speer**, and **Stuart Smith**, are an out-of-this-world team. Thank you!

Knocking it out of the park, the **Simon & Schuster audio division** continues to put unbelievable points on the board. The job they do not only producing the audio versions of my books but also selling and marketing them is amazing. I want to thank every brilliant person under their banner, including **Chris Lynch**, **Tom Spain**, **Sarah Lieberman**, **Desiree Vecchio**, and **Armand Schultz**. Thank you.

Like Scot Harvath, when you choose someone to watch your back, you want that person to be off-the-charts talented. That's what I have in my sharpshooter, **Al Madocs** of the Atria/Emily Bestler Books Production Department. No matter what the mission requires, Al is always there with a smile and a can-do attitude. Al, a million thank-yous would never be enough. You're the best. Thanks for everything.

This year, we wanted to enhance our "look," and that job fell to the peerless **Jimmy Iacobelli** of the Atria/Emily Bestler Books and Pocket Books Art Departments. The *Near Dark* artwork—especially when you see it on the hardcover edition—is nothing short of stunning. Jimmy, I tip my creative hat to you. Extremely well done, sir. Thank you.

My unbelievable copyeditor, **Fred Chase**, did such a terrific job keeping me on the straight and narrow. Thank you so much for your professionalism and hard work.

Twenty novels—and every one of them lovingly overseen by my formidable agent and dear friend, **Heide Lange** of **Sanford J. Greenburger Associates**. Heide is the representative every author dreams of having. She is brilliant, an absolute savant when it comes to publishing, gives great counsel, and is a highly respected negotiator. No matter where you encounter her in the process, she will always treat you fairly. Simply put, they don't make them better than Heide Lange. Thank you for such an incredible journey.

Heide is backed up by a tremendous team that I am thankful for every day, including the fabulous **Samantha Isman**, **Iwalani Kim**, and everyone else at **Sanford J. Greenburger Associates**. Thank you, all, for everything. I really appreciate all of you.

Even closer to home, **Yvonne Ralsky** is one of the most brilliant people I have ever known. And that brilliance is exceeded only by her sense of humor and wonderful outlook on life. I consider it an incredible privilege to know you, work with you, and call you my friend. Thank you for all that you have done for me.

One day, I am going to write a nonfiction book about all of the twists and turns in Hollywood. At the center of it, will be the dashing **Scott Schwimer**—my wonderful friend and absolutely dynamite entertainment attorney. Scottie, I love you tons and tons. Thank you for everything—especially your love, laughter, and infectious optimism.

Now I get to thank **my incredibly accommodating**, **unbelievably understanding**, **and absolutely beautiful family**. Thank you for your unconditional love and unwavering support. It means the world to me. I love you more than you will ever know.